DEVIL'S WALTZ

DEVIL'S WALTZ

JONATHAN KELLERMAN

BANTAM BOOKS
NEW YORK · TORONTO · LONDON · SYDNEY · AUCKLAND

DEVIL'S WALTZ
A Bantam Book/February 1993

Library of Congress Cataloging-in-Publication Data

Kellerman, Jonathan.
    Devil's waltz : a novel / Jonathan Kellerman.
    p.   cm.
    ISBN 0-553-09205-7
    I. Title.
PS3561.E3865D48   1993
813'.54—dc20   92-18089
                                              CIP

Published simultaneously in the United States and Canada

Bantam Books are published by Bantam Books, a division of Bantam
Doubleday Dell Publishing Group, Inc. Its trademark, consisting of the
words "Bantam Books" and the portrayal of a rooster, is Registered in U.S.
Patent and Trademark Office and in other countries. Marca Registrada.
Bantam Books, 666 Fifth Avenue, New York, New York 10103.

PRINTED IN THE UNITED STATES OF AMERICA

BVG   0   9   8   7   6   5   4   3   2   1

To my son, Jesse,
a gentleman and a scholar

Special thanks to Reuben Eagle,
Allan Marder, Yuki Novick,
Michael Samet, Dennis Payne,
and Harry Weisman, M.D.

Ring out old shapes of foul disease;
Ring out the narrowing lust of gold.

—ALFRED, LORD TENNYSON

DEVIL'S WALTZ

1

It was a place of fear and myth, home of miracles and the worst kind of failure.

I'd spent a quarter of my life there, learning to deal with the rhythm, the madness, the starched *whiteness* of it all.

Five years' absence had turned me into a stranger, and as I entered the lobby anxiety tickled my belly.

Glass doors, black granite floors, high, concave travertine walls advertising the names of dead benefactors.

Glossy depot for an unguided tour of uncertainty.

Spring, outside, but in here time had a different meaning.

A group of surgical interns—God, they were taking them young—slouched by on paper-soled scrub slippers, humbled by double shifts. My own shoes were leather-bottomed and they clacked on the granite.

Ice-slick floors. I'd just started my internship when they'd been installed. I remembered the protests. Petitions against the illogic of polished stone in a place where children ran and walked and limped and wheeled. But some philanthropist had liked the look. Back in the days when philanthropists had been easy to come by.

Not much granite visible this morning; a crush of humanity filled the lobby, most of it dark-skinned and cheaply dressed, queued up at the glassed-in booths, waiting for the favors of stone-faced clerks. The clerks avoided eye contact and worshipped paper. The lines didn't seem to be moving.

Babies wailed and suckled; women sagged; men swallowed curses and stared at the floor. Strangers bumped against one another and sought refuge in the placebo of banter. Some of the children— those who still looked like children—twisted and bounced and struggled against weary adult arms, breaking away for precious seconds of freedom before being snagged and reeled back in. Others—pale, thin, sunken, bald, painted in unnatural colors— stood there silently, heartbreakingly compliant. Sharp words in foreign tongues crackled above the drone of the paging operators. An occasional smile or bit of cheer brightened the inertial gloom, only to go out like a spark from a wet flint.

As I got closer I smelled it.

Rubbing alcohol, antibiotic bitters, the sticky-ripe liqueur of elixir and affliction.

Eau de Hospital. Some things never changed. But I had; my hands were cold.

I eased my way through the crowd. Just as I got to the elevators, a heavyset man in a navy-blue rent-a-cop uniform stepped out of no-where and blocked my way. Blond-gray crewcut and a shave so close his skin looked wet-sanded. Black-frame glasses over a triangular face.

"Can I help you, sir?"

"I'm Dr. Delaware. I have an appointment with Dr. Eves."

"I need to see some ID, sir."

Surprised, I fished a five-year-old clip-on badge out of my pocket. He took it and studied it as if it were a clue to something. Looked up at me, then back at the ten-year-old black-and-white photo. There was a walkie-talkie in his hand. Holstered pistol on his belt.

I said, "Looks like things have tightened up a bit since I was last here."

"This is expired," he said. "You still on staff, sir?"

"Yes."

He frowned and pocketed the badge.

I said, "Is there some kind of problem?"

"New badges required, sir. If you go right past the chapel, over to Security, they can shoot your picture and fix you up." He touched the badge on his lapel. Color photograph, ten-digit ID number.

"How long will that take?" I said.

"Depends, sir." He looked past me, as if suddenly bored.

"On what?"

"How many are ahead of you. Whether your paperwork's current."

I said, "Listen, my appointment with Dr. Eves is in just a couple of minutes. I'll take care of the badge on my way out."

" 'Fraid not, sir," he said, still focused somewhere else. He folded his arms across his chest. "Regulations."

"Is this something recent?"

"Letters were sent to the medical staff last summer."

"Must have missed that one." Must have dropped it in the trash, unopened, like most of my hospital mail.

He didn't answer.

"I'm really pressed for time," I said. "How about if I get a visitor's badge to tide me over?"

"Visitor's badges are for visitors, sir."

"I'm visiting Dr. Eves."

He swung his eyes back to me. Another frown—darker, contemplative. He inspected the pattern on my tie. Touched his belt on the holster side.

"Visitor's badges are over at Registration," he said, hooking a thumb at one of the dense queues.

He crossed his arms again.

I smiled. "No way around it, huh?"

"No, sir."

"Just past the chapel?"

"Just past and turn right."

"Been having crime problems?" I said.

"I don't make the rules, sir. I just enforce them."

He waited a moment before moving aside, followed my exit with his squint. I turned the corner, half expecting to see him trailing, but the corridor was empty and silent.

The door marked SECURITY SERVICES was twenty paces down. A sign hung from the knob: BACK IN above a printed clock with movable hands set at 9:30 A.M. My watch said 9:10. I knocked anyway. No answer. I looked back. No rent-a-cop. Remembering a staff elevator just past Nuclear Medicine, I continued down the hall.

Nuclear Medicine was now COMMUNITY RESOURCES. Another closed door. The elevator was still there but the buttons were missing; the machine had been switched to key-operated. I was looking for the nearest stairway when a couple of orderlies appeared, wheeling an empty gurney. Both were young, tall, black, sporting geometrically carved hip-hop hairstyles. Talking earnestly about the Raiders game. One of them produced a key, inserted it into the lock, and turned. The elevator doors opened on walls covered with padded batting. Junk-food wrappers and a piece of dirty-looking gauze littered the floor. The orderlies pushed the gurney in. I followed.

General Pediatrics occupied the eastern end of the fourth floor, separated from the Newborn Ward by a swinging wooden door. I knew the outpatient clinic had been open for only fifteen minutes but the small waiting room was already overflowing. Sneezes and coughs, glazed looks and hyperactivity. Tight maternal hands gripped babes and toddlers, paperwork, and the magic plastic of Medi-Cal cards. To the right of the reception window was a set of double doors marked PATIENTS REGISTER FIRST over a Spanish translation of same.

I pushed through and walked past a long white corridor tacked with safety and nutrition posters, county health bulletins, and bilingual exhortations to nurture, vaccinate, and abstain from alcohol and dope. A dozen or so examining rooms were in use, their chart-racks brimming over. Cat-cries and the sounds of comfort seeped from under the doors. Across the hall were files, supply cabinets, and a refrigerator marked with a red cross. A secretary tapped a computer keyboard. Nurses hustled between the cabinets and the exam rooms. Residents spoke into chin-cradled phones and trailed after fast-stepping attending physicians.

The wall right-angled to a shorter hallway lined with doctors' offices. Stephanie Eves's open door was the third in a set of seven.

The room was ten by twelve, with institutional-beige walls relieved by bracket shelves filled with books and journals, a couple of Miró posters, and one cloudy window with an eastern view. Beyond the glint of car-tops, the peaks of the Hollywood hills seemed to be dissolving into a broth of billboards and smog.

The desk was standard hospital-issue phony walnut and chrome, pushed up against one wall. A hard-looking chrome and orange-cloth chair competed for space with a scuffed brown Naugahyde recliner. Between the chairs a thrift-shop end table supported a coffee maker and a struggling philodendron in a blue ceramic pot.

Stephanie sat at the desk, wearing a long white coat over a wine-and-gray dress, writing on an outpatient intake form. A chin-high stack of charts shadowed her writing arm. When I stepped into the room she looked up, put down her pen, smiled, and stood.

"Alex."

She'd turned into a good-looking woman. The dull-brown hair, once worn shoulder-length, limp, and barretted, was short, frosted at the tips, and feathered. Contact lenses had replaced granny glasses, revealing amber eyes I'd never noticed before. Her bone structure seemed stronger, more sculpted. She'd never been heavy; now she was thin. Time hadn't ignored her as she entered the dark side of thirty; a mesh of feathers gathered at the corners of her eyes and there was some hardness at the mouth. Makeup handled all of it well.

"Good to see you," she said, taking my hand.

"Good to see you, Steph."

We hugged briefly.

"Can I get you something?" She pointed to the coffee machine, arm jangling. Gold vermeil bracelets looped her wrist. Gold watch on the other arm. No rings. "Plain old coffee or real *café au lait*? This little guy actually steams the milk."

I said no thanks and looked at the machine. Small, squat, black matte and brushed steel, logo of a German manufacturer. The carafe was tiny—two cups' worth. Next to it sat a petite copper pitcher.

"Cute, huh?" she said. "Gift from a friend. Gotta do something to bring a little style into this place."

She smiled. Style was something she'd never cared about. I smiled back and settled in the recliner. A leatherbound book sat on a nearby table. I picked it up. Collected poems of Byron. Bookmark from a store named Browsers—up on Los Feliz, just above Hollywood. Dusty and crowded, with an emphasis on verse. Lots of junk, a few treasures. I'd gone there as an intern, during lunch hour.

Stephanie said, "He's some writer. I'm trying to expand my interests."

I put the book down. She sat in her desk chair and wheeled around facing me, legs crossed. Pale-gray stockings and suede pumps matched her dress.

"You look great," I said.

Another smile, casual but full, as if she'd expected the compliment but was still pleased by it. "You, too, Alex. Thanks for coming on such short notice."

"You piqued my interest."

"Did I?"

"Sure. All those hints of high intrigue."

She half turned toward the desk, removed a chart from the stack, let it rest in her lap but didn't open it.

"Yup," she said, "it's a challenging one, that's for sure."

Standing suddenly, she walked to the door, closed it, and sat back down.

"So," she said, "how does it feel to be back?"

"Almost got busted on the way in."

I told her about my encounter with the security guard.

"Fascist," she said cheerfully, and my memory banks reactivated: grievance committees over which she'd presided. White coat disdained for jeans, sandals, bleached cotton blouses. *Stephanie, not Doctor. Titles are exclusionary devices of the power elite. . . .*

I said, "Yeah, it was kind of paramilitary," but she just gazed at the chart in her lap.

"High intrigue," she said. "What we've got is a whodunit, howdunit—a *did-anyone-do-it*. Only this is no Agatha Christie thing, Alex. This is a real-life mess. I don't know if you can help, but I'm not sure what else to do."

Voices from the corridor filtered in, squalls and scolding and fleeing footsteps. Then a child's cry of terror pierced the plaster.

"This place is a zoo," she said. "Let's get out of here."

A door at the rear of the clinic opened to a stairway. We descended to the first basement level. Stephanie moved fast, almost jogging down the steps.

The cafeteria was nearly empty—one orange-topped table occupied by a male intern reading the sports section, two others shared by slumping couples who looked as if they'd slept in their clothes. Parents spending the night. Something we'd fought for.

Empty trays and dirty dishes cluttered some of the other tables. A hair-netted orderly circulated slowly, filling salt shakers.

On the eastern wall was the door to the doctors' dining room: polished teak panels, finely etched brass nameplate. Some philanthropist with a nautical bent. Stephanie bypassed it and led me to a booth at the far end of the main room.

"Sure you don't want coffee?" she said.

Remembering the hospital mud, I said, "Already filled my caffeine quota."

"I know what you mean."

She ran her hand through her hair and we sat.

"Okay," she said. "What we've got is a twenty-one-month-old white female, full-term pregnancy, normal delivery, APGAR of nine. The only significant historical factor is that just before this child was born, a male sib died of sudden infant death syndrome at age one year."

"Any other children?" I said, taking out a note pad and pen.

"No, there's just Cassie. Who looked fine until she was three months old, at which time her mother reported going in at night to check on her and finding her not breathing."

"Checking because she was nervous about SIDS?"

"Exactly. When she wasn't able to rouse the baby, she administered CPR, got her going. Then they brought her into the E.R. By the time I arrived she looked fine, nothing remarkable on exam. I admitted her for observation, did all the usual tests. Nothing. After discharge we set the family up with a sleep monitor and an alarm. Over the next few months the bell went off a few times but they were always false positives—the baby was breathing fine. The graphs show some tracings that could be very brief apnea but there are also lots of movement artifacts—the baby thrashing around. I figured maybe she was just restless—those alarms aren't foolproof—and put down the first episode to some quirky thing. But I did have the pulmonologists look at her because of her brother's SIDS. Negative. So we decided just to keep a close eye on her during the high-risk period for crib death."

"A year?"

She nodded. "I played it safe—fifteen months. Started with weekly outpatient checkups, tapered off so that by nine months I was willing to let them go till the one-year exam. Two days after the nine-month checkup they're back at E.R., middle-of-the-night respiratory problems—the baby woke up gasping, with a croupy bark. More CPR by mom and they bring her in."

"Isn't CPR kind of extreme for croup? Did the baby actually pass out?"

"No, she never lost consciousness, just gasped a lot. Mom may have been overreacting, but with her losing the first child, who could blame her? By the time I got to the E.R., the baby looked fine, no fever, no distress. No surprise, either. Cool night air can clear up croup. I ran a chest X-ray and bloodwork, all normal. Prescribed decongestants, fluids, and rest and was ready to send them home but the mother asked me to admit her. She was convinced there was something serious going on. I was almost certain there wasn't, but we'd been seeing some scary respiratory things recently, so I admitted her, ordered daily bloodwork. Her counts were normal and after a couple of days of getting stuck, she was going hysterical at the sight of a white coat. I discharged her, went back to weekly outpatient follow-up, during which the baby would have nothing to do with me. Minute I walk into the exam room she screams."

"The fun part of being a doctor," I said.

She gave a sad smile, glanced over at the food servers. "They're closing up. Want anything?"

"No thanks."

"If you don't mind, I haven't had breakfast yet."

"Sure, go ahead."

She walked briskly to the metal counters and came back with half a grapefruit on a plate and a cup of coffee. She took a sip of the coffee and grimaced.

"Maybe it needs some steamed milk," I said.

She wiped her mouth with a napkin. "Nothing can save this."

"Least it doesn't cost anything."

"Says who?"

"What? No more free coffee for the docs?"

"Them days are gone, Alex."

"Another tradition bites the dust," I said. "The old budgetary blues?"

"What else? Coffee and tea are forty-nine cents a cup now. Wonder how many cups it'll take to balance the books."

She ate some grapefruit. I fiddled with my pen and said, "I remember how hard you guys fought to get the interns and residents in on the freebie."

She shook her head. "Amazing what seemed important back then."

"Money problems worse than usual?"

"Afraid so." She frowned, put her spoon down and pushed the grapefruit away. "Anyway, back to the case. Where was I?"

"The baby screaming at you."

"Right. Okay, again things start to look good, so again I taper off and terminate, set up an appointment in two months. Three days later, back in the E.R., two A.M. Another croup thing. Only this time the mother says the kid *did* pass out—actually turned blue. More CPR."

"Three days after you terminated," I said, making a note. "Last time it was two."

"Interesting, huh? Okay, I do an E.R. checkup. The baby's blood pressure is up a bit and she's breathing rapidly. But getting plenty of oxygen in. No wheeze, but I was thinking either acute asthma or some sort of anxiety reaction."

"Panic at being back in the hospital again?"

"That, or just the mother's distress rubbing off on her."

"Was the mother showing a lot of overt distress?"

"Not really, but you know how it is with mothers and kids—the vibes. On the other hand, I wasn't ready to rule out something physical. A baby passing out is something to take seriously."

"Sure," I said, "but it could also have been a tantrum gone too far. Some kids learn young how to hold their breath and pass out."

"I know, but this happened in the middle of the night, Alex, not after some power struggle. So I admit her again, order allergy tests, complete pulmonary functions—no asthma. I also start thinking of rarer stuff: membrane problems, an idiopathic brain thing, an enzyme disorder. They're up on Five for a week, real merry-go-round, consults by every specialty in the house, lots of poking and probing. Poor little thing's freaking out as soon as the door to her room opens, no one's coming up with a diagnosis, and the whole time she's in, there are no breathing difficulties. Reinforcing my anxiety theory. I discharge them and the next time I see them in the office, I do nothing but try to play with her. But she still won't have anything to do with me. So I gently raise the anxiety issue with mom but she's not buying."

"How'd she take that?" I said.

"No anger—that's not this lady's style. She just said she couldn't see it, the baby being so young. I told her phobias could occur at any age, but I clearly wasn't getting through. So I backed off, sent them home, gave her some time to think about it. Hoping that as the baby approached one year and the SIDS risk dropped, mom's fears would diminish and the baby would start to relax too. Four days later they were back in the E.R., croup, gasping, mom's in tears, *begging* for an admit. I put the baby in but ordered no tests. Nothing even remotely invasive, just observation. And the baby looked perfect—not even a sniffle. At that point I took the mom aside and leaned more heavily on the psychological angle. Still no sale."

"Did you ever bring up the first child's death?"

She shook her head. "No. I thought of it but at the time it just didn't seem right, Alex. Overloading the lady. I figured I had a good feel for her—I was the attending doc when they brought the first child in dead. Handled the whole post-mortem . . . I carried him to the morgue, Alex."

She closed her eyes, opened them but focused away from me.

"What hell," I said.

"Yeah—and it was a chance thing. They were Rita's private patients, but she was out of town and I was on call. I didn't know them from Adam but I got stuck doing the death conference, too. I tried to do some basic counseling, gave them referrals to grief groups, but they weren't interested. When they came back a year and a half later, wanting me to take care of the *new* baby, I was really surprised."

"Why?"

"I would have predicted they'd associate me with the tragedy, a kill-the-messenger kind of thing. When they didn't, I figured I'd handled them well."

"I'm sure you did."

She shrugged.

I said, "How'd Rita react to your taking over?"

"What choice did she have? She wasn't around when they needed her. She was going through her own problems at the time. Her husband—you know who she was married to, don't you?"

"Otto Kohler."

"The famous conductor—that's how she used to refer to him: 'My husband, the famous conductor.' "

"He died recently, didn't he?"

"Few months ago. He'd been sick for a while, series of strokes. Since then, Rita's been gone even more than usual and the rest of us have been picking up a lot of the slack. Mostly, she attends conventions and presents old papers. She's actually going to retire." Embarrassed smile. "I've been considering applying for her position, Alex. Do you see me as a division head?"

"Sure."

"Really?"

"Sure, Steph. Why not?"

"I don't know. The position's kind of . . . inherently authoritarian."

"To some extent," I said. "But I'd imagine the position can adapt to different styles of leadership."

"Well," she said, "I'm not sure I'd make a good leader. I don't really like telling people what to do. . . . Anyway, enough about that. I'm getting off track. There were two more passing-out episodes before I brought up the psych thing again."

"Two more," I said, looking at my notes. "I've got a total of five."

"Correct."

"How old's the baby by now?"

"Just under a year. And a hospital veteran. Two more admits, negative for everything. At that point I sat mom down and *strongly* recommended a psych consult. To which she reacted with . . . here, let me give you the exact quote."

She opened the chart and read softly: " 'I know that makes sense, Dr. Eves, but I just *know* Cassie's sick. If you'd only seen her—lying there, cyanotic.' End of quote."

"She phrased it that way? 'Cyanotic'?"

"Yup. She has a medical background. Studied to be a respiratory tech."

"And both her kids stop breathing. Interesting."

"Yes." Hard smile. "At the time I didn't realize how interesting. I was still caught up in the puzzle—trying to arrive at a diagnosis, worrying when the next crisis was going to be and if I'd be able to do anything about it. To my surprise it didn't happen for a while."

She looked at the chart again. "A month passes, two, three, still no sign of them. I'm happy the baby's okay but I'm also starting to wonder if maybe they've just found themselves another doc. So I called the home, talked to mom. Everything's fine. Then I realized that in the heat of everything, the baby had never had her one-year exam. I schedule it, find everything intact, with the exception that she's a little slow vocally and verbally."

"How slow?"

"No retardation or anything like that. She just made very few sounds—in fact I didn't hear anything from her at all, and mom said she was pretty quiet at home, too. I tried to do a Bailey test, but couldn't because the baby wouldn't cooperate. My guesstimate was about a two-month lag, but you know at that age it doesn't take much to tip the scales, and given all the stress the poor thing's been through, no big deal. But brilliant me. Bringing up language development got mom worried about *that*. So I sent them over to ENT and Speech and Hearing, who found her ears and laryngeal structure one hundred percent normal and concurred with my assessment: possible mild delay in reaction to medical trauma. I gave the mom suggestions about stimulating speech and didn't hear from them for another two months."

"Baby's fourteen months old," I said, writing.

"And back in the E.R., four days later. But not with breathing probs. This time she's spiking a temp—a hundred and five. Flushed and dry, and breathing fast. To be honest, Alex, I was almost *happy* to see the fever—at least I had something organic to work with. Then the white count came back normal, nothing viral or bacterial. So I ran a toxicology. Clean. Still, lab tests aren't perfect—even our error rates are running ten to twenty percent. And that spike was real—I took the temp myself. We bathed her and Tylenoled her down to a hundred and two, admitted her with a fever-of-unknown-origin diagnosis, pushed fluids, put her through some real hell: spinal tap to rule out meningitis, even though her ears were clear and her neck was supple, because for all we knew she had one heck of a headache she couldn't tell us about. Plus twice-daily bloodwork—she went bananas, had to be held down. Even with that, she managed to dislodge the needle a couple of times."

She exhaled and pushed the grapefruit farther away. Her forehead had moistened. Swabbing it with a napkin, she said, "First time I've told it like this from the beginning."

"You haven't had any case conferences?"

"No, we don't do much of that anymore. Rita's basically use-less."

I said, "How did the mother react to all the procedures?"

"Some tears, but basically she stayed composed. Able to comfort the baby, cuddling her when it was over. I made sure she never was involved in holding the baby down—integrity of the mother-child bond. See, your lectures stuck, Alex. Of course the *rest* of us felt like Nazis."

She wiped her brow again. "Anyway, the blood tests kept coming back normal but I held off discharge until she'd had no fever for four days running."

Sighing, she burrowed her fingers through her hair and flipped through her chart.

"Next fever spike: the kid's fifteen months old, mother claims a hundred and six."

"Dangerous."

"You bet. E.R. doc records a hundred and four and a half, bathes and doses it down to a hundred and one and a half. And mom reports new symptoms: retching, projectile vomiting, diarrhea. And black *stools.*"

"Internal bleeding?"

"Sounds like it. That made *everyone* sit up. The diaper she had on did show some evidence of diarrhea, but no blood. Mom said she threw the bloody one out, would try to retrieve it. On exam, the kid's rectal area was a little red, some irritation at the external edges of the sphincter. But no bowel distension that I can palpate—her belly's nice and soft, maybe a bit tender to the touch. But that's hard to gauge 'cause she's freaking out, nonstop, at being examined."

"Raw rectum," I said. "Any scarring?"

"No, no, nothing like that. Just mild irritation, consistent with diarrhea. Obstruction or appendicitis needed to be ruled out. I called in a surgeon, Joe Leibowitz—you know how thorough he is. He examined her, said there was nothing that justified cutting her open but we should admit her and watch her for a while. We put an I.V. in—*great* fun—did a complete panel, and this time there was a slightly elevated white count. But still within normal limits, nothing that would jibe with a hundred and four and a half. Next day she was down to one hundred. Day after that, ninety-nine point two, and her tummy didn't seem to hurt. Joe said definitely no appendicitis, call in GI. I got a consult from Tony Franks and he evaluated her for early signs of irritable bowel syndrome, Crohn's disease, liver problems. Negative. Another tox panel, a careful diet history. I called in Allergy and Immunology again, to test her for some weird hypersensitivity to something."

"Was she on formula?"

"Nope, a breast-fed baby, though by that time she was totally on solids. After a week she was looking perfect. Thank God we didn't cut her open."

"Fifteen months old," I said. "Just past the high-risk period for SIDS. So the respiratory system quiets and the gut starts acting up?"

Stephanie gave me a long, searching look. "Want to hazard a diagnosis?"

"Is that all of it?"

"Un-uh. There were two other GI crises. At sixteen months— four days after an appointment with Tony in Gastro clinic—and a month and a half later, following his final appointment with them."

"Same symptoms?"

"Right. But both those times, mom actually brought in bloody diapers and we worked them over for every possible pathogen—I mean we're talking typhoid, cholera, tropical maladies that have never been seen on this continent. Some sort of environmental toxin—lead, heavy metals, you name it. But all we found was a little healthy blood."

"Are the parents in some sort of work that would expose the child to weird pollutants?"

"Hardly. She's a full-time mom and he's a college professor."

"Biology?"

"Sociology. But before we get off on the family structure, there's more. Another type of crisis. Six weeks ago. Bye-bye gut, hello new organ system. Want to take a guess which one?"

I thought for a moment. "Neurological?"

"Bingo." She reached over and touched my arm. "I feel so vindicated calling you in."

"Seizures?"

"Middle of the night. Grand mal, according to the parents, right down to the frothing at the mouth. The EEG showed no abnormal wave activity and the kid had all her reflexes, but we put her through a CAT scan, another spinal, and all the high-tech neuro-radiology video games, on the chance she had some kind of brain tumor. That *really* scared me, Alex, because when I thought about it I realized a tumor could have caused *everything* that had been happening, right from the beginning. A growth impinging on different brain centers, causing different symptoms as it grew."

She shook her head. "Wouldn't *that* have been a happy situation? Me talking psychosomatic and there's an astrocytoma or something growing inside her? Thank God all her scans were totally clean."

"Did she look post-seizural when you saw her in the E.R.?"

"In terms of being drowsy and listless, she did. But that's also consistent with a little kid being dragged to the hospital in the middle of the night and put through the wringer. Still, it scared me—that there could be something organic I was missing. I asked Neurology to follow up. They did for a month, found nothing, terminated. Two weeks later—*two days ago*—another seizure. And I really need your help, Alex. They're up in Five West, right now. And that's the whole kaboodle, history-wise. Ready to give me some wisdom now?"

I scanned my notes.

Recurrent, unexplained illnesses. Multiple hospitalizations.

Shifting organ systems.

Discrepancies between symptoms and lab tests.

Female child showing panic at being treated or handled.

Mother with a paramedical training.

Nice mother.

Nice mother who might just be a monster. Scripting, choreographing, and directing a Grand Guignol, and casting her own child as unwitting star.

Rare diagnosis, but the facts fit. Up until twenty years ago nobody had heard of it.

"Munchausen syndrome by proxy," I said, putting my notes down. "Sounds like a textbook case."

Her eyes narrowed. "Yes, it does. When you hear it all strung together like this. But when you're right in the middle of it . . . even now I can't be sure."

"You're still considering something organic?"

"I have to until I can prove otherwise. There was another case—last year, over at County. *Twenty-five* consecutive admits for recurrent weird infections during a six-month period. Also a female child, attentive mother who looked too calm for the staff's peace of mind. *That* baby was really going downhill and they were just about ready to call in the authorities when it turned out to be a rare immunodeficiency—three documented cases in the literature, special tests that had to be done at NIH. Moment I heard about it, I had Cassie tested for the same thing. Negative. But that doesn't mean there isn't some other factor I haven't caught. New stuff keeps popping up—I can barely keep up with the journals."

She moved her spoon around in her coffee.

"Or maybe I'm just denying—trying to make myself feel better for not seeing the Munchausen thing sooner. Which is why I called you in—I need some direction, Alex. Tell me which way to go with this."

I thought for a while.

Munchausen syndrome.

A.k.a. *pseudologia fantastica*.

A.k.a. factitious illness disorder.

An especially grotesque form of pathological lying, named after Baron von Munchausen, the world-class prevaricator.

Munchausen is hypochondriasis gone mad. Patients fabricating disease by mutilating and poisoning themselves, or just lying. Playing mind games with physicians and nurses—with the health-care system itself.

Adult Munchausen patients manage to get hospitalized repeatedly, medicated needlessly, even cut open on the operating table.

Pitiful, masochistic, and perplexing—a twist of the psyche that still defies comprehension.

But what we were considering here was beyond pity. It was an evil variant:

Munchausen by proxy.

Parents—mothers, invariably—faking illness in their own offspring. Using their children—especially daughters—as crucibles for a hideous concoction of lies, pain, and disease.

I said, "So much of it fits, Steph. Right from the beginning.

The apnea and passing out could be due to smothering—those movement artifacts on the monitor could mean she was struggling."

She winced. "God, yes. I just did some reading, found a case in England where movement artifacts tipped them off to the baby being smothered."

"Plus, with mom being a respiratory tech, breathing could be the first system she'd choose to mess with. What about the intestinal stuff? Some kind of poisoning?"

"Most likely, but it's nothing the tox panel could come up with when they tested."

"Maybe she used something short-acting."

"Or an inert irritant that activated the bowel mechanically, but passed right through."

"And the seizures?"

"Same thing, I guess. I don't *know*, Alex. I really don't *know*." She squeezed my arm again. "I've got no evidence at all and what if I'm wrong? I need you to be objective. Give Cassie's mom the benefit of the doubt—maybe I'm misjudging her. Try to get into her head."

"I can't promise a miracle, Steph."

"I know. But *anything* you can do will be helpful. Things could get really messy with this one."

"Did you tell the mother I'd be consulting?"

She nodded.

"Is she more amenable to a psych consult now?"

"I wouldn't say amenable, but she agreed. I think I convinced her by backing away from any suggestion that stress was *causing* Cassie's problems. Far as she's concerned, *I* think the seizures are bona fide organic. But I did press the need for helping Cassie adjust to the trauma of hospitalization. Told her epilepsy would mean Cassie can expect to see a lot more of this place and we're going to have to help her deal with it. I said you were an expert on medical trauma, might be able to do some hypnosis thing to relax Cassie during procedures. That sound reasonable?"

I nodded.

"Meanwhile," she said, "you can be analyzing the mother. See if she's a psychopath."

"If it is Munchausen by proxy, we may not be looking for a psychopath."

"What then? What kind of nut does this to her own kid?"

"No one really knows," I said. "It's been a while since I looked at the literature, but the best guess used to be some kind of mixed personality disorder. The problem is, documented cases are so rare, there really isn't a good data base."

"It's still that way, Alex. I looked up sources over at the med school and came up with very little."

"I'd like to borrow the articles."

"I read them there, didn't check them out," she said. "But I think I still have the references written down somewhere. And I think I remember that mixed personality business—whatever that means."

"It means we don't know, so we're fudging. Part of the problem is that psychologists and psychiatrists depend on information we get from the patient. And taking a history from a Munchausen means relying upon a habitual liar. But the stories they tell, once you expose them, *do* seem to be fairly consistent: early experience with serious physical illness or trauma, families that overemphasized disease and health, child abuse, sometimes incest. Leading to very poor self-esteem, problems with relationships, and a pathological need for attention. Illness becomes the arena in which they act out that need—that's why so many of them enter health professions. But lots of people with those same histories *don't* become Munchausens. And the same history applies both to Munchausens who abuse themselves and the proxies who torment their kids. In fact, there's some sugges-tion that Munchausen-by-proxy parents start out as self-abusers and switch, at some point, to using their kids. But as for why and when that happens, no one knows."

"Weird," she said, shaking her head. "It's like a dance. I feel I'm waltzing around with her, but she's leading."

"Devil's waltz," I said.

She shuddered. "I know we're not talking hard science, Alex, but if you could just dig your way in there, tell me if you think she's doing it. . . ."

"Sure. But I am a bit curious why you didn't call in the hospital Psych department."

"Never liked the hospital Psych department," she said. "Too Freudian. Hardesty wanted to put everyone on the couch. It's a moot point, anyway. There is no Psych department."

"What do you mean?"

"They were all fired."

"The whole department? When?"

"Few months ago. Don't you read your staff newsletter?"

"Not very often."

"Obviously. Well, Psych's dissolved. Hardesty's county contract was canceled and he never wrote any grants, so there was no financial backup. The board decided not to pick up the cost."

"What about Hardesty's tenure? The others—weren't Greiler and Pantissa tenured, too?"

"Probably. But tenure, as it turns out, comes from the med school, not the hospital. So they've still got their titles. Salaries are a whole other story. Quite a revelation for those of us who thought we had job security. Not that anyone fought for Hardesty. Everyone thought he and his guys were deadwood."

"No more Psych department," I said. "No more free coffee. What else?"

"Oh, plenty. Does it affect you, there being no Psych department—in terms of your staff privileges, I mean?"

"No, my appointment's in pediatrics. Oncology, actually, though it's been years since I've seen any cancer patients."

"Good," she said. "Then there won't be any procedural hassles. Any more questions before we go up?"

"Just a couple of observations. If it is Munchausen by proxy, there's some time pressure—the usual picture is an escalating pattern. Sometimes kids die, Steph."

"I know," she said miserably, pressing her fingertips to her temples. "I know I may need to confront the mother. That's why I have to be sure."

"The other thing is the first child—the boy. I assume you're considering him a possible homicide."

"Oh, God, yes. That's really been eating at me. When my suspicions about the mother started to gel, I pulled his chart and went over it with a fine-tooth comb. But there was nothing iffy. Rita's ongoing notes were good—he was perfectly healthy before he died and the autopsy was inconclusive, as so many of them are. Now here I am with a living, breathing child and I can't do a thing to help *her*."

"Sounds like you're doing everything you can."

"Trying, but it's so damned frustrating."

I said, "What about the father? We haven't talked about him."

"I don't really have a good feel for him. Mother's clearly the primary caretaker and it's her I've been dealing with most of the time. Once I started to think of it as a possible Munchausen by proxy, she seemed especially important to focus on, because aren't mothers always the ones?"

"Yes," I said, "but in some cases the father turns out to be a passive accomplice. Any sign he suspects something?"

"If he has, he hasn't told me. He doesn't seem especially passive—nice enough. So is she, for that matter. They're both nice, Alex. That's one of the things that makes it so difficult."

"Typical Munchausen scenario. The nurses probably love them."

She nodded.

"What's the other?" I said.

"The other what?"

"Thing that makes it so difficult."

She closed her eyes and rubbed them and took a long time to answer.

"The other thing," she said, "and this may sound horribly cold-hearted and political, is who they *are*. Socially. Politically. The child's full name is Cassie Brooks *Jones*—set off any buzzers?"

"No," I said. "Jones isn't exactly memorable."

"Jones, as in Charles L. Junior. Hotshot financier? The hospital's primary money manager?"

"Don't know him."

"That's right—you don't read your newsletters. Well, as of eight months ago he's also chairman of the board. There was a big shake-up."

"The budget?"

"What else. Anyway, here's the genealogy: Charles Junior's only son is Charles the Third—like royalty. He goes by *Chip*—Cassie's daddy. The mom is Cindy. The dead son was Chad—Charles the Fourth."

"All *C*s," I said. "Sounds like they like order."

"Whatever. The main thing is, Cassie is Charles Junior's only *grandchild*. Isn't that wonderful, Alex? Here I am with a potential Munchausen by proxy that could explode in everyone's face, and the patient's the only grandchild of the guy who took away the free coffee."

3

We got up from the table and she said, "If you don't mind, we can take the stairs up."

"Morning aerobics? Sure."

"You hit thirty-five," she said, smoothing her dress and buttoning her white coat, "and the old basal metabolism goes to hell. Got to work hard not to be lumpy. Plus, the elevators still move on Valium Standard Time."

We walked toward the cafeteria's main exit. The tables were completely empty now. A brown-uniformed maintenance worker was wet-mopping the floor, and we had to step gingerly to maintain traction.

I said, "The elevator I took to your office was converted to key lock. Why the need for all the security?"

"The official line is crime prevention," she said. "Keeping all the street craziness out of here. Which to some extent is valid—there *have* been increased problems, mostly during the night shift. But can you remember a time when East Hollywood didn't get bad after dark?"

We reached the door. Another maintenance man was locking it and when he saw us, he gave a world-weary look and held it open for us.

Stephanie said, "Reduced hours—another budget cut."

Out in the hallway, things had gotten frantic. Doctors blew past in boisterous groups, filling the air with fast talk. Families traipsed through, wheeling doll-sized veteran journeyors to and from the ordeals wrought by science.

A silent crowd was assembled at the elevator doors, clumped like human droplets, waiting for any of three lifts that had settled simultaneously on the third floor. Waiting, always the waiting . . .

Stephanie moved through deftly, nodding at familiar faces but never stopping. I followed close behind, avoiding collision with I.V. poles.

When we entered the basement stairwell, I said, "What kind of crime problems have there been?"

"The usual, but more so," she said, climbing. "Car thefts, vandalism, purse snatchings. Some muggings out on Sunset. And a couple of nurses were assaulted in the parking lot across the street a few months ago."

"Sexual assaults?" I said, taking two steps at a time in order to keep up.

"That was never made clear. Neither of them came back to talk about it. They were night-shift floats, not regular staff. What I *heard* was that they were beaten up pretty badly and had their purses stolen. The police sent a community relations officer who gave us the usual personal safety lecture and admitted that, bottom line, there was little anyone could do to guarantee safety unless the hospital was turned into an armed camp. The women on the staff screamed a lot and the administration promised to have Security patrol more regularly."

"Any follow-through?"

"Guess so—you see more uniforms in the lots and there've been no attacks since then. But the protection came with a whole bunch of other stuff no one asked for. Robocops on campus, new badges, frequent hassles like the one you just went through. Personally, I think we played right into the administration's hands—gave them an excuse for exercising more control. And once they get it, they'll never relinquish it."

"C students getting revenge?"

She stopped climbing and looked down at me over her shoulder, smiling sheepishly. "You *remember* that?"

"Vividly."

"Pretty mouthy back then, wasn't I?"

"The fire of youth," I said. "And they deserved it—talking down to you in front of everyone, that 'Dr. *Ms.*' stuff."

"Yeah, they *were* a pretty cheeky bunch, weren't they." She resumed the climb, but more slowly. "Banker's hours, martini lunches, sitting around shmoozing in the caf and sending *us* memos about increasing efficiency and cutting costs."

A few steps later she stopped again. "C students—I can't believe I actually said that. Her cheeks were aflame. "I *was* obnoxious, wasn't I?"

"Inspired, Steph."

"More like *per*spired. Those were crazy times, Alex. Totally crazy."

"Sure were," I said. "But don't dismiss what we accomplished: equal pay for female staff, parents rooming in, the playrooms."

"And let us not forget free coffee for the house staff."

A few steps later: "Even so, Alex, so much of what we obsessed on seems so misdirected. We focused on personalities but the problem was the system. One bunch of C students leaves, another arrives, and the same old problems go on. Sometimes I wonder if I've stayed here too long. Look at you—away from it for all these years and you look better than ever."

"So do you," I said, thinking of what she'd just told me about trying for the division-head position.

"Me?" She smiled. "Well, you're *gallant* to say so, but in my case, it's not due to personal fulfillment. Just clean living."

The fifth floor housed children aged one to eleven who were not in need of high-tech care. The hundred beds in the east ward took up two thirds of the floor space.

The remaining third was set aside for a twenty-bed private unit on the west side, separated from the ward by teak doors lettered THE HANNAH CHAPELL SPECIAL UNIT in brass.

Chappy Ward. Off limits to the hoi polloi and trainees, maintained by endowments, private insurance, and personal checks; not a Medi-Cal form in sight.

Private meant Muzak flowing from concealed ceiling speakers, carpeted floors instead of linoleum, one patient per room in place of three or more, TVs that worked almost all the time, though they were still black-and-white antiques.

This morning, nearly all twenty rooms were empty. A trio of bored-looking R.N.'s stood behind the counter at the nursing station. A few feet away a unit clerk filed her nails.

"Morning, Dr. Eves," said one of the nurses, addressing Stephanie but watching me and looking none too friendly. I wondered why and smiled at her anyway. She turned away. Early fifties, short, chunky, grainy-skinned, long-jawed, sprayed blond hair. Powder-blue uniform trimmed with white. Atop the stiff hair, a starched cap; I hadn't seen one of those in a long time.

The two other nurses, Filipinas in their twenties, glanced at each other and moved away as if spurred by a silent code.

Stephanie said, "Morning, Vicki. How's our girl doing?"

"So far so good." Reaching over, the blond nurse pulled a chart out of the slot marked 505W and handed it to Stephanie. Her nails were stubby and gnawed. Her gaze settled on me again. The old charm was still not working.

"This is Dr. Alex Delaware," said Stephanie, thumbing through the chart, "our consulting psychologist. Dr. Delaware, Vicki Bottomley, Cassie's primary care nurse."

"Cindy said you'd be coming by," said the nurse, making it sound like bad news. Stephanie kept reading.

"Pleased to meet you," I said.

"Pleased to meet *you*." A challenging sullenness in her voice made Stephanie look up.

"Everything okay, Vicki?"

"Peachy," said the nurse, flashing a smile as jovial as a slap across the face. "Everything's fine. She held down most of her breakfast, fluids and P/O meds—"

"What meds?"

"Just Tylenol. An hour ago. Cindy said she had a headache—"

"Tylenol One?"

"Yes, Dr. Eves, just the kid stuff, liquid, one teaspoon—it's all in there." She pointed to the chart.

"Yes, I see," said Stephanie, reading. "Well, that's all right for today, Vicki, but next time no meds—not even OTC stuff—without my approval. I need to authorize *everything,* other than food and beverage, that passes between this child's lips. Okay?"

"Sure," said Bottomley, smiling again. "No problem. I just thought—"

"No harm done, Vicki," said Stephanie, reaching over and patting the nurse's shoulder. "I'm sure I would have okayed Tylenol. It's just that with this kid's history we've got to be super-careful to tease out drug reactions."

"Yes, Dr. Eves. Is there anything else?"

Stephanie read more of the chart, then closed it and handed it back. "No, not at the moment, unless there's something you want to report."

Bottomley shook her head.

"Okay, then. I'm going to go in and introduce Dr. Delaware. Anything about Cassie you want to share?"

Bottomley removed a bobby pin from her hair and stuck it back in, fastening blond strands to the cap. Her eyes were wide-set and long-lashed, a soft, pretty blue in the tense, gritty terrain of her face.

She said, "Like what?"

"Anything Dr. Delaware should know, to help Cassie and her parents, Vicki."

Bottomley stared at Stephanie for a moment, then turned to me, glaring. "There's nothing wrong with them. They're just regular people."

I said, "I hear Cassie gets pretty anxious about medical procedures."

Bottomley put her hands on her hips. "Wouldn't *you,* if you got stuck as much as she does?"

Stephanie said, "Vicki—"

"Sure," I said, smiling. "It's a perfectly normal reaction, but sometimes normal anxiety can be helped by behavioral treatment."

Bottomley gave a small, tight laugh. "Maybe so. Good luck."

Stephanie started to say something. I touched her arm and said, "Why don't we get going?"

"Sure." To Bottomley: "Remember, nothing P/O except food and drink."

Bottomley held on to her smile. "Yes, Doctor. Now, if it's all right with you, I'd like to leave the floor for a few minutes."

Stephanie looked at her watch. "Break time?"

"No. Just wanted to go down to the gift shop and get Cassie a LuvBunny—you know those stuffed bunnies, the cartoons on TV? She's crazy about them. I figure with you people in there, she should be fine for a few minutes."

Stephanie looked at me. Bottomley followed her glance with what seemed to be satisfaction, gave another tight laugh, and left. Her walk was a brisk waddle. The starched cap floated along the empty corridor like a kite caught in a tailwind.

Stephanie took my arm and steered me away from the station.

"Sorry, Alex. I've never seen her like that."

"Has she been Cassie's nurse before?"

"Several times—almost from the beginning. She and Cindy have developed a good rapport and Cassie seems to like her too. When Cassie comes in, they ask for her."

"She seems to have gotten pretty possessive."

"She does have a tendency to get involved, but I've always looked at that as a positive thing. Families love her—she's one of the most committed nurses I've ever worked with. With morale the way it is, commitment's hard to find."

"Does her commitment extend to home visits?"

"Not as far as I know. The only home things were a couple I did, with one of the residents, at the very beginning, to set up the sleep monitor—" She touched her mouth. "You're not suggesting she had something to do with—"

"I'm not suggesting anything," I said, wondering if I was, because Bottomley had chapped my hide. "Just throwing out ideas."

"Hmm . . . well, that's some idea. Munchausen nurse? I guess the medical background fits."

"There've been cases," I said. "Nurses and doctors looking for attention, and usually they're the really possessive ones. But if Cassie's problems have always started at home and resolved in the hospital, that would rule her out, unless Vicki's a permanent resident at the Jones household."

"She isn't. At least not as far as I know. No, of course she isn't—I'd know if she was."

She looked unsure. Beaten down. I realized what a toll the case was taking.

"I would like to know why she was so hostile to me," I said. "Not for personal reasons but in terms of the dynamics of this family. If Vicki and the mother are tight and Vicki doesn't like me, that could sour my consult."

"Good point . . . I don't know *what's* eating at her."

"I assume you haven't discussed your suspicion of Cindy with her?"

"No. You're really the first person I've talked to about it. That's why I phrased my no-meds instructions in terms of drug reactions. Cindy's also been asked not to bring food from home for the same reason. Vicki and the nurses on the other shifts are supposed to log everything Cassie eats." She frowned. "Of course if Vicki's overstepping her bounds, she might not be following through. Want me to have her transferred? Nursing Ad would give me hell, but I suppose I could swing it pretty quickly."

"Not on my account. Let's keep things stable for the time being."

We walked behind the station. Stephanie retrieved the chart and studied it again.

"Everything looks okay," she said finally. "But I'll have a talk with her anyway."

I said, "Let me have a look."

She gave me the chart. Her usual neat handwriting and detailed notes. They included a family-structure chart that I spent some time on.

"No grandparents on the mother's side?"

She shook her head. "Cindy lost her parents young. Chip lost his mom, too, when he was a teenager. Old Chuck's the only grandparent left."

"Does he get up here much to visit?"

"From time to time. He's a busy man."

I continued reading. "Cindy's only twenty-six . . . maybe Vicki's a mother figure for her."

"Maybe," she said. "Whatever it is, I'll keep a tight leash on her."

"Don't come down too hard right now, Steph. I don't want to be seen by Vicki—or Cindy—as someone who makes anyone's life harder. Give me a chance to get to know Vicki. She could turn out to be an ally."

"Okay," she said. "This human relations stuff is your area. But let me know if she continues to be difficult. I don't want *anything* getting in the way of solving this thing."

The room was inundated with LuvBunnies—on the windowsill, nightstand, the bed tray, atop the TV. A bucktoothed, rainbow-hued welcoming party.

The rails of the bed were lowered. A beautiful child lay sleeping—a tiny bundle barely swelling the covers.

Her heart-face was turned to one side; her rosebud mouth, pink and parted. Buttermilk skin, chubby cheeks, nubbin nose. Her hair was sleek, straight, and black and trickled onto her shoulders. The bangs were moist and they stuck to her forehead. A ring of lace collar was visible above the blanket hem. One hand was concealed; the other, dimpled and clenched, gathered the fabric. Its thumb was the size of a lima bean.

The sleeper sofa by the window was unfolded to a single bed that had been made up. Military corners, pillow smooth as eggshell. A flowered vinyl overnight bag sat on the floor next to an empty food tray.

A young woman sat cross-legged on the edge of the mattress, reading *TV Guide*. As soon as she saw us she put down the magazine and got up.

Five five, firm figure, slightly long-waisted. Same shiny dark hair as her daughter's, parted in the middle, tied back loosely and gathered in a thick braid that nearly reached her waist. Same facial cast as Cassie's, too, stretched by maturity to something just barely longer than the perfect oval. Fine nose; straight, wide, unpainted mouth with naturally dark lips. Big brown eyes. Bloodshot.

No makeup, scrubbed complexion. A girlish woman. Twenty-six but she could easily have passed for a college student.

From the bed came a soft, breathy sound. Cassie sighing. All of us looked over at her. Her eyelids remained closed but they fluttered. Threads of lavender vein were visible beneath the skin. She rolled over, facing away from us.

I thought of a bisque doll.

All around us, the LuvBunnies leered.

Cindy Jones looked down at her daughter, reached over and smoothed hair out of the child's eyes.

Turning back to us, she ran her hands over her clothes, hurriedly, as if searching for unfastened buttons. The clothes were simple—plaid cotton shirt over faded jeans and medium-heeled sandals. A pink plastic Swatch watch. Not the post-deb, VIP daughter-in-law I'd expected.

"Well," whispered Stephanie, "looks like someone's snoozing away. Get any sleep yourself, Cindy?"

"A little." Soft voice, pleasant. She didn't have to whisper.

"Our mattresses have a way to go, don't they?"

"I'm fine, Dr. Eves." Her smile was tired. "Actually, Cassie slept great. She woke once, around five, and needed a cuddle. I held her and sang to her for a while and finally she fell back around seven. Guess that's why she's still out."

"Vicki said she had a headache."

"Yes, when she woke. Vicki gave her some liquid Tylenol and that seemed to work."

"Tylenol was the right thing to give her, Cindy. But in the future all medications—even over-the-counter stuff—will have to be approved by me. Just to play it safe."

The brown eyes opened wide. "Oh. Sure. I'm sorry."

Stephanie smiled. "No big deal. I just want to be careful. Cindy, this is Dr. Delaware, the psychologist we spoke about."

"Hello, Dr. Delaware."

"Hello, Mrs. Jones."

"Cindy." She extended a narrow hand and smiled shyly. Likable. I knew my job wasn't going to be easy.

Stephanie said, "As I told you, Dr. Delaware's an expert on

anxiety in children. If anyone can help Cassie cope, he can. He'd like to talk with you right now, if this is a good time."

"Oh . . . sure. This is fine." Cindy touched her braid and looked worried.

"Terrific," said Stephanie. "If there's nothing you need from me, I'll be going."

"Nothing I can think of right now, Dr. Eves. I was just wondering if you'd . . . come up with anything?"

"Not yet, Cindy. Yesterday's EEG was totally normal. But, as we've discussed, with children this age that's not always conclusive. The nurses haven't charted any seizurelike behavior. Have you noticed anything?"

"No . . . not really."

"Not really?" Stephanie took a step closer. She was only an inch taller than the other woman but seemed much larger.

Cindy Jones passed her upper lip under her top teeth, then released it. "Nothing—it's probably not important."

"It's okay, Cindy. Tell me anything, even if you think it's irrelevant."

"Well, I'm sure it's nothing, but sometimes I wonder if she's tuning out—not listening when I talk to her? Kind of staring off into space—like a petit mal? I'm sure it's nothing and I'm just seeing it because I'm looking for things now."

"When did you start noticing this?"

"Yesterday, after we were admitted."

"You never saw it at home?"

"I . . . no. But it could have been happening and I just didn't notice. Or maybe it's nothing. It probably is nothing—I don't know."

The pretty face began to buckle.

Stephanie patted her and Cindy moved toward the gesture, almost imperceptibly, as if to gain more comfort from it.

Stephanie stepped back, breaking contact. "How often have these staring episodes been occurring?"

"Maybe a couple of times a day. It's probably nothing—just her concentrating. She's always been good at concentrating—when she plays at home she concentrates really well."

"Well, that's good—the fact that she's got a good attention span."

Cindy nodded but she didn't look reassured.

Stephanie drew an appointment book out of a coat pocket, ripped out a back page and handed it to Cindy. "Tell you what, next time you see this staring, make a record of the exact time and call in Vicki or whoever's on duty to have a look, okay?"

"Okay. But it doesn't last long, Dr. Eves. Just a few seconds."

"Just do the best you can," said Stephanie. "In the meantime, I'll leave you and Dr. Delaware to get acquainted."

Pausing for a moment to look at the sleeping child, she smiled at both of us and left.

When the door closed, Cindy looked down at the bed. "I'll fold this up so you'll have somewhere to sit." There were delicate lavender veins under her skin, too. At the temples, throbbing.

"Let's do it together," I said.

That seemed to startle her. "No, that's okay."

Bending, she took hold of the mattress and lifted. I did likewise and the two of us turned the bed back into a sofa.

She smoothed the cushions, stood back, and said, "Please."

Feeling as if I were in a geisha house, I complied.

She walked over to the green chair and removed the LuvBunnies. Placing them on the nightstand, she pulled the chair opposite the couch and sat, feet flat on the floor, a hand on each slender thigh.

I reached over, took one of the stuffed animals from the window ledge, and stroked it. Through the glass the treetops of Griffith Park were green-black and cloudlike.

"Cute," I said. "Gifts?"

"Some of them are. Some we brought from home. We wanted Cassie to feel at home here."

"The hospital's become a second home, hasn't it?"

She stared at me. Tears filled the brown eyes, magnifying them. A look of shame spread across her face.

Shame? Or guilt?

Her hands shot up quickly to conceal it.

She cried silently for a while.

I got a tissue from the box on the bed table and waited.

She uncovered her face. "Sorry."

"No need to be," I said. "There aren't too many things more stressful than having a sick child."

She nodded. "The worst thing is not knowing—watching her suffer and not knowing . . . If only someone could figure it out."

"The other symptoms resolved. Maybe this will too."

Looping her braid over one shoulder, she fingered the ends. "I sure hope so. But . . ."

I smiled but said nothing.

She said, "The other things were more . . . typical. Normal—if that makes any sense."

"Normal childhood diseases," I said.

"Yes—croup, diarrhea. Other kids have them. Maybe not as severe, but they have them, so you can understand those kinds of things. But seizures . . . that's just not *normal*."

"Sometimes," I said, "kids have seizures after a high fever. One or two episodes and then it never recurs."

"Yes, I know. Dr. Eves told me about that. But Cassie wasn't spiking a temp when she had hers. The other times—when she had gastrointestinal problems—there were fevers. She was burning up, then. A hundred and *six*." She tugged the braid. "And then that went away and I thought we were going to be okay, and then the seizures just came out of nowhere—it was really frightening. I heard something in her room—like a knocking. I went in and she was shaking so hard the crib was rattling."

Her lips began to quiver. She stilled them with a hand. Crushed the tissue I'd given her with the other.

I said, "Scary."

"*Terrifying,*" she said, looking me in the eye. "But the worst thing was watching her suffer and not being able to do anything. The helplessness—it's the worst thing. I knew better than to pick her up, but still . . . Do you have children?"

"No."

Her eyes left my face, as if she'd suddenly lost interest. Sighing, she got up and walked to the bed, still carrying the crumpled tissue. She bent, tucked the blanket higher around the little girl's neck, and kissed Cassie's cheek. Cassie's breathing quickened for a second, then slowed. Cindy remained at the bedside, watching her sleep.

"She's beautiful," I said.

"She's my *pudding* pie."

She reached down, touched Cassie's forehead, then drew back her arm and let it drop to her side. After gazing down for several more seconds, she returned to the chair.

I said, "In terms of her suffering, there's no evidence seizures are painful."

"That's what Dr. Eves says," she said doubtfully. "I sure hope so . . . but if you'd have seen her afterwards—she was just *drained*."

She turned and stared out the window. I waited a while, then said, "Except for the headache, how's she doing today?"

"Okay. For the little she's been up."

"And the headache occurred at five this morning?"

"Yes. She woke up with it."

"Vicki was already on shift by then?"

Nod. "She's pulling a double—came on last night for the eleven-to-seven and stayed for the seven-to-three."

"Pretty dedicated."

"She is. She's a big help. We're lucky to have her."

"Does she ever come out to the house?"

That surprised her. "Just a couple of times—not to help, just to visit. She brought Cassie her first LuvBunny, and now Cassie's in love with them."

The look of surprise remained on her face. Rather than deal with it, I said, "How did Cassie let you know her head hurt?"

"By pointing to it and crying. She didn't tell me, if that's what you mean. She only has a few words. *Daw* for dog, *bah-bah* for bottle, and even with those, sometimes she still points. Dr. Eves says she's a few months behind in her language development."

"It's not unusual for children who've been hospitalized a lot to lag a bit. It's not permanent."

"I try to work with her at home—talking to her as much as I can. I read to her when she'll let me."

"Good."

"Sometimes she likes it but sometimes she's really jumpy—especially after a bad night."

"Are there a lot of bad nights?"

"Not a lot, but they're hard on her."

"What happens?"

"She wakes up as if she's having a bad dream. Tossing and turning and crying. I hold her and sometimes she falls back to sleep. But sometimes she's up for a long time—kind of weepy. The morning after, she's usually jumpy."

"Jumpy in what way?"

"Has trouble concentrating. Other times she can concentrate on something for a long time—an hour or more. I look for those times, try to read to her, talk to her. So that her speech will pick up. Any other suggestions?"

"Sounds like you're on the right track," I said.

"Sometimes I get the feeling she doesn't talk because she doesn't have to. I guess I can tell what she wants, and I give it to her before she has to talk."

"Was that what happened with the headache?"

"Exactly. She woke up crying and tossing around. First thing I did was touch her forehead to see if she was warm. Cool as a cucumber. Which didn't surprise me—it wasn't a scared cry. More of a pain cry.

By now I can tell the difference. So I started asking her what hurt and she finally touched her head. I know it doesn't sound scientific, but you just kind of develop a feel for a child—almost like radar."

Glance at the bed. "If her CAT scan hadn't come back normal that same afternoon, I would have really been scared."

"Because of the headache?"

"After you're here long enough, you see things. Start thinking of the worst things that can happen. It still scares me when she cries out at night—I never know what's going to happen."

She broke into tears again and dabbed at her eyes with the crumpled tissue. I gave her a fresh one.

"I'm really sorry, Dr. Delaware. I just can't stand to see her hurt."

"Of course," I said. "And the irony is that the very things that are being done to help her—the tests and procedures—are causing her the most pain."

She took a deep breath and nodded.

I said, "That's why Dr. Eves asked me to see you. There are psychological techniques that can help children deal with procedural anxiety and, sometimes, even reduce the pain itself."

"Techniques," she said, echoing the way Vicki Bottomley had, but with none of the nurse's sarcasm. "That would be great—I'd sure appreciate anything you could do. Watching her go through her bloodwork is like . . . It's just horrible."

I remembered what Stephanie had said about her composure during procedures.

As if reading me, she said, "Every time someone walks in that door with a needle, I just freeze inside, even though I keep smiling. My smiles are for Cassie. I try really hard not to get upset in front of her but I know she's got to feel it."

"The radar."

"We're so close—she's my one and only. She just looks at me and she knows. I'm not helping her but what can I do? I can't just leave her alone with them."

"Dr. Eves thinks you're doing great."

Something in the brown eyes. A momentary hardening? Then a tired smile.

"Dr. Eves is wonderful. We . . . She was the . . . She's really been wonderful with Cassie, even though Cassie won't have anything more to do with her. I know all these illnesses have been horrible for her, too. Every time the E.R. calls her, I feel bad about putting *her* through it again."

"It's her job," I said.

She looked as if I'd struck her. "I'm sure with her it's more than just a job."

"Yes, it is." I realized the LuvBunny was still in my hand. I was squeezing it.

Fluffing its tummy, I put it back on the ledge. Cindy watched me, stroking her braid.

"I didn't mean to snap," she said, "but what you just said— about Dr. Eves doing her job—it made me think about *my* job. Being a mother. I don't seem to be pulling that off too well, do I? No one *trains* you for that."

She looked away.

"Cindy," I said, leaning forward, "this is a tough thing to go through. Not exactly business as usual."

A smile danced across her lips for just an instant. Sad madonna smile.

Madonna-monster?

Stephanie had asked me to keep an open mind but I knew I was using her suspicions as a point of departure.

Guilty till proven innocent?

What Milo would call limited thinking. I resolved to concentrate on what I actually observed.

Nothing grossly pathologic, so far. No obvious signs of emotional imbalance, no overt histrionics or pathologic attention-seeking. Yet I wondered if she hadn't succeeded—in her own quiet way—in keeping the focus squarely on herself. Starting off talking about Cassie but ending with her maternal failings.

Then again, hadn't I elicited confession? Using shrink looks, shrink pauses and phrases to open her up?

I thought of the way she presented herself—the rope of braid that served as her worry beads, the lack of makeup, conspicuously plain clothes on a woman of her social rank.

All of it could be seen as reverse drama. In a room full of socialites she'd be noticed.

Other things clogged my analytical sieve as I tried to fit her to a Munchausen-by-proxy profile.

The easy usage of hospital jargon: *Spiking temps . . . pulling a double.*

Cyanotic . . .

Leftovers from her respiratory-tech training? Or evidence of an untoward attraction to things medical?

Or maybe nothing more ominous than too many hours spent in this place. During my years on the wards I'd met plumbers and housewives and teamsters and accountants—parents of chronically ill kids who slept and ate and lived at the hospital and ended up sounding like first-year residents.

None of them had poisoned their kids.

Cindy touched her braid and looked back at me.

I smiled, trying to look reassuring, wondering about her certainty that Cassie and she were able to communicate on a near-telepathic level.

Blurred ego boundaries?

The kind of pathologic overidentification that feeds into child abuse?

Then again, what mother didn't claim—often correctly—a radarlike link with her baby? Why suspect this mother of anything more than good bonding?

Because this mother's babies didn't lead healthy, happy lives.

Cindy was still looking at me. I knew I couldn't go on weighing every nuance and still come across as genuine.

I glanced over at the child in the bed, as perfect as a bisque doll. Her mother's voodoo doll?

"You're doing your best," I said. "That's all anyone can ask."

I hoped it sounded more sincere than I felt. Before Cindy could respond, Cassie opened her eyes, yawned, rubbed her lids and sat up groggily. Both hands were out from under the covers now. The one that had been concealed was puffy and bore needle bruises and yellow Betadine stains.

Cindy rushed over to her and held her. "Good *morning,* baby." New music in her voice. She kissed Cassie's cheek.

Cassie gazed up at her and let her head rest against Cindy's abdomen. Cindy stroked her hair and held her close. Yawning again,

Cassie looked around until her eyes settled on the LuvBunnies on the nightstand.

Pointing to the stuffed animals, she began making urgent whining noises:

"Eh, eh."

Cindy reached over and snagged a pink animal. "Here you go, baby. It's *Funny*Bunny and he's saying, 'Good *morning,* Miss Cassie Jones. Did you have a good *dream?*' "

Talking softly, slowly, in the goofy, eager-to-please voice of a kiddy-show host.

Cassie snatched the doll. Holding it to her chest, she closed her eyes and swayed, and for a moment I thought she'd fall back asleep. But a moment later the eyes opened and stayed that way. Big and brown, just like her mother's.

Her big-eyed gaze jumped around the room once more, swinging in my direction and stopping.

We made eye contact.

I smiled.

She screamed.

5

Cindy held her and rocked her and said, "It's okay. He's our friend."

Cassie threw the LuvBunny on the floor, then began sobbing for it.

I picked it up and held it out to her. She shrank back and clung to her mother. I gave Cindy the doll, took a yellow bunny from the shelf, and sat back down.

I began to play with the animal, manipulating its arms, chatting nonsense. Cassie continued crying and Cindy kept up a quiet, comforting patter, too soft to hear. I stayed with the bunny. After a minute or so, Cassie's volume dropped a notch.

Cindy said, "Look, honey—you see? Dr. Delaware likes the bunnies, too."

Cassie gulped, gasped, and let out a wail.

"No, he's not going to hurt you, honey. He's our friend."

I stared at the doll's overbite and shook one of its paws. A white heart on its belly bore yellow letters: *SillyBunny* and the trademark ®. A tag near its crotch said MADE IN TAIWAN.

Cassie paused for breath.

Cindy said, "It's okay, honey, everything's okay."

Whimper and sniff from the bed.

"How 'bout a story, baby, okay? Once upon a time there was a princess named Cassandra who lived in a great big castle and had wonderful dreams about candy and whipped-cream clouds. . . ."

Cassie stared up. Her bruised hand touched her lips.

I placed the yellow bunny on the floor, opened my briefcase, and took out a notebook and a pencil. Cindy stopped talking for a moment, then resumed her story. Cassie was calm now, caught up in another world.

I started to draw. A bunny. I hoped.

A few minutes later it was clear the Disney folk had nothing to worry about, but I thought the end product managed to be cute and sufficiently rabbitlike. I added a hat and a bow tie, reached into the case again, and found the box of colored markers I kept there along with other tools of the trade.

I began coloring. The markers squeaked. Rustles came from the bed. Cindy stopped telling her story.

"Oh, look, honey, Dr. Delaware's *drawing*. What are you drawing, Dr. Delaware?"

Before I could answer, the word *doctor* precipitated another tear-storm.

Again, maternal comfort squelched it.

I held up my masterpiece.

"Oh, look, honey, it's a *bunny*. And he's wearing a hat. And a bow tie—isn't that *silly*?"

Silence.

"Well, *I* think it's silly. Do you think he's one of the LuvBunnies, Cass?"

Silence.

"Did Dr. Delaware draw a LuvBunny?"

Whimper.

"C'mon, Cass, there's nothing to worry about. Dr. Delaware won't do anything to hurt you. He's the kind of doctor who never gives shots."

Bleats. It took a while for Cindy to calm her down. Finally she was able to resume her story. Princess Cassandra riding a white horse . . .

I drew a companion for Mr. HatBunny. Same rodent face but short ears, polka-dot dress—Ms. Squirrel. I added an amorphous-looking acorn, pulled the page out of the notebook, reached over and placed it on the bed near Cassie's feet.

She whipped her head around just as I got back to my seat.

Cindy said, "Oh, look, he's done a . . . *prairie* dog, too. And she's a *girl*, Cass—look at her dress. Isn't that *funny*? And she's got big *dots* all over her dress, Cass. That's so *funny*—a prairie dog in a dress!"

Warm, womanly laughter. At the tail end, a child's giggle.

"So *silly*. I wonder if she's going to a *party* with that dress . . . or maybe she's going to go *shopping* or something, huh? Wouldn't that be silly, a prairie dog going shopping at the *mall*? Going with her friend Mr. Bunny, and he's got that silly hat on—the two of them are really dressed up silly. Maybe they'll go to Toys "Я" Us and get their *own* dolls—wouldn't *that* be something, Cass? Yeah, that would be silly. *Boy,* Dr. Delaware sure makes silly pictures—wonder what he's going to do now!"

I smiled and lifted my pencil. Something easy: hippopotamus . . . just a bathtub with legs . . .

"What's your bunny's name, Dr. Delaware?"

"Benny."

"Benny *Bunny*—that's *ridiculous*!"

I smiled, concealing my artistic struggle. The bathtub was looking too fierce. . . . The problem was the grin . . . too aggressive—more like a dehorned rhino . . . What would Freud say about that?

I performed reconstructive surgery on the critter's mouth.

"Benny the *Hat* Bunny—didja *hear* that, Cass?"

High-pitched, little-kid laughter.

"And what about the prairie dog, Dr. Delaware? What's *her* name?"

"Priscilla . . ." Working away. The hippo finally hippolike, but still something wrong . . . the grin venal—the greasy smirk of a carny barker . . . Maybe a dog would have been easier . . .

"Pri*scil*la the prairie dog! Do you believe *that*!"

"*Pilla!*"

"Yes, Priscilla!"

"*Pilla!*"

"Very *good,* Cass! That's excellent! Pri*scil*la. Can you say that again?"

Silence.

"Pri*scil*la—*Pri-scil-la.* You just said it. Here, watch my mouth, Cass."

Silence.

"Okay, you don't have to if you don't want to. Let's get back to Princess Cassandra Silversparkle, riding Snowflake up into the Shiny Country . . ."

The hippo was finally done. Scarred by smudges and eraser abrasions, but at least it didn't look as if it had a rap sheet. I placed it on top of the bedcovers.

"Oh, look, Cass. We know what this is, don't we? A *hippopotamus*—and he's holding a . . ."

"A yo-yo," I said.

"A *yo*-yo! A hippo with a *yo*-yo—that is *really* silly. You know what I think, Cass? I think Dr. Delaware can be pretty silly when he wants to, even though he's a doctor. What do *you* think?"

I faced the little girl. Our eyes locked once more. Hers flickered. The rosebud mouth began to pout, lower lip curling. Hard to imagine anyone being capable of hurting her.

I said, "Would you like me to draw some more?"

She looked at her mother and grabbed Cindy's sleeve.

"Sure," said Cindy. "Let's see what other silly things Dr. Delaware can draw, okay?"

Minuscule nod from Cassie. She buried her head in Cindy's blouse.

Back to the drawing board.

A mangy hound, a cross-eyed duck, and a spavined horse later, she was tolerating my presence.

I edged the chair closer to the bed, gradually. Chatted with Cindy about games and toys and favorite foods. When Cassie seemed to be taking me for granted, I pushed right up against the mattress and taught Cindy a drawing game—the two of us alternating turning squiggles into objects. Child analyst's technique for building rapport and getting to the unconscious in a nonthreatening way.

Using Cindy as a go-between even as I studied her.

Investigated her.

I drew an angular squiggle and handed the paper to her. She and Cassie were snuggled together; they could have been a poster for National Bonding Week. Cindy turned the squiggle into a house and handed the paper back, saying, "Not very good, but . . ."

Cassie's lips turned up a bit. Then down. Her eyes closed and she pressed her face against Cindy's blouse. Grabbed a breast and squeezed. Cindy lowered the hand gently and placed it in her own lap. I saw the puncture marks on Cassie's flesh. Black dots, like snakebites.

Cindy made easy, cooing sounds. Cassie nuzzled, shifted position, and gathered a handful of blouse.

Sleepy again. Cindy kissed the top of her head.

I'd been trained to heal, trained to believe in the open, honest therapeutic relationship. Being in this room made me feel like a con man.

Then I thought about raging fevers and bloody diarrhea and convulsions so intense they rattled the crib, remembered a little baby boy who'd died in his crib, and my self-doubts turned stale and crumbled.

By 10:45, I'd been there for more than half an hour, mostly watching Cassie lie in Cindy's arms. But she seemed more comfortable with me, even smiling once or twice. Time to pack up and declare success.

I stood. Cassie started to fuss.

Cindy sniffed the air, wrinkled her nose, and said, "Uh-oh."

Gently, she rolled Cassie onto her back and changed the little girl's diaper.

Powdered, patted, and reclothed, Cassie remained restless. Pointing at the floor, she said, "Ah! Ah! Ah! Ah!"

"Out?"

Emphatic nod. *"Ahd!"*

She got on her knees and tried to stand on the bed, wobbling on the soft mattress. Cindy held her under the arms, lifted her off, and placed her on the floor. "You want to walk around? Let's get some slippers on you." The two of them walked to the closet. Cassie's pajama bottoms were too long for her and they dragged on the floor. Standing, she looked even tinier. But sturdy. Good steady walk, good sense of balance.

I picked up my briefcase.

Kneeling, Cindy put fuzzy pink bunny slippers on Cassie's feet. These rodents had clear plastic eyes with movable black beads for pupils and each time Cassie moved, her feet hissed.

She tried to jump, barely got off the ground.

Cindy said, "Good jump, Cass."

The door opened and a man came in.

He looked to be in his late thirties. Six two or so, and very slim. His hair was dark-brown, wavy, and thick, combed straight back and left long enough to curl over his collar. He had a full face at odds with the lanky physique, rounded further by a bushy, cropped brown beard flecked with gray. His features were soft and pleasant. A gold stud pierced his left earlobe. The clothes he had on were loose-fitting but well cut: blue-and-white striped button-down shirt under a gray tweed sport coat; baggy, pleated black cords; black running shoes that looked brand-new.

A coffee cup was in one hand.

"It's Daddy!" said Cindy.

Cassie held out her arms.

The tall man put the cup down and said, "Morning, ladies." Kissing Cindy's cheek, he scooped Cassie up.

The little girl squealed as he held her aloft. He brought her close with one swift, descending motion.

"How's my baby?" he said, pressing her to his beard. His nose disappeared under her hair and she giggled. "How's the little *grande dame* of the diaper set?"

Cassie put both of her hands in *his* hair and pulled.

"Ouch!"

Giggle. Yank.

"Double ouch!"

Baby-guffaw.

"Ouch-a-*roo*!"

They played a bit longer; then he pulled away and said, "Whew. You're too rough for me, Spike!"

Cindy said, "This is Dr. Delaware, honey. The psychologist? Doctor, Cassie's dad."

The man turned toward me, holding on to Cassie, and extended his free hand. "Chip Jones. Good to meet you."

His grip was strong. Cassie was still yanking on his hair, messing it. He seemed impervious.

"I minored in psych," he said, smiling. "Forgot most of it." To Cindy: "How's everything?"

" 'Bout the same."

He frowned. Looked at his wrist. Another Swatch.

Cindy said, "On the run?"

"Unfortunately. Just wanted to see your faces." He picked up the coffee cup and held it out to her.

"No, thanks."

"You're sure?"

"Nah, I'm fine."

"Stomach?"

She touched her abdomen and said, "Just feeling a little woozy. How long can you stay?"

"In and out," he said. "Got a twelve o'clock class, then meetings for the rest of the day—probably dumb to drive all the way over, but I missed you guys."

Cindy smiled.

Chip kissed her, then Cassie.

Cindy said, "Daddy can't stay, Cass. Bummer, huh?"

"Dah-dee."

Chip gave Cassie's chin a gentle tweak. She continued playing with his beard. "I'll try to kick by later this evening. Stay as long as you need me."

"Great," said Cindy.

"*Dah-dee.*"

"Dah-dee," said Chip. "Dah-dee love you. You cute." To Cindy: "Not a good idea at all, coming for two minutes. Now I'm really gonna miss you."

"We miss you too, Daddy."

"I was in the neighborhood," he said. "So to speak—this side of the hill, at least."

"The U?"

"Yup. Library duty." He turned to me: "I teach over at West Valley C.C. New campus, not much in terms of reference resources. So when I have some serious research to do, I go over to the university."

"My alma mater," I said.

"That so? I went to school back east." He tickled Cassie's belly. "Get any sleep at all, Cin?"

"Plenty."

"Sure?"

"Uh-huh."

"Want some herb tea? I think I've got some chamomile in the car."

"No, thanks, hon. Dr. Delaware has some techniques to help Cassie deal with the p-a-i-n."

Chip looked at me while stroking Cassie's arm. "That would be terrific. This has been an incredible ordeal." His eyes were slate-blue with a slight droop, very deep-set.

"I know it has," I said.

Chip and Cindy looked at each other, then at me.

"Well," I said, "I'll be shoving off now. Come by to see you tomorrow morning."

I bent and whispered goodbye to Cassie. She batted her lashes and turned away.

Chip laughed. "What a flirt. It's inborn, isn't it?"

Cindy said, "Your techniques. When can we talk about that?"

"Soon," I said. "First I need to get a rapport with Cassie. I think we did pretty well today."

"Oh. Sure. We did great. Didn't we, pudding?"

"Is ten o'clock a good time for you?"

"Sure," said Cindy. "We're not going anywhere."

Chip looked at her and said, "Dr. Eves didn't say anything about discharge?"

"Not yet. She wants to keep observing."

He sighed. "Okay."

I walked to the door.

Chip said, "I've got to be running, myself, Doctor. If you can hold on for one sec, I'll walk out with you."

"Sure."

He took his wife's hand.

I closed the door, walked to the nursing station, and went behind the desk. Vicki Bottomley was back from the gift shop, sitting in the unit clerk's chair, reading *RN*. No one else was around. A box wrapped with Western Peds gift-shop paper sat on the counter, next to a coil of catheter tubing and a stack of insurance forms.

She didn't look up as I lifted Cassie's chart from the rack and began leafing through. I skimmed through the medical history and came upon Stephanie's psychosocial history. Wondering about the age difference between Chip and Cindy, I looked up his biographical data.

Charles L. Jones III. Age: 38. Educational level: Master's degree. Occupation: College professor.

Sensing someone looking at me, I lowered the chart and saw Vicki whipping her head back toward her magazine.

"So," I said, "how were things down in the gift shop?"

She lowered the journal. "Is there something specific you need from me?"

"Anything that would help me work with Cassie's anxiety."

Her pretty eyes narrowed. "Dr. Eves already asked me that. You were right here."

"Just wondering if something occurred to you in the meantime."

"Nothing *occurred*," she said, "I don't know anything—I'm just the nurse."

"The nurse often knows more than anybody."

"Tell it to the salary committee." She lifted the magazine high, concealing her face.

I was considering my response when I heard my name called. Chip Jones strode toward me.

"Thanks for waiting."

The sound of his voice made Vicki stop reading. She straightened her cap and said, "Hi, Dr. Jones." A sweet smile spread across her face, honey on stale bread.

Chip leaned on the counter, grinned, and shook his head. "There you go again, Vicki, trying to promote me." To me: "I'm A.B.D.—that's 'all but dissertation,' Vicki—but generous Ms. Bottomley here keeps trying to graduate me before I earn it."

Vicki managed to work up another dirt-eating smile. "Degree or not, what's the difference?"

"Well," said Chip, "it might make quite a difference to someone like Dr. Delaware here, who genuinely earned his."

"I'm sure it *does*."

He heard the acid in her voice and gave her a quizzical look. She got flustered and looked away.

He noticed the gift box. "Vicki. Again?"

"It's just a little something."

"That's very sweet of you, Vicki, but totally unnecessary."

"I wanted to, Dr. Jones. She's such an angel."

"That she is, Vicki." He smiled. "Another bunny?"

"Well, she likes them, Dr. Jones."

"*Mister,* Vicki—if you insist on using a title, how about Herr Professor? It has a nice classical ring to it, wouldn't you agree, Dr. Delaware?"

"Absolutely."

He said, "I'm prattling—this place addles me. Thank you again, Vicki. You're very sweet."

Bottomley went scarlet.

Chip turned to me. "Ready if you are, Doctor."

We walked through the teak doors into the hustle of Five East. A child being wheeled somewhere was crying, a little boy hooked to an I.V. and turbaned with bandages. Chip took it in, frowning but not talking.

As we approached the elevators he shook his head and said, "Good old Vicki. What a shameless brown-noser. But she got kind of uppity with you back there, didn't she?"

"I'm not her favorite person."

"Why?"

"I don't know."

"Ever have any hassles with her before?"

"Nope. Never met her before."

He shook his head. "Well, I'm sorry for you, but she seems to be taking really good care of Cassie. And Cindy likes her. I think she reminds Cindy of her aunt—she had an aunt who raised her. Also a nurse, real tough egg."

After we passed a gaggle of dazed-looking medical students, he said, "It's probably territorial—Vicki's reaction to you. Some kind of turf battle, wouldn't you say?"

"Could be."

"I notice a lot of that kind of thing around here. Possessiveness over patients. As if they're commodities."

"Have you experienced that personally?"

"Oh, sure. Plus, our situation heightens the tension. People think that we're worth kissing up to, because we've got some sort of direct line to the power structure. I assume you know who my dad is."

I nodded.

He said, "It rubs me the wrong way, being treated differently. I worry about it leading to substandard care for Cassie."

"In what way?"

"I don't know, nothing specific—I guess I'm just not comfortable with being an exception. I don't want anyone missing something important because they hung back or broke routine out of fear of offending our family. Not that Dr. Eves isn't great—I have nothing but respect for her. It's more the whole system—a feeling I get when I'm here."

He slowed his pace. "Maybe I'm just talking through my hat. The frustration. Cassie's been sick with one thing or another for virtually her whole life and no one's figured out what's wrong yet, and we also . . . What I'm saying is that this hospital's a highly formalized structure and whenever the rules change in a formalized structure, you run the risk of structural cracks. That's my field of interest: Formal Org—Formal Organizations. And let me tell you, this is some organization."

We reached the elevators. He punched the button and said, "I hope you can help Cassie with the shots—she's gone through an absolute nightmare. Cindy, too. She's a fantastic mother, but with this kind of thing, self-doubts are inevitable."

"Is she blaming herself?" I said.

"Sometimes. Even though it's totally unjustified. I try to tell her, but . . ."

He shook his head and put his hands together. The knuckles were white. Reaching up, he rotated his earring.

"The strain on her's been incredible."

"Must be rough on you, too," I said.

"It hasn't been fun, that's for sure. But the worst of it falls on Cindy. To be honest, we've got your basic, traditional, sex role—stereotyped marriage—I work; she takes care of things at home. It's by mutual choice—what *Cindy* really wanted. I'm involved at home to some extent—probably not as much as I should be—but child rearing's really Cindy's domain. God knows she's a hell of a lot better at it than I am. So when something goes wrong in that sphere, she takes all the responsibility on her shoulders."

He stroked his beard and shook his head. "Now, *that* was an impressive bit of defensive pedantry, wasn't it? Yes, sure, it's been *damned* rough on me. Seeing someone you love . . . I assume you know about Chad—our first baby?"

I nodded.

"We hit *bottom* with that, Dr. Delaware. There's just no way to . . ." Closing his eyes, he shook his head again. Hard, as if trying to dislodge mental burrs.

"Let's just say it wasn't anything I'd wish on my worst enemy."

He jabbed the elevator button, glanced at his watch. "Looks like we caught the local, Doctor. Anyway, we were just coming out of it—Cindy and I. Pulling ourselves together and starting to enjoy Cassie when *this* mess hit the fan . . . Unbelievable."

The elevator arrived. Two candy-stripers and a doctor exited, and we stepped in. Chip pushed the ground-floor button and settled with his back against the compartment's rear wall.

"You just never know what life's going to throw you," he said. "I've always been stubborn. Probably to a fault—an obnoxious individualist. Probably because a lot of conformity was shoved down my throat at an early age. But I've come to realize I'm pretty conservative. Buying into the basic values: Live your life according to the rules and things will eventually work out. Hopelessly naïve, of course. But you get into a certain mode of thinking and it feels right, so you keep doing it. That's as good a definition of faith as any, I guess. But I'm fast losing mine."

The elevator stopped at four. A Hispanic woman in her fifties and a boy of around ten got on. The boy was short, stocky, bespectacled. His blunt face bore the unmistakable cast of Down's syndrome. Chip smiled at them. The boy didn't appear to notice him. The woman looked very tired. No one talked. The two of them got off at three.

When the door closed, Chip kept staring at it. As we resumed our descent he said, "Take that poor woman. She didn't expect that—child of her old age and now she has to take care of him forever. Something like that'll shake up your entire worldview. That's what's happened to me—the whole child-rearing thing. No more assumptions about happy endings."

He turned to me. The slate eyes were fierce. "I really hope you can help Cassandra. As long as she has to go through this shit, let her be spared some of the pain."

The elevator landed. The moment the door opened, he was out and gone.

When I got back to the General Peds clinic, Stephanie was in one of the exam rooms. I waited outside until she came out a few minutes later, followed by a huge black woman and a girl of around five. The girl wore a red polka-dot dress and had coal-black skin, cornrows, and beautiful African features. One of her hands gripped Stephanie's; the other held a lollipop. A tear stream striped her cheek, lacquer on ebony. A round pink Band-Aid dotted the crook of one arm.

Stephanie was saying, "You did great, Tonya." She saw me and mouthed, "My office," before returning her attention to the girl.

I went to her consult room. The Byron book was back on the shelf, its gilded spine conspicuous among the texts.

I thumbed through a recent copy of *Pediatrics*. Not long after, Stephanie came in, closed the door, and sank into her desk chair.

"So," she said, "how'd it go?"

"Fine, outside of Ms. Bottomley's continuing antagonism."

"She get in the way?"

"No, just more of the same." I told her about the scene with the nurse and Chip. "Trying to get on his good side but it probably backfired. He sees her as a shameless ass-kisser, though he does think she takes good care of Cassie. And his analysis of why she resents me is probably right-on: competing for the attentions of the VIP patient."

"Attention seeking, huh? There's a bit of Munchausen symptomology."

"Yup. In addition, she did visit the home. But only a couple of times, a while back. So it still doesn't seem likely she could have caused anything. But let's keep our eyes on her."

"I already started, Alex. Asked around about her. The nursing office thinks she's tops. She gets consistently good ratings, no complaints. And as far as I can tell there's been no unusual pattern of illness in any of her patients. But my offer's still open—she causes too much hassle, she's transferred."

"Let me see if I can work things out with her. Cindy and Chip like her."

"Even though she's an ass-kisser."

"Even though. Incidentally, he feels that way about the entire hospital. Doesn't like getting special treatment."

"In what way?"

"No specific complaints, and he made a point of saying he likes *you*. He's just got a general concern that something could be missed because of who his father is. More than anything, he looks weary. They both do."

"Aren't we all," she said. "So what's your initial take on mama?"

"She wasn't what I expected—neither of them was. They seem more health-food restaurant than country club. And they're also different from each other. She's very . . . I guess the best word for it is *basic*. Unsophisticated. Especially for a honcho's daughter-in-law. I can see Chip growing up rich, but he's not exactly corporate son."

"The earring?"

"The earring, his choice of profession, his general demeanor. He talked about getting conformity shoved at him throughout childhood and rebelling. Maybe marrying Cindy was part of it. There's a twelve-year difference between them. Was she his student?"

"Could be, I don't know. Is that relevant in terms of Munchausen?"

"Not really. I'm just getting my feet wet. In terms of a Munchausen profile, it's too early to tell much about her. She does toss some jargon into her speech and she's highly identified with Cassie—feels the two of them have an almost telepathic link. The physical resemblance between them is strong—Cassie's like a miniature of her. That could enhance the identification, I suppose."

"Meaning if Cindy hates herself she could be projecting it on to Cassie?"

"It's possible," I said. "But I'm a long way off from interpretation. Did Chad also resemble her?"

"I saw him dead, Alex." She covered her face, rubbed her eyes, looked up. "All I remember was that he was a pretty little boy. Gray, like one of those cherub statues you put in a garden. Tell the truth, I tried *not* to look at him."

She picked up a demitasse cup, looked ready to throw it.

"God, what a nightmare. Carrying him down to the morgue. The staff elevator was jammed. I was just standing around, holding this *bundle*. Waiting. People passing right by me, gabbing—I wanted to scream. Finally I walked over to the public elevators, rode down with a bunch of other people. Patients, parents. Trying not to look at *them*. So they wouldn't know what I was carrying."

We sat for a while. Then she said, "Espresso," leaned over toward the little black machine and turned it on. A red light glowed. "Loaded and ready to go. Let's caffeine our troubles away. Oh, let me give you those references."

She took a piece of paper from the desk and handed it to me. List of ten articles.

"Thanks."

"Notice anything else," she said, "about Cindy?"

"No *belle indifférence* or dramatic attention seeking, so far. On the contrary, she seemed very low-key. Chip did mention that the aunt who raised her was a nurse, so we've got a possible early exposure to health-related issues, on top of her being a respiratory tech. But that's really pretty thin, by itself. Her child-rearing skills seem good—exemplary, even."

"What about the relationship with her husband? Pick up any stress there?"

"No. Have you?"

She shook her head. Smiled. "But I thought you guys had tricks."

"Didn't bring my bag this morning. Actually, they seem to get along pretty well."

"One big happy family," she said. "Have you ever seen a case like this before?"

"Never," I said. "Munchausens avoid psychologists and psychiatrists like the plague because we're proof no one's taking their diseases seriously. The closest I've come are doctor-hoppers—parents convinced something's wrong with their kids, running from specialist to specialist even though no one can find any real symptoms. When I was in practice I used to get referrals from doctors driven crazy by them. But I never treated them for long. When they showed up at all, they tended to be pretty hostile and almost always dropped out quickly."

"Doctor-hoppers," she said. "Never thought of them as mini-Munchausens."

"Could be the same dynamic at a milder level. Obsession with health, seeking attention from authority figures while dancing around with them."

"The waltz," she said. "What about Cassie? How's she functioning?"

"Exactly as you described—she freaked out when she saw me, but calmed down eventually."

"Then you're doing better than I am."

"I don't stick her with needles, Steph."

She gave a sour smile. "Maybe I went into the wrong field. Anything else you can tell me about her?"

"No major pathology, maybe some minor language delay. If her speech doesn't get better in the next six months, I'd have it checked out with a full psych battery, including neuropsych testing."

She began ordering the piles on her desk. Swiveled and faced me.

"Six months," she said. "If she's still alive by then."

The waiting room was hot with bodies and impatience. Several of the mothers flashed hopeful looks at Stephanie as she walked me out. She smiled, said, "Soon," and ushered me into the hall.

A group of men—three white-coated doctors and one business suit in gray flannel—was heading our way. The lead white-coat noticed us and called out, "Dr. Eves!"

Stephanie grimaced. "Wonderful."

She stopped and the men came abreast. The white-coats were all in their fifties and had the well-fed, well-shaven look of senior attending physicians with established practices.

Business-suit was younger—mid-thirties—and hefty. Six feet, 230 or so, big round shoulders padded with fat under a broad columnar head. He had short dishwater hair and bland features, except for a nose that had been broken and reset imperfectly. A wispy narrow mustache failed to give the face any depth. He looked like an ex-jock playing the corporate game. He stood behind the others, too far away for me to read his badge.

The lead doctor was also thickset, and very tall. He had wide razor-edge lips and thinning curly hair the color of silver plate that he wore longish and winged at the sides. A heavy, outthrusting chin gave his face the illusion of forward movement. His eyes were quick and brown, his skin pinkish and gleaming as if fresh from the sauna. The two doctors flanking him were medium-sized, gray-haired, and bespectacled. In one case, the hair was a toupee.

Chin said, "How're things in the trenches, Dr. Eves?" in a deep, adenoidal voice.

Stephanie said, "Trenchlike."

He turned to me and did some eyebrow calisthenics.

Stephanie said, "This is Dr. Delaware, a member of our staff."

He shot his hand out. "Don't believe it's been my pleasure. George Plumb."

"Pleased to meet you, Dr. Plumb."

Vise-grip handshake. "Delaware," he said. "What division are you with, Doctor?"

"I'm a psychologist."

"Ah."

The two gray-haired men looked at me but didn't talk or move. Suit seemed to be counting the holes in the acoustical ceiling.

"He's with pediatrics," said Stephanie. "Serving as a consultant on the Cassie Jones case—helping the family cope with the stress."

Plumb swung his eyes back to her. "Ah. Very good." He touched her arm lightly. She endured it for a moment, then backed away.

He renewed his smile. "You and I need to confer, Stephanie. I'll have my girl call yours and set it up."

"I don't have a girl, George. The five of us share one *woman* secretary."

The gray twins looked at her as if she were floating in a jar. Suit was somewhere else.

Plumb kept smiling. "Yes, the ever-changing nomenclature. Well, then my *girl* will call your *woman*. Be well, Stephanie."

He led his entourage away, stopped several yards down the hall, and ran his eyes up and down a wall, as if measuring.

"What are you going to dismantle now, boys?" said Stephanie under her breath.

Plumb resumed walking and the group disappeared around a corner.

I said, "What was that all about?"

"That was about *Doctor* Plumb, our new chief administrator and CEO. Papa Jones's boy—Mr. Bottom Line."

"M.D. administrator?"

She laughed. "What, the coat? No, he's no doc. Just some kind of asinine Ph.D. or something—" She stopped, colored. "Jeez, I'm sorry."

I had to laugh. "Don't worry about it."

"I'm *really* sorry, Alex. You know how I feel about psychologists—"

"Forget it." I put my arm over her shoulder. She slipped hers around my waist.

"My mind is going," she said softly. "I am definitely falling apart."

"What's Plumb's degree in?"

"Business or management, something like that. He uses it to the hilt—insists on being called Doctor, wears a white coat. Most of his lackeys have doctorates, too—like Frick and Frack over there: Roberts and Novak, his numbers crunchers. They all love to traipse into the doctors' dining room and take over a table. Show up at medical meetings and rounds for no apparent reason, walking around staring and measuring and taking notes. Like the way Plumb just stopped and sized up that wall. I wouldn't be surprised if the carpenters show up soon. Dividing three offices into six, turning clinical space into administrative offices. And now he wants to *confer* with me—there's something to look forward to."

"Are you vulnerable?"

"Everyone is, but General Peds is at the bottom of the barrel. We've got no fancy technology or heroics to make headlines. Most of what we do's outpatient, so our reimbursement level's the lowest in the hospital. Since Psych's gone." She smiled.

"Even technology doesn't seem immune," I said. "This morning, when I was looking for an elevator, I went by where Nuclear Medicine used to be and the suite had been given over to something called Community Services."

"Another of Plumb's coups. But don't worry about the Nukers—they're okay. Moved upstairs to Two, same square footage, though patients have trouble finding them. But some of the other divisions have had real problems—Nephrology, Rheumatology, your buddies in Oncology. They're stuck in trailers across the street."

"Trailers?"

"As in Winnebago."

"Those are major divisions, Steph. Why do they put up with it?"

"No choice, Alex. They signed away their rights. They were supposed to be housed in the old Hollywood Lutheran Tower— Western Peds bought it a couple of years ago, after Lutheran had to divest because of *their* budget problems. The board promised to build fantastic suites for anyone who moved over there. Construction was supposed to start last year. The divisions that agreed were moved to the trailers and their old space was given to someone else. Then they discovered—*Plumb* discovered—that even though enough money had been raised to make a down payment on the tower and do some of the remodeling, insufficient funds had been allocated to do the rest and to *maintain* it. Trifling matter of thirteen million dollars. Try raising that in this climate—heroes are already in short supply because we've got a charity hospital image and no one wants their name on a bunch of doctors' offices."

"Trailers," I said. "Melendez-Lynch must be overjoyed."

"Melendez-Lynch went *adios,* last year."

"You're kidding. Raoul *lived* here."

"Not anymore. Miami. Some hospital offered him chief of staff, and he took it. I hear he's getting triple the salary and half the headaches."

"It *has* been a long time," I said. "Raoul had all those research grants. How'd they let him get away?"

"Research doesn't matter to these people, Alex. They don't want to pay the overhead. It's a whole new game." She let her arm fall from my waist. We began walking.

"Who's the other guy?" I said. "Mr. Gray Suit."

"Oh, him." She looked unnerved. "That's Huenengarth— *Presley* Huenengarth. Head of security."

"He looks like an enforcer," I said. "Muscle for those who don't pay their bills?"

She laughed. "That wouldn't be so terrible. The hospital's bad debt is over eighty percent. No, he doesn't seem to do much of anything, except follow Plumb around and *lurk*. Some of the staff think he's spooky."

"In what way?"

She didn't answer for a moment. "His manner, I guess."

"You have any bad experiences with him?"

"Me? No. Why?"

"You look a little antsy talking about him."

"No," she said. "It's nothing personal—just the way he acts to everyone. Showing up when you're not expecting him. Materializing around corners. You'll come out of a patient's room and he'll just *be* there."

"Sounds charming."

"*Très*. But what's a *girl* to do? Call Security?"

I rode down to the ground floor alone, found Security open, endured a uniformed guard's five-minute interrogation, and finally earned the right to have a full-color badge made.

The picture came out looking like a mug shot. I snapped the badge onto my lapel and took the stairs down to the sub-basement level, heading for the hospital library, ready to check out Stephanie's references.

The door was locked. An undated memorandum taped to the door said new library hours were three to five P.M., Monday through Wednesday.

I checked the adjoining reading room. Open but unoccupied. I stepped into another world: oiled paneling, tufted leather chesterfields and wing chairs, worn but good Persian rugs over a shoe-buffed herringbone oak floor.

Hollywood seemed planets away.

Once the study of a Cotswolds manor house, the entire room had been donated years ago—before I'd arrived as an intern—transported across the Atlantic and reconstructed under the financial guidance of an Anglophile patron who felt doctors need to relax in high style. A patron who'd never spent time with a Western Peds doctor.

I strode across the room and tried the connecting door to the library. Open.

The windowless room was pitch-dark and I turned on the lights.

Most of the shelves were empty; a few bore thin stacks of mismatched journals. Careless piles of books sat on the floor. The rear wall was bare.

The computer I'd used to run Medline searches was nowhere in sight. Neither was the golden-oak card catalogue with its hand-lettered parchment labels. The only furniture was a gray metal table. Taped to the top was a piece of paper. An inter-hospital memo, dated three months ago.

TO: Professional Staff
FROM: G. H. Plumb, MBA, DBA, Chief Executive Officer
SUBJECT: Library Restructure

In accordance with repeated requests by the Professional Staff and a subsequent confirmatory decision by the Research Committee, the Board of Directors in General Assembly, and the Finance Subcommittee of the Executive Board, the Medical Library reference index will be converted to a fully computerized system utilizing Orion and Melvyl-type standard library data search programs. The contract for this conversion has been put out to competitive bid and, after careful deliberation and cost/benefit computation, has been awarded to BIO-DAT, Inc., of Pittsburgh, Pennsylvania, a concern specializing in medical and scientific research probe systems and health-care workstation integration. BIO-DAT officials have informed us that the entire process should take approximately three weeks, once they are in full receipt of all relevant data. Accordingly, the library's current card files will be shipped to BIO-DAT headquarters in Pittsburgh for the duration of the conversion process, and returned to Los Angeles for purposes of storage and archival activity, once the conversion has been terminated. Your cooperation and forbearance during the conversion period is solicited.

Three weeks had stretched to three months.

I ran my finger along the metal table and ended up with a dust-blackened tip.

Turning off the light, I left the room.

* * *

Sunset Boulevard was a bouillabaisse of rage and squalor mixed with immigrant hope and livened by the spice of easy felony.

I drove past the flesh clubs, the new-music caverns, titanic show-biz billboards, and the anorexically oriented boutiques of the Strip, crossed Doheny and slipped into the dollar-shrines of Beverly Hills. Passing my turnoff at Beverly Glen, I headed for a place where serious research could always be done. The place where Chip Jones had done his.

The Biomed library was filled with the inquisitive and the obligated. Sitting at one of the monitors was someone I recognized.

Gamine face, intense eyes, dangling earrings, and a double pierce on the right ear. The tawny bob had grown out to a shoulder-length wedge. A line of white collar showed over a navy-blue crew-neck.

When had I last seen her? Three years or so. Making her twenty.

I wondered if she'd gotten her Ph.D. yet.

She was tapping the keys rapidly, bringing data to the screen. As I neared I saw that the text was in German. The word *neuropeptide* kept popping out.

"Hi, Jennifer."

She spun around. "Alex!" Big smile. She gave me a kiss on the cheek and got off her stool.

"Is it Dr. Leavitt yet?" I said.

"This June," she said. "Wrapping up my dissertation."

"Congratulations. Neuroanatomy?"

"Neurochemistry—much more practical, right?"

"Still planning on going to med school?"

"Next fall. Stanford."

"Psychiatry?"

"I don't know," she said. "Maybe something a bit more . . . concrete. No offense. I'm going to take my time and see what appeals to me."

"Well, there's certainly no hurry—what are you, twelve years old?"

"Twenty! I'll be twenty-one next month."

"A veritable crone."

"Weren't you young, too, when you finished?"

"Not that young. I was shaving."

She laughed again. "It's great to see you. Hear from Jamey at all?"

"I got a postcard at Christmas. From New Hampshire. He's renting a farm there. Writing poetry."

"Is he . . . all right?"

"He's better. There was no return address on the card and he wasn't listed. So I called the psychiatrist who treated him up in Carmel and she said he'd been maintaining pretty well on medication. Apparently he's got someone to take care of him. One of the nurses who worked with him up there."

"Well, that's good," she said. "Poor guy. He had so much going for and against him."

"Good way to put it. Have you had any contact with the other people in the group?"

The group. *Project 160*. As in IQ. Accelerated academics for kids with genius intellects. A grand experiment; one of its members ended up accused of serial murder. I'd gotten involved, taken a joyride into hatred and corruption. . . .

". . . is at Harvard Law and working for a judge, Felicia's studying math at Columbia, and David dropped out of U. of Chicago med school after one semester and became a commodities trader. In the pits. He always was kind of an eighties guy. Anyway, the project's defunct—Dr. Flowers didn't renew the grant."

"Health problems?"

"That was part of it. And of course the publicity about Jamey didn't help. She moved to Hawaii. I think she wanted to minimize her stress—because of the M.S."

Catching up with the past for the second time today, I realized how many loose ends I'd let dangle.

"So," she said, "what brings you here?"

"Looking up some case material."

"Anything interesting?"

"Munchausen syndrome by proxy. Familiar with it?"

"I've heard of Munchausen—people abusing their bodies to fake disease, right? But what's the proxy part?"

"People faking disease in their children."

"Well, *that's* certainly hideous. What kinds of illnesses?"

"Almost anything. The most common symptoms are breathing problems, bleeding disorders, fevers, infections, pseudoseizures."

"By *proxy,*" she said. "The *word* is unnerving—so calculated, like some sort of business deal. Are you actually working with a family like that?"

"I'm evaluating a family to see if that's what's going on. It's still in the differential diagnosis stage. I have some preliminary references, thought I'd review the literature."

She smiled. "Card-file, or have you become computer-friendly?"

"Computer. If the screen talks English."

"Do you have a faculty account for SAP?"

"No. What's that?"

" 'Search and Print.' New system. Journals on file—complete texts scanned and entered. You can actually call up entire articles and have them printed. Faculty only, if you're willing to pay. My chairman got me a temporary lectureship and an account of my own. He expects me to publish my results and put his name on it. Unfortunately, foreign journals haven't been entered into the system yet, so I've got to locate those the old-fashioned way."

She pointed to the screen. "The master tongue. Don't you just love these sixty-letter words and umlauts? The grammar's nuts, but my mother helps me with the tough passages."

I remembered her mother. Heavyset and pleasant, fragrant of dough and sugar. Blue numbers on a soft white arm.

"Get an SAP card," she said. "It's a kick."

"Don't know if I'd qualify. My appointment's across town."

"I think you would. Just show them your faculty card and pay a fee. It takes about a week to process."

"I'll do it later, then. Can't wait that long."

"No, of course not. Listen, I've got plenty of time left on my account. My chairman wants me to use all of it up so he can ask for a bigger computer budget next year. If you want me to run you a search, just let me finish up with this, and we'll find all there is to know about people who *proxy* their kids."

*　　*　　*

We rode up to the SAP room at the top of the stacks. The search system looked no different from the terminals we'd just left: computers arranged in rows of partitioned cubicles. We found a free station and Jennifer searched for Munchausen-by-proxy references. The screen filled quickly. The list included all the articles Stephanie had given me, and more.

"Looks like the earliest one that comes up is 1977," she said. "*Lancet.* Meadow, R. 'Munchausen syndrome by proxy: The hinterland of child abuse.' "

"That's the seminal article," I said. "Meadow's the British pediatrician who recognized the syndrome and named it."

"The hinterland . . . that's ominous too. And here's a list of related topics: Munchausen syndrome, child abuse, incest, dissociative reactions."

"Try dissociative reactions first."

For the next hour we sifted through hundreds of references, distilling a dozen more articles that seemed to be relevant. When we were through, Jennifer saved the file and typed in a code.

"That'll link us to the printing system," she said.

The printers were housed behind blue panels that lined two walls of the adjoining room. Each contained a small screen, a card slot, a keyboard, and a mesh catch-bin under a foot-wide horizontal slit that reminded me of George Plumb's mouth. Two of the terminals weren't in use. One was marked OUT OF ORDER.

Jennifer activated the operative screen by inserting a plastic card in the slot, then typing in a letter-number code, followed by the call letters of the first and last articles we'd retrieved. Seconds later the bin began to fill with paper.

Jennifer said, "Automatically collated. Pretty nifty, huh?"

I said, "Melvyl and Orion—those are basic programs, right?"

"*Neanderthal.* One step above cards."

"If a hospital wanted to convert to computerized search and had a limited budget, could it go beyond that?"

"Sure. Way beyond. There are tons of new software programs. Even an office practitioner could go beyond that."

"Ever hear of a company called BIO-DAT?"

"No, can't say that I have, but that doesn't mean anything—

I'm no computer person. For me it's just a tool. Why? What do they do?"

"They're computerizing the library at Western Pediatric Hospital. Converting reference cards to Melvyl and Orion. Supposed to be a three-week job but they've been at it for three months."

"Is it a huge library?"

"No, quite a small one, actually."

"If all they're doing is probe and search, with a print-scanner it could be done in a couple of days."

"What if they don't have a scanner?"

"Then they're Stone Age. That would mean hand-transfer. Actually typing in each reference. But why would you hire a company with such a primitive setup when— Ah, it's finished."

A thick sheaf of papers filled the bin.

"Presto-gizmo, all the gain, none of the pain," she said. "One day they'll probably be able to program the stapling."

I thanked her, wished her well, and drove home with the fat bundle of documents on the passenger seat. After checking in with my service, going through the mail, and feeding the fish—the koi who'd survived infancy were thriving—I gulped down half a roast beef sandwich left over from last night's supper, swigged a beer, and started in on my homework.

People who proxied their kids . . .

Three hours later, I felt scummy. Even the dry prose of medical journals had failed to dim the horror.

Devil's waltz . . .

Poisoning by salt, sugar, alcohol, narcotics, expectorants, laxatives, emetics, even feces and pus used to create "bacteriologically battered babies."

Infants and toddlers subjected to a staggering list of torments that brought to mind Nazi "experiments." Case after case of children in whom a frighteningly wide range of phony diseases had been induced—virtually every pathology, it seemed, could be faked.

Mothers most frequently the culprits.

Daughters, almost always the victims.

The criminal profile: model mommy, often charming and personable, with a background in medicine or a paramedical field. Unusual calmness in the face of disaster—blunted affect masquerading as good coping. A hovering, protective nature—one specialist even warned doctors to look out for "overly caring" mothers.

Whatever that meant.

I remembered how Cindy Jones's tears had dried the moment Cassie had awakened. How she'd taken charge, with cuddles, fairy tales, the maternal breast.

Good child rearing or something evil?

Something else fit too.

Another *Lancet* article by Dr. Roy Meadow, the pioneer researcher. A discovery, in 1984, after examining the backgrounds of thirty-two children with manufactured epilepsy:

Seven siblings, dead and buried.

All expired from crib death.

7

I read some more until seven, then worked on the galley proofs of a monograph I'd just gotten accepted for publication: the emotional adjustment of a school full of children targeted by a sniper a year ago. The school's principal had become a friend of mine, then more. Then she went back to Texas to attend to a sick father. He died and she never returned.

Loose ends . . .

I reached Robin at her studio. She'd told me she was elbow-deep in a trying project—building four matching Stealth bomber-shaped guitars for a heavy metal band with neither budget nor self-control—and I wasn't surprised to hear the strain in her voice.

"Bad time?"

"No, no, it's good talking to someone who isn't drunk."

Shouts in the background. I said, "Is that the boys?"

"Being boys. I keep booting them out and they keep coming back. Like mildew. You'd think they'd have something to keep them busy—trashing their hotel suite, maybe—but— Uh-oh, hold on. *Lucas,* get *away* from there! You may need your fingers some day.

Sorry, Alex. He was drumming near the circular saw." Her voice softened: "Listen, I've got to go. How about Friday night—if that's okay with you?"

"It's okay. Mine or yours?"

"I'm not sure exactly when I'll be ready, Alex, so let me come by and get you. I promise no later than nine, okay?"

"Okay."

We said our goodbyes and I sat thinking about how independent she'd become.

I took out my old Martin guitar and finger-picked for a while. Then I went back into my study and reread the Munchausen articles a couple of times over, hoping to pick up something—some clinical cue—that I might have missed. But no insights were forthcoming; all I could think of was Cassie Jones's chubby face turned into something gray and sepulchral.

I wondered if it was even a question of science—if all the medical wisdom in the world was going to take me where I needed to go.

Maybe time for a different kind of specialist.

I phoned a West Hollywood number. A sultry female voice said, "You've reached Blue Investigations. Our office is closed. If you wish to leave a nonemergency message, do so after the first tone. In an emergency, wait until two tones have sounded."

After the second beep, I said, "It's Alex, Milo. Call me at home," and picked up my guitar again.

I'd played ten bars of "Windy and Warm" when the phone rang.

A voice that sounded far away said, "What's the emergency, pal?"

"*Blue* Investigations?"

"As in cop."

"Ah."

"Too abstract?" he said. "Do you get a porno connotation?"

"No, it's fine—very L.A. Whose voice is on the message?"

"Rick's sister."

"The dentist?"

"Yeah. Good pipes, huh?"

"Terrific. She sounds like Peggy Lee."

"Gives you fever when she drills your molars."

"When'd you go private?"

"Yeah, well, you know how it is—the lure of the dollar. Just a little moonlighting, actually. Long as the department keeps force-feeding me tedium during the day, might as well get paid well for it on the off hours."

"Not loving your computers yet?"

"Hey, I love 'em but they don't love me. 'Course, now they're saying the goddam things give off bad vibes—literally. Electromagnetic crap, probably slowly destroying this perfect body." A burst of static washed over the tail end of the sentence.

"Where are you calling from?" I said.

"Car phone. Wrapping up a job."

"Rick's car?"

"*Mine.* My phone too. It's a new age, Doctor. Rapid communication and even faster decay. Anyway, what's up?"

"I wanted to ask your advice on something—a case I'm working on—"

"Say no more—"

"I—"

"I mean it, Alex. *Say. No. More.* Cellular and privacy don't mix. Anyone can listen in. Hold tight."

He cut the line. My doorbell rang twenty minutes later.

"I was close," he said, tramping into my kitchen. "Wilshire near Barrington, paranoid lover surveillance."

In his left hand was an LAPD note pad and a black mobile phone the size of a bar of soap. He was dressed for undercover work: navy-blue Members Only jacket over a shirt of the same color, gray twill pants, brown desert boots. Maybe five pounds lighter than the last time I'd seen him—but that still added up to at least 250 of them distributed unevenly over 75 inches: long thin legs, protruberant gut, jowls surrendering to gravity and crowding his collar.

His hair had been recently cut—clipped short at back and sides, left full at the top. The black thatch hanging over his forehead showed a few strands of white. His sideburns reached the bottom of his ear lobes, a good inch longer than department regulations—but that was the least of the department's problems with him.

Milo was oblivious to fashion. He'd had the same look since I'd known him. Now Melrose trendies were adopting it; I doubted he'd noticed.

His big, pockmarked face was night-shift pale. But his startling green eyes seemed clearer than usual.

He said, "*You* look wired."

Opening the refrigerator, he bypassed the bottles of Grolsch, removed an unopened quart jar of grapefruit juice, and uncapped it with a quick twist of two thick fingers.

I handed him a glass. He filled it, drained it, filled again and drank.

"Vitamin C, free enterprise, snappy-sounding business title— you're moving too fast for me, Milo."

Putting the glass down, he licked his lips. "Actually," he said, "*Blue*'s an acronym. Big Lug's Uneasy Enterprise—Rick's idea of wit. Though I admit it was accurate at the time—jumping into the private sector wasn't exactly your smooth transition. But I'm glad I did it, because of the bread. I've become serious about financial security in my old age."

"What do you charge?"

"Fifty to eighty per hour, depending. Not as good as a shrink, but I'm not complaining. City wants to waste what it taught me, have me sit in front of a screen all day, it's their loss. By night, I'm getting my detective exercise."

"Any interesting cases?"

"Nah, mostly petty bullshit surveillance to keep the paranoids happy. But at least it gets me out on the street."

He poured more juice and drank. "I don't know how long I can take it—the day job."

He rubbed his face, as if washing without water. Suddenly, he looked worn, stripped of entrepreneurial cheer.

I thought of all he'd been through during the last year. Breaking the jaw of a superior who'd put his life in danger. Doing it on live television. The police department settling with him because going public could have proved embarrassing. No charges pressed, six months' unpaid leave, then a return to West L.A. Robbery/Homicide with a one-notch demotion to Detective II. Finding out, six months later, that no detective jobs were open at West L.A., or any other division, due to "unforeseen" budget cuts.

They shunted him—"temporarily"—to a data-processing job at Parker Center, where he was put under the tutelage of a flagrantly effeminate civilian instructor and taught how to play with computers. The department's not-so-subtle reminder that assault was one thing, but what he did in bed was neither forgotten nor forgiven.

"Still thinking of going to court?" I said.

"I don't know. Rick wants me to fight to the death. Says the way they reneged proves they'll never give me a break. But I know if I take it to court, that's it for me in the department. Even if I win."

He removed his jacket and tossed it on the counter. "Enough bullshit self-pity. What can I do for *you*?"

I told him about Cassie Jones, gave him a mini-lecture on Munchausen syndrome. He drank and made no comment. Looked almost as if he were tuning out.

I said, "Have you heard of this before?"

"No. Why?"

"Most people react a little more strongly."

"Just taking it all in . . . Actually, it reminded me of something. Several years ago. There was this guy came into the E.R. at Cedars. Bleeding ulcer. Rick saw him, asked him about stress. Guy says he's been hitting the bottle very heavy 'cause he's guilty about being a murderer and getting away with it. Seems he'd been with a call girl, gotten mad and cut her up. Badly—real psycho slasher thing. Rick nodded and said uh-huh; then he got the hell out of there and called Security—then me. The murder had taken place in Westwood. At the time I was in a car with Del Hardy, working on some robberies over in Pico-Robertson, and the two of us bopped over right away, Mirandized him, and listened to what he had to say.

"The turkey was *overjoyed* to see us. *Vomiting* out details like we were his salvation. Names, addresses, dates, weapon. He denied any other murders and came up clean for wants and warrants. A real middle-of-the-road type of guy, even owned his own business— carpet cleaning, I think. We booked him, had him repeat his confession on tape, and figured we'd picked up a dream solve. Then we proceeded to round up verifying details and found nothing. No crime, no physical evidence of any murder at that particular date and place; no hooker had ever lived at that address or anywhere nearby. No hooker fitting the name and description he'd given us had ever existed *anywhere* in L.A. So we checked unidentified victims, but none of the Jane Does in the morgue fit, and no moniker in Vice's files matched the one he said his girl used. We even ran checks in other cities, contacted the FBI, figuring maybe he got disoriented—some kind of psycho thing—and mixed up his locale. *He* kept insisting it had happened exactly the way he was telling it. Kept saying he wanted to be punished.

"After three straight days of this: *nada*. Guy's got a court-appointed attorney against his will, and the lawyer's screaming at us to make a case or let his client go. Our lieutenant is putting the pressure on—put up or shut up. So we keep digging. Zilch.

"At this point we begin to suspect we've been had, and confront the guy. He denies it. Really convincing—De Niro could have taken lessons. So we go over it *again*. Backtracking, double-checking, driving ourselves crazy. And still come up empty. Finally, we're convinced it's a scam, get overtly pissed off at the guy—major league bad-cop/bad-cop. *He* reacts by getting pissed off, too. But it's an embarrassed kind of anger. Slimy. Like he knows he's been found out and is being extra-indignant in order to put us on the defensive."

He shook his head and hummed the *Twilight Zone* theme.

"What happened?" I said.

"What could happen? We let him walk out and never heard from the asshole again. We could have busted him for filing a false report, but that would have bought us lots of paperwork and court time, and for what? Lecture and a fine on a first offense knocked down to a misdemeanor? No, thank you. We were really steamed, Alex. I've never *seen* Del so mad. It had been a heavy week, plenty of real crimes, very few solutions. And *this* bastard yanks our chains with total *bullshit*."

Remembered anger colored his face.

"Confessors," he said. "Attention-seeking, jerking everyone around. Doesn't that sound like your Munchausen losers?"

"Sounds a lot like them," I said. "Never thought of it that way."

"See? I'm a regular font of insight. Go on with your case."

I told him the rest of it.

He said, "Okay, so what do you want? Background checks on the mother? Both parents? The nurse?"

"I hadn't thought in those terms."

"No? What, then?"

"I really don't know, Milo. I guess I just wanted some counsel."

He placed his hands atop his belly, bowed his head, and raised it. "Honorable Buddha on duty. Honorable Buddha counsels as following: Shoot all bad guys. Let some other deity sort them out."

"Be good to know who the bad guys are."

"Exactly. That's why I suggested background checks. At least on your prime suspect."

"That would have to be the mother."

"Then she gets checked first. But as long as I'm punching buttons, I can throw in any others as a bonus. More fun than the payroll shit they're punishing me with."

"What would you check for?"

"Criminal history. It's a police data bank. Will your lady doctor friend be in on the fact that I'm checking?"

"Why?"

"I like to know my parameters when I snoop. What we're doing is technically a no-no."

"No. Let's keep her out of it—why put her in jeopardy?"

"Fine."

"In terms of a criminal history," I said, "Munchausens generally present as model citizens—just like your carpet cleaner. And we already know about the first child's death. It's been written off as SIDS."

He thought. "There'd be a coroner's report on that, but if no one had any suspicions of foul play, that's about it. I'll see what I can do about getting hold of the paperwork. You might even be able to do it yourself—check hospital records. If you can be discreet."

"Don't know if I can. The hospital's a different place now."

"In what way?"

"Lots more security—kind of heavy-handed."

"Well," he said, "you can't fault that. That part of town's gotten real nasty."

He got up, went to the fridge, found an orange and began peeling it over the sink. Frowning.

I said, "What is it?"

"I'm trying to frame some strategy on this. Seems to me the only way to solve something like this would be to catch the bad guy in the act. The kid gets sick at home?"

I nodded.

"So the only way to do it would be to surveil their house electronically. Hidden audio and video. Trying to record someone actually poisoning the baby."

"The Colonel's games," I said.

That made him frown.

"Yeah, exactly the kind of stuff that prick would delight in . . . He moved, you know."

"Where?"

"Washington, D.C. Where else? New enterprise for him. Corporation with one of those titles that tells you nothing about what it does. Ten to one he's living off the government. I got a note and a business card in the mail a while back. Congrats for entering the informational age and some free software to do my taxes."

"He knew what you were doing?"

"Evidently. Anyway, back to your baby-poisoner. Bugging her house. Unless you got a court order, anything you came up with would be inadmissible. But a court order means strong evidence, and all you've got are suspicions. Not to mention the fact that Grandpa's a pooh-bah, and you've got to tread extra carefully."

He finished peeling the orange, put it down, washed his hands, and began pulling apart the sections. "This one may be a heartbreaker—please don't tell me how cute the kid is."

"The kid's adorable."

"Thank you very much."

I said, "There were a couple of cases in England, reported in one of the pediatrics journals. They videotaped mothers smothering babies, and all *they* had were suspicions."

"They taped at home?"

"In the hospital."

"Big difference. And for all I know, the law's different in England. . . . Let me think on it, Alex. See if there's anything creative we *can* do. In the meantime I'll start playing with local records, NCIC, on the off chance that any of them has been naughty before, and we can build up *something* to get a warrant. Old Charlie's taught me well—you should see me ride those data bases."

"Don't put *yourself* in jeopardy," I said.

"Don't worry. The preliminary searches are no more than what an officer does every time he pulls someone over for a traffic stop. If and when I dig deeper, I'll be careful. Have the parents lived anyplace other than L.A.?"

"I don't know," I said. "I really don't know much about them, better start learning."

"Yeah, you dig your trench; I'll dig mine." He hunched over the counter, thinking out loud: "They're upper-crusties, which could mean private schools. Which is tough."

"The mother might be a public school girl. She doesn't come across as someone who was born to money."

"Social climber?"

"No, just simple. He's a college teacher. She might have been one of his students."

"Okay," he said, opening his note pad. "What else? Maybe military service for him, maybe officer's training—another tough nut to crack. Charlie *has* managed to hack into some of the military files, but nothing fancy, just V.A. benefits, cross-referencing, that kind of stuff."

"What do you guys do, play around with confidential data banks?"

"More like he plays, I watch. Where does the father teach?"

"West Valley Community College. Sociology."

"What about mom? Any job?"

"No, she's a full-time mom."

"Takes her job seriously, huh. Okay, give me a name to work with."

"Jones."

He looked at me.

I nodded.

His laughter was deep and loud, almost drunken.

The next morning, I arrived at the hospital at 9:45. The doctors' lot was nearly full and I had to drive up to the top level to find a space. A uniformed guard was leaning against a concrete abutment, half-concealed by shadows, smoking a cigarette. He kept his eyes on me as I got out of the Seville and didn't stop looking until I'd snapped my new badge to my lapel.

The private ward was as quiet as it had been yesterday. A single nurse sat at the desk and the unit clerk read *McCall's.*

I read Cassie's chart. Stephanie had been by for morning rounds, reported Cassie symptom-free but decided to keep her in for at least another day. I went to 505W, knocked, and entered.

Cindy Jones and Vicki Bottomley were sitting on the sleeper couch. A deck of cards rested in Vicki's lap. The two of them looked up.

Cindy smiled. "Good morning."

"Good morning."

Vicki said, "Okay," and stood.

Cassie's bed had been cranked to an upright position. She sat playing with a Fisher-Price house. Other amusements, including a quorum of LuvBunnies, were scattered on the bedcover. A breakfast tray held a bowl of partially eaten oatmeal and a plastic cup of something red. Cartoon action flashed on the TV but the sound was off. Cassie was preoccupied with the house, arranging furniture and plastic figures. An I.V. pole was pushed into a corner.

I placed a new drawing on the bed. She glanced at it for a moment, then returned to her play.

Vicki was in rapid motion, handing the cards to Cindy, then clasping Cindy's hand briefly between both of hers. Avoiding eye contact with me, she walked over to the bed, tousled Cassie's head, and said, "See you, punkin."

Cassie looked up for an instant. Vicki tousled her hair again and left.

Cindy stood. A pink blouse replaced yesterday's plaid. Same jeans and sandals.

"Let's see, what did Dr. Delaware draw for you today?" She picked up the drawing. Cassie reached out and took it from her.

Cindy put an arm around her shoulder. "An elephant! Dr. Delaware drew you a cute blue elephant!"

Cassie brought the paper closer. "Eh-fa."

"Good, Cass, that's great! Did you hear that, Dr. Delaware? Elephant?"

I nodded. "Terrific."

"I don't know what you did, Dr. Delaware, but since yesterday she's been talking more. Cass, can you say elephant again?"

Cassie closed her mouth and crumpled the paper.

Cindy said, "Oh, my," cuddled her and stroked her cheek. Both of us watched Cassie labor to unfold the picture.

When she finally succeeded she said, "Eh-fa!" compressed the paper again, tighter, into a fist-sized ball, then looked at it, perplexed.

Cindy said, "Sorry, Dr. Delaware. Looks like your elephant isn't doing too well."

"Looks like Cassie is."

She forced a smile and nodded.

Cassie made another attempt to straighten the paper. This time, thimble-sized fingers weren't up to the task and Cindy helped her. "There you go, honey. . . . Yes, she's feeling great."

"Any problems with procedures?"

"There haven't been any procedures. Not since yesterday morning. We've just been sitting here—it's . . ."

"Something the matter?" I said.

She brought her braid forward and smoothed the fringe.

"People must think I'm crazy," she said.

"Why do you say that?"

"I don't know. It was a stupid thing to say—I'm sorry."

"What's the matter, Cindy?"

She turned away and played with her braid some more. Then she sat back down. Picking up the deck of cards, she passed it from hand to hand.

"It's just that . . ." she said, speaking so softly I had to move closer, "I . . . each time I bring her here she gets better. And then I take her home, thinking everything's going to be okay, and it is for a while, and then . . ."

"And then she gets sick again."

Keeping her head down, she nodded.

Cassie mumbled something to a plastic figure. Cindy said, "That's good, baby," but the little girl didn't seem to hear.

I said, "And then she gets sick all over again and you're let down."

Cassie threw the figure down, picked up another, and began shaking it.

Cindy said, "And then all of a sudden, she's okay—just like now. That's what I meant—about being crazy. Sometimes *I* think I'm crazy."

She shook her head and returned to Cassie's bedside. Taking a lock of the child's hair between her fingers, she let it slip away. Peering into the playhouse, she said, "Well, look at that—they're all eating what you made for dinner!" Her voice was so cheerful it made the roof of my mouth ache.

She stayed there, playing with Cassie's hair, pointing at the dolls, and prompting. Cassie made imitative sounds. Some of them sounded like words.

I said, "How about we go down for a cup of coffee? Vicki can stay with Cassie."

Cindy looked up. One hand rested on Cassie's shoulder. "No— no, I'm sorry, Dr. Delaware, I couldn't. I never leave her," she said.

"Never?"

She shook her head. "Not when she's in here. I know that sounds crazy, too, but I can't. You hear too many . . . things."

"What kinds of things?"

"Accidents—someone getting the wrong medicine. Not that I'm actually worried—this is a great hospital. But . . . I just need to be here. I'm sorry."

"It's okay. I understand."

"I'm sure it's more for me than for her, but . . ." She bent and hugged Cassie. Cassie squirmed and continued playing. Cindy gave me a helpless look.

"I know I'm being overprotective," she said.

"Not considering what you've been through."

"Well . . . thanks for saying that."

I pointed to the chair.

She gave a weak smile and sat down.

"It must be a real strain," I said. "Being here so often. It's one thing working in a hospital, but being dependent is something else."

She looked puzzled. "Working in a hospital?"

"You were a respiratory tech, right?" I said. "Didn't you do it at a hospital?"

"Oh, that. That was such a long time ago. No, I never got that far—didn't graduate."

"Lost interest?"

"Kind of." Picking up the box of cards, she tapped one knee. "Actually, going into R.T. in the first place was my aunt's idea. She was an R.N. Said a woman should have a skill even if she didn't use it, and that I should find something that would always be in demand, like health care. With the way we were ruining the air, people smoking, she felt there'd always be a call for R.T.'s."

"Your aunt sounds like someone with strong opinions."

She smiled. "Oh, she was. She's gone now." Rapid eyeblink.

"She was a fantastic person. My parents passed on when I was a kid and she basically raised me by herself."

"But she didn't encourage you to go into nursing? Even though she was an R.N.?"

"Actually she recommended *against* nursing. Said it was too much work for too little pay and not enough . . ."

She gave an embarrassed smile.

"Not enough respect from the doctors?"

"Like you said, Dr. Delaware, she had strong opinions on just about everything."

"Was she a hospital nurse?"

"No, she worked for the same G.P. for twenty-five years and they bickered the whole time like an old married couple. But he was a really nice man—old-fashioned family doctor, not too good about collecting his bills. Aunt Harriet was always on him for that. She was a real stickler for details, probably from her days in the army—she served in Korea, on the front. Made it to captain."

"Really," I said.

"Uh-huh. Because of her I tried out the service, too. Boy, this is really taking me back a few years."

"You were in the army?"

She gave a half-smile, as if expecting my surprise. "Strange for a girl, huh? It happened in my senior year in high school. The recruiter came out on careers day and made it sound pretty attractive—job training, scholarships. Aunt Harriet thought it would be a good idea, too, so that clinched it."

"How long were you in?"

"Just a few months." Her hands worked her braid. "A few months after I arrived I got sick and had to be discharged early."

"Sorry to hear that," I said. "Must have been serious."

She looked up. Blushing deeply. Yanking the braid.

"It was," she said. "Influenza—real bad flu—that developed into pneumonia. Acute viral pneumonia—there was a terrible epidemic in the barracks. Lots of girls got sick. After I recovered, they said my lungs might be weakened and they didn't want me in anymore." Shrug. "So that was it. My famous military career."

"Was it a big disappointment?"

"No, not really. Everything worked out for the best." She looked at Cassie.

"Where were you stationed?"

"Fort Jackson. Down in South Carolina. It was one of the few places they trained only women. It was the summer—you don't think of pneumonia in the summer, but a germ's a germ, right?"

"True."

"It was really humid. You could shower and feel dirty two seconds later. I wasn't used to it."

"Did you grow up in California?"

"California native," she said, waving an imaginary flag. "Ventura. My family came out from Oklahoma originally. Gold Rush days. One of my great-grandmothers was part Indian—according to my aunt, that's where the hair comes from."

She hefted the braid, then dropped it.

" 'Course, it's probably not true," she said, smiling. "Everyone wants to be Indian now. It's kind of fashionable." She looked at me: "Delaware. With that name you could be part Indian too."

"There's a family myth that says so—one third of one great-great-grandfather. I guess what I *am* is a mongrel—little bit of everything."

"Well, good for you. That makes you all-American, doesn't it?"

"Guess so," I said, smiling. "Was Chip ever in the service?"

"Chip?" The idea seemed to amuse her. "No."

"How'd the two of you meet?"

"At college. I did a year at WVCC, after R.T. school. Took Soc One-oh-one and he was my teacher."

Another look at Cassie. Still busy with the house. "Do you want to do your techniques now?"

"It's still a little soon," I said. "I want her to really trust me."

"Well . . . I think she does. She loves your drawings—we saved all the ones she didn't destroy."

I smiled. "It's still best to take it slow. And if she's not having any procedures, there's no need to rush."

"True," she said. "For all that's happening here, I guess we could go home right now."

"Do you want to?"

"I always want to. But what I *really* want is for her to get *better*."
Cassie glanced over and Cindy lowered her voice to a whisper again:
"Those seizures *really* scared me, Dr. Delaware. It was like . . ." She
shook her head.

"Like what?"

"Like something out of a movie. This is terrible to say, but it reminded me of *The Exorcist*." She shook her head. "I'm sure Dr. Eves will
get to the bottom of whatever's going on, eventually. Right? She said
we should stay at least one more night, maybe two, for observation. It's
probably for the best, anyway. Cassie's always so healthy *here*."

Her eyes moistened.

"Once you do go home," I said, "I'd like to come out and visit."

"Oh, sure . . ." Unasked questions flooded her face.

"In order to keep working on the rapport," I said. "If I can get
Cassie totally comfortable with me when she's not having procedures,
I'll be in a better position to help her when she does need me."

"Sure. That makes sense. Thank you, that's very kind. I . . .
didn't know doctors still made house calls."

"Once in a while. We call them home visits now."

"Oh. Well, sure, that would be great. I really appreciate your
taking the time."

"I'll call you after you're discharged and set up an appointment.
Why don't you give me your address and phone number?"

I tore a sheet out of my datebook and handed it to her along with
a pen.

She wrote and handed it back.

Fine, round hand, light touch.

> *Cassie B. Jones's house:*
> *19547 Dunbar Court*
> *Valley Hills, Ca.*

A phone number with an 818 area code.

"That's out at the north end of Topanga Boulevard," she said.
"Near the Santa Susanna Pass."

"Pretty good ride to the hospital."

"Sure is." She wiped her eyes again. Bit her lip and tried to
smile.

"What is it?" I said.

"I was just thinking. When we come in, it's always the middle of the night and the freeway's clear. Sometimes I hate the night."

I squeezed her hand. Her fingers were slack.

I released them, looked at the paper again, folded it and put it in my pocket.

"Cassie B.," I said. "What does the B. stand for?"

"Brooks—that was my maiden name. It's sort of a tribute to Aunt Harriet. It's not exactly feminine, I guess. Brooke with an *e* would have been more of a girl's name. Like Brooke Shields. But I wanted to remember Aunt Harriet." She glanced sideways. "What're they doing now, Cass? Cleaning up the dishes?"

"Dih."

"Good! *Dish*es!"

She got up. I rose too. "Any questions before I go?"

"No . . . I don't think so."

"Then I'll stop by tomorrow."

"Sure. Great. Cass? Dr. Delaware's leaving. Say bye-bye?"

Cassie raised her eyes. Each hand clutched a plastic doll.

I said, "Bye-bye, Cassie."

"Bah-bah."

"Great!" said Cindy. "That was really great!"

"Bah . . . bah." The hands clapped, dolls clicking upon impact. "Bah! Bah!"

I walked over to the bed. Cassie looked up at me. Shiny eyes. Neutral expression. I touched her cheek. Warm and buttery.

"Bah!" A tiny finger probed my arm, just for a second. The puncture wound was healing nicely.

"Bye, cutie."

"Bah!"

Vicki was at the nursing station. I said hi, and when she didn't answer, I noted my visit in Cassie's chart, walked to Five East, and took the stairs down to the ground floor. Leaving the hospital, I drove to a gas station at Sunset and La Brea and used a pay phone to call Milo at Parker Center.

The line was busy. I tried twice more, same result, dialed Milo's home, and listened to Rick's sister do Peggy Lee.

One beep sounded. I talked quickly: "Hey, Mr. Blue, no emergency, but some data that might save you some time. Dad was never in the army but *mom* was—how's that for a switch? Maiden name: Brooks, as in babbling. She spent her time at Fort Jackson, South Carolina. Discharged early, due to a bout of viral pneumonia, she claims. But she blushed and got a little antsy when talking about it, so maybe it's not the whole truth. Maybe she misbehaved and got kicked out. She's twenty-six now, was a senior in high school when she joined up, so that gives you a time range to work with."

Returning to the car, I drove the rest of the way home thinking about pneumonia, respiratory therapy, and a baby boy lying still and gray in his crib. By the time I arrived, I was feeling short of breath.

I changed into shorts and a T-shirt, reviewed my chat with Cindy.

People must think I'm crazy. . . . Sometimes I think I'm crazy.

Guilt? A veiled confession? Or just tantalizing me?

Waltzing.

She'd been totally cooperative until I'd suggested we leave the room.

The "overly caring" Munchausen mother? Or simply the reasonable anxiety of a woman who's lost one child and suffered plenty with another?

I recalled the nervous surprise she'd shown when I told her of my plans for a home visit.

Something to hide? Or just surprise—a logical reaction—because doctors *didn't* do house calls anymore?

Another risk factor: Her mother-figure, the nurse. A woman who came across, even in Cindy's loving recollection, as something of a martinet.

A nurse who worked for a doctor but fought with him. Who disparaged physicians.

She'd guided Cindy into health care but away from nursing.

Ambivalence about doctors? About the health-care power structure? Preoccupation with sickness and treatment?

Had all that been communicated to Cindy at a young age?

Then there was the matter of her own illnesses—the flu and pneumonia that had disrupted her career plans.

Everything worked out for the best.

The blush, the yanking at her braid. The discharge was definitely a sensitive topic.

I got on the kitchen phone, obtained the 803 area code for South Carolina and dialed Information there. Fort Jackson turned out to be in Columbia. I wrote down the number and called it.

A drawling female voice answered. I asked for the base's chief medical officer.

"You want the commander of the hospital?"

"Yes, please."

"One moment."

A second later: "Colonel Hedgeworth's office."

"This is Dr. Delaware, from Los Angeles, California. I'd like to speak with the colonel, please."

"What was that name, sir?"

"Delaware." I added my professional title and medical school affiliation.

"Colonel Hedgeworth is out of the office, sir. Would you care to speak with Major Dunlap?"

"That would be fine."

"Please hold."

Half a dozen beats, then another drawling voice. Male baritone: "Major Dunlap."

"Major, this is Dr. Alex Delaware, from L.A." I repeated my credentials.

"Uh-huh. What can I do for you, Doctor?"

"We've been doing some pilot research—contagion patterns of viral epidemics, influenza and pneumonia, specifically—in relatively closed environments such as prisons, private schools, and military bases. Contrasting it with control groups in the general population."

"Epidemiological research?"

"We're working out of the Pediatrics department. Still in the process of assembling a preliminary data base, and Fort Jackson came up as a possible target site."

"Uh-huh," he said. Long pause. "Have you got a research grant on this?"

"Not yet, just some preliminary seed money. Whether or not we apply for full funding depends on how the data base shapes up. If we do write a proposal it would be as a collaborative effort—the target sites, plus us. We'd carry all the overhead, would just need access to facts and figures."

He chuckled. "We give you our stats and you put our names on any papers you write?"

"That would be part of it, but we'd always be open to scientific input."

"What med school was that?"

I told him.

"Uh-huh." Another laugh. "Well, I guess that would be pretty attractive, if I still cared about that kind of thing. But yeah, sure, I guess you can put our names down, for the time being—conditionally, no commitment. Got to check it with Colonel Hedgeworth, though, before I finalize anything."

"When will he be back?"

He laughed again. "*She'll* be back in a couple of days. Give me your number."

I gave him my home exchange, saying, "That's a private line, easier to reach."

"And what was your name?"

"Delaware."

"Like in the state?"

"Exactly."

"And you're with Pediatrics?"

"Yes," I said. Technically true, but I hoped he wouldn't delve too deeply and find out I had a clinical appointment but hadn't lectured in years.

"Fine," he said. "Get back to you soon as I can. If you don't hear from me in, say, a week—call back."

"Will do, Major. Thanks."

"No problem."

"In the meantime, though, if you could give me one bit of information, I'd appreciate it."

"What's that?"

"Do you recall any epidemics of either influenza or pneumonia at your base during the last ten years?"

"Ten years? Hmm. I haven't been here that long. We did have a meningitis outbreak a couple of years ago, but that was bacterial. Very nasty."

"We're limiting the inquiry to viral respiratory illnesses."

"Well," he said, "I guess the information's somewhere— hold on."

Two minutes passed.

"Captain Katz, how can I help you?"

I repeated my request.

"That far back wouldn't be on our computer," he said. "Can I get back to you on that?"

"Sure. Thanks."

Another exchange of numbers.

I put the receiver down, clogged with frustration, knowing the information was on someone's hard drive or floppy disc, accessible, instantly, at the push of the right button.

Milo didn't call back until four.

"Been trying to keep up with your Joneses," he said. "The coroner has a death form on file for the first kid. Charles Lyman Jones the Fourth. Nothing suspicious—sudden infant death syndrome, certified by your friend Stephanie and backed up by a Rita Kohler, M.D."

"She's the head of the General Pediatrics division. Stephanie's boss. She was originally their doctor, was out of town when Chad died."

"Uh-huh. Well, it all looks kosher. Now, in terms of the parents, here's what I've got so far. They live out in the West Valley and pay their property taxes on time—lots of taxes, 'cause they own lots of property. Fifty parcels."

"Fifty? Where?"

"Right where they live—the entire surrounding tract is theirs. Not bad for a college teacher, huh?"

"College teacher with a trust fund."

"No doubt. Other than that, they seem to live pretty simple and straight. Charles Lyman the Third drives a 1985 Volvo 240 four-door, received a speeding ticket last year and two parking citations, all paid. Cindy Brooks Jones drives a Plymouth Voyager van and is pure as the driven snow, infraction-wise. Ditto your surly nurse, if she's Victoria June Bottomley, DOB 4/24/36, with an address in Sun Valley."

"Sounds like her."

"So far, Beaver Cleaverland."

"You obviously didn't get my message."

"No. When and where?"

"Around eleven. I left it with Rick's sister."

"I didn't get any emergency call."

"That's 'cause I did a *one* beeper," I said. "Respecting your business procedures." I recounted the suspicions my talk with Cindy had aroused and my call to South Carolina.

"Joe Sleuth," he said. "Just can't control yourself."

"Hey, with your fees, I figured anything I could do myself would be a bargain."

He grunted. "*Knowing* me is a bargain. Pneumonia, huh? So what're you saying? Her lungs clog, it messes her plans up, so she fucks up her kids' lungs—whatchacallit, projecting?"

"Something like that. On top of that, she was trained in respiratory therapy."

"Then why would she move away from respiratory stuff? Why the stomach problems and the seizures?"

"I don't know, but the facts remain: Lung sickness disrupted her life. And/or gave her a lot of attention."

"So she passed it on to the kids in order to get more attention for herself? Or got *mad* at being sick and took it *out* on the kids?"

"Either. Neither. Both. I don't know. Maybe I'm just blowing air—no pun intended."

"That comment about being nuts. You think she suspects she's under watch?"

"It's possible. Or maybe she was just playing around with me. She's on edge, but who wouldn't be, with a child constantly sick? That's the problem with this whole case—anything I see can be explained several different ways. What does stick in my mind is the way she blushed and fiddled with her hair when she talked about the army. I'm wondering if the pneumonia story could be a cover for a psychiatric discharge or something else she doesn't want coming out. I'm hoping the army can confirm it, one way or the other."

"When's the army gonna call you back?"

"The guy I spoke to didn't commit himself. Said their health records that far back aren't computerized. Would health data be included in the military data banks Charlie's hacked into?"

"Don't know, but I'll ask him."

"Thanks."

"How's the baby doing?"

"Full recovery. No neurological problems that would have caused her to seize. Stephanie wants to watch her for a day or two. Mom says she wouldn't *mind* going home, but makes no effort to push it—Miss Compliant, doctor knows all. She's also claiming Cassie's talking more since I met her. She's certain it's something I did."

"The old kiss-up?"

"Munchausen moms are notorious for it—the staff generally loves them."

"Well," he said, "enjoy it while it lasts. You dig up some dirt on this lady, she's not gonna be kissing you anywhere."

9

After he hung up, I took the mail, the morning paper, and a month's worth of bills to a deli in West L.A. The place was nearly full—old people hunched over soup, young families with small children, two uniformed policemen at the rear joshing with the owner, mountainous sandwiches sharing table space with their walkie-talkies.

I sat at the corner table at the front, to the left of the counter, and had smoked turkey on onion roll, cole slaw, and Dr. Brown's CelRay soda.

Good stuff, but hospital thoughts intruded on my digestion.

At 9:00 P.M. I decided to go back to the hospital for an unscheduled visit. See how Mrs. Charles Lyman Jones the Third reacted to that.

Black night; the shadows on Sunset seemed to be moving in slow motion and the boulevard turned spooky nearer to the good side of town. After a few miles of hollow eyes, Thorazine shuffles, and scary motels, Western Peds's child-shaped logo and brightly lit Emergency Room arrow signaled a welcome outpost.

The parking lot was nearly deserted now. Small amber bulbs in grilled cases hung from the concrete ceiling, casting a hard-focus glow on every other parking slot. The remaining spaces were totally dark, creating a zebra-stripe effect. As I walked to the stairs I felt as if someone were watching me. When I looked back, I was alone.

The lobby was empty, too, the marble floors mirrors of nothing. One woman sat behind the Information window, methodically hand-stamping some papers. The page operator was getting paid for showing up. A clock ticked loudly. The smell of adhesive tape and a faint but definite sweat-spoor lingered, remembrances of stress gone by.

Something else I'd forgotten: Hospitals are different at night. The place was as spooky as the streets.

I took the elevator up to Five and walked through the ward, unnoticed. The doors to most of the rooms were closed; handwritten signs provided occasional distraction: *Protective Isolation*, *Infection Watch/No Visitors*. . . . The few doors that were open emitted TV sounds and the cricket-clicks of metered I.V.'s. I passed sleeping children and others entranced by the cathode ray. Parents sat, stiff as plaster. Waiting.

Chappy Ward's teak doors vacuum-sucked me into dead silence. No one was at the desk.

I walked over to 505 and rapped very softly. No answer. I opened the door and looked in.

Cassie's side rails were raised. She slept, guarded by stainless steel. Cindy slept, too, on the sofa bed, positioned so that her head was close to Cassie's feet. One of her hands extended through the bars, touching Cassie's sheet.

I closed the door softly.

A voice behind me said, "They're sleeping."

I turned.

Vicki Bottomley glared at me, hands on meaty hips.

"Another double shift?" I said.

She rolled her eyes and began walking off.

"Hold on," I said. The sharpness in my voice surprised both of us.

She stopped, turned slowly. "What?"

"What's the problem, Vicki?"

"There is no problem."

"I think there is."

"You're entitled." She started to leave again.

"Hold it." The empty corridor amplified my voice. Or maybe I really was that angry.

She said, "I've got work to do."

"So do I, Vicki. Same patient, as a matter of fact."

She stretched one arm toward the chart rack. "Be my guest."

I walked up to her. Close enough to crowd. She backed away. I moved forward.

"I don't know what your problem with me is, but I suggest we deal with it."

"I don't have any problem with anyone."

"Oh? Is what I've seen so far your usual level of charm?"

The pretty blue eyes blinked. Though they were dry, she wiped them quickly.

"Listen," I said, retreating a step, "I don't want to get into anything personal with you. But you've been hostile to me from the beginning and I'd like to know why."

She stared at me. Opened her mouth. Closed it.

"It's nothing," she said. "I'll be okay—no problem, I promise. Okay?"

She held out her hand.

I reached for it.

She gave me fingertips. A quick shake and she turned and started to walk away.

I said, "I'm going down to get some coffee. Care to join me?"

She stopped but didn't turn around.

"Can't. On duty."

"Want me to bring a cup up for you?"

Now she turned quickly. "What do you *want*?"

"Nothing," I said. "With your double-shifting, I figured you could use some coffee."

"I'm *fine*."

"I've heard you're terrific."

"What does that mean?"

"Dr. Eves thinks a lot of you. As a nurse. So does Cindy."

Her arms clamped across her chest, as if she were holding herself together. "I do my job."

"Do you see me getting in the way of that?"

Her shoulders climbed. She seemed to be phrasing an answer. But all she said was, "No. Everything will be okay. Okay?"

"Vicki—"

"I *promise*," she said. "*Please?* Can I *go* now?"

"Sure," I said. "Sorry if I came on too strong."

She clamped her lips together, pivoted, and returned to her station.

I went to the Five East elevators. One lift was stuck on the sixth floor. The other two arrived simultaneously. Chip Jones stepped out of the central door, a cup of coffee in each hand. He had on faded jeans, a white turtleneck, and a denim jacket that matched the pants.

"Dr. Delaware."

"Professor."

He laughed and said, "Please," and stepped out into the hall. "How are my ladies doing?"

"They're both sleeping."

"Thank God. When I spoke to Cindy this afternoon, she sounded exhausted. I brought this from downstairs"—raising one cup—"to help fuel her. But sleep is what she really needs."

He began walking toward the teak doors. I tagged along. "Are we keeping you from hearth and home, Doctor?"

I shook my head. "Been and returned."

"Didn't know psychologists kept that kind of schedule."

"We don't when we can avoid it."

He smiled. "Well, the fact that Cindy's sleeping this early means Cassie must be getting healthy enough for her to relax. So that's good."

"She told me she never leaves Cassie."

"Never."

"Must be hard on her."

"Unbelievably hard. At first I tried to ease her away from it, but after being here a few times and seeing other mothers, I realized it was normal. Rational, actually. It's self-defense."

"Against what?"

"Screw-ups."

"Cindy talked about that, too," I said. "Have you seen a lot of medical error around here?"

"As a parent or as Chuck Jones's son?"

"Is there a difference?"

He gave a small, hard smile. "You bet there is. As Chuck Jones's son, I think this place is pediatric paradise, and I'll say so in the next banquet journal if they ask me. As a parent, I've seen things—the inevitable human errors. I'll give you an example—one that really shook me. A couple of months ago, the whole fifth floor was buzzing. Seems there was this little boy being treated for some kind of cancer—getting an experimental drug, so maybe there wasn't much hope anyway. But that's not the point. Someone misread a decimal point and he got a massive overdose. Brain damage, coma, the whole bit. All the parents on the floor heard the resuscitation page and saw the emergency team rush in. Heard his mother screaming for help. Including us—I was out in the hall, actually heard his mother scream for help."

He winced. "I saw her a couple of days later, Dr. Delaware. When he was still being respirated. She looked like a concentration camp victim. That look of being beaten down and betrayed? All because of one decimal point. Now that kind of thing probably happens all the time, on a smaller scale—things that can be smoothed over. Or don't even get picked up in the first place. So you can't blame parents for wanting to keep an eye out, can you?"

"No," I said. "Sounds like you don't have much confidence in this place."

"On the contrary, I do," he said impatiently. "Before we decided to have Cassie treated here, we did research—Dad notwithstanding. So I know this is *the* best place in the city for sick kids. But when it's your child, statistics don't matter much, do they? And human error is inevitable."

I held the doors to Chappy Ward open for him and he carried the coffee in.

Vicki's chunky form was visible through the glass door of the supply room behind the nursing station. She was placing something on a high shelf. We passed her and went to Cassie's room.

Chip stuck his head in, retracted it, and said, "Still out." Looking down at the cups, he held one out to me. "No sense wasting bad coffee."

"No, thanks," I said.

He laughed softly. "The voice of experience, huh? Has it always been this bad?"

"Always."

"Look at this—little *Exxon Valdez* we've got here." A faint, rainbowed slick floated on the black surface. Grimacing, he raised the other cup to his lips. "Yum—essence of grad school. But I need it to keep conscious."

"Long day?"

"On the contrary—too short. They seem to get shorter as you get older, don't they? Short and crammed with busywork. Then there's having to drive back and forth between work and home and here. Our glorious freeways—humanity at its nadir."

"Valley Hills means the Ventura Freeway," I said. "That's about as bad as it gets."

"Vile. When we were home-hunting, I purposely picked a place close to work to avoid commuting." He shrugged. "Best-laid plans. Sometimes I sit bumper to bumper and imagine it's what hell would be like."

He laughed again, sipped.

I said, "I'll be experiencing it firsthand in a couple of days— making a home visit."

"Yes, Cindy mentioned it. Ah, here comes Ms. Night-ingale. . . . Hello, Vicki. Burning the midnight oil again?"

I turned and saw the nurse marching toward us, smiling, cap bobbing.

"Evening, Professor Jones." She sucked in air, as if preparing to power-lift, then nodded at me.

Chip handed her the untouched coffee. "Drink it or toss it."

"Thank you, Professor Jones."

He cocked his head at Cassie's door. "How long have the Sleeping Beauties been snoozing?"

"Cassie went down around eight. Mrs. Jones, around eight forty-five."

He looked at his watch. "Could you do me a favor, Vicki? I'm going to walk Dr. Delaware out, maybe get something to eat while I'm down there. Please have me paged if they wake up."

"If you like I can go down and get you something, Professor."

"No, thanks. I need to stretch—freewayitis."

Vicki clucked sympathetically. "Of course. I'll let you know soon as someone's up."

When we got to the other side of the teak doors, he stopped and said, "What do you think about the way we're being handled?"

"Handled in what way?"

He resumed walking. "Handled medically—this current hospitalization. No real evaluation's going on, as far as I can tell. No one's really checking Cassie out physically. Not that I mind—thank God she doesn't have to endure those godawful needles. But the message I'm starting to get is *placebo*. Hold our hands, send in a shrink—nothing personal—and let whatever's going on with Cassie just wind itself down."

"Do you find that insulting?"

"Not insulting—well, maybe a little. As if it's all in our heads. Believe me, it isn't. You people here haven't seen what we have—the blood, the seizures."

"You've seen all of it?"

"Not all of it. Cindy's the one who gets up at night. I tend to be a solid sleeper. But I've seen enough. You can't argue with blood. So why isn't more being done?"

"I can't answer for anyone else," I said. "But my best guess is, no one really knows what to do and they don't want to be unnecessarily intrusive."

"I suppose so," he said. "And, hey, for all I know it's exactly the right approach to take. Dr. Eves seems smart enough. Maybe Cassie's symptoms *are*—what's the term—self-restricting?"

"Self-limiting."

"Self-limiting." He smiled. "Doctors propagate more euphemisms than anyone. . . . I pray to God it *is* self-limiting. Be more than happy to remain an unsolved medical mystery if Cassie finally stays healthy. But hope comes hard by now."

"Chip," I said, "I haven't been called in because anyone thinks Cassie's problems are psychosomatic. My job is to help her deal with anxiety and pain. The reason I want to visit your home is to build up rapport with her in order to be useful for her when she needs me."

"Sure," he said. "I understand."

He looked at the ceiling and tapped one foot. A couple of nurses walked by. His eyes followed their trail, absently.

"I guess what I really have trouble handling is the irrationality," he said. "As if we're all floating around in some sea of random events. What the *hell* is making her *sick?*"

He punched the wall.

I sensed that anything I said would make matters worse, but I knew silence wouldn't help much either.

The elevator door opened and we stepped in.

"Pissed-off parents," he said, punching the DOWN button hard. "Pleasant way to end *your* day."

"My job."

"Some job."

"Beats honest labor."

He smiled.

I pointed to the cup in his hand. "That's got to be cold. How about we both get some fresh sludge?"

He thought for a moment. "Sure, why not?"

The cafeteria was closed, so we went down the hall, past the Residents' Lounge, where a row of vending machines stood next to the locker room. A thin young woman in surgical scrubs was walking away with two handfuls of candy bars. Chip and I each bought black coffee and he purchased a plastic-wrapped packet containing two chocolate chip cookies.

Farther down the corridor was a sitting area: orange plastic chairs arranged in an L, a low white table bearing food wrappers and out-of-date magazines. The Path Lab was a stone's throw away. I thought of his little boy and wondered if he'd make the association. But he ambled over and sat down, yawning.

Unwrapping the cookies, he dunked one in the coffee, said, "Health food," and ate the soggy part.

I sat perpendicular to him and sipped. The coffee was terrible but oddly comforting—like a favorite uncle's stale breath.

"So," he said, dunking again, "let me tell you about my daughter. Terrific disposition, good eater, good sleeper—she slept through at five weeks. For anyone else, good news, right? After what happened to Chad, it scared the *shit* out of us. We wanted her *awake*—used to take turns going in there, waking her up, poor thing. But what amazes me is how resilient she is—the way she just keeps bouncing back. You wouldn't think anything that small could be so tough.

"I feel kind of ridiculous, even discussing her with a psychologist. She's a *baby,* for God's sake—what kind of neuroses could she have? Though I guess with all this she could end up with plenty, couldn't she? All the stress. Are we talking major psychotherapy for the rest of her life?"

"No."

"Has anyone ever studied it?"

"There's been quite a bit of research," I said. "Chronically ill children tend to do better than experts predict—people do, in general."

"Tend to?"

"Most do."

He smiled. "I know. It's not physics. Okay, I'll allow myself some momentary optimism."

He tensed, then relaxed—deliberately, as if schooled in meditation. Letting his arms drop and dangle and stretching his legs. Dropping his head back and massaging his temples.

"Doesn't it get to you?" he said. "Listening to people all day? Having to nod and be sympathetic and tell them they're okay."

"Sometimes," I said. "But usually you get to know people, start to see their humanity."

"Well, this is sure the place to remind you of that—'A rarer spirit never did steer humanity; but you, gods, will give us some *faults* to make us men.' Words, Willy Shakespeare; italics, mine. I know it sounds pretentious, but I find the old bard reassures me—something for every situation. Wonder if *he* spent any time in hospitals."

"He may have. He lived during the height of the black plague, didn't he?"

"True . . . Well"—he sat up and unwrapped the second cookie—"all credit to you, I couldn't do it. Give me something neat and clean and theoretical, anytime."

"I never thought of sociology as hard science."

"Most of it isn't. But Formal Org has all sorts of nifty models and measurable hypotheses. The illusion of precision. I delude myself regularly."

"What kinds of things do you deal with? Industrial management? Systems analysis?"

He shook his head. "No, that's the applied side. I'm theoretical—setting up models of how groups and institutions function on a structural level, how components mesh, phenomenologically. Ivory tower stuff, but I find it great fun. I was schooled in the ivory tower."

"Where's that?"

"Yale, undergrad; University of Connecticut, grad. Never finished my dissertation after I found out teaching turns me on a lot more than research."

He stared down the empty basement corridor, watching the occasional passage of wraithlike white-coated figures in the distance.

"Scary," he said.

"What is?"

"This place." He yawned, glanced at his watch. "Think I'll go up and check on the ladies. Thanks for your time."

We both stood.

"If you ever need to talk to me," he said, "here's my office number."

He put his cup down, reached into a hip pocket, and pulled out an Indian silver money clasp inlaid with an irregular turquoise. Twenty-dollar bill on the outside, credit cards and assorted papers underneath. Removing the entire wad, he shuffled through it and found a white business card. Placing it on the table, he retrieved a blue Bic from another pocket and wrote something on the card, then handed it to me.

Snarling tiger logo, WVCC TYGERS circling it. Below that:

WEST VALLEY COMMUNITY COLLEGE
DEPARTMENT OF SOCIAL SCIENCES
(818) 509-3476

Two lines at the bottom. He'd filled them in using dark block letters:

CHIP JONES
EXT. 2359

"If I'm in class," he said, "this'll connect you to the message center. If you want me around when you come visiting at the house, try to give me a day's notice."

Before I could reply, heavy rapid footsteps from the far end of the hall made both of us turn. A figure came toward us. Athletic gait, dark jacket.

Black leather jacket. Blue slacks and hat. One of the rent-a-cops patrolling the halls of Pediatric Paradise for signs of evil?

He came closer. A mustachioed black man with a square face and brisk eyes. I got a look at his badge and realized he wasn't Security. LAPD. Three stripes. A sergeant.

"Excuse me, gentlemen," he said, speaking softly but giving us the once-over. His name tag read PERKINS.

Chip said, "What is it?"

The cop read my badge. It seemed to confuse him. "You're a doctor?"

I nodded.

"How long have you gentlemen been out here in the hall?"

Chip said, "Five or ten minutes. What's wrong?"

Perkins's gaze shifted to Chip's chest, taking in the beard, then the earring. "You a doctor too?"

"He's a parent," I said. "Visiting his child."

"Got a visiting badge, sir?"

Chip pulled one out and held it in front of Perkins's face.

Perkins chewed his cheek and swung back to me. He gave off a barbershop scent. "Have either of you seen anything unusual?"

"Such as?" said Chip.

"Anything out of the ordinary, sir. Someone who doesn't belong."

"Doesn't belong," said Chip. "Like somebody healthy?"

Perkins's eyes became slits.

I said, "We haven't seen anything, Sergeant. It's been quiet. Why?"

Perkins said, "Thank you," and left. I watched him slowing for a moment as he passed the pathology lab.

*   *   *

Chip and I took the stairs to the lobby. A crowd of night-shifters crowded the east end, pressing toward the glass doors that led outside. On the other side of the glass the darkness was cross-cut with the cherry-red pulse of police lights. White lights, too, refracting in starbursts.

Chip said, "What's going on?"

Without turning her head, a nurse nearby said, "Someone got attacked. In the parking lot."

"Attacked? By whom?"

The nurse looked at him, saw he was a civilian and moved away.

I looked around for a familiar face. None. Too many years.

A pale, thin orderly with short platinum hair and a white Fu Manchu said, "Enough, already," in a nasal voice. "All I want to do is go *home*."

Someone groaned a chorus.

Unintelligible whispers passed through the lobby. I saw a uniform on the other side of the glass, blocking the door. A burst of radio talk leaked through from the outside. Lots of movement. A vehicle swung its lights toward the glass, then turned away and sped off. I read a flash of letters: AMBULANCE. But no blinkers or siren.

"Whyn't they just bring her in here?" said someone.

"Who says it's a *her*?"

A woman said, "It's *always* a her."

"Dinja hear? No howler," someone answered. "Probably not an emergency."

"Or maybe," said the blond man, "it's too late."

The crowd rippled like gel in a petri dish.

Someone said, "I tried to get out the back way but they had it blocked. I'm like, this sucks."

"I think I heard one of them say it was a doctor."

"Who?"

"That's all I heard."

Buzz. Whisper.

Chip said, "Wonderful." Turning abruptly, he began pushing his way toward the rear of the crowd, back into the hospital. Before I could say anything, he was gone.

*   *   *

Five minutes later, the glass door opened and the crowd surged forward. Sergeant Perkins slipped through and held out a tan palm. He looked like a substitute teacher before an unruly high school class.

"Can I have your attention for a moment?" He waited for silence, finally settled for relative quiet. "An assault's occurred in your parking lot. We need you to file out one by one and answer some questions."

"What kind of assault?"

"Is he okay?"

"Who was it?"

"Was it a doctor?"

"Which lot did it happen in?"

Perkins did the slit-eye again. "Let's get this over with as quickly as possible, folks, and then you can all go home."

The man with the white Fu Manchu said, "How about telling us what happened so we can *protect* ourselves, Officer?"

Supportive rumblings.

Perkins said, "Let's just take it easy."

"No, *you* take it easy," said the blond man. "All you guys do is give *jay*walking tickets out on the boulevard. Then, when something real happens, you ask your questions and disappear and leave us to clean up the mess."

Perkins didn't move or speak.

"Come *on,* man," said another man, black and stooped, in a nursing uniform. "Some of us have *lives.* Tell us what happened."

"Yeah!"

Perkins's nostrils flared. He stared out at the crowd a while longer, then opened the door and backed out.

The people in the lobby twanged with anger.

A loud voice said, *"Deputy Dawg!"*

"Damned jaywalking brigade."

"Yeah, buncha stiffs—hospital sticks us across the street and then we get busted trying to get to work on time."

Another hum of consensus. No one was talking anymore about what had happened in the lot.

The door opened again. Another cop came through, young, white, female, grim.

"Okay, everyone," she said. "If you'll just file out one by one, the officer will check your ID and then you can go."

"Yo," said the black man. "Welcome to San Quentin. What's next? Body searches?"

More tunes in that key, but the crowd started to move, then quieted.

It took me twenty minutes to get out the door. A cop with a clipboard copied my name from my badge, asked for verifying identification, and recorded my driver's license number. Six squad cars were parked in random formation just outside the entrance, along with an unmarked sedan. Midway down the sloping walkway to the parking structure stood a huddle of men.

I asked the cop, "Where did it happen?"

He crooked a finger at the structure.

"I parked there."

He raised his eyebrows. "What time did you arrive?"

"Around nine-thirty."

"P.M.?"

"Yes."

"What level did you park on?"

"Two."

That opened his eyes. "Did you notice anything unusual at that time—anyone loitering or acting in a suspicious manner?"

Remembering the feeling of being watched as I left my car, I said, "No, but the lighting was uneven."

"What do you mean by uneven, sir?"

"Irregular. Half the spaces were lit; the others were dark. It would have been easy for someone to hide."

He looked at me. Clicked his teeth. Took another glance at my badge and said, "You can move on now, sir."

I walked down the pathway. As I passed the huddle I recognized one of the men. Presley Huenengarth. The head of hospital Security was smoking a cigarette and stargazing, though the sky was starless. One of the other suits wore a gold shield on his lapel and was talking. Huenengarth didn't seem to be paying attention.

Our eyes met but his gaze didn't linger. He blew smoke through his nostrils and looked around. For a man whose system had just failed miserably, he looked remarkably calm.

Wednesday's paper turned the assault into a homicide.

The victim, robbed and beaten to death, had indeed been a doctor. A name I didn't recognize: Laurence Ashmore. Forty-five years old, on the staff at Western Peds for just a year. He'd been struck from behind by the assailant and robbed of his wallet, keys, and the magnetized card key that admitted his car to the doctors' lot. An unnamed hospital spokesperson emphasized that all parking-gate entry codes had been changed but admitted that entry on foot would continue to be as easy as climbing a flight of stairs.

Assailant unknown, no leads.

I put the paper down and looked through my desk drawers until I found a hospital faculty photo roster. But it was five years old, predating Ashmore's arrival.

Shortly after eight I was back at the hospital, finding the doctors' lot sealed with a metal accordion gate and cars stack-parked in the circular drive fronting the main entrance. An ALL FULL sign was posted at the mouth of the driveway, and a security guard handed me a mimeographed sheet outlining the procedure for obtaining a new card key.

"Where do I park in the meantime?"

He pointed across the street, to the rutted outdoor lots used by nurses and orderlies. I backed up, circled the block, and ended up queuing for a quarter hour. It took another ten minutes to find a space. Jaywalking across the boulevard, I sprinted to the front door. Two guards instead of one in the lobby, but there was no other hint that a life had been snuffed out a couple of hundred feet away. I knew death was no stranger to this place but I'd have thought murder rated a stronger reaction. Then I looked at the faces of the people coming and going and waiting. Nothing like worry and grief to narrow one's perspective.

I headed for the rear stairway and noticed an up-to-date roster just past the Information desk. Laurence Ashmore's picture was on the top left. Specialty in Toxicology.

If the portrait was recent, he'd been a young-looking forty-five. Thin, serious face. Dark, unruly hair, hyphen mouth, horn-rimmed eyeglasses. Woody Allen with dyspepsia. Not the type to pose much of a challenge for a mugger. I wondered why it had been necessary to kill him for his wallet, then realized what an idiotic question that was.

As I prepared to ride up to Five, sounds from the far end of the hospital caught my attention. Lots of white coats. A squadron of people moving across my line of sight, rushing toward the patient-transport elevator.

Wheeling a child on a gurney, one orderly pushing, another holding an I.V. bottle and keeping pace.

A woman I recognized as Stephanie. Then two people in civvies. Chip and Cindy.

I went after them and caught up just as they entered the lift. Barely squeezing in, I edged my way next to Stephanie.

She acknowledged me with a twitch of her mouth. Cindy was holding one of Cassie's hands. She and Chip both looked defeated and neither of them glanced up.

We rode up in silence. As we got off the elevator Chip held out his hand and I grasped it for a second.

The orderlies wheeled Cassie through the ward and through the teak doors. Within moments her inert form had been lowered to the bed, the I.V. hooked up to a drip monitor, and the side rails raised.

Cassie's chart was on the gurney. Stephanie picked it up and said, "Thanks, guys." The orderlies left.

Cindy and Chip hovered near the bed. The room lights were off and slivers of gray morning peeked through the split of drawn drapes.

Cassie's face was swollen, yet it appeared drained—an inflated husk. Cindy took her hand once more. Chip shook his head and wrapped his arm around his wife's waist.

Stephanie said, "Dr. Bogner will be by again and so should that Swedish doctor."

Faint nods.

Stephanie cocked her head. The two of us stepped out into the hall.

"Another seizure?" I said.

"Four A.M. We've been in the E.R. since then, working her over."

"How's she doing?"

"Stabilized. Lethargic. Bogner's doing all of his diagnostic tricks but he's not coming up with much."

"Was she in any danger?"

"No mortal danger, but you know the kind of damage repetitive seizures can do. And if it's an escalating pattern, we can probably expect lots more." She rubbed her eyes.

I said, "Who's the Swedish doctor?"

"Neuroradiologist named Torgeson, published quite a bit on childhood epilepsy. He's giving a lecture over at the medical school. I thought, why not?"

We walked to the desk. A young dark-haired nurse was there now. Stephanie wrote in the chart and told her, "Call me immediately if there are any changes."

"Yes, Doctor."

Stephanie and I walked down the hall a bit.

"Where's Vicki?" I said.

"Home sleeping. I hope. She went off shift at seven, but was down in the E.R. until seven-thirty or so, holding Cindy's hand. She wanted to stay and do another shift, but I insisted she leave—she looked totally wiped out."

"Did she see the seizure?"

Stephanie nodded. "So did the unit clerk. Cindy pressed the call button, then ran out of the room, crying for help."

"When did Chip show up?"

"Soon as we had Cassie stabilized, Cindy called him at home and he came right over. I guess it must have been around four-thirty."

"Some night," I said.

"Well, at least we've got outside corroboration of the seizures. Kid's definitely grand mal."

"So now everyone knows Cindy's not nuts."

"What do you mean?"

"Yesterday she talked to me about people thinking she was crazy."

"She actually *said* that?"

"Sure did. The context was her being the only one who saw Cassie get sick, the way Cassie would recover as soon as she got to the hospital. As if her credibility was suspect. It could have been frustration, but maybe she knows she's under suspicion and was bringing it up to test my reaction. Or just to play games."

"How did you react?"

"Calm and reassuring, I hope."

"Hmm," she said, frowning. "One day she's worrying about her credibility; then all of a sudden we've got something organic to work with?"

"The timing *is* awfully cute," I said. "Who else besides Cindy was with Cassie last night?"

"No one. Not constantly. You think she slipped her something?"

"Or pinched her nose. Or squeezed her neck—carotid sinus pressure. Both came up when I was scanning the Munchausen literature and I'm sure there are a few more tricks that haven't been documented yet."

"Tricks a respiratory tech might know . . . Damn. So how in blazes do you detect something like that?"

She pulled her stethoscope from around her neck. Looped it around one hand and unwrapped it. Facing the wall, she pressed her forehead to it and closed her eyes.

"Are you going to put her on anything?" I said. "Dilantin or phenobarb?"

"I can't. Because if she doesn't have a bona fide disorder, meds can do more harm than good."

"Won't they suspect something if you don't medicate her?"

"Maybe . . . I'll just tell them the truth. The EEG tracings are inconclusive and I want to find the exact cause for the seizures before I dose her up. Bogner'll back me up on that—he's mad because *he* can't figure it out."

The teak doors swung open and George Plumb shot through, jaw leading, white coat flapping. He held the door for a man in his late sixties wearing a navy-blue pin-stripe suit. The man was much shorter than Plumb—five six or seven—stocky and bald, with a rapid, bowlegged walk and a malleable-looking face that appeared to have taken plenty of direct hits: broken nose, off-center chin, grizzled eyebrows, small eyes set in a sunburst pucker of wrinkles. He wore steel-rimmed eyeglasses, a white shirt with a spread collar, and a powder-blue silk tie fastened in a wide Windsor. His wingtips gleamed.

The two of them came straight to us. The short man looked busy even when standing still.

"Dr. Eves," said Plumb. "And Dr. . . . Delaware, was it?"

I nodded.

The short man seemed to be opting out of the introductions. He was looking around the ward—that same measuring appraisal Plumb had conducted two days ago.

Plumb said, "How's our little girl doing, Dr. Eves?"

"Resting," said Stephanie, focusing on the short man. "Good morning, Mr. Jones."

Quick turn of the bald head. The short man looked at her, then at me. Intense focus. As if he were a tailor and I were a bolt of cloth.

"What exactly happened?" he said in a gravelly voice.

Stephanie said, "Cassie experienced an epileptic seizure early this morning."

"Damn." The short man punched one hand with the other. "And still no idea what's causing it?"

"Not yet, I'm afraid. Last time she was admitted we ran every relevant test, but we're running them again and Dr. Bogner's coming over. There's also a visiting professor from Sweden who's arriving any minute. Childhood epilepsy's his specialty. Though when I spoke with him on the phone he felt we'd done everything right."

"Damn." The puckered eyes turned on me. A hand shot out. "Chuck Jones."

"Alex Delaware."

We shook hard and fast. His palm felt like a rasp blade. Everything about him seemed to run on fast-forward.

Plumb said, "Dr. Delaware is a psychologist, Chuck."

Jones blinked and stared at me.

"Dr. Delaware's been working with Cassie," said Stephanie, "to help her with her fear of needles."

Jones made a noncommittal sound, then said, "Well, let me know what goes on. Let's get to the bottom of this damned folderol."

He walked toward Cassie's room. Plumb followed like a puppy.

When they were inside I said, "Folderol?"

"How'd you like to have him for a grandpa?"

"He must love Chip's earring."

"One thing he doesn't love is shrinks. After Psychiatry was abolished a bunch of us went to him, trying to get some sort of mental health services restored. We might as well have asked him for an interest-free loan. Plumb was setting you up just now, when he told Jones what you do."

"The old corporate pissing game? Why?"

"Who knows? I'm just telling you so you'll keep your guard up. These people play a different game."

"Duly noted," I said.

She looked at her watch. "Time for clinic."

We left Chappy and headed for the elevator.

She said, "So what are we going to do, Alex?"

I considered telling her what I'd put Milo up to. Decided to keep her out of it. "From my reading, the only thing that seems to work is either catching someone in the act or having a direct confrontation that gets them to confess."

"Confrontation? As in coming out and accusing her?"

I nodded.

"I can't exactly do that at this point, can I?" she said. "Now that

she's got witnesses to a bona fide seizure and I'm bringing in specialists. Who knows, maybe I'm totally off-base and there really *is* some
kind of epilepsy, I don't know. . . . I received a letter from Rita this
morning. Express mail from New York—she's touring the art gal-
leries. 'How are things progressing on the case?' Am I 'making any
headway' in my '*diagnosis?*' I got the feeling someone went around me
and called her."

"Plumb?"

"Uh-huh. Remember that meeting he wanted? We had it yesterday and it turned out to be all sweetness and light. Him telling me
how much he appreciates my commitment to the institution. Letting
me know the financial situation is lousy and going to get lousier but
implying that if I don't make waves, I can have a better job."

"Rita's."

"He didn't come out and say it but that was the message.
It would be just like him to then go and call *her,* set *her* against
me. . . . Anyway, none of that's important. What do I do about
Cassie?"

"Why don't you wait to see what this Torgeson says? If he feels
the seizures have been manufactured, you'd have more ammunition
for an eventual confrontation."

"Confrontation, huh? Can't wait."

As we neared the waiting room I commented on how little impact
Laurence Ashmore's murder seemed to have made.

"What do you mean?"

"No one's talking about it."

"Yes. You're right—it's terrible, isn't it. How hardened we get.
Caught up in our own stuff."

A few steps later she said, "I didn't really know him—
Ashmore. He kept to himself—kind of antisocial. Never attended a
staff meeting, never RSVP'd to party invitations."

"With those kinds of social skills, how'd he get any referrals?"

"He didn't *want* referrals—didn't do any clinical work. Pure
research."

"Lab rat?"

"Beady eyes and all. But I heard he was smart—knew his

toxicology. So when Cassie started coming in with those respiratory things, I asked him to go over Chad's chart."

"You tell him why?"

"You mean that I was suspicious? No. I wanted him to go in with an open mind. I just asked him to look for anything out of the ordinary. He was very reluctant. Almost resentful—as if I was imposing. A couple of days later I got a phone message saying he hadn't found anything. As in, don't bug me again!"

"How'd he pay his way? Grants?"

"I assume."

"I thought the hospital was discouraging them—didn't want to pay overhead."

"I don't know," she said. "Maybe he brought in his own overhead."

She frowned. "No matter what his social skills, what happened to him is horrible. There was a time, no matter how ugly things got out on the street, if you wore a white coat, or a steth around your neck, you were safe. Now that's all broken down. Sometimes it feels as if everything's breaking down."

We reached the clinic. The waiting room was overflowing and as noisy as a steam drill.

She said, "Enough whining. No one's forcing me. What I *wouldn't* mind is some time off."

"Why don't you take some?"

"Got a mortgage."

Several mothers waved at her and she returned the greetings. We passed through the door to the medical suite and headed for her office. A nurse said, "Morning, Dr. Eves. Your dance card is full."

Stephanie smiled gamely. Another nurse came up and handed her a stack of charts.

She said, "Merry Christmas to you, too, Joyce," and the nurse laughed and hurried off.

"See you," I said.

"Sure. Thanks. Oh, by the way, I learned something else about Vicki. A nurse I used to work with on Four told me she thought Vicki had a bad family situation. Alcoholic husband who roughed her up quite a bit. So maybe she's just a bit frayed—down on men. She still bugging you?"

"No. Actually we had a confrontation of our own and reached a truce of sorts."

"Good."

"She may be down on men," I said. "But not on Chip."

"Chip's no man. He's the boss's son."

"Touché," I said. "An abusive husband might explain why *I* put her teeth on edge. She could have turned to a therapist for help, gotten nowhere, developed a resentment. . . . Of course, major family stress could also lead her to act out in other ways—become a hero at work in order to raise her self-esteem. How'd she handle the seizure?"

"Competently. I wouldn't call it heroic. She calmed Cindy down, made sure Cassie was okay, then called me. Cool under fire, everything by the book."

"Textbook nurse, textbook case."

"But like you said before, how could she be involved, when all the other crises started at home?"

"But this one didn't. No, in all fairness, I can't say I really suspect her of anything. It just twangs my antennae that her home life's troubled and she comes over here and shines. . . . I'm probably just focusing on her because she's been such a pain."

"Fun referral, huh?"

"High intrigue, just like you said."

"I always keep my promises." Another glance at her watch. "Got to get through my morning exams, then drive out to Century City to pick up Torgeson. Got to make sure his car doesn't get caught up in the parking mess. Where'd they stick you?"

"Across the street, like everyone else."

"Sorry."

"Hey," I said, feigning insult, "some of us are international hotshots and some of us park across the street."

"Guy sounds like a cold fish over the phone," she said, "but he *is* hot stuff—served on the Nobel Committee."

"Hoo-hah."

"Hoo-hah in spades. Let's see if we can frustrate him too."

*   *   *

I called Milo from a pay phone and left him another one-beep message: "Vicki Bottomley has a husband who drinks and may beat her up. It probably doesn't mean anything, but could you please check if there are any domestic violence calls on record and if so, get me the dates?"

Textbook nurse . . .

Textbook Munchausen by proxy.

Textbook crib death.

Crib death evaluated by the late Dr. Ashmore.

The doctor who didn't see patients.

Just a grisly coincidence, no doubt. Stick around any hospital long enough and grisly becomes routine. But, not knowing what else to do, I decided to have a closer look at Chad Jones's chart myself.

Medical Records was still on the basement floor. I waited in line behind a couple of secretaries bearing requisition slips and a resident carrying a laptop computer, only to be informed that deceased patients' files were housed one floor down, in the sub-basement, in a place called SPI—status permanently inactive. It sounded like something the military had invented.

On the wall just outside the sub-basement stairwell was a map with one of those red YOU ARE HERE arrows in the lower left-hand corner. The rest was an aerial view of a grid of corridors. The actual hallways were walled with white tile and floored with gray linoleum patterned with black-and-pink triangles. Gray doors, red plaques. The hallway was fluorescent-lit and had the vinegary smell of a chem lab.

SPI was in the center of the webwork. Small box. Hard to extrapolate from two dimensions to the long stretch of corridor before me.

I began walking and reading door signs. BOILER ROOM. FURNITURE STORAGE. A series of several doors marked SUPPLIES. Lots of others that said nothing at all.

The hallway angled to the right.

CHEMICAL SPECTROGRAPHY. X-RAY ARCHIVES. SPECIMEN FILES. A double-width slab that said: MORGUE: NO UNAUTHORIZED ADMITTANCE.

I stopped. No smell of formalin, not a hint of what existed on the other side. Just silence and the acetic bite, and a chill that could have been due to a low thermostat setting.

I pictured the map in my head. If my memory was functioning properly, SPI was another right turn, a left, then a short jog. I started walking again, realized I hadn't seen another person since I'd been down here. The air got colder.

I picked up my pace, had managed to slip into a thought-free speed-walk when a door on the right wall swung open so suddenly I had to dodge to avoid getting hit.

No sign on this one. Two maintenance men in gray work clothes emerged from behind it carrying something. Computer. PC, but a big one—black and expensive-looking. As they huffed away, two more workers came out. Another computer. Then a single man, sleeves rolled up, biceps bunched, carrying a laser printer. A five-by-eight index card taped to the printer's console read L. ASHMORE, M.D.

I stepped past the door and saw Presley Huenengarth standing in the doorway, holding an armful of printout. Behind him were blank beige walls, charcoal-colored metal furniture, several more computers in various states of disconnection.

A white coat on a hook was the sole hint that anything more organic than differential equations had been contemplated here.

Huenengarth stared at me.

I said, "I'm Dr. Delaware. We met a couple of days ago. Over at General Pediatrics."

He gave a very small nod.

"Terrible thing about Dr. Ashmore," I said.

He nodded again, stepped back into the room, and closed the door.

I looked down the hall, watching the maintenance men carry off Ashmore's hardware and thinking of grave robbers. Suddenly a room full of post-mortem files seemed a warm and inviting prospect.

11

Status permanently inactive was a long narrow room lined with metal floor-to-ceiling shelves and human-width aisles. The shelves were filled with medical charts. Each chart bore a black tab. Hundreds of consecutive tabs created wavy, inch-thick black lines that seemed to cut the files in half.

Access was blocked by a waist-high counter. Behind it sat an Asian woman in her forties, reading a tabloid-sized Asian-language newspaper. Rounded characters—Thai or Laotian, I guessed. When she saw me she put it down and smiled as if I were delivering good news.

I asked to see the chart for Charles Lyman Jones IV. The name didn't appear to mean anything to her. She reached under the counter and produced a three-by-five card titled SPI REQUISITION. I filled it out, she took it, said "Jones," smiled again, and went into the files.

She looked for a while, walking up and down the aisles, pulling out charts, lifting tabs, consulting the slip. When she returned she was empty-handed.

"Not here, Doctor."

"Any idea where it might be?"

She shrugged. "Someone take."

"Someone's already checked it out?"

"Must be, Doctor."

"Hmm," I said, wondering who'd be interested in a two-year-old death file. "This is pretty important—for research. Is there any way I could talk to that someone?"

She thought for a moment, smiled, and pulled something else out from under the counter. El Producto cigar box. Inside were stacks of SPI requisition forms held together with spring clasps. Five stacks. She spread them on the counter. The top slips all bore the signature of pathologists. I read the patients' names, saw no evidence of alphabetization or any other system of classification.

She smiled again, said "Please," and returned to her newspaper.

I removed the clasp from the first pile and sifted through the forms. It soon became obvious that a system did exist. The slips had been classified by date of *request,* each stack representing a month, each piece of paper placed in daily chronological order. Five stacks because this was May.

No shortcuts—every slip had to be examined. And if Chad Jones's chart had been checked out before January 1, the form wouldn't be here at all.

I began reading the names of dead children. Pretending they were just random assemblages of letters.

A moment later I found what I was looking for, in the February stack. A slip dated February 14 and signed by someone with very poor penmanship. I studied the cramped scrawl, finally deciphered the last name as Herbert. D. Kent Herbert, or maybe it was *Dr.* Kent Herbert.

Other than the signature, the date, and a hospital phone extension, the slip was blank; POSITION/TITLE, DEPARTMENT, REASON FOR REQUEST hadn't been filled out. I copied the extension and thanked the woman behind the counter.

"Everything okay?" she said.

"Do you have any idea who this is?"

She came over and peered at the form.

"Habert . . . no. I just work here one month." Another smile. "Good hospital," she said cheerfully.

I began to wonder if she had any idea what she was filing.

"Do you have a hospital directory?"

She looked confused.

"A hospital phone book—the little orange ones?"

"Ah." She bent and produced one from under the counter.

No Herberts in the medical roster. In the following section, listing nonmedical staff, I found a Ronald Herbert, tagged as Assistant Food Services Manager. But the extension didn't match the one on the slip and I couldn't see a catering specialist having an interest in sudden infant death.

I thanked her and left. Just before the door closed, I heard her say, "Come again, Doctor."

I retraced my steps through the sub-basement, passing Laurence Ashmore's office again. The door was still closed and when I stopped to listen, I thought I heard movement on the other side.

I kept going, looking for a phone, finally spotted a pay unit just past the elevators. Before I got to it the elevator door opened and Presley Huenengarth stood there, looking at me. He hesitated, then walked out of the lift. Standing with his back to me, he removed a pack of Winstons from his suit pocket and took a long time cracking the seal.

The elevator door started to shut. I checked it with the heel of my hand and got on. The last thing I saw before it closed was the security man's placid stare behind a rising cloud of smoke.

After riding up to the first floor I used an in-house phone near Radiation Therapy to dial D. Kent Herbert's extension. The hospital's main switchboard answered.

"Western Pediatrics."

"I was dialing extension two-five-oh-six."

"One moment and I'll connect you, sir." A series of clicks and mechanical burps, then: "Sorry, sir, that extension's been disconnected."

"Since when?"

"I don't know, sir."

"Any idea whose extension it was?"

"No, sir. Who were you trying to reach?"

"D. Kent Herbert."

"Is that a doctor?"

"I don't know."

Pause. "One moment . . . The only Herbert I have listed is Ronald, in Food Services. Would you like me to connect you?"

"Why not?"

Five rings.

"Ron Herbert." Crisp voice.

"Mr. Herbert, this is Medical Records, calling about the chart you requisitioned?"

"Come again?"

"The medical chart you checked out in February? From SPI?"

"You must have the wrong guy, pal. This is the cafeteria."

"You never requested an SPI chart on February 14 of this year?"

Laughter. "Now why the heck would I do that?"

"Thank you, sir."

"No prob. Hope you find what you're after."

I hung up, took the stairs to the ground floor and entered the throng in the lobby. Easing my way through hard-packed bodies, I made it to the Information counter and, after spotting a hospital directory near the clerk's hand, slid it toward me.

The clerk, a dyed-blond black woman, was answering a Spanish-speaking man's question in English. Both of them looked tired and the acid of strife embittered the air. The clerk noticed the book in my hand and looked down her nose at me. The man's gaze followed. The queue behind him swayed and rumbled like a giant serpent.

"You can't have that," said the clerk.

I smiled, pointed at my badge, and said, "Just want to borrow it for a minute."

The clerk rolled her eyes and said, "Just for a minute, that's all."

I moved to the far end of the counter and flipped the book open to the first page, running my eyes and my index finger down the numbers column on the right side of each page, prepared to scan hundreds of extensions until I found 2506. But I hit the jackpot after only a couple of dozen.

ASHMORE, L. W.   (TOX.)   2506

I replaced the book and thanked the clerk. She glared again, snatched it, and placed it out of reach.

"Half a minute," I said. "Do I get a refund?"

Then I saw the faces of the people waiting in line and regretted being a wise-ass.

I went up to see Cassie, but there was a DO NOT DISTURB sign on her door and the nurse on duty told me both she and Cindy were sleeping.

On my way out of the hospital, my thoughts were intruded upon by someone calling my name. Looking up, I saw a tall, mustachioed man approaching from the main entrance. Late thirties, white coat, rimless glasses, Ivy League clothes. The mustache was an extravagant waxed black handlebar. The rest of him seemed arranged around it.

He waved.

I reached into the past and drew out a name.

Dan Kornblatt. Cardiologist. Former UC San Francisco chief resident. His first year at the hospital had been my last. Our relationship had been limited to case conferences and casual chats about the Bay Area—I'd done a fellowship at Langley Porter and Kornblatt delighted in pushing the proposition that no civilization existed south of Carmel. I remembered him as long on brains and short on tact with peers and parents, but tender with his young patients. Four other doctors were walking with him, two women, two men, all young. The five of them moved rapidly, accompanied by swinging arms—physical fitness or a strong sense of purpose. As they got closer I saw that Kornblatt's hair had grayed at the temples and his hawk face had taken on a few seams.

"Alex Delaware. My, my."

"Hi, Dan."

"To what do we owe the honor?"

"Here on a consult."

"Really? Gone private?"

"A few years ago."

"Where?"

"The West Side."

"But of course. Been back up to the *real* city lately?"

"Not lately."

"Me neither. Not since two Christmases ago. Miss that Tadich Grill, all that real-city culture."

He made introductions all around. Two of the other doctors were residents, one was a Cardiology fellow and one of the women—a short, dark, Mideastern woman—was an attending physician. Obligatory smiles and handshakes all around. Four names that passed right through me.

Kornblatt said, "Alex, here, was one of our star psychologists. Back when we had them." To me: "Speaking of which, I thought you guys were *verboten* around here. Has something changed in that regard?"

I shook my head. "It's just an isolated consult."

"Ah. So where you heading? Out?"

I nodded.

"If you're not crunched for time, why don't you come with us? Emergency staff meeting. Are you still on staff? Yeah, you must be if you're doing a consult." His brows creased. "How'd you manage to avoid the Psychiatry bloodbath?"

"Through a technicality. My affiliation was in Pediatrics, not Psychiatry."

"Pediatrics—that's interesting. Good loophole." To the others: "You see, there's always a loophole."

Four knowing looks. None of them was over thirty.

Kornblatt said, "So, you wanna hang with us? The meeting's an important one—that is, if you're still feeling sufficiently affiliated to care what goes on around here."

"Sure," I said, and fell in alongside him. "What's the topic?"

"The decline and fall of the Western Peds Empire. As evidenced by the murder of Larry Ashmore. Actually, it's a memorial for him." He frowned. "You heard about what happened, didn't you?"

I nodded. "Terrible."

"Symptomatic, Alex."

"Of what?"

"What's happened to this place. Look at the way the whole thing's been handled by the administration. A physician gets *murdered* and no one even bothers to send around a memo. Not that *dered* and no one even bothers to send around a memo. Not that they're paper-shy when it comes to disseminating *their* directives."

"I know," I said. "I happened to read one. On the door of the library."

He scowled and his mustache flared. "*What* library?"

"I saw that too."

"Sucks," he said. "Every time I have research to do I've got to drive over to the med school."

We walked across the lobby and came up against the queues. One of the doctors noticed a patient waiting in line, said "I'll join you in a moment," and left the group to greet the child.

"Don't miss the meeting," Kornblatt called after her, without breaking step. When we were clear of the crowd, he said, "No library, no Psych department, no overhead for grants, total hiring freeze. *Now,* there's talk about more cutbacks in all departments—straight across the board. *Entropy.* The bastards probably plan to tear the place down and sell the real estate."

"Not in this market."

"No, I'm serious, Alex. We don't make money and these are bottom-line people. Pave it over, put in lots of parking lots."

"Well," I said, "they might start by paving the ones across the street."

"Don't hold your breath. We are *peons* to these guys. Just another form of service staff."

"How'd they get control?"

"Jones—the new chairman—was managing the hospital's investments. Supposedly did a really good job, so when hard times got harder the board claimed they needed a financial pro and voted him in. He, in turn, fired all the old administration and brought in his own army."

Another crowd milled near the doors. Lots of tapping feet, weary head shakes, and needless punches of the buttons. Two of the lifts were stuck on upper floors. An OUT OF ORDER sign was taped across the door of the third.

"Onward, troops," said Kornblatt, pointing to the stairwell and increasing his pace to a near-run. All of them vaulted the first flight with the zest of triathlon junkies. When we got to the top, Kornblatt was bouncing like a boxer.

"Go, team!" he said, pushing the door open.

The auditorium was a few paces down. A couple of doctors were lounging near the entrance, which was topped by a handwritten banner that said ASHMORE MEMORIAL.

I said, "Whatever happened to Kent Herbert?"

Kornblatt said, "Who?"

"Herbert. The toxicologist. Didn't he work with Ashmore?"

"I didn't know *anyone* worked with Ashmore. The guy was a loner, a real—" He stopped himself. "Herbert? No, can't say I remember him."

We entered the big fan-shaped lecture hall; rows of gray cloth seats sloped sharply to a wooden lecture pit. A dusty green board on wheels stood at the rear of the pit. The upholstery on the seats was dingy and some of the cushions were tattered. The light, fluctuating hum of occasional conversation filled the room.

The auditorium held at least five hundred chairs but no more than seventy were occupied. The spotty attendance gave it the look of a pass-fail class. Kornblatt and his entourage headed down toward the front of the room, shaking hands and trading a few high-fives along the way. I hung back and sat by myself in the uppermost row.

Lots of white coats—full-time staffers. But where were the private practitioners? Unable to attend on short notice or choosing to stay away? Western Peds had always suffered from town-gown tension, but the full-timers and the physicians out in "the real world" had always managed to achieve a grudging symbiosis.

As I looked around some more, I was struck by another scarcity: gray heads. Where were all the senior people I'd known?

Before I could mull that, a man holding a cordless microphone stepped into the pit and called for quiet. Thirty-five; soft, pale baby face under a big blond Afro. His white coat was slightly yellowed and too big for him. Under it he wore a black shirt, and a brown knit tie.

He said, "Please," and the hum died. A few beepers went off, then silence.

"Thanks to all of you for coming. Could someone get the door?"

Faces turned. I realized I was closest to the exit, got up and shut the door.

"Okay," said Afro. "The first order of business is a moment of silence for our colleague Dr. Laurence Ashmore, so if you could all please rise. . . ."

Everyone stood. Heads drooped. A long minute passed.

Afro said, "Okay, please be seated." Walking to the board, he picked up a piece of chalk and wrote:

AGENDA

1. ASHMORE MEMORIAL
2.
3.
4. . . . ?

Stepping away from the board, he said, "Is there someone who wants to say a few words about Dr. Ashmore?"

Silence.

"Let me say, then, that I know I speak for all of us in condemning the brutality of what happened to Larry. And in offering our deepest sympathy to his family. In lieu of flowers, I propose we get together a fund and donate it to an organization of the family's choice. Or our choice, if it would be too disruptive to ask the family at this point. We can decide now, or at a later date, depending on what people feel. Anyone care to comment?"

A short-haired woman in the third row said, "How about the Poison Control Center? He was a toxicologist."

"Poison Control Center sounds good," said Afro. "Anyone second that?"

A hand rose in the middle of the room.

"Thanks, Barb. So moved. Anyone know the family? To inform them of our plan?"

No response.

He looked at the woman who'd made the suggestion. "Barb, would you be in charge of collecting the funds?"

She nodded.

"All right, people, bring your donations to Barb Loman's office in Rheumatology and we'll see that the Poison Control Center gets the money, posthaste. Anything more along those lines?"

"Data," said someone. "As in, we don't have any."

"Could you stand and clarify, Greg?" said Afro.

A stocky, bearded man in a checked shirt and wide, floral, retro tie rose. I thought I remembered him, as a resident, without the beard. An Italian name . . .

". . . I'm saying, John, is that security stinks around here. What happened to him could have happened to any of us, and since it's *our* lives on the line we deserve to have full access to information. Exactly what happened, the progress of the police's investigation, as well as any measures we can take to assure our safety."

"There aren't any!" a bespectacled black man across the room called out. "Not unless the administration makes a real commitment to genuine security—twenty-four-hour guards at every entrance to the lot and at each and every stairwell."

"That means money, Hank," said the bearded man. "Good luck."

A ponytailed woman with dishwater hair got up.

"The money *would* be available, Greg," she said, "if they got their priorities straight. What we *don't* need are more paramilitary types obstructing our patients in the halls. What we *do* need is exactly what you and Hank just said: *genuine* security, including self-defense classes, karate, Mace, personal training, whatever. Especially for female staff. The nurses deal with this kind of threat every single day, coming from across the street. Especially the night shift—you know how a couple of them were beat up, and—"

"I know tha—"

". . . the open lots have no security at all. As all of us are learning, from direct experience. I drove in at five this morning on an emergency call, and let me tell you, it felt scary, people. I also have to say I think it was a *serious* mistake to limit this meeting to physicians. This is no time for elitism. There are nurses and ancillary staff out there suffering just like we are, working for the same goals. We should be getting together, empowering each other, not fraction-ating."

No one spoke.

The ponytailed woman looked around the auditorium and sat down.

Afro said, "Thank you, Elaine, your point is well taken. Though

I certainly don't think any deliberate attempt was made to be exclusionary."

"Well," said the ponytailed woman, standing again, "was anyone else other than physicians informed?"

Afro smiled. "This was an ad hoc *medical* staff meeting, Elaine, so it's only natural that physicians would—"

"Don't you think the rest of the staff *cares,* John?"

"Of course," said Afro. "I—"

"Western Peds women are *terrified!* Wake up, people! Everyone needs to be empowered. If you recall, the last two assault victims were women and—"

"Yes, I do recall, Elaine. We all do. And I assure you that in the event other meetings are scheduled—and it's certainly clear to me that they need to be—a definite effort will be made to reach out."

Elaine contemplated debate, then shook her head and sat.

Afro returned to the board, chalk poised. "I suppose we've moved on to another item, de facto, haven't we. Staff security?"

Scattered nods. The lack of group coherence was almost tangible. It reminded me of so many other meetings, years ago. Endless discussions, little or no resolution . . .

Afro placed a check next to ASHMORE MEMORIAL, wrote STF SECURITY on the next line, and faced the assembly.

"Okay. Any suggestions beyond guards and karate?"

"Yeah," said a balding, swarthy, thick-shouldered man. "Guns."

A few chuckles.

Afro gave a tight smile. "Thank you, Al. Was that the way things were handled in Houston?"

"You bet, John. S and W in every black bag. That's Smith and Wesson, for all you pacifist types."

Afro made a gun with his thumb and forefinger, pointed it at Bald, and winked. "Anything else, Al, short of turning the hospital into an armed camp?"

Dan Kornblatt stood. "I hate to say it but I think we're lapsing into tunnel vision here. What we need to do is address the larger issues."

"In what sense, Dan?"

"In the sense of our purpose—the institution's purpose."

Afro looked puzzled. "Are we through, then, with item two?"

Kornblatt said, "*I* certainly am. Security is just a symptom of the greater malaise."

Afro waited a moment, then checked off STF SECURITY.

"What malaise is that, Dan?"

"Chronic, end-stage apathy—institutionally *sanctioned* apathy. Just look around. How many private physicians are there on staff, John? Two hundred? Just take a look what percentage cared enough to brown-bag it today and make a statement with their presence."

"Dan—"

"Wait, let me finish. There's a *reason* so few private people are here. And it's the same reason they avoid sending their paying patients here if they can find semi-decent local facilities. Same reason so many of *our* top people have gone elsewhere. We've been tagged as a stepchild—an institutional *loser.* And the community's bought *into* that because the board itself *and* the administration hold this institution in low regard. And so do we. I'm sure we've all had enough psych to know what happens to the self-image of a kid who keeps being told he's a loser. He starts believing it. Same thing applies to—"

The door opened wide. Heads turned. George Plumb entered and straightened his tie, a blood-red paisley against a white shirt and light-gray raw silk suit. His shoes clicked as he descended to the pit. When he got to the bottom he stood next to Afro, as if assuming his rightful position.

"Afternoon, ladies and gentlemen," he said.

Kornblatt said, "We were just talking about institutional apathy, George."

Plumb gave a thoughtful look and placed one fist under his chin. "I was under the impression this was a memorial for Dr. Ashmore."

Afro said, "It was, but we've covered some additional ground."

Plumb turned and studied the writing on the board. "Quite a chunk of ground, it seems. Might I backtrack and talk a bit about Dr. Ashmore?"

Silence. Then nods. Looking disgusted, Kornblatt sat down.

"First of all," said Plumb, "I want to communicate the sympathy of the board of directors and the administration for the loss of Dr. Laurence Ashmore. Dr. Ashmore was a noted researcher and his absence will be profoundly felt. In lieu of flowers, Mrs. Ashmore has requested that funds be sent to UNICEF. My office will be pleased to handle all donations. Second, I want to assure you that progress *has* been made fabricating new parking cards. The cards are ready and can be picked up from Security between three and five, today and tomorrow. We regret any inconvenience. However, I'm sure all of you recognize the necessity of changing the keys. Any questions?"

The stocky bearded man named Greg said, "What about real security—guards at each stairwell?"

Plumb smiled. "I was just getting to that, Dr. Spironi. Yes, both the police and our own security staff inform us that the stairwells are a problem, and though the cost will be considerable, we are prepared to implement twenty-four-hour guards, one man per shift, for each level of the physicians' lot, as well as one guard per shift for each of the three open lots across the boulevard. That adds up to a total parking staff of fifteen guards, meaning a net hire of eleven guards added to the four already on staff. The cost, including benefits and insurance, should amount to slightly under four hundred thousand dollars."

"Four hundred!" said Kornblatt, springing to his feet. "Almost forty thousand a cop?"

"*Guards,* not cops, Dr. Kornblatt. Cops would cost much, much more. As I said, the figure includes benefits, insurance, workman's compensation, supplies and equipment, and site-specific ancillary costs such as orientation and in-house training. The company with which we've contracted has an excellent track record and their proposal includes self-defense and crime-prevention education for the entire staff. The administration didn't feel it was appropriate to bargain-hunt in this matter, Dr. Kornblatt. However, if you'd like to shop around for a more competitive price, be our guest. Bear in mind, however, that time is an issue—we want to restore a sense of security and well-being for everyone, with maximal haste."

Lacing his hands across his abdomen, he looked at Kornblatt.

The cardiologist said, "Last time I checked, *my* job was treating kids, George."

"Precisely," said Plumb. Turning his back on Kornblatt, he said, "Any additional questions?"

There was a moment of silence, as long as the one honoring Ashmore's memory.

Kornblatt stood and said, "I don't know about the rest of you but I'm feeling co-opted."

Plumb said, "Co-opted? In what sense, Dr. Kornblatt?"

"In the sense, George, that this was supposed to be a physicians' meeting and you've just walked in and taken over."

Plumb rubbed his jaw. Looked at the doctors. Smiled. Shook his head.

"Well," he said, "that certainly wasn't my intent."

"Maybe not, George, but it's sure coming out that way."

Plumb stepped forward, toward the front row. Lowering one leg to the cushion of an empty seat, he rested his elbow on the bent knee. Chin on hand again, and he was Rodin's "Thinker."

"Coopting," he said. "All I can say is that was not my intention."

Afro said, "George, what Dan—"

"No need to explain, Dr. Runge. The tragic incident with Dr. Ashmore has left all of us on edge."

Maintaining the thinker's pose, he turned back to Kornblatt: "I must say, Doctor, that I'm surprised to be hearing that kind of sectarian talk from you in particular. If I recall correctly, you drafted a memorandum last month calling for greater communication between the administration and the professional staff. I believe the term you used was cross-pollination?"

"I was talking about decision-making, George."

"And that's exactly what I'm attempting to do, Dr. Kornblatt. Cross-pollinate vis-à-vis security decisions. In that spirit I reiterate my offer to you—to any of you. Come up with your own security proposals. If you can develop one as comprehensive as ours, at equal or lower cost, the administration and the board will be more than happy to entertain it seriously. I mean that. I'm sure I don't need to remind you of the institution's financial situation. That four hundred thousand will have to come from somewhere."

"Patient care, no doubt," said Kornblatt.

Plumb gave a sad smile. "As I've stressed in the past, patient-care reduction is always the court of last resort," he said. "But each month strips us closer and closer to the bone. No one's fault—it's just present-day reality. In fact, perhaps it's good we've wandered afield of the issue of Dr. Ashmore's murder and are talking about it in open forum. To some extent, fiscal and security issues dovetail—both stem from demographic issues outside of anyone's control."

"There goes the neighborhood?" said Spironi.

"Unfortunately, Doctor, the neighborhood has *already* gone."

"So what do you suggest?" said Elaine, the ponytailed woman. "Closing down?"

Plumb shifted his gaze to her sharply. Lifting his foot from the chair, he straightened and sighed.

"What I suggest, Dr. Eubanks, is that we all remain painfully aware of the realities that, for all intents and purposes, imprison us. Institution-specific problems that augment the already difficult state of health care in this city, county, state, and to some extent, the entire country. I suggest that all of us work within a *realistic* framework in order to keep this institution going at some level."

"*Some* level?" said Kornblatt. "That sounds like more cuts a-comin', George. What's next, another pogrom, like Psychiatry? Or radical surgery on every division, like the rumors we've been hearing?"

"I really don't think," said Plumb, "that this is the right time to get into that kind of detail."

"Why not? It's an open forum."

"Because the facts simply aren't available at present."

"So you're not denying there will be cuts, soon?"

"No, Daniel," said Plumb, straightening and placing his hands behind his back. "I couldn't be honest and deny it. I'm neither denying nor confirming, because to do either would be to perform a disservice to you as well as to the institution. My reason for attending this meeting was to pay respect to Dr. Ashmore and to express solidarity—personal and institutional—with your well-intentioned memorial for him. The political nature of the meeting was never made clear to me and had I known I was intruding, I would have steered clear. So please excuse that intrusion, right now—though if I'm not mistaken, I do spot a few other Ph.D.'s out there." He looked at me briefly. "Good day."

He gave a small wave and headed up the stairs.

Afro said, "George—Dr. Plumb?"

Plumb stopped and turned. "Yes, Dr. Runge?"

"We do—I'm sure I speak for all of us in saying this—we do appreciate your presence."

"Thank you, John."

"Perhaps if this leads to greater communication between administration and the professional staff, Dr. Ashmore's death will have acquired a tiny bit of meaning."

"God willing, John," said Plumb. "God willing."

After Plumb left, the meeting lost its steam. Some of the doctors stayed behind, clustering in small discussion groups, but most disappeared. As I exited the auditorium I saw Stephanie coming down the hall.

"Is it over?" she said, walking faster. "I got hung up."

"Over and done. But you didn't miss much. No one seemed to have much to say about Ashmore. It started to evolve into a gripe session against the administration. Then Plumb showed up and took the wind out of the staff's sails by offering to do everything they were demanding."

"Like what?"

"Better security." I told her the details, then recounted Plumb's exchange with Dan Kornblatt.

"On a brighter note," she said, "we seem finally to have found something physical on Cassie. Look here."

She reached into her pocket and drew out a piece of paper. Cassie's name and hospital registration number were at the top. Below was a column of numbers.

"Fresh from this morning's labs."

She pointed to a number.

"Low sugar—hypoglycemia. Which could easily explain the grand mal, Alex. There were no focal sites on the EEG and very little if any wave abnormality—Bogner says it's one of those profiles that's open to interpretation. I'm sure you know that happens all the time in kids. So if we hadn't found low sugar, we would have really been stumped."

She pocketed the paper.

I said, "Hypoglycemia never showed up in her tests before, did it?"

"No, and I checked for it each time. When you see seizures in a kid you always look at sugar and calcium imbalance. The layman thinks of hypoglycemia as something minor but in babies it can really trash their nervous systems. Both times after her seizures, Cassie had normal sugar, but I asked Cindy if she'd given her anything to drink before she brought her into the E.R. and she said she had—juice or soda. Reasonable thing to do—kid looks dehydrated, get some fluids in her. But that, plus the time lag getting over here, could very well have messed up the other labs. So in some sense it's good she seized here in the hospital and we were able to check her out right away."

"Any idea why her sugar's low?"

She gave a grim look. "*That's* the question, Alex. Severe hypoglycemia with seizures is usually more common in infants than in toddlers. Preemies, babies of diabetic mothers, perinatal problems—anything that messes up the pancreas. In older kids, you tend to think more in terms of infection. Cassie's white count is normal, but maybe what we're seeing are residual effects. Gradual damage to the pancreas brought about by an old infection. I can't rule out metabolic disorders either, even though we checked for that back when she had breathing problems. She could have some sort of rare glycogen-storage problem that we don't have an assay for."

She looked up the hall and blew out air. "The other possibility's an insulin-secreting pancreatic tumor. Which is not good news."

"None of them sound like good news," I said.

"No, but at least we'll know what we're dealing with."

"Have you told Cindy and Chip?"

"I told them Cassie's sugar was low and she probably doesn't have classical epilepsy. I can't see any reason to go into any more detail while we're still groping for a diagnosis."

"How'd they react?"

"They were both kind of passive—wiped out. Like, 'Give me one more punch in the face.' Neither of them got much sleep last night. He just left to go to work and she's bunked out on the couch."

"What about Cassie?"

"Still drowsy. We're working on getting her sugar stabilized. She should be okay soon."

"What's in store for her, procedure-wise?"

"More blood tests, a tomographic scan of her gut. It may be necessary, eventually, to open her up surgically—get an actual look at her pancreas. But that's a ways off. Got to get back to Torgeson. He's reviewing the chart in my office. Turned out to be a nice guy, really casual."

"Is he reviewing Chad's chart too?"

"I called for it but they couldn't find it."

"I know," I said. "I was looking for it, too—for background. Someone named D. Kent Herbert pulled it—he worked for Ashmore."

"Herbert?" she said. "Never heard of him. Why would Ashmore be wanting the chart when he wasn't even interested the first time?"

"Good question."

"I'll put a tracer on it. Meantime, let's concentrate on Ms. Cassie's metabolic system."

We headed for the stairs.

I said, "Would hypoglycemia explain the other problems— breathing difficulties, bloody stools?"

"Not directly, but all the problems could have been symptoms of a generalized infectious process or a rare syndrome. New stuff is always coming at us—every time an enzyme is discovered, we find someone who doesn't have it. Or it could even be an *atypical* case of something we *did* test for that just didn't register in her blood for some God-knows-why reason."

She talked quickly, animatedly. Pleased to be dueling with familiar enemies.

"Do you still want me involved?" I said.

"Of course. Why do you ask?"

"Sounds like you've moved away from Munchausen and think it's genuine."

"Well," she said, "it would be nice for it to *be* genuine. And *treatable*. But even if that is the case, we're probably talking chronic disease. So they can use the support, if you don't mind."

"Not at all."

"Thanks much."

Down the stairs. At the next floor I said, "Could Cindy—or anyone else—have somehow caused the hypoglycemia?"

"Sure, if she gave Cassie a middle-of-the-night shot of insulin. I thought of that right away. But that would have required a lot of expertise with timing and dosage."

"Lots of practice injections?"

"Using Cassie as a pincushion. Which I can buy, theoretically. Cindy has plenty of time with Cassie. But given Cassie's reaction to needles, if her mom was sticking her, wouldn't she be freaking out every time she saw her? And I'm the only one she seems to despise. . . . Anyway, I never noticed any unusual injection marks when I did the physical."

"Would they be obvious, given all the other sticks she's had?"

"Not obvious, but I'm careful when I do my exams, Alex. The kids' bods get gone over pretty thoroughly."

"Could the insulin have been administered other than by injection?"

She shook her head as we continued to descend. "There *are* oral hypoglycemics, but their metabolites would show up on the tox panel."

Thinking of Cindy's health discharge from the army, I said, "Any diabetes in the family?"

"Someone sharing their insulin with Cassie?" She shook her head. "Back at the beginning, when we were looking at Cassie's metabolics, we had both Chip and Cindy tested. Normal."

"Okay," I said. "Good luck pinning it down."

She stopped and gave me a light kiss on the cheek. "I appreciate your comments, Alex. I'm so thrilled to be dealing with biochemistry, I run the risk of narrowing my perspective."

*   *   *

Back on the first floor I asked a guard where to find the Personnel office. He looked me over and told me right here, on the first floor.

It turned out to be exactly where I remembered it. Two women sat at typewriters; a third filed papers. The filer came up to me. She was straw-haired and hatchet-faced, in her late fifties. Under her ID was a circular badge that looked homemade, bearing a photo of a big hairy sheepdog. I told her I wanted to send a condolence card to Dr. Laurence Ashmore's widow and asked for his home address.

She said, "Oh, yes, isn't it terrible? What's this place coming to?" in a smoker's voice, and consulted a folder the size of a small-town phone book. "Here you go, Doctor—North Whittier Drive, over in Beverly Hills." She recited a street address in the 900's.

North Beverly Hills—prime real estate. The 900 block placed it just above Sunset. Prime of the prime; Ashmore had lived on more than research grants.

The clerk sighed. "Poor man. Just goes to show you, you can't buy your safety."

I said, "Isn't that the truth?"

"Isn't it, though?"

We traded wise smiles.

"Nice dog," I said, indicating the badge.

She beamed. "That's my honey—my champ. I breed true Old English, for temperament and working ability."

"Sounds like fun."

"It's more than that. Animals give without expecting anything in return. We could learn a few things from them."

I nodded. "One more thing. Dr. Ashmore had someone working with him—D. Kent Herbert? The medical staff would like him to be informed of the charity fund the hospital's establishing in Dr. Ashmore's honor but no one's been able to locate him. I was appointed to get hold of him but I'm not even sure he's still working here, so if you have some sort of an address, I'd be much obliged."

"Herbert," she said. "Hmm. So you think he terminated?"

"I don't know. I think he was still on the payroll in January or February, if that helps."

"It might. Herbert . . . let's see."

Walking to her desk, she pulled another thick folder from a wall shelf.

"Herbert, Herbert, Herbert . . . Well, I've got two here, but neither of them sound like yours. Herbert, Ronald, in Food Services, and Herbert, Dawn, in Toxicology."

"Maybe it's Dawn. Toxicology was Dr. Ashmore's specialty."

She screwed up her face. "Dawn's a girl's name. Thought you were trying to find a man."

I gave a helpless shrug. "Probably a mixup—the doctor who gave me the name didn't actually know this person, so both of us assumed it was a man. Sorry for the sexism."

"Oh, don't worry about *that,*" she said. "I don't mess with all that stuff."

"Does this Dawn have a middle initial 'K'?"

She looked down. "Yes, she does."

"Then, there you go," I said. "The name I was given was D. *Kent.* What's her job description?"

"Um, five thirty-three A—let me see . . ." Thumbing through another book. "That looks like a research assistant, Level One."

"Did she transfer to another department in the hospital, by any chance?"

Consulting yet another volume, she said, "Nope. Looks like a termination."

"Hmm . . . Do you have an address for her?"

"Nope, nothing. We throw out personal stuff thirty days after they're gone—got a real space problem."

"When exactly did she terminate?"

"That I can tell you." She flipped a few pages and pointed to a code that I couldn't comprehend. "Here we go. You're right—about her being here in February. But that was her last month—she gave notice on the fifteenth, went officially off payroll on the twenty-eighth."

"The fifteenth," I said. The day after pulling Chad Jones's chart.

"That's right. See right here? Two slash fifteen?"

I stuck around for a few more minutes, listening to a story about her dogs. But I was thinking about two-legged creatures.

*   *   *

It was 3:45 when I drove out of the parking lot. A few feet from the exit a motorcycle cop was giving a jaywalking ticket to a nurse. The nurse looked furious; the cop's face was a blank tablet.

Traffic on Sunset was obstructed by a four-car fender-bender, and the accompanying turmoil wrought by rubberneckers and somnolent traffic officers. It took almost an hour to reach the inanimate green stretch that was Beverly Hills' piece of the boulevard. Tile-roofed ego monuments perched atop hillocks of Bermuda grass and dichondra, embellished by hostile gates, tennis court sheeting, and the requisite battalions of German cars.

I passed the stadium-sized weed-choked lot that had once housed the Arden mansion. The weeds had turned to hay, and all the trees on the property were dead. The Mediterranean palace had served briefly as a twenty-year-old Arab sheik's plaything before being torched by persons unknown—aesthetic sensibilities offended by puke-green paint and moronic statuary with blacked-in pubic hair, or just plain xenophobia. Whatever the reason for the arson, rumors had been circulating for years about subdivision and rebuilding. But the real estate slump had taken the luster off that kind of optimism.

A few blocks later the Beverly Hills Hotel came into view, ringed by a motorcade of white stretch limos. Someone getting married or promoting a new film.

As I approached Whittier Drive, I decided to keep going. But when the letters on the street sign achieved focus, I found myself making a sudden right turn and driving slowly up the jacaranda-lined street.

Laurence Ashmore's house was at the end of the block, a three-story, limestone Georgian affair on a double lot at least two hundred feet wide. The building was blocky, and impeccably maintained. A brick circular drive scythed through a perfect flat lawn. The land-scaping was spare but good, with a preference for azaleas, camellias, and Hawaiian tree ferns—Georgian goes tropical. A weeping olive tree shaded half the lawn. The other half was sun-kissed.

To the left of the house was a porte-cochere long enough to shelter one of the stretches I'd just seen at the hotel. Beyond the

wooden gates were treetops and the flaming red clouds of bougainvillea.

Prime of the prime. Even with the slump, at least four million.

A single car was parked in the circular drive. White Olds
Cutlass, five or six years old. A hundred yards in either direction the
curb was vacant. No black-garbed callers or bouquets on the door-
stop. Shuttered windows; no sign of occupancy. The placard of a
security company was staked in the perfect, clipped grass.

I drove on, made a U-turn, passed the house again and continued home.

Routine calls from my service; nothing from Fort Jackson. I called the
base anyway and asked for Captain Katz. He came on quickly.

I reminded him who I was and told him I hoped I hadn't
interrupted his dinner.

He said, "No, that's fine, I was going to call you. Think I found
what you're after."

"Great."

"One second—here it is. Influenza and pneumonia epidemics
over the last ten years, right?"

"Exactly."

"Well, far as I can tell, we only had one major flu epidemic—
one of the Thai strains—back in '73. Which is before your
time."

"Nothing since?"

"Doesn't look like it. And no pneumonia, period. I mean, I'm
sure we've had plenty of isolated flu cases, but nothing that would
qualify as an epidemic. And we're real good about keeping those
kinds of records. Only thing we usually have to worry about, in terms
of contagion, is bacterial meningitis. You know how tough that can
be in a closed environment."

"Sure," I said. "Have you had epidemics of meningitis?"

"A few. The most recent was two years ago. Before that, '83,
then '78 and '75—almost looks cyclical, come to think of it. Might
be worth checking *that* out, see if someone can come up with a
pattern."

"How serious were the outbreaks?"

"Only one I observed personally was two years ago, and that was serious enough—soldiers died."

"What about sequellae—brain damage, seizure disorders?"

"Most probably. I don't have the data handy but I can get hold of them. Thinking of changing your research protocol?"

"Not quite yet," I said. "Just curious."

"Well," he said, "that can be a good thing, curiosity. At least out in the civilian world."

Stephanie had her hard data, and now I had mine.

Cindy had lied about her discharge.

Maybe Laurence Ashmore found some data too. Saw Cassie's name on the admission and discharge sheets and got curious.

What else could have caused him to take another look at Chad Jones's chart?

He'd never be able to tell me, but maybe his former assistant could.

I called 213, 310, and 818 Informations for a listing on Dawn Kent Herbert and got nowhere. Expanded my search to 805, 714, and 619 with the same result, then phoned Milo at Parker Center. He picked up and said, "Heard about your homicide last night."

"I was at the hospital when it happened." I told him about being questioned, the scene in the lobby. Feeling as if I'd been watched when I left the parking structure.

"Be careful, bucko. I got your message on Bottomley's hubby, but I've got no domestic violence calls to her address and there's no one on NCIC who could be her hubby. But she does have a trouble-maker living there. Reginald Douglas Bottomley, D.O.B. '70. Which would probably make him her son or maybe an errant nephew."

"What'd he do to get in trouble?"

"Lots—he's got a sheet long enough to cover Abdul-Jabbar's bed. Sealed juvenile file, then a bunch of DUIs, possession, shoplifting, petty theft, burglary, robbery, assault. Lots of busts, a few convictions, a teensy bit of jail time, mostly at County. Got a call in to a detective over at Foothill Division, see what he knows. What's the relevance of Bottomley's home situation to the little kid?"

"Don't know," I said. "Just looking for stress factors that might get her to act out. Probably because she was getting on my nerves. 'Course, if Reggie turned out bad because Vicki abused him, that would tell us something. Meanwhile, I've got something that definitely is relevant. Cindy Jones lied about her military discharge. I just talked to Fort Jackson and there was no pneumonia epidemic in '83."

"That so?"

"She might have had pneumonia, but it wasn't part of any outbreak. And she made a point about the epidemic."

"Seems a stupid thing to lie about."

"The Munchausen game," I said. "Or maybe she was covering up something. Remember I told you the discharge seemed a sensitive topic for her—how she blushed and yanked her braid? The public health officer at the army base said there *was* an epidemic in '83— just about the time Cindy would have been in. But it was bacterial *meningitis.* Which can lead to seizures. Giving us a link to another organ system Cassie's had problems with. In fact, she had a grand mal seizure last night. In the hospital."

"That's a first."

"Yup. First time anyone but Cindy saw it."

"Who else did?"

"Bottomley and the ward clerk. And what's interesting is, yesterday Cindy was talking to me about how Cassie always gets sick at home, then recovers right away in the hospital. So people start thinking her mother's crazy. And here we are, a few hours later, with eyewitnesses and chemical corroboration. The lab tests turned up hypoglycemia, and now Stephanie's convinced Cassie's really sick. But hypoglycemia can be faked, Milo, by anything that alters the blood sugar, like a shot of insulin. I mentioned that to Stephanie, but I'm not sure she's hearing it. She's really geared up, looking for rare metabolic diseases."

"Pretty sharp about-face," he said.

"I can't say that I blame her. After months of dealing with this, she's frustrated and wants to practice medicine, not play psychological guessing games."

"You, on the other hand . . ."

"I've got an evil mind—too much time hanging around you."

"Yeah," he said. "Well, I can see your point about the meningitis, if that's what the mom had. Seizures for all—like mother, like daughter. But you don't know that yet. And if she was covering up, why would she bring up the discharge in the first place? Why even tell you she was in the army?"

"Why'd your confessor make up his story? If she's a Munchausen, she'd get off on *teasing* me with half-truths. It would sure be nice to get hold of her discharge papers, Milo. Find out exactly what *did* happen to her in South Carolina."

"I can try, but it'll take time."

"Something else. I went looking for Chad Jones's post-mortem chart today but it was missing. Pulled by Ashmore's research assistant in February and never returned."

"Ashmore? The one who was killed?"

"The very same. He was a toxicologist. Stephanie had already asked him to review the chart half a year ago, when she started getting suspicious about Cassie. He did it reluctantly—pure researcher, didn't work with patients. And he told her he'd found nothing. So why would he pull the chart again, unless *he* discovered something new about Cassie?"

"If he didn't work with patients, how would he know about Cassie in the first place?"

"By seeing her name on the A and D's—the admission and discharge sheets. They come out daily and every doctor gets them. Seeing Cassie on them time after time might have finally gotten him curious enough to review her brother's death. The assistant's a woman by the name of Dawn Herbert. I tried to get hold of her but she quit the hospital the day after she pulled the chart—talk about more cute timing. And now Ashmore's dead. I don't want to sound like some kind of conspiracy nut, but it's weird, isn't it? Herbert might be able to clear things up, but there's no address or phone number listed for her from Santa Barbara down to San Diego."

"Dawn Herbert," he said. "As in the other Hoover."

"Middle name of Kent. As in Duke of."

"Fine. I'll try to squeeze in a trace before I go off shift."

"I appreciate it."

"Show it by feeding me. Got any decent grub in the house?"

"I suppose—"

"Better yet, *haute cuisine.* I'll pick. Gluttonous, overpriced, and on your credit card."

He showed up at eight, holding out a white box. On the cover was a cartoon of a grinning, grass-skirted islander finger-spinning a huge disc of dough.

"Pizza?" I said. "What happened to *haute* and overpriced?"

"Wait till you see the bill."

He carried the box into the kitchen, slit the tape with his fingernail, lifted the lid, removed a slice from the pie, and ate it standing at the counter. Then he pulled off a second wedge, handed it to me, got another one for himself, and sat at the table.

I looked at the slice in my hand. Molten desert of cheese, landscaped with mushrooms, onions, peppers, anchovies, sausage, and lots of things I couldn't identify. "What is this—pineapple?"

"And mango. And Canadian bacon and bratwurst and chorizo. What you've got there, pal, is authentic Spring Street Pogo-Pogo pizza. The ultimate democratic cuisine—little bit of every ethnicity, a lesson in gastronomic democracy."

He ate and spoke with his mouth full: "Little Indonesian guy sells it from a stand, near the Center. People line up."

"People line up to pay parking fines too."

"Suit yourself," he said, and dug in again, holding one hand under the slice to catch dripping cheese.

I went to the cupboard, found a couple of paper plates, and put them on the table, along with napkins.

"Whoa, the good china!" He wiped his chin. "Drink?"

I took two cans of Coke from the fridge. "This okay?"

"If it's cold."

Finishing his second slice, he popped his can and drank.

I sat and took a bite of pizza. "Not bad."

"Milo knows grub." He guzzled more Coke. "Regarding your Ms. Dawn K. Herbert, no wants or warrants. Another virgin."

He reached into his pocket, took out a piece of paper, and handed it to me. Typewritten on it was:

Dawn Kent Herbert, DOB 12/13/63, 5'5",
170 lb., brown and brown. Mazda Miata.

Under that was an address on Lindblade Street, in Culver City.

I thanked him and asked him if he'd heard anything new on the Ashmore murder.

He shook his head. "It's going down as your routine Hollywood mugging."

"Right guy to mug. He was rich." I described the house on North Whittier.

"Didn't know research paid that well," he said.

"It doesn't. Ashmore must have had some sort of independent income. That would explain why the hospital hired him at a time when they're getting rid of doctors and discouraging research grants. He probably brought some kind of endowment with him."

"Paid his way in?"

"It happens."

"Let me ask you this," he said. "In terms of your Ashmore-getting-curious theory. Cassie's been in and out of the hospital since she was born. Why would he wait until February to start snooping?"

"Good question," I said. "Hold on for a sec."

I went to the library and fetched the notes I'd taken on Cassie's medical history. Milo had sat down at the table and I joined him, turning pages.

"Here we are," I said. "February 10. Four days before Herbert pulled Chad's chart. It was Cassie's second hospitalization for stomach problems. The diagnosis was gastric distress of unknown origin, possible sepsis—the main symptom was bloody diarrhea. Which could have made Ashmore think of some specific kind of poisoning. Maybe his toxicology training overcame his apathy."

"Not enough for him to talk to Stephanie."

"True."

"So maybe he looked and didn't find anything."

"Then why not return the chart?" I said.

"Sloppy housekeeping. Herbert was supposed to but didn't. Knew she was leaving and didn't give a damn about her paperwork."

"When I see her I'll ask her."

"Yeah. Who knows, maybe she'll give you a ride in her Miata."

"Zoom zoom," I said. "Anything new on Reginald Bottomley?"

"Not yet. Fordebrand—the Foothill guy—is on vacation, so I've got a call in to the guy who's catching for him. Let's hope he cooperates."

He put the Coke down. Tension wounded his face and I thought I knew why. He was wondering if the other detective knew who *he* was. Would *bother* to return his call.

"Thanks," I said. "For everything."

"*De nada.*" He shook the can. Empty. Leaning on the counter with both elbows, he faced me.

"What's the matter?" I said.

"You sound low. Beaten down."

"Guess I am—all this theorizing and Cassie's no safer."

"Know what you mean," he said. "Best thing's to stay focused, not drift too far afield. It's a risk on cases with bad solve-prospects— God knows I've had plenty of them. You feel powerless, start throwing wild punches and end up no wiser and a helluva lot older."

He left shortly after that and I called Cassie's hospital room. It was after nine and direct access to patients had been cut off. I identified myself to the hospital operator and was put through. Vicki answered.

"Hi, it's Dr. Delaware."

"Oh . . . what can I do for you?"

"How's everything?"

"Fine."

"Are you in Cassie's room?"

"No—out here."

"At the desk?"

"Yes."

"How's Cassie doing?"

"Fine."

"Sleeping?"

"Uh-huh."

"What about Cindy?"

"Her too."

"Busy day for everyone, huh?"

"Uh-huh."

"Has Dr. Eves been by recently?"

"Around eight—you want the exact time?"

"No, thanks. Anything new, in terms of the hypoglycemia?"

"You'd have to ask Dr. Eves that."

"No new seizures?"

"Nope."

"All right," I said. "Tell Cindy I called. I'll be by tomorrow."

She hung up. Despite her hostility, I felt a strange—almost corrupt—sense of power. Because I knew about her unhappy past and she was unaware of it. Then I realized that what I knew put me no closer to the truth.

Far afield, Milo said.

I sat there, feeling the power diminish.

The next morning I woke up to clean spring light. I jogged a couple of miles, ignoring the pain in my knees and fixing my thoughts on the evening with Robin.

Afterward I showered, fed the fish, and read the paper while eating breakfast. Nothing more on the Ashmore homicide.

I called Information, trying to match a phone number to the address Milo had given me for Dawn Herbert. None was listed and neither of the two other Herberts residing in Culver City knew any Dawn.

I hung up, not sure it made much of a difference. Even if I located her, what explanation would I use to ask her about Chad's file?

I decided to concentrate on the job I'd been trained to do. Dressing and clipping my hospital badge to my lapel, I left the house, turned east on Sunset, and headed for Hollywood.

I reached Beverly Hills within minutes and passed Whittier Drive without slowing. Something on the opposite side of the boulevard caught my eye:

White Cutlass, coming from the east. It turned onto Whittier and headed up the 900 block.

At the first break in the median, I hung a U. By the time I reached the big Georgian house, the Olds was parked in the same place I'd seen it yesterday and a black woman was stepping out on the driver's side.

She was young—late twenties or early thirties—short and slim. She had on a gray cotton turtleneck, black ankle-length skirt, and black flats. In one hand was a Bullock's bag; in the other, a brown leather purse.

Probably the housekeeper. Out doing a department store errand for Ashmore's grieving widow.

As she turned toward the house she saw me. I smiled. She gave me a quizzical look and began walking over slowly, with a short, light step. As she got closer I saw she was very pretty, her skin so dark it was almost blue. Her face was round, bottomed by a square chin; her features clean and broad like those of a Nubian mask. Large, searching eyes focused straight at me.

"Hello. Are you from the hospital?" British accent, public-school refined.

"Yes," I said, surprised, then realized she was looking at the badge on my lapel.

Her eyes blinked, then opened. Irises in two shades of brown—mahogany in the center, walnut rims.

Pink at the periphery. She'd been crying. Her mouth quivered a bit.

"It's very kind of you to come," she said.

"Alex Delaware," I said, extending my hand out the driver's window. She put the shopping bag on the grass and took it. Her hand was narrow and dry and very cold.

"Anna Ashmore. I didn't expect anyone so soon."

Feeling stupid about my assumptions, I said, "I didn't know Dr. Ashmore personally, but I did want to pay my respects."

She let her hand drop. Somewhere in the distance a lawn mower belched. "There's no formal service. My husband wasn't religious." She turned toward the big house. "Would you like to come in?"

*   *   *

The entry hall was two stories of cream plaster floored with black marble. A beautiful brass banister and marble stairs twisted upward to the second story. To the right, a large yellow dining room gleamed with dark, fluid Art Nouveau furniture that the real housekeeper was polishing. Art filled the wall behind the stairs, too—a mix of contemporary paintings and African batiks. Past the staircase, a short foyer led to glass doors that framed a California postcard: green lawn, blue pool sun-splashed silver, white cabanas behind a trellised colonnade, hedges and flower beds under the fluctuating shade of more specimen trees. Scrambling over the tiles of the cabana roof was a splash of scarlet—the bougainvillea I'd seen from the street.

The maid came out of the dining room and took Mrs. Ashmore's bag. Anna Ashmore thanked her, then pointed left, to a living room twice the size of the dining room, sunk two steps down.

"Please," she said, descending, and flipping a switch that ignited several floor lamps.

A black grand piano claimed one corner. The east wall was mostly tall, shuttered windows that let in knife-blades of light. The floors were blond planks under black-and-rust Persian rugs. A coffered white ceiling hovered over apricot plaster walls. More art: the same mix of oils and fabric. I thought I spotted a Hockney over the granite mantel.

The room was chilly and filled with furniture that looked straight out of the Design Center. White Italian suede sofas, a black Breuer chair, big, pockmarked post-Neanderthal stone tables, and a few smaller ones fashioned of convoluted brass rods and topped with blue-tinted glass. One of the stone tables fronted the largest of the sofas. Centered on it was a rosewood bowl filled with apples and oranges.

Mrs. Ashmore said, "Please," again, and I sat down directly behind the fruit.

"Can I offer you something to drink?"

"No, thank you."

She settled directly in front of me, straight and silent.

In the time it had taken to walk from the entry, her eyes had filled with tears.

"I'm sorry for your loss," I said.

She wiped her eyes with a finger and sat even straighter. "Thank you for coming."

Silence filled the room and made it seem even colder. She wiped her eyes again and laced her fingers.

I said, "You have a beautiful home."

She lifted her hands and made a helpless gesture. "I don't know what I'll do with it."

"Have you lived here long?"

"Just one year. Larry owned it long before that, but we never lived in it together. When we came to California, Larry said this should be our place."

She shrugged, raised her hands again, and let them drop back to her knees.

"Too big, it's really ridiculous. . . . We talked about selling it. . . ." Shaking her head. "Please—have something."

I took an apple from the bowl and nibbled. Watching me eat seemed to comfort her.

"Where did you move from?" I said.

"New York."

"Had Dr. Ashmore ever lived in Los Angeles before?"

"No, but he'd been here on buying trips—he had many houses. All over the country. That was his . . . thing."

"Buying real estate?"

"Buying and selling. Investing. He even had a house in France for a short while. Very old—a château. A duke bought it and told everyone it had been in his family for hundreds of years. Larry laughed at that—he hated pretentiousness. But he did love the buying and selling. The freedom it brought him."

I understood that, having achieved some financial independence myself by riding the land boom of the mid-seventies. But I'd operated on a far less exalted level.

"Upstairs," she said, "is all empty."

"Do you live here by yourself?"

"Yes. No children. Please—have an orange. They're from the tree in back, quite easy to peel."

I picked up an orange, removed its rind, and ate a segment. The sound of my jaws working seemed deafening.

"Larry and I don't know many people," she said, reverting to the present-tense denial of the brand-new mourner.

Remembering her remark about my arriving earlier than expected, I said, "Is someone from the hospital coming out?"

She nodded. "With the gift—the certificate of the donation to UNICEF. They're having it framed. A man called yesterday, checking to see if that was all right—giving to UNICEF."

"A man named Plumb?"

"No . . . I don't believe so. A long name—something German."

"Huenengarth?"

"Yes, that's it. He was very nice, said kind things about Larry."

Her gaze shifted, distractedly, to the ceiling. "Are you certain I can't get you something to drink?"

"Water would be fine."

She nodded and rose. "If we're lucky, the Sparkletts man has come. Beverly Hills water is disagreeable. The minerals. Larry and I don't drink it."

While she was gone, I got up and inspected the paintings. Hockney verified. Watercolor still life in a Plexiglas box frame. Next to that, a small abstract canvas that turned out to be a De Kooning. A Jasper Johns word salad, a Jim Dine bathrobe study, a Picasso satyr-and-nymph gambol in China ink. Lots of others I couldn't identify, interspersed with the earth-toned batiks. The wax pressings were tribal scenes and geometric designs that could have been talismans.

She returned with an empty glass, a bottle of Perrier, and a folded linen napkin on an oval lacquer tray. "I'm sorry, there's no spring water. I trust this will be acceptable."

"Of course. Thank you."

She poured the water for me and took her seat again.

"Lovely art," I said.

"Larry bought it in New York, when he worked at Sloan-Kettering."

"The cancer institute?"

"Yes. We were there for four years. Larry was very interested in cancer—the rise in frequency. Patterns. How the world was being poisoned. He worried about the world."

She closed her eyes again.

"Did the two of you meet there?"

"No. We met in my country—the Sudan. I'm from a village in the South. My father was the head of our community. I was schooled in Kenya and England because the big universities in Khartoum and Omdurman are Islamic and my family was Christian. The South is Christian and animist—do you know what that is?"

"Ancient tribal religions?"

"Yes. Primitive, but very enduring. The northerners resent that—the endurance. Everyone was supposed to embrace Islam. A hundred years ago they sold the southerners as slaves; now they try to enslave us with religion."

Her hands tightened. The rest of her remained unchanged.

"Was Dr. Ashmore doing research in the Sudan?"

She nodded. "With the U.N. Studying disease patterns—that's why Mr. Huenengarth felt the donation to UNICEF would be an appropriate tribute."

"Disease patterns," I said. "Epidemiology?"

She nodded. "His training was in toxicology and environmental medicine, but he did that only briefly. Mathematics was his true love, and with epidemiology he could combine mathematics with medicine. In the Sudan he studied the pace of bacterial contagion from village to village. My father admired his work and assigned me to help him take blood from the children—I'd just finished my nursing degree in Nairobi and had returned home." She smiled. "I became the needle lady—Larry didn't like hurting the children. We became friends. Then the Muslims came. My father was killed—my entire family. . . . Larry took me with him on the U.N. plane, to New York City."

She recounted the tragedy matter-of-factly, as if numbed by repeated insults. I wondered if exposure to suffering would help her deal with her husband's murder when the pain hit full force, or would make matters worse.

She said, "The children of my village . . . were slaughtered when the northerners came. The U.N. did nothing, and Larry became angry and disillusioned with them. When we got to New York he wrote letters and tried to talk to bureaucrats. When they wouldn't receive him, his anger grew and he turned inward. That's when the buying started."

"To deal with his anger?"

Hard nod. "Art became a kind of refuge for him, Dr. Delaware. He called it the highest place man could go. He would buy a new piece, hang it, stare at it for hours, and talk about the need to surround ourselves with *things* that couldn't hurt us."

She looked around the room and shook her head.

"Now I'm left with all of it, and most of it doesn't mean much to me." She shook her head again. "Pictures and the memory of his anger—he was an angry man. He even earned his money angrily."

She saw my puzzled look. "Please excuse me—I'm drifting. What I'm referring to is the way he started. Playing blackjack, craps—other games of chance. Though I guess *playing* isn't the right word. There was nothing playful about it—when he gambled he was in his own world, didn't stop to eat or sleep."

"Where did he gamble?"

"Everywhere. Las Vegas, Atlantic City, Reno, Lake Tahoe. The money he made there he invested in other schemes—the stock market, bonds." She waved an arm around the room.

"Did he win most of the time?"

"Nearly always."

"Did he have some kind of system?"

"He had many. Created them with his computers. He was a mathematical *genius*, Dr. Delaware. His systems required an extraordinary memory. He could add columns of numbers in his head, like a human computer. My father thought he was magical. When we took blood from the children, I had him do numbers tricks for them. They watched and were amazed, and didn't feel the sting."

She smiled and covered her mouth.

"He thought he could go on forever," she said, looking up, "making a profit at the casinos' expense. But they caught on and told him to leave. This was in Las Vegas. He flew to Reno but the casino there knew also. Larry was furious. A few months later he returned to the first casino in different clothing and an old man's beard. Played for higher stakes and won even more."

She stayed with that memory for a while, smiling. Talking seemed to be doing her good. That helped me rationalize my presence.

"Then," she said, "he just stopped. Gambling. Said he was

bored. Began buying and selling real estate . . . He was so good at it. . . . I don't know what to do with all this."

"Do you have any family here?"

She shook her head and clasped her hands. "Not here or any-where. And Larry's parents are gone too. It's so . . . ironic. When the northerners came, shooting women and children, Larry looked at them in the face and screamed at them, calling them terrible names. He wasn't a big man. . . . Did you ever meet him?"

I shook my head.

"He was very small." Another smile. "Very small—behind his back my father called him a monkey. Affectionately. A monkey who thought he was a lion. It became a village joke and Larry didn't mind at all. Perhaps the Muslims believed he *was* a lion. They never hurt him. Allowed him to take me away on the plane. A month after we got to New *York,* I was robbed on the street by a drug addict. Terrified. But the city never frightened Larry. I used to joke that he frightened it. My fierce little monkey. And now . . ."

She shook her head. Covered her mouth again and looked away. Several moments passed before I said, "Why did you move to Los Angeles?"

"Larry was unhappy at Sloan-Kettering. Too many rules, too much politics. He said we should move to California and live in this house—it was the best piece of property he'd bought. He thought it was foolish that someone else should enjoy it while we lived in an apartment. So he evicted the tenant—some kind of film producer who hadn't paid his rent."

"Why did he choose Western Pediatrics?"

She hesitated. "Please don't be offended, Doctor, but his reason-ing was that Western Peds was a hospital in . . . decline. Money problems. So his financial independence meant he'd be left alone to pursue his research."

"What kind of research was he doing?"

"Same as always, disease patterns. I don't know much about it—Larry didn't like to talk about his work." She shook her head. "He didn't talk much at all. After the Sudan, the cancer patients in New York, he wanted nothing to do with real people and their pain."

"I've heard he kept to himself."

She smiled tenderly. "He loved to be alone. Didn't even want a secretary. He said he could type faster and more accurately on his word processor, so what was the purpose?"

"He had research assistants, didn't he? Like Dawn Herbert."

"I don't know names, but yes, from time to time he'd hire graduate students from the university, but they never met his standards."

"The university over in Westwood?"

"Yes. His grant paid for lab assistance and there were tasks that he needn't have bothered himself with. But he was never happy with the work of others. The truth is, Doctor, Larry just didn't like depending on anyone else. Self-reliance became his religion. After my robbery in New York, he insisted we both learn self-defense. Said the police were lazy and didn't care. He found an old Korean man in lower Manhattan who taught us karate, kick-fighting—different techniques. I attended two or three lessons, then stopped. It seemed illogical—how could our hands protect us against a drug addict with a gun? But Larry kept going and practiced every night. Earned a belt."

"Black belt?"

"A brown one. Larry said brown was enough; anything more would have been ego."

Lowering her face, she cried softly into her hands. I took a napkin from the lacquer tray, stood by her chair, and had it ready when she looked up. Her hand gripped my fingers hard enough to sting, then let go. I sat back down.

She said, "Is there anything else I can get you?"

I shook my head. "Is there something I can do for you?"

"No, thank you. Just your coming to visit was gracious—we don't know many people."

She looked around the room once more.

I said, "Have you made funeral arrangements?"

"Through Larry's attorney . . . Apparently Larry planned it all out. The details—the plot. There's a plot for me too. I never knew. He took care of everything. . . . I'm not sure when the funeral will be. In these . . . cases, the coroner . . . Such a stupid way to . . ."

Her hand flew to her face. More tears.

"This is terrible. I'm being childish." She dabbed at her eyes with the napkin.

"It's a terrible loss, Mrs. Ashmore."

"Nothing I haven't seen before," she said quickly. Suddenly her voice was hard, plated with anger.

I kept quiet.

"Well," she said, "I suppose I'd better attend to business."

I got up. She walked me to the door. "Thank you for coming, Dr. Delaware."

"If there's anything I can do—"

"That's very kind, but I'm certain I'll be able to handle things as they come up."

She opened the door.

I said goodbye and the door closed behind me.

I began walking toward the Seville. The gardening noises had died and the street was beautiful and silent.

When I entered room 505 W, Cassie followed me with her eyes but the rest of her didn't move.

The drapes were drawn, and yellow light came from the half-open door of the bathroom. I saw wet clothes hanging over the shower rod. The bed rails were down and the room had the gluey smell of old bandages.

A metered I.V. line was still attached to Cassie's left arm. Clear fluid from a hanging bottle slow-dripped through the tubing. The whirr of the I.V. meter seemed louder. LuvBunnies surrounded Cassie. An untouched breakfast tray sat on the table.

I said, "Hi, sweetie."

She gave a small smile, closed her eyes, and moved her head back and forth the way a blind child might.

Cindy came out of the bathroom and said, "Hi, Dr. Delaware." Her braid was gathered atop her head and her blouse was untucked.

"Hi. How're you managing?"

"Okay."

I sat on the edge of Cassie's bed. Cindy came over and stood next to me. The pressure of my weight made Cassie's eyes open again. I smiled at her, touched her fingers. Her stomach rumbled and she shut her eyes once more. Her lips were dry and chapped. A small scrap of dead skin hung from the upper one. Each breath ruffled it.

I took her free hand. She didn't resist. Her skin was warm and silky, soft as a dolphin's belly.

I said, "Such a good girl," and saw her eyes move behind the lids.

"We had a rough night," said Cindy.

"I know. Sorry to hear it." I looked down at the hand in mine. No new wounds but plenty of old ones. The thumbnail was tiny, square-edged, in need of cleaning. I exerted gentle pressure and the digit rose, remained extended for a moment, then lowered, tapping the top of my hand. I repeated the pressure and the same thing happened. But her eyes remained shut and her face had grown loose. Within moments she was sleeping, breathing in time with the I.V. drip.

Cindy reached down and stroked her daughter's cheek. One of the bunnies fell to the floor. She picked it up and placed it next to the breakfast tray. The tray was farther away than she'd estimated and the movement threw her off balance. I caught her elbow and held it. Through the sleeve of her blouse, her arm was thin and pliable. I let go of it but she held on to my hand for a moment.

I noticed worry lines around her eyes and mouth, saw where aging would take her. Our eyes met. Hers were full of wonder and fear. She stepped away from me and went to sit on the sleeper couch.

I said, "What's been happening?" though I'd read the chart before coming in.

"Sticks and tests," she said. "All kinds of scans. She didn't get any dinner until late and couldn't hold it down."

"Poor thing."

She bit her lip. "Dr. Eves says the appetite loss is either anxiety or some sort of reaction to the isotopes they used in the scans."

"That sometimes happens," I said. "Especially when there are a lot of tests and the isotopes build up in the system."

She nodded. "She's pretty tired. I guess you can't draw with her today."

"Guess not."

"It's too bad—the way it worked out. You didn't have time to do your techniques."

"How'd she tolerate the procedures?"

"Actually, she was so tired—after the grand mal—that she was kind of passive."

She looked over at the bed, turned away quickly, and put the palms of her hands on the sofa, propping herself up.

Our eyes met again. She stifled a yawn and said, "Excuse me."

"Anything I can help with?"

"Thanks. Can't think of any."

She closed her eyes.

I said, "I'll let you rest," and walked to the door.

"Dr. Delaware?"

"Yes?"

"That home visit we spoke about," she said. "When we finally do get out of here, you're still planning on doing it, aren't you?"

"Sure."

"Good."

Something in her voice—a stridency I'd never heard before—made me stand there and wait.

But she just said "Good" again, and looked away, resigned. As if a critical moment had come and gone. When she started to play with her braid, I left.

No sign of Vicki Bottomley; the nurse on shift was a stranger. After completing my own notes, I reread Stephanie's, the neurologist's, and those of the consulting endocrinologist—someone named Alan Macauley, with strong, large handwriting.

The neurologist had found no abnormality on two successive EEGs and deferred to Macauley, who reported no evidence of any metabolic disorder, though his lab tests were still being analyzed. As far as medical science could tell, Cassie's pancreas was structurally and biochemically normal. Macauley suggested further genetic tests and scans to rule out some sort of brain tumor, and recommended further "intensive psychological consultation per Dr. Delaware."

I'd never met the man and was surprised to be referred to by name. Wanting to know what he meant by "intensive," I looked up his number in a hospital directory and called it.

"Macauley."

"Dr. Macauley, this is Alex Delaware—the psychologist who's seeing Cassie Jones."

"Lucky you. Been to see her recently?"

"About a minute ago."

"How's she doing?"

"Wiped out—post-seizural fatigue, I guess."

"Probably."

"Her mother said she didn't hold her dinner down."

"Her mother, huh? . . . So, what can I do for you?"

"I read your notes—about psychological support. Wondered if you had any suggestions."

Long pause.

"Where are you now?" he said.

"Chappy Ward nursing station."

"Okay, listen, I've got Diabetes Clinic in about twenty minutes. I can get there a little early—say in five. Why don't you catch me? Three East."

He waved when he saw me coming and I realized I'd seen him the day before at Ashmore's memorial. The husky, dark, bald man who'd talked about Texas and guns, a Smith & Wesson in every black bag.

Standing, he looked even bigger, with thick sloping shoulders and stevedore arms. He had on a white polo shirt over pressed jeans and western ostrich boots. His badge was pinned just above the jockey-and-horse logo. His stethoscope was in one hand. The other hand made aeronautic movements—nosedives and fast climbs—as he talked to a gangly boy of around seventeen.

Fifteen minutes before clinic was scheduled to start and the Endocrinology waiting room was filling up. Nutritional posters hung on the walls. Children's books and battered magazines were stacked on the table, along with brochures and packets of artificial sweetener.

Macauley slapped the boy's back and I heard him say, "You're doing great—keep it up. I know sticking yourself sucks the big hairy one, but depending on *Mommy* to stick you sucks even worse, doesn't it? So keep her the heck out of your life and go have some fun."

"Yeah, right," said the boy. He had a big chin and big nose. Big jug ears, each pierced with three gold wire loops. Well over six feet, but Macauley made him look small. His skin was oily-looking and sallow, spotted with pimples on cheeks and brow. His hair had been mowed in a new-wave do with more levels and angles than an architect's wet dream. "Party on," he said glumly.

"Hey, party *hearty,* man," said Macauley, "just as long as it's sugar-free."

"Fuck," said the boy.

"Now, *that's* okay, Kev. *That* you can do to your horny little heart's content, long as you use a condom."

The boy grinned despite himself.

Macauley slapped him again and said, "Okay, scram, get, vamoose, clear out of here. I've got *sick* people to deal with."

"Yeah, right." The boy pulled out a pack of cigarettes, stuck a smoke in his mouth, but didn't light it.

Macauley said, "Hey, turkey, your lungs are someone else's problem."

The boy laughed and shambled off.

Macauley came over to me. "Noncompliant adolescents with brittle diabetes. When I die I *know* I'm going to heaven, 'cause I've already been to hell."

He shot a thick arm forward. The hand at the end of it was big but his grip was restrained. His face was basset with a touch of bull terrier: thick nose, full lips, small, drooping dark eyes. The baldness and perpetual five o'clock shadow gave him a middle-aged look, but I guessed he was thirty-five or so.

"Al Macauley."

"Alex Delaware."

"Meeting of the Als," he said. "C'mon out of here before the natives grow restless."

He took me behind swinging doors just like those in Stephanie's clinic, past a similar mix of clerks, nurses, residents, ringing phones, and scratching pens, to an examining room decorated with a sugar-content chart issued by one of the big fast-food chains. The five food groups with an emphasis on burgers and fries.

"What can I do for you?" he said, sitting on a stool and spinning back and forth in small semicircles.

"Any insights on Cassie?" I said.

"Insights? Isn't that your department?"

"In a perfect world it would be, Al. Unfortunately, reality's refusing to cooperate."

He snorted and ran his hand over his head, smoothing nonexistent hair. Someone had left a rubber reflex hammer on the examining table. He picked it up and touched the tip to his knee.

"You recommended intensive psych support," I said, "and I just wondered—"

"If I was being an especially sensitive guy or if I thought the case was suspicious, right? The answer is b. I read your notes in the chart, asked around about you, and found out you were good. So I figured I'd put in my two cents."

"Suspicious," I said. "As in Munchausen by proxy?"

"Call it what you want—I'm a gland-hand, not a shrink. But there's nothing wrong with the kid's metabolism, I can tell you that."

"You're sure of that?"

"Look, this isn't the first time I've been involved in the case—I worked her up months ago, when she supposedly presented with bloody stools. No one ever actually *saw* the stools except the mom, and red spots on a diaper don't make it in my book. We could be talking diaper rash. And my first go-round was *rigorous.* Every endocrine test in the book, some that weren't."

"Someone saw this latest seizure."

"I know that," he said impatiently. "The nurse and the U.C. And low sugar does explain it, physiologically. But what it *doesn't* explain is *why.* She's got no genetic or metabolic abnormality of any kind, no glycogen storage disorder, and her pancreas is functioning perfectly. At this point, all I'm doing is plowing old ground and throwing in some experimental assays I borrowed from the med school—basic science stuff they're still getting baselines on. We might just have the most tested two-year-old kid in the Western Hemisphere. Wanna call Guinness?"

"What about something idiopathic—a rare variant of a known disease?"

He looked at me, passed the hammer from hand to hand. "Anything's possible."

"But you don't think so."

"What I *don't* think is that there's anything wrong with her glands. This is a healthy kid, presenting with hypoglycemia because of something else."

"Something someone gave her?"

He tossed the hammer up in the air and snagged it with two fingers. Repeated the exercise a couple more times, then said, "What do *you* think?" He smiled. "Always wanted to do that with one of you guys. Seriously, though, yeah, that's what I think. It's logical, isn't it, considering the history? And that sib who died."

"Did you consult on his case?"

"No, why would I? That was respiratory. And I'm not saying that was necessarily ominous—babies do die of SIDS. But in this case it makes you think, doesn't it?"

I nodded. "When I heard about the hypoglycemia, one of the first things I thought about was insulin poisoning. But Stephanie said there were no fresh injection marks on Cassie's body."

He shrugged. "Could be. I didn't do a complete physical. But there are ways to stick someone and be subtle: Use a really small needle—a newborn spike. Pick a site that's easy to miss—the folds of the buttocks, knee folds, between the toes, right under the scalp. My doper patients get creative all the time, and insulin goes right into the skin. Little pinprick like that can heal really quickly."

"Have you mentioned your suspicions to Stephanie?"

He nodded. "Sure I did, but she's still hopped up on something esoteric. Between you and me, I didn't get the feeling she wanted to hear it. Not that it matters to me personally. I'm off the case—quits, vamoose. Out of *here,* as a matter of fact."

"Leaving the hospital?"

"You bet. One more month, then off for quieter pastures. I need the time I have left to wrap up my own cases. It's gonna be a mess— lots of angry families. So the last thing I want to do is muck around in Chuck Jones's family affairs when there's nothing I can do about it anyway."

"*Because* it's his family?"

He shook his head. "It would be nice to say yup, that's it, the whole thing's politics. But actually, it's the case itself. She could be *anyone's* granddaughter and we'd still be spitting into the wind because we have no facts. Just look at you and me, right here. *You* know what's going on; *I* know what's going on; Stephanie *used* to know what was going on until she got all horny about the hypoglycemia. But knowing doesn't mean a thing, legally, does it? 'Cause we can't do anything. That's what I hate about abuse cases—someone accuses parents; they deny it, walk away or just ask for another doc. And even if you *could* prove something was going on, you'd get into a circus of lawyers, paperwork, years in court, dragging *our* reputations through the mud. Meantime the kid's a basket case and you couldn't even get a restraining order."

"Sounds like you've had experience."

"My wife's a county social worker. The system's so overloaded, even kids with broken bones aren't considered a priority anymore. But it's the same all over—I had a case back in Texas, diabetic kid. The mother was *witholding* insulin and we still had a hell of a time keeping the kid safe. And she was a nurse. Top O.R. gal."

"Speaking of nurses," I said, "what do you think of Cassie's primary R.N.?"

"Who's that? Oh, yeah, Vicki. I think Vicki's a cranky bitch but generally real good at what she does—" The droopy eyes perked. "Her? Shit, I never thought about that, but that doesn't make sense, does it? Till this last seizure, the problems started at home?"

"Vicki visited the home, but only a couple of times. Not enough to do all the damage."

"Besides," he said, "it's always the mother, isn't it, these Munchausens? And this one's strange—at least in my uneducated opinion."

"How so?"

"I don't know. She's just too damned nice. Especially considering how inept we've been diagnosing her kid. That were me, I'd be pissed, demanding action. But she keeps smiling. Smiles *too* much for my taste. 'Hi, Doctor, how are you, Doctor?' Never trust a smiler, Al. I was married to one the first time. Those white teeth were always hiding something—you can probably give me all the psychodynamics behind it, right?"

I shrugged and said, "Perfect world."

He laughed. "Lot of good you are."

I said, "Any impressions of the father?"

"Never met him. Why? Is he strange too?"

"I wouldn't say strange. He's just not what you'd expect of Chuck Jones's son. Beard, earring. Doesn't seem to have much affection for the hospital."

"Well, at least he and Chuck have something in common. . . . Far as I'm concerned the case is a loser and I'm tired of losing. That's why I punted to you. And now you're telling me you've got squat. Too bad."

He retrieved the hammer, tossed it, caught it, used it to drum the top of the table.

I said, "Would hypoglycemia explain any of Cassie's earlier symptoms?"

"Maybe the diarrhea. But she also had fevers, so there was probably some kind of infectious process going on. In terms of the breathing problems, it's also possible. Mess with the metabolism, *anything's* possible."

He picked up his stethoscope and looked at his watch. "Got work to do. Some of the kids out there, this'll be the last time I see them."

I got up and thanked him.

"For what? I've accomplished squat on this one."

I laughed. "Same way I feel, Al."

"Consultancy blues. You know the story of the oversexed rooster who was bothering the hens in the henhouse? Sneaking up behind 'em and jumping their bones, just generally making a nuisance of himself? So the farmer had him castrated and turned him into a *consultant.* Now he just sits on the fence, watching and giving advice to the other roosters. Trying to remember what it felt like."

I laughed again. We left the exam room and returned to the waiting room. A nurse came up to Macauley and handed him a pile of charts without comment. She looked angry as she walked away.

"Good morning to you, too, darling," he said. To me: "I'm a rotten deserter. Next few weeks are gonna be my punishment."

He looked out at the turmoil and his hound face sagged.

"Does quieter pastures mean private practice?" I said.

"Group practice. Small town in Colorado, not far from Vail. Ski in the winter, fish in the summer, find new modes of mischief for the rest of the year."

"Doesn't sound too bad."

"Shouldn't be. No one else in the group does endocrinology, so maybe I'll even have a chance to use my training once in a while."

"How long have you been at Western Peds?"

"Two years. One and a half too long."

"The financial situation?"

"That's a big part of it but not all of it. I was no Pollyanna when I came here, knew an inner-city hospital would always be struggling to balance the books. It's the attitude that bugs me."

"Grandpa Chuck?"

"And his boys. They're trying to run this place like just another company. We could be manufacturing widgets for all they're concerned. *That's* what grinds—their not understanding. Even the gypsies know things are bad—you know about our Hollywood gypsies?"

"Sure," I said. "Big white Cadillacs, twelve to a car, camp-outs in the hallways, the barter system."

He grinned. "I've been paid with food, spare parts for my MG, an old mandolin. Actually, it's a better reimbursement rate than I get from the government. Anyway, one of my diabetics is one of them. Nine years old, in line to be king of the tribe. His mother's this good-looking woman, educated, about a hundred years of living behind her. Usually when she comes in she's full of laughs, buttering me up, telling me I'm God's answer to medical science. This time she was really quiet, as if she was upset about something. And it was just a routine exam—the boy's doing well, medically. So I asked her what the matter was and she said, 'This place, Dr. Al. Bad vibrations.' She was narrowing her eyes at me like some storefront fortuneteller. I said, what do you mean? But she wouldn't explain, just touched my hand and said, 'I like you, Dr. Al, and Anton likes you. But we won't be coming back here. Bad vibrations.' "

He hefted the charts and transferred them to one hand. "Pretty dicey, huh?"

I said, "Maybe we should consult her on Cassie."

He smiled. Patients continued to stream in, even though there was no room for them. Some of them greeted him and he responded with winks.

I thanked him again for his time.

He said, "Sorry we won't have a chance to work together."

"Good luck in Colorado."

"Yup," he said. "You ski?"

"No."

"Me neither . . ." He looked back at the waiting room, shook his head. "What a place . . . Originally, I was gonna be a surgeon, slice and dice. Then, when I was a second-year med student, I came down with diabetes. No dramatic symptoms, just some weight loss that I didn't think much about because I wasn't eating properly. I went into shock in the middle of gross anatomy lab, collapsed on top of my cadaver. It was just before Christmas. I got home and my family handled it by passing the honey-baked ham right by me, no one saying anything. *I* handled *that* by rolling my pants up, hoisting my leg up on the table and jabbing it, in front of everyone. Eventually, I figured it was time to forget about scalpels and think about people. That's what appealed to me about *this* place—working with kids and families. But when I got here I found out that was all gone. Bad vibes is right. That gypsy lady could tell the *moment* she walked in the door. It might sound nuts to you, but she crystallized what had been going on in my head for a while. Sure, Colorado's gonna be boring—sniffles and sneezes and diaper rash. And I haven't been here long enough to collect any pension, so financially the two years have been a wash. But at least I won't be sitting on the fence. Cock-a-doodle-doo."

Robin called at seven to say she was on her way over. She was at my door a half hour later, hair drawn back and French-braided, accentuating the sweet, clean lines of her neck. She wore black teardrop earrings and a cool-pink denim dress that hugged her hips. In her arms were bags of Chinese takeout.

When we'd lived together, Chinese had been the cue for dinner in bed. Back in the good old days I'd have led her into the bedroom, Joe Suave. But two years apart and a reconciliation that was still confusing had shaken my instincts. I took the bags, placed them on the dining room table, and kissed her lightly on the lips.

She put an arm around me, pressed the back of my head, and enlarged the kiss.

When we broke for breath she said, "I hope this is okay—not going out?"

"I've been out plenty today."

"Me too. Delivering the Stealths to the *boys'* hotel. They wanted me to stay and party."

"They've got better taste in women than in music."

She laughed, kissed me again, pulled back, and did some exaggerated heavy breathing.

"Enough with the hormones," she said. "First things first. Let me heat this up and we'll have ourselves an indoor picnic."

She took the food into the kitchen. I hung back and watched her move. All these years I'd never tired of watching her move.

The dress was nouveau-rodeo sweetheart—lots of leather fringe and old lace on the yoke. She wore ankle-high boots that echoed sharply on the kitchen floor. Her braid swung as she walked. So did the rest of her but I found myself looking at the braid. Shorter than Cindy Jones's and auburn instead of dark-brown, but it got me thinking about the hospital again.

She deposited the bags on the counter, started to say something, then realized I hadn't followed her in. Looking over her shoulder, she said, "Something the matter, Alex?"

"No," I lied, "just admiring."

One of her hands darted to her hair and I realized she was nervous. That made me want to kiss her again.

I said, "You look gorgeous."

She flashed a smile that tightened my chest and held out her arms. I went into the kitchen.

"Tricky," she said later, trying to knit my chest hair with chopsticks.

"The idea," I said, "is to show your devotion by knitting me a sweater. Not turning me into one."

She laughed. "Cold moo goo. What a gourmet treat."

"At this moment, wet sand on toast would be okay." I stroked her face.

Placing the chopsticks on the nightstand, she moved closer. Our sweaty flanks stuck together and made wet-plastic noises. She turned her hand into a glider and flew it over my chest, barely touching skin. Propping herself up, she bumped her nose against mine, kissed my chin. Her hair was still braided. As we'd made love, I'd held it, passing the smooth rope between my fingers, finally letting go when I began to lose control, for fear of hurting her. Some of the curly strands had come loose and they tickled my face. I smoothed them back and nuzzled her under her chin.

Her head lifted. She massaged my chest some more, stopped, inspected, looped a finger under a single hair, and said, "Hmm."

"What?"

"A *gray* one—isn't that *cute.*"

"Adorable."

"It is, Alex. You're *maturing.*"

"What's that, the euphemism of the day?"

"The *truth,* Doctor. Time's a sexist pig—women decay; men acquire a vintage. Even guys who weren't all that cute when they were young have a second shot at studliness if they don't let themselves go completely to seed. The ones like you, who were adorable to begin with, can really clean up."

I started panting.

"I'm serious, Alex. You'll probably get all craggy and wise— look like you really understand the mysteries of life."

"Talk about false advertising."

She inspected each of my temples, turning my head gently with strong fingers and burrowing through the hair.

"This is the ideal place to start silvering," she said in a teacher's voice. "Maximum class-and-wisdom quotient. Hmm, nope, I don't see anything yet, just this one little guy, down here." Touching a nail to the chest hair, she brushed my nipple again. "Too bad you're still a callow youth."

"Hey, babe, let's party."

She put her head back down and reached lower, under the blanket.

"Well," she said, "there's something to be said for callow too."

We moved to the living room and listened to some tapes she'd brought. The new Warren Zevon casting cold light upon the dark side of life—a novel in miniature. A Texas genius named Eric Johnson who produced musical textures from the guitar that made me want to burn my instruments. A young woman named Lucinda Williams with a beautiful, bruised voice and lyrics straight from the heart.

Robin sat on my lap, curled small, her head on my chest, breathing shallowly.

When the music was over she said, "Is everything okay?"

"Sure. Why?"

"You seem a little distracted."

"Don't mean to be," I said, wondering how she could tell.

She sat up and undid her braid. Her curls had matted and she began separating the strands. When she'd fluffed them and restored the natural perm, she said, "Anything you want to talk about?"

"It really isn't anything," I said. "Just work—a tough case. I'm probably letting it get to me too much."

I expected her to let that go, but she said, "Confidential, right?" with just a trace of regret.

"Limited confidentiality," I said. "I'm a consultant and this one may spill over into the criminal justice system."

"Oh. *That* kind of case."

She touched my face. Waited.

I told her the story of Cassie Jones, leaving out names and identifying marks.

When I finished, she said, "Isn't there anything that can be done?"

"I'm open to suggestions," I said. "I've got Milo running background checks on the parents and the nurse, and I'm doing my best to get a feel for all of them. Problem is, there isn't a shred of real evidence, just logic, and logic isn't worth much, legally. The only fishy thing so far is the mother lying to me about being the victim of an influenza epidemic when she was in the army. I called the base and managed to find out there'd been no epidemic."

"Why would she lie about something like that?"

"The real reason she was discharged could be something she wants to hide. Or, if she's a Munchausen personality, she just likes lying."

"Disgusting," she said. "A person doing that to their own flesh and blood. To any kid . . . How does it feel to be back at the hospital?"

"Kind of depressing, actually. Like meeting an old friend who's gone downhill. The place seems gloomy, Rob. Morale's low, cash flow's worse than ever, lots of staff have left—remember Raoul Melendez-Lynch?"

"The cancer specialist?"

"Uh-huh. He was *married* to the hospital. I watched him weather crisis after crisis and keep on ticking. Even he's gone—took a job in Florida. *All* the senior physicians seem to be gone. The faces I pass in the halls are new. And young. Or maybe I'm just getting old."

"Mature," she said. "Repeat after me: ma-ture."

"I thought I was callow."

"Mature *and* callow. Secret of your charm."

"Top of all that, the crime problems out on the street are leaking in more and more. Nurses beaten and robbed . . . A couple of nights ago there was a murder in one of the parking lots. A doctor."

"I know. I heard it on the radio. Didn't know you were back working there or I would have freaked."

"I was there the night it happened."

Her fingers dug into my hand, then loosened. "Well, that's reassuring. . . . Just be careful, okay? As if my saying it makes a difference."

"It does. I promise."

She sighed and put her head on my shoulder. We sat there without talking.

"I'll be careful," I said. "I mean it. Old guys can't afford to be reckless."

"Okay," she said. A moment later: "So that's why you're down. I thought it might be me."

"You? Why?"

She shrugged. "The changes—everything that's happened."

"No way," I said. "You're the bright spot in my life."

She moved closer and rested a hand on my chest. "What you said before—the hospital being gloomy? I've *always* thought of hospitals that way."

"Western Peds was different, Rob. It used to be . . . vital. Everything meshing together like this wonderful organic *machine.*"

"I'm sure it was, Alex," she said softly. "But when you get down to it, no matter how vital or caring a hospital is, it's always going to be a place of death, isn't it? Mention the word *hospital* to me and what comes to my mind is my dad. Lying there, all tubed and punctured and helpless. Mom screaming for the nurse every time he moaned, no one really caring . . . The fact that *your* place treats kids only makes it worse, as far as I'm concerned. 'Cause what's worse than suffering kids? I never understood how you stayed there as long as you did."

"You build up a shell," I said. "Do your job, let in just enough emotion so you can be useful to your patients. It's like that old toothpaste commercial. The invisible shield."

"Maybe that's what's really bothering you, coming back after all these years, and your shield's gone."

"You're probably right." I sounded glum.

"Some shrink I am," she said.

"No, no. It's good talking about it."

She snuggled up against me. "You're sweet to say so, whether it's true or not. And I'm glad you told me what's on your mind. You never used to talk much about your work. The few times I tried, you changed the subject, so I could tell you weren't comfortable with it and I never pushed. I know part of it was confidentiality, but I really wasn't after gory details, Alex. I just wanted to know what you were going through so I could support you. I guess you were protecting me."

"Maybe I was," I said. "But to tell the truth, I never really knew you wanted to hear any of it."

"Why's that?"

"You always seemed more interested in—how can I say this— angles and planes."

She gave a small laugh. "Yeah, you're right. I never was much for touchy-feely. In fact, when we first met, the one thing that I wasn't sure I liked about you was that you were a psychologist. Not that it stopped me from chasing you shamelessly, but it did surprise me—being attracted to a shrink. I didn't know a thing about psychology, never even took a course in college. Probably because of Dad. He was always making comments about crazy psychiatrists, crooked doctors. Going on about how anyone who didn't work with his hands couldn't be trusted. But as I got to know you and saw how serious you were about what you did, I loosened up. Tried to learn—I even read some of your psych books. Did you know that?"

I shook my head.

She smiled. "At night, in the library. I used to sneak in when you were sleeping and I couldn't. *Schedules of Reinforcement. Cognitive Theory.* Pretty strange stuff for a woodchopper like me."

"I never knew," I said, amazed.

She shrugged. "I was . . . embarrassed. I don't really know why. Not that I was trying to be an expert or anything. Just wanted to be closer to you. I'm sure I didn't send out a clear message . . . not sympathetic enough. I guess what I'm saying is, I hope we can continue this way. Letting each other in a little more."

"Sure we can," I said. "I never found you unsympathetic, just—"

"Preoccupied? Self-obsessed?"

She looked up at me with another chest-tightening smile. Big white upper incisors. The ones I liked to lick.

"Strongly focused," I said. "You're one a them artsy-fartsy creative types. Need intense concentration."

"Strongly focused, huh?"

"Definitely."

She laughed. "We've definitely got a thing for each other, Dr. Delaware. Probably chemical—pheromones or whatever."

"That we do, that we do."

She put her head on my chest. I stroked her hair and thought of her going into the library, reading my books.

"Can we try again?" I said. "Will you come back?"

She tensed hard as bone.

"Yes," she said. "God, yes."

She sat up, took my face in her hands and kissed it. Scrambled on me, straddling me, her arms down over my shoulders, gripping.

I ran my hands over her back, held her hips, raised myself to her. We fused once more, rocked and rolled together, silent and intent.

Afterward she lay back, panting. I was breathing hard, too, and it took a long time to wind down.

I rolled on my side and wrapped my arms around her. She pressed her belly up against mine, glued herself to me.

We stayed together for a long while. When she started to get restless, the way she always did, and began to pull away, I didn't let her go.

16

She stayed the night and, as usual, was up early.

What wasn't usual was her sticking around for another hour to drink coffee and read the paper. She sat next to me at the table, one hand on my knee, finishing the arts section as I skimmed the sports scores. Afterward, we went down to the pond and threw pellets to the fish. The heat had come on early for spring, overpowering the ocean currents, and the air smelled like summer vacation.

Saturday, but I felt like working.

She remained at my side. We touched a lot but the signs of her restlessness were beginning: flexing muscles, random glances, minuscule lags in the conversation that only a lover or a paranoiac would have noticed.

I said, "Got a busy one planned?"

"Just a few things to catch up on. How about you?"

"The same. I'm planning to hit the hospital sometime today."

She nodded, put both arms around my waist, and we walked back up to the house, entwined. After she got her purse we descended to the carport.

A new truck was parked next to the Seville. Royal-blue Chevy pickup with a white racing stripe along the side. New car registration sticker on the windshield.

"Nice," I said. "When'd you get it?"

"Yesterday. The Toyota developed serious engine problems and the estimates I got ranged from one to two thousand, so I thought I'd treat myself."

I walked her to the truck.

She said, "Dad would've liked it. He was always a Chevy man— didn't have much use for anything else. When I drove the other one I sometimes felt he was looking over my shoulder, scowling and telling me Iwo Jima stories."

She got in, put her bag on the passenger seat, and stuck her face out the window for a kiss.

"Yum," she said. "Let's do it again soon, cutie. What was your name again? Felix? Ajax?"

"Mr. Clean."

"How true," she said, laughing as she sped away.

I paged Stephanie, and the operator came back on the line saying Dr. Eves would call back. I hung up, pulled out my Thomas Guide, and pinpointed Dawn Herbert's address on Lindblade Street. I'd just located it when the phone rang.

"Steph?"

"No, *Mile*. Am I interrupting something?"

"Just waiting for a callback from the hospital."

"And of course you don't have call-waiting."

"Of course."

Milo gave a long, equine snort that the phone amplified into something thunderous. "Have you had your gas lamps converted to Dr. Edison's miracle wires yet?"

"If God had wanted man to be electric, he would have given him batteries."

He snort-laughed. "I'm at the Center. Phone me as soon as you're finished with *Steph*."

He hung up. I waited another ten minutes before Stephanie's call came in.

"Morning, Alex," she said. "What's up?"

"That's what I wanted to ask you."

"Nothing much. I saw her about an hour ago," she said. "She's feeling better—awake, alert, and screaming at the sight of me."

"What's the latest on the hypoglycemia?"

"The metabolic people say there are no metabolic problems, her pancreas has been examined from every possible angle—clean as a whistle—and my Swedish friend and everyone else is back on Munchausen. So I guess *I'm* back to square one, too."

"How long are you planning to keep her in?"

"Two or three days, then back home if nothing else comes up. I know it's dangerous letting her out, but what can I do, turn the hospital into her foster home? Unless you've got some suggestions."

"None yet."

"You know," she said, "I really let myself go with that sugar thing. Thinking it was real."

"Don't bludgeon yourself. It's a crazy case. How did Cindy and Chip react to the continuing uncertainty?"

"I only saw Cindy. The usual quiet resignation."

Remembering Al Macauley's comment, I said, "Any smiles?"

"Smiles? No. Oh, you mean those spacey ones she sometimes gives? No. Not this morning. Alex, I'm worried sick over this. By discharging Cassie, what am I sentencing her to?"

Having no balm, I offered a Band-Aid. "At least discharging her will give me the chance to make a home visit."

"While you're there, why don't you sneak around and look for hot clues?"

"Such as?"

"Needles in bureau drawers, insulin spansules in the fridge. I'm kidding—no, actually I'm only half-kidding. I'm *this* close to confronting Cindy, let the chips fall. The next time that little girl gets sick, I just may do it, and if they get mad and go elsewhere, at least I'll know I did everything I could— Oops, that's me on page— Neonatology, one of my preemies. Gotta go, Alex. Call me if you learn anything, okay?"

*   *   *

I phoned Milo back. "Working weekends?"

"Did a trade with Charlie. Saturdays on in exchange for some flexibility in my moonlighting. How's old *Steph*?"

"Off organic disease, back on Munchausen. No one can find an organic reason for the hypoglycemia."

"Too bad," he said. "Meantime, I've got the lowdown on Reggie Bottomley, the nurse's bad seed. Guy's been dead for a couple of years. For some reason his name never got off the files. Suicide."

"How?"

"He went into the bathroom, got naked, sat on the toilet, smoked crack, jacked off, then turned his head into bad fruit with a shotgun. Very messy. The Tujunga detective—a gal, actually, named Dunn—said Vicki was home when it happened, watching TV in the next room."

"Jesus."

"Yeah. The two of them had just had some kind of spat over Reggie's dissolute life-style and Reggie stomped off, got his works out of his dresser drawer and the gun, locked himself in the can, and kaboom. Mom heard the shot, couldn't get the door open, tried to use a hatchet and still couldn't do it. The paramedics found her sitting on the floor, crying and screaming for him to please come out, talk it over. They broke the door down and when they saw what he looked like, tried to hold her back. But she got a look at some of it. So that could explain her sour disposition."

"Oh, man," I said. "What a thing to go through. Anything on the family history that led up to the suicide?"

"Dunn said there was no history of child abuse—she saw it as basically a nice mom with a rotten kid. And she busted Reggie lots of times, knew him well."

"What about dad?"

"Died when Reggie was little. Heavy drinker, like you said. Reggie was in trouble right out of the chute, smoking dope and moving on up the pharmaceutical ladder. Dunn describes him as a little skinny jerk, learning disabilities, not too bright, couldn't hold a job. Incompetent criminal, too—got caught all the time, but he was so pitiful-looking, judges usually went easy on him. He didn't get violent until near the end—the assault rap. And even that was relatively dinky—bar fight, he used a pool cue on some other scrote's head. Dunn said he was getting feistier because of the crack, it was just a matter of time before he ended up prematurely *muerto.* According to her, mom was the long-suffering type, tried her best. End of story. It tell you anything about mom as a suspect?"

"Not really. Thanks anyway."

"What's your next step?"

"Lacking anything else, I guess a visit with Dawn Herbert. I spoke to Ashmore's wife yesterday, and she said he hired grad students from the university. So maybe Herbert has enough technical knowledge to know what Ashmore was looking for in Chad's chart."

"Ashmore's wife? What'd you do, pay a grief call?"

"Yes. Nice lady. Ashmore was quite an interesting fellow." I told him about the couple's time in the Sudan, Ashmore's gambling systems and investments.

"Blackjack, huh? Must have been good."

"She said he was a math genius—computer wizard. Brown belt in several martial arts, too. Not exactly easy prey for a mugger."

"No? I know you used to do all that good stuff, and I never wanted to disillusion you, but I've seen plenty of martial *artists* with tags on their toes. It's one thing in a *dojo,* bowing and jumping around and screaming like there's a hatpin in your colon. Whole different story out on the streets. Incidentally, I checked with Hollywood Division on Ashmore's murder and they're giving a low solve probability. Hope the widow isn't pinning her hopes on law enforcement."

"The widow is still too dazed to hope."

"Yeah . . ."

"What?"

"Well," he said, "I've been thinking a lot about your case—the psychology of this whole Munchausen thing—and it seems to me we've missed a potential suspect."

"Who?"

"Your buddy Steph."

"Stephanie? Why?"

"Female, medical background, likes to test authority, wants to be in the center of things."

"I never thought of her as attention-seeking."

"Didn't you tell me she was some big radical in the old days, Chairman of the interns' union?"

"Sure, but she seemed sincere. Idealistic."

"Maybe. But look at it this way: Treating Cassie puts her smack at the center of things, and the sicker the kid is, the more Stephanie gets the spotlight. Playing rescuer, big hero, rushing over to the Emergency Room and taking charge. The fact that Cassie's a big shot's kid makes it even tastier, from that standpoint. And these sudden shifts she's making—Munchausen one day, pancreatic disease the next, then back to Munchausen. Doesn't that have a *hysterical* feeling to it? Your goddam waltz?"

I digested all that.

"Maybe there's a *reason* the kid goes nuts when she sees her, Alex."

"But the same logic that applies to Vicki applies to her," I said. "Until this last seizure, all of Cassie's problems began at home. How could Stephanie have been involved?"

"Has *she* ever been out to the home?"

"Just early on—once or twice, setting up the sleep monitor."

"Okay, what about this? The first problems the kid had were real—the croup, or whatever. Steph treated them and found out being doctor to the chairman of the board's grandchild was a kick. Power trip—you yourself said she plans on being head of the department."

"If that was her goal, *curing* Cassie would have made her look a lot better."

"The parents haven't dropped her yet, have they?"

"No. They think she's great."

"There you go. She gets them to depend on her, and tinkers with Cassie—best of both worlds. And you yourself told me Cassie gets sick soon after appointments. What if that's because Stephanie's doing something to her—dosing her up during a checkup and sending her home like a medical time bomb?"

"What could she have done with Cindy right there in the exam room?"

"How do you know she was there?"

"Because she never leaves Cassie's side. And some of those

medical visits were with other doctors—specialists, not Stephanie."

"Do you know for a fact that Stephanie didn't also see the kid the same day the specialists did?"

"No. I guess I could look at the outpatient chart and find out."

"If she even charted it. It could have been something subtle—checking the kid's throat and the tongue depressor's coated with something. Whatever, it's something to consider, right?"

"Doctor sends baby home with more than a lollipop? That's pretty obscene."

"Any worse than a mother poisoning her own child? The other thing you might want to think of, in terms of her motivation, is revenge: She hates Grandpa because of what he's doing to the hospital, so she gets to him through Cassie."

"Sounds like you've been doing a lot of thinking."

"Evil mind, Alex. They used to pay me for it. Actually, what got me going was talking to Rick. He'd heard of Munchausen—the adult type. Said he'd seen nurses *and* doctors with those tendencies. Mistakes in dosage that aren't accidental, heroes rushing in and saving the day—like pyromaniac firemen."

"Chip talked about that," I said. "Medical errors, dosage miscalculations. Maybe he senses something about Stephanie without realizing it. . . . So why's she calling me in? To play with me? We never worked that closely together. I can't mean that much to her, psychologically."

"Calling you in proves she's doing a thorough job. And you've got a rep as a smart guy—real challenge for her if she's a Munchie. Plus, all the other shrinks are gone."

"True, but I don't know . . . Stephanie?"

"There's no reason to get an ulcer over it—it's all theory. I can peel 'em off, right and left."

"It makes my stomach turn, but I'll start looking at her more closely. Guess I'd better watch what I say to her, stop thinking in terms of teamwork."

"Ain't it always that way? One guy, walking the road alone."

"Yeah . . . Meantime, as long as we're peeling off theories, how about this one? We're not making headway because we're concentrating on one bad guy. What if there's some kind of collusion going on?"

"Who?"

"Cindy and Chip are the obvious choice. The typical Munchausen husband is described as passive and weak-willed. Which doesn't fit Chip at all. He's a savvy guy, smart, opinionated. So if his wife's abusing Cassie, why isn't he aware of it? But it could also be Cindy and Vicki—"

"What? Some romantic thing?"

"Or just some twisted mother-*daughter* thing. Cindy rediscovering her dead aunt in Vicki—another tough R.N. And Vicki, with her own child rearing a failure, ripe for a surrogate daughter. It's possible their pathology's meshed in some bizarre way. Hell, maybe Cindy and *Stephanie* have a thing going. And maybe it *is* romantic. I don't know anything about Stephanie's private life. Back in the old days she hardly seemed to have one."

"Long as you're piling it on, what about dad and Stephanie?"

"Sure," I said. "Dad and doc, dad and nurse—Vicki sure kisses up plenty to Chip. Nurse and doc, et cetera. *Ad nauseum. E pluribus unum.* Maybe it's *all* of them, Milo. Munchausen team—the Orient Express gone pediatric. Maybe half the damn world's psychopathic."

"Too conservative an estimate," he said.

"Probably."

"You need a vacation, Doc."

"Impossible," I said. "So much psychopathology, so little time. Thanks for reminding me."

He laughed. "Glad to brighten your day. You want me to run Steph through the files?"

"Sure. And as long as you're punching keys, why not Ashmore? Dead men can't sue."

"Done. Anyone else? Take advantage of my good mood and the LAPD's hardware."

"How about me?"

"Already did that," he said. "Years ago, when I thought we might become friends."

I took a ride to Culver City, hoping Dawn Herbert stayed home on Saturday morning. The drive took me past the site of the cheesy apartment structure on Overland where I'd spent my student/intern days. The body shop next door was still standing, but my building had been torn down and replaced with a used-car lot.

At Washington Boulevard, I headed west to Sepulveda, then continued south until a block past Culver. I turned left at a tropical fish store with a coral-reef mural painted on the windows and drove down the block, searching for the address Milo had pulled out of the DMV files.

Lindblade was packed with small, boxy, one-story bungalows with composition roofs and lawns just big enough for hopscotch. Liberal use of texture-coat; the color of the month was butter. Big Chinese elms shaded the street. Most of the houses were neatly maintained, though the landscaping—old birds of paradise, arborvitaes, spindly tree roses—seemed haphazard.

Dawn Herbert's residence was a pale-blue box one lot from the corner. An old brown VW bus was parked in the driveway. Travel decals crowded the lower edge of the rear window. The brown paint was dull as cocoa powder.

A man and a woman were gardening out in front, accompanied by a large golden retriever and a small black mutt with spaniel pretensions.

The people were in their late thirties or early forties. Both had pasty, desk-job complexions lobstered with patches of fresh sunburn on upper arm and shoulder, light-brown hair that hung past their shoulders, and rimless glasses. They wore tank tops, shorts, and rubber sandals.

The man stood at a hydrangea bush, clippers in hand. Shorn flowers clumped around his feet like pink fleece. He was thin and sinewy, with mutton-chop sideburns that trailed down his jaw, and his shorts were held up by leather suspenders. A beaded band circled his head.

The woman wore no bra and as she knelt, bending to weed, her breasts hung nearly to the lawn, brown nipples visible. She looked to be the man's height—five nine or ten—but probably outweighed him by thirty pounds, most of it in the chest and thighs. A possible match for the physical dimensions on Dawn Herbert's driver's license but at least a decade too old for the '63 birthdate.

As I pulled up I realized that the two of them looked vaguely familiar. But I couldn't figure out why.

I parked and turned off the engine. Neither of them looked up. The little dog started to bark, the man said, "Down, Homer," and continued clipping.

That was a cue for the bark to go nuclear. As the mutt scrunched his eyes and tested the limits of his vocal cords, the retriever looked on, bemused. The woman stopped weeding and searched for the source of irritation.

She found it and stared. I got out of the car. The mutt stood his ground but went into the face-down submissive posture.

I said, "Hey, boy," bent and petted him. The man lowered his clippers. All four of them were staring at me now.

"Morning," I said.

The woman stood. Too *tall* for Dawn Herbert, too. Her thick, flushed face would have looked right at a barn raising.

"What can I do for you?" she said. Her voice was melodious and I was certain I'd heard it before. But where?

"I'm looking for Dawn Herbert."

The look that passed between them made me feel like a cop.

"That so?" said the man. "She doesn't live here anymore."

"Do you know where she does live?"

Another exchange of glances. More fear than wariness.

"Nothing ominous," I said. "I'm a doctor, over at Western Pediatric Hospital—in Hollywood. Dawn used to work there and she may have some information on a patient that's important. This is the only address I have for her."

The woman walked over to the man. It seemed like a self-defense move but I wasn't clear who was protecting who.

The man used his free hand to brush petals off his shorts. His bony jaw was set hard. The sunburn had gotten his nose, too, and the tip was raw.

"You come all the way here just to get information?" he said.

"It's complicated," I said, fudging for enough time to build a credible story. "An important case—a small child at risk. Dawn checked his medical chart out of the hospital and never returned it. Normally I'd have gone to Dawn's boss. A doctor named Ashmore. But he's dead. Mugged a couple of days ago in the hospital parking lot—you may have heard about it."

New look on their faces. Fear and bafflement. The news had

obviously caught them off guard and they didn't know how to respond. Finally they chose suspicion, locking hands and glaring at me.

The retriever didn't like the tension. He looked back at his masters and started to whine.

"Jethro," said the woman, and the dog quieted. The black mutt perked up his ears and growled.

She said, "Mellow out, Homer," in a singsong voice, almost crooning it.

"Homer and Jethro," I said. "Do they play their own instruments or use backup?"

Not a trace of a smile. Then I finally remembered where I'd seen them. Robin's shop, last year. Repair customers. A guitar and a mandolin, the former in pretty bad shape. Two folkies with a lot of integrity, some talent, not much money. Robin had done five hundred bucks' worth of work for some self-produced record albums, a plate of home-baked muffins, and seventy-five in cash. I'd watched the transaction, unnoticed, from up in the bedroom loft. Later, Robin and I had listened to a couple of the albums. Public domain songs, mostly—ballads and reels, done traditionally and pretty well.

"You're Bobby and Ben, aren't you?"

Being recognized cracked their suspicion and brought back the confusion.

"Robin Castagna's a friend of mine," I said.

"That so?" said the man.

"She patched up your gear last winter. Gibson A-four with a headstock crack? D-eighteen with loose braces, bowed neck, bad frets, and a popped bridge? Whoever baked those muffins was good."

"Who *are* you?" said the woman.

"Exactly who I said I was. Call Robin—she's at her shop, right now. Ask her about Alex Delaware. Or if you don't want to bother, could you please tell me where I can find Dawn Herbert? I'm not out to hassle her, just want to get the chart back."

They didn't answer. The man placed a thumb behind one of his suspender straps.

"Go call," the woman told him.

He went into the house. She stayed behind, watching me, breathing deeply, bosoms flopping. The dogs watched me too. No one spoke. My eyes caught motion from the west end of the block and I turned and saw a camper back out of a driveway and lumber toward Sepulveda. Someone on the opposite side of the street was flying an American flag. Just beyond that, an old man sat slumped in a lawn chair. Hard to be sure but I thought he was watching me too.

Belle of the ball in Culver City.

The suspendered man came back a few minutes later, smiling as if he'd run into the Messiah. Carrying a pale-blue plate. Cookies and muffins.

He nodded. That and his smile relaxed the woman. The dogs began wagging their tails.

I waited for someone to ask me to dance.

"Get this, Bob," he said to the woman. "This boy's her main squeeze."

"Small world," said the woman, finally smiling. I remembered her singing voice from the album, high and clear, with a subtle vibrato. Her speaking voice was nice too. She could have made money delivering phone sex.

"That's a terrific woman you've got there," she said, still check-ing me out. "Do you appreciate her?"

"Every day."

She nodded, stuck out her hand, and said, "Bobby Murtaugh. This is Ben. You've already been introduced to *these* characters."

Greetings all around. I petted the dogs and Ben passed the plate. The three of us took muffins and ate. It felt like a tribal ritual. But even as they chewed, they looked worried.

Bobby finished her muffin first, ate a cookie, then another, chewing nonstop. Crumbs settled atop her breasts. She brushed them off and said, "Let's go inside."

The dogs followed us in and kept going, into the kitchen. A moment later I heard them slurping. The front room was flat-ceilinged and darkened by drawn shades. It smelled of Crisco and sugar and wet canine. Tan walls, pine floor in need of finishing, odd-sized home-made bookshelves, several instrument cases where a coffee table would have been. A music stand in the corner was stacked with sheet music. The furniture was heavy Depression-era stuff—thrift-shop treasures. On the walls were a Vienna Regulator that had stopped at two o'clock, a framed and glassed Martin guitar poster, and several handbills commemorating the Topanga Fiddle and Banjo Contest.

Ben said, "Have a seat."

Before I could comply, he said, "Sorry to tell you this, friend, but Dawn's dead. Someone killed her. That's why we got freaked out when you mentioned her name, and the other murder. I'm sorry."

He looked down at the muffin plate and shook his head.

"We still haven't gotten it out of our heads," said Bobby. "You can still sit down. If you want to."

She sank into a tired green sofa. Ben sat next to her, balancing the plate on one bony knee.

I lowered myself to a needlepoint chair and said, "When did it happen?"

"A couple of months ago," said Bobby. "March. It was on a weekend—middle of the month, the tenth, I think. No, the ninth." Looking at Ben.

"Something like that," he said.

"I'm pretty sure it was the ninth, babe. It was the weekend of Sonoma, remember? We played on the ninth and came back to L.A. on the tenth—'member how late it was because of the problems with the van in San Simeon? Least that's when he said it happened—the cop. The ninth. It *was* the ninth."

He said, "Yeah, you're right."

She looked at me: "We were out of town—playing a festival up north. Had car trouble, got stuck for a while, and didn't get back till late on the tenth—early morning of the eleventh, actually. There was a cop's business card in the mailbox with a number to call. Homicide detective. We didn't know what to do and didn't call him, but he called us. Told us what happened and asked us lots of questions. We didn't have anything to tell him. The next day he and a couple of other guys came by and went through the house. They had a warrant and everything, but they were okay."

A glance at Ben. He said, "Not too bad."

"They just wanted to go through her stuff, see if they could find anything that might relate. 'Course they didn't—that was no surprise. It didn't happen here and they told us from the beginning they didn't suspect anyone she knew."

"Why's that?"

"He—this detective—said it was . . ." She closed her eyes and reached for a cookie. Managed to find it and ate half.

"According to the cop, it was a sick psycho thing," said Ben. "He said she was really . . ."

Shaking his head.

"A mess," said Bobby.

"They didn't find anything here," said Ben. The two of them looked shaken.

"What a thing to come home to," I said.

"Oh, yeah," said Bobby. "It really scared us—to have it be someone we knew." She reached for another cookie, even though half of the first one was still in her hand.

"Was she your roommate?"

"Tenant," said Bobby. "We own the house." Saying it with wonderment. "We have a spare bedroom, used to use it as a practice room, do some home recording. Then I lost my job over at the day-care center, so we decided to rent it out for the money. Put a card up on the bulletin board at the university 'cause we figured a student might want just a room. Dawn was the first to call."

"How long ago was this?"

"July."

She ate both cookies. Ben patted her thigh and squeezed it gently. The soft flesh cottage-cheesed. She sighed.

"What you said before," he said, "about this medical chart. Was her taking it uncool?"

"She was supposed to return it."

They looked at each other.

"Did she have a 'taking' problem?" I said.

"Well," he said, uncomfortably.

"Not at first," said Bobby. "At first she was a great tenant—cleaned up after herself, minded her own business. Actually, we didn't see her much because we had our day jobs, and then sometimes we'd go out to sing at night. When we didn't, we went to sleep early. She was out all the time—real night owl. It was a pretty good arrangement."

"Only problem," said Ben, "was her coming in at all hours, because Homer's a good watchdog and when she came in he used to bark and wake us up. But we couldn't very well tell her when to come in and out, could we? Mostly, she was okay."

"When did she start taking things?"

"That was later," he said.

"A couple of months after she arrived," said Bobby. "At first we didn't put it together. It was just small stuff—pens, guitar picks. We don't own anything valuable, except the instruments, and stuff gets lost, right? Look at all those one-of-a-kind socks, right? Then it got more obvious. Some cassette tapes, a six-pack of beer—which she could have had if she'd asked. We're pretty free with our food, even though the deal was she was supposed to buy her own. Then some jewelry—a couple pairs of my earrings. And one of Ben's bandannas, plus an antique pair of suspenders he got up in Seattle. Real nice, heavy leather braces, the kind they don't make anymore. The last thing she took was the one that bothered me the most. An old English brooch I got handed down from my grandmother—silver and garnet. The stone was chipped but it had sentimental value. I left it out on the dresser and the next day it was gone."

"Did you ask her about it?" I said.

"I didn't come out and accuse her, but I did ask her if she'd seen it. Or the earrings. She said no, real casual. But we knew it had to be her. Who else could it have been? She's the only other person ever stepped in here, and things never disappeared until she came."

"It must have been an emotional problem," said Ben. "Klepto-mania, or something like that. She couldn't have gotten any serious money for any of it. Not that she needed dough. She had plenty of clothes and a brand-new car."

"What kind of car?"

"One of those little convertibles—a Mazda, I think. She got it after Christmas, didn't have it when she first started living with us or we might have asked for a little more rent, actually. All we charged her was a hundred a month. We thought she was a starving student."

Bobby said, "She definitely had a head problem. I found all the junk she stole out in the garage, buried under the floorboards, in a box, along with a picture of her—like she was trying to stake claim to it, put away a little squirrel's nest or something. To tell the truth, she was greedy, too—I know that's not charitable but it's the truth. It wasn't until later that I put two and two together."

"Greedy in what way?"

"Grabbing the best for herself. Like if there'd be a half-gallon of fudge ripple in the freezer, you'd come back and find all the fudge dug out and just the vanilla left. Or with a bowl of cherries, all the dark ones would be picked out."

"Did she pay her rent on time?"

"More or less. Sometimes she was a week or two late. We never said anything, and she always paid, eventually."

Ben said, "But it was turning into a tense scene."

"We were getting to the point where we would have asked her to leave," said Bobby. "Talked about how to do it for a couple of weeks. Then we got the gig in Sonoma and got all tied up, practicing. Then we came home and . . ."

"Where was she murdered?"

"Somewhere downtown. A club."

"A nightclub?"

Both of them nodded. Bobby said, "From what I gather it was one of those New Wave places. What was the name of it, Ben? Something Indian, right?"

"Mayan," he said. "The Moody Mayan. Or something like that." Thin smile. "The cop asked us if we'd been there. Right."

"Was Dawn a New Waver?"

"Not at first," said Bobby. "I mean, when we met her she was pretty straight-looking. Almost too straight—kind of prim, actually. We thought she might think *we* were too loose. Then gradually she punked up. One thing she was, was smart, I'll tell you that. Always reading textbooks. Studying for a Ph.D. Biomathematics or something like that. But at night she used to change—she'd dress up to go out. That's what Ben meant by her having the clothes—punk stuff, lots of black. She used to smear on that temporary hair dye that washes right out. And all this Addams Family makeup—sometimes she'd mousse up her hair and spike it. Like a costume. The next morning she'd be straight again, going to work. You wouldn't have recognized her."

"Did she actually get killed at this club?"

"I don't know," she said. "We really weren't listening to the details, just wanted the cops to get her stuff out of here, get the whole thing out of our systems."

"Do you remember the detective's name?"

"Gomez," they said in unison.

"Ray Gomez," said Bobby. "He was a Los Lobos fan and he liked doo-wop. Not a bad guy."

Ben nodded. Their knees were pressed up against each other, white from pressure.

"What a thing to happen," she said. "Is this child going to suffer because Dawn stole the chart?"

"We can work around it," I said. "It just would have been nice to have."

"Shame," said Ben. "Sorry we can't help you. The police took all her stuff and I didn't see any medical chart in there. Not that I was looking that close."

"What about the things she stole?"

"No," said Bobby, "no charts there, either. Not too thorough of the cops not to find it, huh? But let me just check, to make sure— maybe inside the flaps or something."

She went into the kitchen and came back shortly with a shoebox and a strip of paper. "Empty—this here's the picture she laid on top. Like she was staking her claim."

I took the photo. One of those black-and-white, four-for-a-quarter self-portraits you get out of a bus terminal machine. Four versions of a face that had once been pretty, now padded with suet and marred by distrust. Straight dark hair, big dark eyes. Bruised eyes. I started to hand it back. Bobby said, "You keep it. I don't want it."

I took another look at the photo before pocketing it. Four identical poses, grim and watchful.

"Sad," I said.

"Yeah," said Bobby, "she never smiled much."

"Maybe," said Ben, "she left it at her office at the U—the chart, I mean."

"Do you know what department she was in?"

"No, but she had an extension there that she gave us. Two-two-three-eight, right?"

"Think so," said Bobby.

I took paper and pen out of my briefcase and copied that down. "She was a doctoral student?"

"That's what she told us when she applied. Biomathematics, or something."

"Did she ever mention her professor's name?"

"She gave a name for a reference," said Bobby, "but to tell the truth we never called it."

Sheepish smile.

"Things were tight," said Ben. "We wanted to get a tenant quickly, and she looked okay."

"The only boss she ever talked about was the guy at the hospital—the one who got killed. But she never mentioned him by name."

Ben nodded. "She didn't like him much."

"Why's that?"

"I dunno. She never went into details—just said he was an asshole, really picky, and she was gonna quit. Then she did, back in February."

"Did she get another job?"

"Not that she told us about," said Bobby.

"Any idea how she paid her bills?"

"Nope, but she always had money to spend."

Ben gave a sick smile.

Bobby said, "What?"

"Her and her boss. She hated him but now they're both in the same boat. L.A. got 'em."

Bobby shuddered and ate a muffin.

Learning about Dawn Herbert's murder and her penchant for stealing got me thinking.

I'd assumed she'd pulled Chad's chart for Laurence Ashmore. But what if she'd done it for herself because she'd learned something damaging to the Jones family and planned to profit from it?

And now she was dead.

I drove to the fish store, bought a forty-pound bag of koi food, and asked if I could use the phone to make a local call. The kid behind the counter thought for a while, looked at the total on the register, and said, "Over there," pointing to an old black dial unit on the wall. Next to it was a big saltwater aquarium housing a small leopard shark. A couple of goldfish thrashed at the water's surface. The shark glided peacefully. Its eyes were steady and blue, almost as pretty as Vicki Bottomley's.

I called Parker Center. The man who answered said Milo wasn't there and he didn't know when he'd be back.

"Is this Charlie?" I said.

"No."

Click.

I dialed Milo's home number. The kid behind the counter was watching me. I smiled and gave him the one-minute index finger while listening to the rings.

Peggy Lee delivered the Blue Investigations pitch. I said, "Dawn Herbert was murdered in March. Probably March 9, somewhere downtown, near a punk music club. The investigating detective was named Ray Gomez. I should be at the hospital within an hour—you can have me paged if you want to talk about it."

I hung up and started walking out. A froth of movement caught the corner of my eye and I turned toward the aquarium. Both the goldfish were gone.

The Hollywood part of Sunset was weekend-quiet. The banks and entertainment firms preceding Hospital Row were closed, and a scatter of poor families and drifters massaged the sidewalk. Auto traffic was thin—mostly weekend workers and tourists who'd gone too far past Vine. I made it to the gate of the doctors' parking structure in less than half an hour. The lot was functioning again. Plenty of spaces.

Before heading up to the wards, I stopped at the cafeteria for coffee.

It was the tail end of lunch hour but the room was nearly empty. Dan Kornblatt was getting change from the cashier just as I stepped up to pay. The cardiologist was carrying a lidded plastic cup. Coffee had leaked out and was running down the cup's sides in mud-colored rivulets. Kornblatt's handlebars drooped and he looked preoccupied. He dropped the change in his pocket and saw me, gave a choppy nod.

"Hey, Dan. What's up?"

My smile seemed to bother him. "Read the paper this morning?" he said.

"Actually," I said, "I just skimmed."

He squinted at me. Definitely peeved. I felt as if I'd gotten the wrong answer on an oral exam.

"What can I say," he snapped, and walked away.

I paid for my coffee and wondered what in the paper was eating him. Looking around the cafeteria for a discarded paper, I failed to spot one. I took a couple of swallows of coffee, tossed the cup, and went to the library's reading room. This time it was locked.

Chappy Ward was deserted and the door to every room but Cassie's was open. Lights off, stripped beds, the tainted meadow smell of fresh deodorization. A man in yellow maintenance scrubs vacuumed the hallway. The piped-in music was something Viennese, slow and syrupy.

Vicki Bottomley sat at the nursing station reading a chart. Her cap sat slightly off-kilter.

I said, "Hi, anything new?"

She shook her head and held out the chart without looking up.

"Go ahead and finish it," I said.

"Finished." She waved the chart.

I took it but didn't open it. Leaning against the counter, I said, "How's Cassie feeling today?"

"Bit better." Still no eye contact.

"When did she wake up?"

"Around nine."

"Dad here yet?"

"It's all in there," she said, keeping her head down and pointing at the chart.

I flipped it open, turned to this morning's pages, and read Al Macauley's summary notes and those of the neurologist.

She picked up some kind of form and began to write.

"Cassie's latest seizure," I said, "sounds like it was a strong one."

"Nothing I haven't seen before."

I put the chart down and just stood there. Finally she looked up. The blue eyes blinked rapidly.

"Have you seen lots of childhood epilepsy?" I said.

"Seen everything. Worked Onco. Took care of babies with brain tumors." Shrug.

"I did oncology, too. Years ago. Psychosocial support."

"Uh-huh." Back to the form.

"Well," I said, "at least Cassie doesn't seem to have a tumor."

No answer.

"Dr. Eves told me she's planning to discharge her soon."

"Uh-huh."

"I thought I'd go out and make a home visit."

Her pen raced.

"You've been out there yourself, haven't you?"

No answer.

I repeated the question. She stopped writing and looked up. "If I have, is there something wrong with that?"

"No, I was just—"

"You were just making talky-talk is what you were doing. Right?" She put the pen down and wheeled backward. A smug smile was on her lips. "Or are you checking me out? Wanting to know if I went out and *did* something to her?"

She wheeled back farther, keeping her eyes on me, still smiling.

"Why would I think that?" I said.

" 'Cause I know the way you people think."

"It was a simple question, Vicki."

"Yeah, right. That's what this has all been about, from the beginning. All this phony talky-talk. You're checking me out to see if I'm like that nurse in New Jersey."

"What nurse is that?"

"The one killed the babies. They wrote a book about it and it was on TV."

"You think you're under suspicion?"

"Aren't I? Isn't it always the nurse who gets blamed?"

"Was the nurse in New Jersey blamed falsely?"

Her smile managed to turn into a grimace without a movement.

"I'm sick of this game," she said, standing and shoving the chair away. "With you people it's always games."

" 'You people' meaning psychologists?"

She folded her hands across her chest and muttered something. Then she turned her back on me.

"Vicki?"

No answer.

"What this is all *about*," I said, fighting to keep my voice even, "is finding out what the hell's going on with Cassie."

She pretended to read the bulletin board behind the desk.

"So much for our little truce," I said.

"Don't worry," she said, turning quickly and facing me. Her voice had risen, a sour reed solo superimposed on the Sacher-torte music.

"Don't worry," she repeated, "I won't get in your way. You want something, just ask. 'Cause you're the *doctor*. And I'll do anything that'll help that poor little baby—contrary to what you think, I *care* about her, okay? Fact is, I'll even go down and get you *coffee* if that impresses you and keeps your attention on her, where it should be. I'm not one of those *feminists* think it's a sin to do something other than push meds. But don't pretend to be my *friend*, okay? Let's both of us just do our jobs without talky-talk, and go about our merry ways, okay? And in answer to your question, I was out at the house exactly two times—months ago. Okay?"

She walked to the opposite end of the station, found another form, picked it up and began reading. Squinting, she held it at arm's length. She needed reading glasses. The smug smile returned.

I said, "*Are* you doing something to her, Vicki?"

Her hands jerked and the paper dropped. She bent to pick it up and her cap fell off. Bowing a second time, she retrieved it and stood up rigidly. She was wearing a lot of mascara and a couple of specks had come loose below one eye.

I didn't budge.

"No!" A whisper with lots of force behind it.

Footsteps turned both of our heads. The maintenance man came out into the hall, pulling his vacuum. He was middle-aged and Hispanic, with old eyes and a Cantinflas mustache.

"Sumtin' else?" he said.

"No," said Vicki. "*Go.*"

He looked at her, raised an eyebrow, then yanked on the machine and towed it toward the teak doors. Vicki watched him, hands clenched.

When he was gone, she said, "That was a *horrible* question! Why do you have to think such *ugly* thoughts—why does *any*one have to be *doing* anything to her? She's sick!"

"All her symptoms are some sort of mystery illness?"

"Why *not*?" she said. "Why not? This is a hospital. That's what we get here—sick *kids*. That's what *real* doctors do. Treat sick *kids*."

I maintained my silence.

Her arms began to rise and she fought to keep them down, like a subject resisting a hypnotist. Where the cap had been, her stiff hair had bunched in a hat-sized dome.

I said, "The real doctors aren't having much luck, are they?"

She exhaled through her nose.

"Games," she said, whispering again. "Always games with you people."

"You seem to know a lot about us people."

She looked startled and swiped at her eyes. Her mascara had started to run and the knuckles came away gray but she didn't notice them; her glare was fixed on me.

I met it, absorbed it.

The smug smile came back on her face. "Is there anything else you want, *sir*?" She pulled bobby pins out of her hair and used them to fasten the wedge of white starch.

"Have you told the Joneses your feelings about therapists?" I said.

"I keep my feelings to myself. I'm a professional."

"Have you told them someone suspects foul play?"

"Of course not. Like I said, I'm a professional!"

"A professional," I said. "You just don't like therapists. Bunch of quacks who promise to help but don't come through."

Her head jerked back. The hat bobbled and one hand shot up to keep it in place.

"You don't know me," she said. "You don't know anything about me."

"That's true," I lied. "And that's become a problem for Cassie."

"That's ridic—"

"Your behavior's getting in the way of her care, Vicki. Let's not discuss it out here anymore." I pointed to the nurse's room behind the station.

She slammed her hands on her hips. "For what?"

"A discussion."

"You have no right."

"Actually, I do. And the only reason you're still on the case is through my good graces. Dr. Eves admires your technical skills but your attitude's getting on her nerves, as well."

"Right."

I picked up the phone. "Call her."

She sucked in her breath. Touched her cap. Licked her lips. "What do you *want* from me?" Trace of whine.

"Not out here," I said. "In there, Vicki. Please."

She started to protest. No words came out. A tremor surged across her lips. She put a hand up to cover it.

"Let's just drop it," she said. "I'm sorry, okay?"

Her eyes were full of fear. Remembering her final view of her son and feeling like a louse, I shook my head.

"No more hassles," she said. "I promise—I really mean it this time. You're right, I *shouldn't* have mouthed off. It's because I'm worried about her, same as you. I'll be fine. Sorry. It won't happen again—"

"Please, Vicki." I pointed to the nurse's room.

"—I swear. Come on, cut me a little slack."

I held my ground.

She moved toward me, hands fisted, as if ready to strike. Then she dropped them. Turned suddenly, and walked to the room. Moving slowly, shoulders down, barely lifting her shoes from the carpet.

The room was furnished with an orange Naugahyde couch and matching chair, and a coffee table. A phone sat on the table next to an unplugged coffee maker that hadn't been used or cleaned in a long time. Cat and puppy posters were taped to the wall above a bumper sticker that read NURSES DO IT WITH TENDER LOVING CARE.

I closed the door and sat on the couch.

"This stinks," she said, without conviction. "You have no right— I *am* calling Dr. Eves."

I picked up the phone, called the page operator and asked for Stephanie.

"Wait," she said. "Hang up."

I canceled the page and replaced the receiver. She did a little toe-heel dance, finally sank into the chair, fiddling with her cap, both feet flat on the ground. I noticed something I hadn't seen before: a tiny daisy drawn in nail polish marker, on her new badge, just above her photo. The polish was starting to flake and the flower looked shredded.

She put her hands in her spreading lap. A condemned-prisoner look filled her face.

"I have work to do," she said. "Still have to change the sheets, check to make sure Dietary gets the dinner order right."

"The nurse in New Jersey," I said. "What made you bring that up?"

"Still on that?"

I waited.

"No big deal," she said. "I told you, there was a book and I read it, that's all. I don't like to read those kinds of things usually, but someone gave it to me, so I read it. Okay?"

She was smiling, but suddenly her eyes had filled with tears. She flailed at her face, trying to dry it with her fingers. I looked around the room. No tissues. My handkerchief was clean and I gave it to her.

She looked at it, ignored it. Her face stayed wet, mascara tracing black cat-scratches through the impasto of her makeup.

"Who gave you the book?" I said.

Her face clogged with pain. I felt as if I'd stabbed her.

"It had nothing to do with Cassie. Believe me."

"Okay. What exactly did this nurse do?"

"Poisoned babies—with lidocaine. But she was no nurse. Nurses love kids. Real nurses." Her eyes shifted to the bumper sticker on the wall and she cried harder.

When she stopped, I held out the handkerchief again. She pretended it wasn't there. "What do you *want* from me?"

"Some honesty—"

"About what?"

"All the hostility I've been getting from you—"

"I said I was sorry about that."

"I don't need an apology, Vicki. My honor isn't the issue and we don't have to be buddies—make talky-talk. But we do have to communicate well enough to take care of Cassie. And your behavior's getting in the way."

"I disag—"

"It *is,* Vicki. And I know it can't be anything I've said or done because you were hostile before I opened my mouth. So it's obvious you have something against psychologists, and I suspect it's because they've failed you—or mistreated you."

"What are you doing? Analyzing me?"

"If I need to."

"That's not fair."

"If you want to keep working the case, let's get it out in the open. Lord knows it's difficult enough as is. Cassie's getting sicker each time she comes in; no one knows what the hell's going on. A few more seizures like the one you saw and she could be at risk for some serious brain damage. We can't afford to get distracted by interpersonal crap."

Her lip shook and scooted forward.

"There's no need," she said, "to swear."

"Sorry. Besides my foul mouth, what do you have against me?"

"Nothing."

"Baloney, Vicki."

"There's really no—"

"You don't like shrinks," I said, "and my intuition is you've got a good reason."

She sat back. "That so?"

I nodded. "There are plenty of bad ones out there, happy to take your money without doing anything for you. I happen not to *be* one of them but I don't expect you to believe that just because I say so."

She screwed up her mouth. Relaxed it. Puckers remained above her upper lip. Her face was streaked and smudged and weary and I felt like the Grand Inquisitor.

"On the other hand," I said, "maybe it's just me you resent— some sort of turf thing over Cassie, your wanting to be the boss."

"That's not it at *all*!"

"Then what *is* it, Vicki?"

She didn't answer. Looked down at her hands. Used a nail to push back a cuticle. Her expression was blank but the tears hadn't stopped.

"Why not get it out into the open and be done with it?" I said. "If it's not related to Cassie, it won't leave this room."

She sniffed and pinched the tip of her nose.

I moved forward and softened my tone: "Look, this needn't be a marathon. I'm not out to expose you in any way. All I want to do is clear the air—work out a real truce."

"Won't leave this room, huh?" Return of the smug smile. "I've heard that before."

Our eyes met. Hers blinked. Mine didn't waver.

Suddenly her arms flew upward, hands scissoring. Ripping her cap from her hair, she hurled it across the room. It landed on the floor. She started to get up, but didn't.

"Damn you!" she said. The top of her head was a bird's nest.

I'd folded the handkerchief and rested it on one of my knees. Such a neat boy, the Inquisitor.

She put her hands to her temples.

I got up and placed a hand on her shoulder, certain she'd fling it off. But she didn't.

"I'm sorry," I said.

She sobbed and started to talk, and I had nothing to do but listen.

She told only part of it. Ripping open old wounds while struggling to hold on to some dignity.

The felonious Reggie transformed into an "active boy with school problems."

"He was smart enough, but he just couldn't find anything that interested him and his mind used to wander all over the place."

The boy growing into a "restless" young man who "just couldn't seem to settle down."

Years of petty crime reduced to "some problems."

She sobbed some more. This time she took my handkerchief.

Weeping and whispering the punch line: her only child's death at nineteen, due to "an accident."

Relieved of his secret, the Inquisitor held his tongue.

She was silent for a long time, dried her eyes, wiped her face, then began talking again:

Alcoholic husband upgraded to blue-collar hero. Dead at thirty-eight, the victim of "high cholesterol."

"Thank God we owned the house," she said. "Besides that, the only other thing Jimmy left us worth anything was an old Harley-Davidson motorcycle—one of those choppers. He was always tinkering with that thing, making a mess. Putting Reggie on the back and racing through the neighborhood. He used to call it his hog. Till Reggie was four he actually thought that's what a hog was."

Smiling.

"It was the first thing I sold," she said. "I didn't want Reggie getting ideas that it was his birthright to just go out and crack himself up on the freeway. He always liked speed. Just like his dad. So I sold it to one of the doctors where I worked—over at Foothill General. I'd worked there before Reggie was born. After Jimmy died, I had to go back there again."

I said, "Pediatrics?"

She shook her head. "General ward—they didn't do peds there. I would have preferred peds, but I needed a place that was close to home, so I could be close to Reggie—he was ten but he still wasn't good by himself. I wanted to be home when he was. So I worked nights. Used to put him in at nine, wait till he was asleep, grab a nap for an hour, then go off at ten forty-five so I could be on shift by eleven."

She waited for judgment.

The Inquisitor didn't oblige.

"He was all alone," she said. "Every night. But I figured with him sleeping it would be okay. What they call latchkey now, but they didn't have a name for it back then. There was no choice—I had no one to help me. No family, no such thing as day care back then. You could only get all-night babysitters from an agency and they charged as much as I was making."

She dabbed at her face. Looked at the poster again, and forced back tears.

"I never stopped worrying about that boy. But after he grew up he accused me of not caring about him, saying I left him because I didn't care. He even got on me for selling his dad's bike—making it into a mean thing instead of because I cared."

I said, "Raising a kid alone," and shook my head in what I hoped was sympathy.

"I used to *race* home at seven in the morning, hoping he'd still be asleep and I could wake him up and pretend I'd been there with him all night. In the beginning it worked, but pretty soon he caught on and he'd start to hide from me. Like a game—locking himself in the bathroom . . ." She mashed the handkerchief and a terrible look came onto her face.

"It's okay," I said. "You don't have to——"

"You don't have kids. You don't understand what it's like. When he was older—a teenager—he'd stay out all night, never calling in, sometimes for a couple days at a time. When I grounded him, he'd sneak out anyway. Any punishment I tried, he just laughed. When I tried to talk to him about it, he threw it back in my face. My working and leaving him. Tit for tat: *you* went out—now *I* go out. He never . . ."

She shook her head.

"Never got a lick of help," she said. "Not one single lick . . . from any of them. *Your* crowd, the experts. Counselors, special-ed experts, you name it. Everyone was an expert except me. 'Cause I was the *problem,* right? They were all good at blaming. Real experts at that. Not that any of them could help him—he couldn't learn a thing in school. It got worse and worse each year and all I got was the runaround. Finally, I took him to . . . one of you. Private clown. All the way over in Encino. Not that I could afford it."

She spat out a name I didn't recognize.

I said, "Never heard of him."

"Big office," she said. "View of the mountains and all these little dolls in the bookshelf instead of books. Sixty dollars an hour, which was a lot back then. Still is . . . specially for a total waste of time. Two years of fakery is what I got."

"Where'd you find him?"

"He came recommended—*highly* recommended—from one of the doctors at Foothill. And I thought he was pretty smart myself, at first. He spent a couple of weeks with Reggie, not telling me anything, then called me in for a conference and told me how Reggie had serious problems because of the way he'd grown up. Said it was gonna take a long time to fix it but he would fix it. *If.* Whole list of *if*s. *If* I didn't put any pressure on Reggie to perform. *If* I respected Reggie as a person. Respected his *confidentiality.* I said what's my part in all this? He said paying the bills and minding my own business. Reggie had to develop his own responsibility—long as I did it for him he'd never straighten out. Not that he kept what *I* said to *him* about Reggie confidential. Two years I paid that faker and at the end of it I got a boy who hated me because of what that man put in his head. It wasn't till later that I found out he'd repeated everything I'd told him. Blown it way up and made it worse."

"Did you complain?"

"Why? *I* was the stupid one. For believing. You wanna know how stupid? After . . . after Reggie . . . after he had his . . . after he was . . . gone—a *year* after, I went to another one. Of your crowd. Because my supervisor thought I should—not that she'd pay for it. And not that I wasn't doing my job properly, 'cause I was. But I wasn't sleeping well or eating or enjoying anything. It wasn't like being alive at all. So she gave me a referral. I figured maybe a woman would be a better judge of character. . . . *This* joker was in Beverly *Hills*. Hundred and *twenty* an hour. Inflation, right? Not that the value went up. Though in the beginning this one seemed even more on the ball than the first one. Quiet. Polite. A real gentleman. And he seemed to understand. I felt . . . talking to him made me feel better. In the beginning. I started to be able to work again. Then . . ."

She stopped, clamping her mouth shut. Shifting her attention from me to the walls to the floor to the handkerchief in her hand. Staring at the sodden cloth with surprise and revulsion.

She dropped it as if it were lice-ridden.

"Forget it," she said. "Water under the dam."

I nodded.

She tossed the handkerchief at me and I caught it.

She said, "Baseball Bob," with reflexive quickness. Laughed. Shut it off.

I put the handkerchief on the table. "Baseball Bob?"

"We used to say that," she said defensively. "Jimmy and me and Reggie. When Reggie was little. When someone would make a good catch, he was Baseball Bob—it was stupid."

"In my family it was 'You can be on my team.' "

"Yeah, I've heard that one."

We sat in silence, resigned to each other, like boxers in the thirteenth round.

She said, "That's it. My secrets. Happy?"

The phone rang. I picked it up. The operator said, "Dr. Delaware, please?"

"Speaking."

"There's a call for you from a Dr. Sturgis. He's been paging you for the last ten minutes."

Vicki stood.

I motioned her to wait. "Tell him I'll call him back."

I hung up. She remained on her feet.

"That second therapist," I said. "He abused you, didn't he?"

"Abuse?" The word seemed to amuse her. "What? Like some kind of abused child?"

"It's pretty much the same thing, isn't it?" I said. "Breaking a trust?"

"Breaking a trust, huh? How about blowing it *up*? But that's okay. I learned from it—it made me stronger. Now I watch myself."

"You never complained about him either?"

"Nope. Told you I'm stupid."

"I—"

"Sure," she said. "That's all I needed, his word against mine— who're they gonna believe? He'd get lawyers to go into my life and dig it all up—Reggie. Probably get *experts* to say I was a liar and a rotten mother . . ." Tears. "I wanted my boy to rest in peace, okay? Even though . . ."

She threw up her hands, put her palms together.

"Even though what, Vicki?"

"Even though he never gave *me* peace." Her voice soared in pitch, teetering on hysteria.

"He blamed me till the *end*. Never got rid of those feelings that first faker planted in his head. *I* was the bad one. *I'd* never cared about him. *I'd* made him not learn, not do his homework. *I* didn't force him to go to school because I didn't care a hoot. It was 'cause of me he dropped out and started . . . running around with bad influences and . . . I was one hundred percent of it, hundred and five. . . ."

She let out a laugh that raised the hair on the back of my neck.

"Wanna hear something *confidential*—kind of stuff *you* people like to hear? *He* was the one gave me that book about that bitch from New Jersey. *That* was his Mother's Day gift to me, okay? All wrapped up in a little box with ribbons and the word *Mom* on it. In printing, 'cause he couldn't do cursive, never mastered it—even his printing was all crooked, like a first-grader's. He hadn't given me a present for years, not since he stopped bringing home his shop projects. But there it was, little gift-wrapped package, and inside this little used paperback book on dead babies. I nearly threw up, but I read it anyway. Trying to see if there was something I'd missed. That he was trying to tell me something I wasn't getting. But there wasn't. It was just plain ugly. She was a monster. No real nurse. And one thing I know—one thing I've worked into my own head, without experts—is that she has nothing to do with me, okay? She and me didn't even live on the same planet. I make kids feel *better*. I'm *good* at that. And I never hurt them, okay? *Never.* And I'm gonna keep helping them the rest of my natural life."

"Can I go now?" she said. "I'd like to wash my face."

Unable to think of a reason to keep her there, I said, "Sure."

She righted her cap. "Listen, I don't need any more grief, okay? The main thing is for Cassie to get better. Not that . . ." She colored and began walking to the door.

"Not that I can do any good in that department?" I said.

"I *meant,* not that it's gonna be *easy.* If you're the one ends up diagnosing her, hats off to you."

"What do you think about the fact that the doctors can't find anything?"

Her hand rested on the doorknob. "Doctors can't find lots of things. If patients knew how much guessing goes on, they'd . . ." She stopped. "I keep on, I'm gonna get myself in trouble again."

"Why are you so certain it's organic?"

"Because what else could it be? These aren't *abusers.* Cindy's one of the best mothers I've ever seen, and Dr. Jones is a real gentleman. And despite *who* they are, you'd never know it, because they don't lord it over anyone, okay? That's *real* class, far as I'm concerned. Go out and see for yourself—they love that little girl. It's just a matter of time."

"Before what?"

"Before someone figures out what's *wrong*. I've seen it lots of times. Doctors can't figure things out so they call it psychosomatic. Then poof, all of a sudden someone finds something that hasn't been looked for before and you've got yourself a new disease. They call that medical progress."

"What do you call it?"

She stared at me. "I call it progress too."

She walked away and I stayed behind, thinking. I'd gotten her to talk but had I learned anything?

My thoughts shifted to the cruel gift her son had given her. Pure spite? Or had he been telling her something?

Had she told *me* about it as part of a game? Told me just what she wanted me to know?

I stayed with it a while and came up with nothing. Cleared my head and walked to 505 W.

Cassie sat propped up in bed, wearing red floral pajamas with white collar and cuffs. Her cheeks were raspberry-pink and her hair was gathered in a topknot tied with a white bow. The I.V. had been disconnected and it stood in the corner, like a metal scarecrow. Depleted glucose bags hung from the arms. The only evidence her veins had been punctured was a small round Band-Aid atop one hand and the yellow Betadine stain below it. Her eyes glistened as they followed me.

Cindy sat near her on the bed, spoon-feeding her cereal. She wore a SAVE THE OCEANS T-shirt over a denim skirt and sandals. Dolphins cavorted across her bustline. She and Cassie looked more similar than ever.

As I approached, Cassie opened a mouth full of cereal-mush. A stray speck dotted her upper lip.

Cindy picked it off. "Swallow, honey. Hi, Dr. Delaware. We didn't expect to see you today."

I put my briefcase down and sat on the foot of the bed. Cassie looked confused but not fearful.

"Why's that?" I said.

"It's the weekend."

"You're here, so I'm here."

"That's very nice of you. Look, sweetie, Dr. Delaware came all the way to see you on a Saturday."

Cassie looked at Cindy, then back at me, still muddled.

Wondering about the mental effects of the seizure, I said, "How's everything?"

"Oh, fine."

I touched Cassie's hand. She didn't move for a second, then drew away, slowly. When I chucked her chin, she looked down at my hand.

"Hi, Cassie," I said.

She continued to stare. Some milk dribbled out of her mouth. Cindy wiped it and closed her mouth gently. Cassie started to chew. Then she parted her lips and said, "Hah," through the mush.

"Right!" said Cindy. "*Hi!* That's great, Cass!"

"Hah."

"We did very well with our food today, Dr. Delaware. Juice and fruit and crackers for breakfast. Then we had our breakfast Krispies for lunch."

"Great."

"Real great." Her voice was tight.

Remembering the short-lived moment of tension last time I'd talked to her—the feeling that she was about to tell me something important—I said, "Is there anything you want to discuss with me?"

She touched Cassie's hair. Cassie started to play with another drawing. "No, I don't think so."

"Dr. Eves tells me you'll be going home soon."

"That's what she says." She adjusted Cassie's topknot. "I'm sure looking forward to it."

"Bet you are," I said. "No more doctors for a while."

She looked at me. "The doctors have been great. I know they're doing their best."

"You've seen some of the best," I agreed. "Bogner, Torgeson, Macauley, Dawn Herbert."

No reaction.

"Got anything planned when you get back home?"

"Just getting back to normal."

Wondering what that meant, I said, "I'd like to come out pretty soon."

"Oh—of course. You can draw with Cassie at her play table. I'm sure we can find a chair to fit you—can't we, Cass?"

"Fip."

"Right! Fi*t*."

"*Fip.*"

"Excellent, Cass. Do you want Dr. Delaware to draw with you at your little bear table?" When Cassie didn't answer she said, "Draw? Draw pictures?" and made scrawling motions with one hand.

"Daw."

"Yes, draw. With Dr. Delaware."

Cassie looked at her, then me. Then she nodded. Then she smiled.

I stayed awhile, providing entertainment and looking for signs of post-seizural damage. Cassie seemed okay but I knew brain effects could be subtle. For the thousandth time I wondered what was going on in her little body.

Cindy was friendly enough, but I couldn't shake the feeling that her enthusiasm for my services had waned. She sat on the sleeper, brushing out her hair while scanning *TV Guide.* The hospital air was cool and dry and the hair crackled with each stroke. Northern light came in through the room's single window, a straw-colored beam that burned through the smog and burst against the fairy-tale wallpaper. The lower edge of the beam touched upon the long dark strands, tracing a metallic streak through them.

It created an odd cosmetic effect and made her look beautiful. I'd never thought of her as desirable—too busy wondering if she was a monster. But seeing her gilded that way made me realize how little she exploited her looks.

Before I could mull that any longer, the door swung open and Chip came in, carrying coffee. He had on navy sweats and running shoes and his hair looked freshly washed. A diamond sparkled in his ear.

His greeting was tavern-buddy friendly but a ribbon of steel ran through the amiability—resistance not unlike Cindy's. It made me wonder if the two of them had discussed me. When he sat down between Cassie and me I got up and said, "See you later."

No one argued, though Cassie kept looking at me. I smiled at her. She stared a while longer before shifting her attention to a drawing. I collected my stuff and headed for the door.

"Bye, Dr. Delaware," said Cindy.

"Bye," said Chip. "Thanks for everything."

I looked over his shoulder at Cassie. Waved at her. She raised a hand and curled her fingers. The topknot was in disarray again. I wanted to swoop her up and take her home with me.

"Bye, sweetie."

"Bah."

I had to get away from the hospital.

Feeling like a teething puppy with nothing to chomp, I turned out of the lot and drove up Hillhurst, heading for a restaurant at the top of the street that I'd learned about from Milo but never went to alone. Continental food of the old school, autographed photos of near-celebrities, dark panel walls saturated with nicotine bitters, waiters without SAG cards.

A sign in the lobby said the restaurant wouldn't be serving for another half hour but the cocktail lounge was accepting sandwich orders.

A middle-aged, tuxedoed woman with improbable red hair worked behind the bar. A few serious drinkers sat at the padded horseshoe chewing ice cubes, snuffling salted freebies, and devoting what little attention they had left to an auto-chase scene on the tube. The TV was mounted on a ceiling bracket. It reminded me of the one I'd just seen in Cassie's room.

The hospital . . . dominating my thoughts the way it had years ago. I loosened my tie, sat down, and ordered a club sandwich and beer. When the bartender turned to prepare it, I went to the pay phone at the back of the lounge and called Parker Center.

"Records," said Milo.

"*Doctor* Sturgis?"

"Well, if it isn't *Doctor* Hard-to-Get. Yeah, I figured easiest way to get some action in that place was use the title."

"If only it were so," I said. "Sorry for the delay getting back to you but I was tied up with Vicki Bottomley, then Cassie and her parents."

"Anything new?"

"Not much, except the Joneses seemed a little cool."

"Maybe you're threatening them. Getting too close."

"Can't see why. As for Vicki, she and I had a little psychodrama—I was trying to clear the air, leaned on her a bit. She accused me of suspecting her of harming Cassie. So I asked her if she was, and she went nuclear. Ended up giving me a sanitized version of her son's story and adding something I hadn't known: Reggie gave her a book as a Mother's Day gift. True-crime thing about some nurse in New Jersey who murdered babies."

"Some gift. Think she was trying to tell you something?"

"I don't know. Maybe I should tell Stephanie to pull her off the case and see what happens. If *Stephanie* can be trusted. Meanwhile, this Dawn Herbert thing. On top of being murdered, she was a bit of a kleptomaniac."

I gave him my blackmail theory. "What do you think?"

"Uh-huh . . . well," he said, clearing his throat, "that's certainly a good question, sir, but that information's not currently available on our present data base."

"Bad time to talk?"

"Yes, sir. Right away, sir." A moment later, he lowered his voice: "Brass coming through on tour, some kind of police-biggie convention this weekend. I'm off in five minutes. How about late lunch, early dinner—let's say half an hour?"

"Started without you," I said.

"What a pal. Where are you?"

I told him.

Still talking quietly, he said, "Good. Order me a pea soup with a ham bone and the breast of chicken with the cornbread stuffing, extra stuffing."

"They're only making sandwiches right now."

"By the time I get there, they'll be serving real food. Tell 'em it's for me. Remember the order?"

"Soup, bone, chicken, extra stuffing."

"They ever remake *The Thirty-nine Steps,* you can play Mr. Memory. Have 'em time the order so nothing's cold. Also a dark draft. The Irish stuff—they'll know what I mean."

I returned to the bar, relayed Milo's order to the bartender, and told her to delay my sandwich until he arrived. She nodded, called the kitchen, then served my beer with a dish of almonds. I asked her if she had a newspaper.

"Sorry," she said, glancing toward the barflies. "No one around here reads. Try the machines out front."

I went back to Hillhurst and caught a faceful of sunglare. Four coin-op newspaper dispensers lined the sidewalk. Three were empty; one of them was vandalized and graffitied. The last one was fully stocked with a tabloid promising SAFE SEX, RAUNCHY GIRLS, AND DIRTY FUN.

I went back into the lounge. The channel had been switched to an old western. Square jaws, moping dogies, and long shots of scrubland. The barflies stared up at the screen, entranced. As if it hadn't been filmed just over the hill, in Burbank.

Thirty-six minutes later Milo appeared, waving me over as he strode past the bar, toward the restaurant section. I took my beer and caught up with him. His jacket was over his shoulder and his tie was tucked into his waistband. The band was crushed by the weight of his belly. A couple of the lushes looked up and watched him, dulled, but still wary. He never noticed. But I knew he would've been pleased to see how much cop-scent he still gave off.

The main dining room was empty except for a busboy running a manual carpet-sweeper over a corner. A stringy old waiter appeared—American Gothic on a crash diet—bearing soft rolls, Milo's ale, and a plate of cherry peppers and stuffed olives.

"Him, too, Irv," said Milo.

"Certainly, Mr. Sturgis."

When the waiter left, Milo touched my beer glass and said, "You're replacing that with dark draft, lad. From the weariness in your eyes, I'd say you've earned it."

"Gee, thanks, Dad. Can I have a two-wheeler without training wheels too?"

He grinned, tugged his tie lower, then loosened the knot completely and pulled it off. Running his hand over his face, he sat back in the booth and snorted.

"How'd you find out about Herbert's murder?" he said.

"From her former landlords." I summarized my talk with Bobby and Ben Murtaugh.

"They seem on the level?"

I nodded. "They're still pretty shaken."

"Well," he said, "there's nothing new on the case. She's on file as a Central Division open. The overall picture is a sadistic-psycho thing. Very little physical evidence."

"Another low-probability one?"

"Uh-huh. Best bet on these wacko ones is the bad guy does it again and gets caught. Nasty one, too. She was hit over the head, had her throat cut and something wooden shoved up her vagina—coroner found splinters. That's about all they've got physically. It happened near a punk club operating out of a garment contractor's place in the Union District. Not far from the Convention Center."

"The Moody Mayan," I said.

"Where'd you hear that?"

"The Murtaughs."

"They got it half right," he said. "It was the Mayan *Mortgage*. Place went out of business a couple of weeks later."

"Because of the murder?"

"Hell, no. If anything, that would have helped business. We're talking the night-crawler scene, Alex. Spoiled kids from Brentwood and Beverly Hills putting on *Rocky Horror Show* duds and playing 'Look, Mom, no common sense.' Blood and entrails—someone *else's*—would be just what they're looking for."

"That fits with what the Murtaughs said about Herbert. Grad student by day, but she used to punk herself up at night. Used the kind of hair dye that washes out the next morning."

"L.A. shuffle," he said. "Nothing's what it seems. . . . Anyway, the place probably closed down because that crowd gets bored easily—the whole kick is to move from place to place. Kind of a metaphor for life itself, huh?"

I did a finger-down-the-throat pantomime.

He laughed.

I said, "Do you know this particular club?"

"No, but they're all the same—fly-by-night setups, no occupancy permits, no liquor licenses. Sometimes they take over an abandoned building and don't bother to pay rent. By the time the landlord catches on or the fire department gets around to shutting them down, they're gone. What'll change it is a couple hundred clowns getting roasted."

He raised his glass and buried his upper lip in foam. He wiped it and said, "According to Central, one of the bartenders saw Herbert leave the club shortly before two A.M. with a guy. He recognized her because she'd been dancing at the club and was one of the few heavyset girls they let in. But he couldn't give any specifics on the guy other than that he was straight-looking and older than her. The time frame fits with the coroner's ETD of between two and four. The coroner also found cocaine and booze in her system."

"A lot?"

"Enough to dull her judgment. If she had any in the first place—which is doubtful, seeing as she was traipsing around the Union District in the wee hours, all alone."

"The landlords said she was smart—Ph.D. student in biomath."

"Yeah. Well, there's smart and there's smart. The actual killing took place on a side street a couple of blocks away from the club. In that little Mazda of hers. The keys were still in the ignition."

"She was killed in the car?"

"Right in the driver's seat, judging from the spatter pattern. Afterward, she slumped across both seats. The body was found just after sunrise by a couple of garment workers arriving for the early shift. Blood had seeped through the door and into the street. The slant of the street made it run down into the curb and pool. It was the pool they noticed."

The waiter brought my ale, a bowl of soup oysters, and Milo's pea soup. He waited while Milo tasted. Milo said, "Perfect, Irv," and the old man nodded and disappeared.

Milo took a couple more spoonfuls, licked his lips, and spoke through the steam. "The Mazda's convertible top was up but there was no blood on the headliner, so the coroner's certain the top was down when it happened. The spatter pattern also indicates that whoever did it was outside the car, standing on the driver's side. Standing over her, maybe a foot or two behind her. He hit her on the head. From the skull damage it must've knocked her out, may even have killed her. Then he used some kind of blade to sever her jugular and her windpipe. Once that was done, he did the mechanical rape, so maybe we've got ourselves a necrophile."

"Sounds like overkill," I said. "Some kind of frenzy."

"Or thoroughness," he said, sipping soup. "He was cool enough to raise the top."

"Was she seen dancing with anyone in the club?"

"Nothing on record. Only reason the bartender remembered her leaving was he was on a smoke break, just outside."

"He wasn't considered a suspect?"

"Nope. Tell you one thing, the asshole who did it came prepared—think about all those weapons. We're talking a predator, Alex. Maybe someone watching the club, prowling the area 'cause he knows there's lots of women around. He waits until he sees exactly what he's been looking for. Lone target, maybe a certain physical type, maybe he's just decided tonight's the night. With the added bonus of a *convertible* on a quiet, dark street. With the *top* down. Which is like 'You are cordially invited to assault me.' "

"Makes sense," I said, feeling my gorge rise.

"A grad student, huh? Too bad she flunked Logic One-A. I'm not trying to blame the victim, Alex, but add the dope and booze to her behavioral pattern and it doesn't sound like a lady with strong instincts for self-preservation. What'd she steal?"

As I told him, he ate more soup, used his spoon to wedge marrow out of the bone, and ate that too.

I said, "The Murtaughs said she seemed to have plenty of money even after she quit her job. And you've just added cocaine to her budget. So blackmail makes some sense, doesn't it? She latches on to the fact that one Jones kid died and the other keeps coming back into the hospital with unexplained illnesses. She steals the evidence and tries to exploit it. And now she's dead. Just like Ashmore."

He put his glass down slowly. "Big leap, from petty pilfering to putting the squeeze on biggies, Alex. And there's no reason, from the facts of the case, to think a psycho didn't cut her up. In terms of where she got her money, we still don't know her family didn't give it to her. For that matter, the coke could have been asset, not a debit—maybe she *dealt* dope, too."

"If she had family money, why would she rent a cheap single room from the Murtaughs?"

"Slumming. We already know she played roles—the whole punk bit. And the thefts she pulled on her landlords were illogical, not for profit. Exactly the kind of thing that's likely to get discovered. She comes across *disorganized* to me, Alex. Not the type to plan and execute a high-level blackmail scheme."

"No one said she was good at it. Look at the way she ended up."

He looked around the empty room as if suddenly concerned about being overheard. He drained his ale glass, then lifted his spoon and pushed the soup bone around his bowl like a kid playing toy boat in a tiny green harbor.

"The way she ended up," he finally said. "So who killed her? Daddy? Mommy? Grandpa?"

"Wouldn't you say hired help? Those types don't do their own dirty work."

"Hired to slice her and do a mechanical rape?"

"Hired to make it look like a 'psycho thing' that'll never get solved unless the psycho does it again. Hell, maybe Ashmore was involved, too, and the same guy was paid to set up a phony mugging."

"Imaginative," he said. "You just sat there with those people, playing with their kid, making chitchat, and thinking all this?"

"You think I'm totally off-base?"

He ate more soup before answering. "Listen, Alex, I've known you long enough to appreciate the way your mind works. I just don't think you have much more than fantasy at this point."

"Maybe so," I said. "But it sure beats thinking about Cassie and everything we're not doing for her."

The rest of the food came. I watched him carve up his chicken. He took a long time to section the meat, showing more surgical skill and deliberation than I'd ever seen before.

"Phony psycho job on Herbert," he said. "Phony mugging for Ashmore."

"He was Herbert's boss. Owned the computers and had done a toxicology check on Chad Jones. It was logical to think he knew whatever Herbert did. Even if he didn't, whoever killed her might have taken care of him, too, just to be careful."

"Why would he be involved in blackmail? He *was* independently wealthy."

"He invested in real estate," I said, "and the market's sliding. What if he was leveraged to the hilt? Or maybe he hadn't quit gambling, as his wife believed. Lost big at the tables and needed some cash. Rich folk can get poor, right? The L.A. shuffle."

"If Ashmore was in on it—and I'm just playing along at this point—why would he want Herbert for a partner?"

"Who says he did? She could have found out on her own— gotten hold of his computer data and decided to free-lance."

He said nothing. Wiped his lips with his napkin, even though he hadn't eaten any chicken.

I said, "One problem, though. Ashmore was killed two months after Herbert. If their murders are related, why take so long to eliminate him?"

He tapped his fingers on the table. "Well . . . another way to look at it is, Ashmore had no knowledge of what Herbert was up to at first, but found out later. From data *she'd* stashed in the computer. And he either tried to capitalize on it, or told the wrong person."

"You know, that dovetails with something I saw the other day. Huenengarth—the head of Security—removing Ashmore's computers the morning after Ashmore's murder. My first impression was he was getting hold of Ashmore's equipment. But maybe what Huenengarth was really after was *in* the machines. The data. He works for Plumb—meaning he really works for Chuck Jones. Guy's a real corporate henchman type, Milo. Plus, his name came up yesterday when I was speaking to Mrs. Ashmore. He was the one who called to offer the hospital's sympathies. Was coming by with the UNICEF certificate and the plaque. Strange job for head of Security, wouldn't you say? Unless his real intention was to learn if Ashmore kept a computer at home and, if he did, to get it out of there."

Milo looked down at his plate. Finally ate. Quickly, mechanically, without much apparent pleasure. I knew how much food meant to him and felt bad for ruining his dinner.

"Intriguing," he said, "but it's still one big *if.*"

"You're right," I said. "Let's give it a rest."

He put his fork down. "There's a basic flaw with all of it, Alex. If Grandpa knew about Junior and/or Mrs. Junior killing Chad, and cared enough about hushing it up to pay blackmail money *and* hire a killer, why would he allow Cassie to be brought back to the same hospital?"

"Maybe he didn't know, until Herbert and/or Ashmore put the arm on him."

"Even so. Why not send Cassie somewhere else for treatment? Why run the risk of dealing with the exact same doctors who'd treated Chad and having them make the same connection the blackmailers had made? It's not like the family wouldn't have been justified. Cassie isn't getting any better—you yourself said Jones Junior's talking about medical errors. No one would blame them for getting a second opinion. Also, it's one thing to say the parents are abusers and Grandpa's protecting them, even to the point of eliminating a blackmailer. But if Grandpa *knew* Cassie was being poisoned, wouldn't he want to step in and stop it?"

"Maybe he's no better than they are," I said.

"Family of psychos?"

"Where do you think it starts?"

"I don't know—"

"Maybe Chuck Jones was an abusive father and that's where Chip learned it. The way he's tearing down the hospital sure doesn't make him Mr. Compassionate."

"Corporate greed is one thing, Alex. Watching your granddaughter get messed with to the point of epileptic seizures is another."

"Yeah," I said, "it's probably all fantasy—getting far afield. Would you please eat? Your pickiness is making me nervous."

He smiled for my benefit and took fork in hand. Both of us faked fascination with our food.

"Huenengarth," he said. "Don't imagine there'd be too many of that name on file. What's the first name?"

"Presley."

He smiled. "Even better. Speaking of which, I ran Ashmore and Steph. He's clean except for a couple of traffic tickets that he didn't get around to paying before he died. She's been clean for a long time, but a few years ago she had a DUI."

"Drunk driving?"

"Uh-huh. Caused a collision, no injuries. First offense, she got probation. Probably got sent to AA or a treatment center."

"So maybe *that's* why she's changed."

"Changed how?"

"Got thin, started putting on makeup, got into fashion. Image of the young professional. She has a designer coffee maker in her office. Real espresso."

"Could be," he said. "Strong coffee's part of the reformed alkie thing—to replace the booze."

Thinking of his off-and-on flirtation with the bottle, I said, "You think it means anything?"

"What, the DUI? You see any evidence she's still boozing?"

"No, but I haven't been looking for any."

"Any clear relationship between alcoholism and Munchausen?"

"No. But whatever problem you've got, booze makes it worse. And if she had the typical Munchausen background—abuse, incest, illness—I could understand her hitting the bottle."

He shrugged. "So you answer your own question. At the very least it means she's got something she'd like to forget. Which makes her like most of us."

As we left the restaurant Milo said, "I'll try to find out what I can about Dawn Herbert, for what it's worth. What's your next step?"

"Home visit. Maybe seeing them in their natural habitat will give me *some* kind of insight."

"Makes sense. Hell, while you're out there you can do a little snooping—you've got the perfect cover."

"That's exactly what Stephanie said. She suggested I nose around in their medicine cabinet. Half-joking."

"Why not? You shrinks get paid to poke and probe. Don't even need a search warrant."

On the way home I stopped off at the Ashmore house—still curious about Huenengarth and wanting to see how the widow was doing. A black wreath hung on the front door and no one answered my ring.

I got back in the car, cranked up the stereo, and made it all the way home without thinking about death and disease. I checked in with my service. Robin had left word she'd be back around six. The morning paper was still on the dining room table, neatly folded, the way she always left it.

Recalling Dan Kornblatt's peevish comment in the cafeteria, I paged through the paper, trying to find what had upset him. Nothing in the front pages or Metro, but it jumped out at me from the second page of the Business section.

I never read the financial pages, but even if I did, I could have missed it. Small piece, lower bottom corner, next to the foreign exchange rates.

The headline read HEALTH CARE IN THE PRIVATE SECTOR: THE OPTIMISM FADES. The gist of the article was that the for-profit hospital business, once seen by Wall Street as a rich financial lode, had turned out to be anything but. That premise was backed up by examples of hospitals and HMOs gone bust, and interviews with financial honchos, one of them George Plumb, formerly CEO of MGS Healthcare Consultants, Pittsburgh, and currently CEO of Western Pediatric Medical Center, Los Angeles.

Pittsburgh . . . The outfit revamping the library with an outmoded computer system—BIO-DAT—was from Pittsburgh too.

One hand feeding the other? I read on.

The honchos' main complaints centered on government meddling and "market-restricting" fee schedules but also touched upon difficulties dealing with insurance companies, the skyrocketing cost of new technologies, the salary demands of doctors and nurses, and the failure of sick people to behave like statistics.

"One AIDS patient, alone, can cost us millions," lamented one East Coast administrator. "And we still haven't seen the light at the end of that tunnel. This is a disease no one knew about when any of the plans were put together. The rules have been changed in the middle of the game."

The HIV epidemic was cited repeatedly by executives, as if the plague were a bit of naughtiness devised to throw the actuaries off track.

Plumb's special contribution to the gripe-fest had to do with the difficulties of running inner-city hospitals due to "unfavorable demographics and social problems that seep into the institution from the surrounding neighborhoods. Add to that, rapidly deteriorating physical plants and shrinking revenues, and the paying consumer and his or her provider is unwilling to contract for care."

When asked for solutions, Plumb suggested that the wave of the future might be "decentralization—replacing the large urban hospital with smaller, easily managed health-care units strategically located in positive-growth suburban areas.

"However," he cautioned, "careful economic analyses need to be done before planning anything of that magnitude. And nonpecuniary issues must also be considered. Many established institutions inspire a high degree of loyalty in those whose memories are grounded in the good old days."

It sounded awfully like a trial balloon—testing public opinion before proposing radical surgery: putting the "physical plant" up for sale and heading for suburban pastures. And if cornered, Plumb could always brush off his comments as detached expert analysis.

Kornblatt's remark about selling off the hospital's real estate began to sound less like paranoia and more like an educated guess.

Of course, Plumb was only a mouthpiece. Speaking for the man I'd just proposed as a possible murder contractor and accessory to child abuse.

I remembered what Stephanie had told me about Chuck Jones's background. Before becoming Western Peds's chairman of the board, he'd managed the hospital's investment portfolio. Who'd know more about the precise value of Western Peds's assets—including the land—than the man who kept the books?

I visualized him and Plumb and the gray-twin numbers crunchers, Roberts and Novak, hunched over a moldy ledger, like predators out of a Thomas Nast cartoon.

Could the hospital's dismal financial situation be due to more than unfortunate demographics and shrinking revenues? Had Jones mismanaged Western Peds's money to the point of crisis, and was he now planning to cover his losses with a flashy real estate sale?

Adding insult to injury by taking a nice fat commission on the deal?

Strategically located in positive-growth suburban areas.

Like the fifty lots Chip Jones owned out in the West Valley?

One hand feeding the other . . .

But to pull off that kind of thing, appearances would have to be kept up, Jones and company exhibiting unwavering loyalty to the urban dinosaur until it drew its last breath.

Pulling the chairman's granddaughter out of treatment wouldn't be part of that.

In the meantime, though, steps could be taken to hasten the dinosaur's death.

Shut down clinical programs. Discourage research. Freeze salaries and keep the wards understaffed.

Encourage senior doctors to leave and replace them with inexperienced help, so that private physicians lost confidence and stopped referring their paying patients.

Then, when redemption was out of the question, give an impassioned speech about insoluble social issues and the need to move fearlessly into the future.

Destroying the hospital to save it.

If Jones and his minions pulled it off, they'd be viewed as visionaries with the courage and foresight to put a tottering almshouse out of its misery and replace it with healing grounds for the upper middle class.

There was a certain vicious beauty to it.

Thin-lipped men planning a war of attrition with flow-charts, balance sheets, computer printouts.

Printouts . . .

Huenengarth confiscating Ashmore's computers.

Was he after data that had nothing to do with sudden infant death syndrome or poisoned babies?

Ashmore had no interest in patient care, but a *strong* attraction to finance. Had he stumbled upon Jones's and Plumb's machinations—overheard something down in the sub-basement, or hacked into the wrong data base?

Had he tried to profit from the knowledge and paid for it?

Big leap, Milo would say.

I remembered the glimpse I'd caught of Ashmore's office before Huenengarth shut the door.

What kind of toxicology research could be carried out without test tubes or microscopes?

Ashmore, crunching numbers and dying because of it . . . Then what of Dawn Herbert? Why had she pulled a dead infant's chart? Why had she been murdered two months before Ashmore?

Separate schemes?

Some sort of collusion?

Big leap . . . And even if any of it was true, what the hell did it have to do with Cassie Jones's ordeal?

I phoned the hospital and requested room 505W. No one answered. Dialing again, I asked to be put through to the Chappy Ward nursing desk. The nurse who picked up had a Spanish accent. She informed me the Jones family was off the floor, taking a walk.

"Anything new?" I said. "In terms of her status?"

"I'm not sure—you'll have to ask the primary. I believe that's Dr. . . . ."

"Eves."

"Yeah, that's right. I'm just a float, not really familiar with the case."

I hung up, looked out the kitchen window at treetops graying under a descending lemon-colored sun. Mulled the financial angle some more.

I thought of someone who might be able to educate me financially. Lou Cestare, once a stocks-and-bonds golden boy, now a chastened veteran of Black Monday.

The crash had caught him off guard and he was still scouring the tarnish from his reputation. But he remained on *my* A list.

Years ago I'd saved up some cash, working eighty hours a week and not spending much. Lou had given me financial security by investing the money in pre-boom beachfront real estate, selling for healthy profits and putting the gain into blue-chip securities and tax-free bonds. Avoiding the speculative stuff, because he knew I'd never be rich from practicing psychology and couldn't afford to lose big.

The income from those investments was still coming in, slow and steady, augmenting what I brought in doing forensic consults. I'd never be able to buy French Impressionist paintings, but if I kept my life-style reasonable, I probably wouldn't have to work when I didn't want to.

Lou, on the other hand, was a very wealthy man, even after losing most of his assets and nearly all of his clients. He split his time now between a boat in the South Pacific and an estate in the Willamette Valley.

I called Oregon and spoke to his wife. She sounded serene, as always, and I wondered if it was strength of character or a good facade. We made small talk for a while and then she told me Lou was up in Washington State, hiking near Mount Rainier with their son, and wasn't expected until tomorrow night or Monday morning. I gave her my want-list. It didn't mean much to her, but I knew she and Lou never talked money.

Wishing her well and thanking her, I hung up.

Then I drank another cup of coffee and waited for Robin to come home and help me forget the day.

21

She was carrying two suitcases and looking cheerful. A third valise was down in her new truck. I brought it up and watched her unpack and hang her clothes. Filling the space in the closet that I'd left empty for more than two years.

Sitting down on the bed, she smiled. "There."

We necked for a while, watched the fish, went out and had rack of lamb at a sedate place in Brentwood where we were the youngest patrons. After returning home, we spent the rest of the evening listening to music, reading, and playing gin. It felt romantic, a little geriatric, and very satisfying. The next morning, we went walking in the glen, pretending we were birdwatchers and making up names for the winged things we saw.

Sunday lunch was hamburgers and iced tea up on the terrace. After we did the dishes she got involved in the Sunday crossword puzzle, biting her pencil and frowning a lot. I stretched out on a lounge chair, feigning relaxation. Shortly after 2:00 P.M. she put the puzzle down, saying, "Forget it. Too many French words."

She lay down beside me. We absorbed sun, until I noticed her starting to fidget.

I leaned over and kissed her forehead.

"Ummm . . . anything I can do for you?" she said.

"No, thanks."

"Sure?"

"Uh-huh."

She tried to sleep, grew more restless.

I said, "I'd like to get over to the hospital some time today."

"Oh, sure . . . As long as you're going out, I might as well get over to the shop, take care of a few odds and ends."

Cassie's room was empty, the bed stripped, the drapes drawn. Vacuum tracks striped the carpet. The bathroom was bare and disinfected; a paper runner was wrapped around the toilet.

As I stepped out of the room a voice said, "Hold it."

I came face to face with a security guard. Wet-sanded triangular face, grim lips, and black-framed glasses. Same hero I'd met the first day, enforcing the badge law.

He blocked the doorway. Looked ready to charge San Juan Hill.

I said, "Excuse me."

He didn't move. There was barely enough space between us for me to glance down and read his badge. *Sylvester, A.D.*

He looked at mine and took a single step backwards. Partial retreat but not enough to allow me through.

"See, got a new one," I said. "All bright and shiny, full color. Now could you please get out of the way so I can go about my business?"

He looked up and down a couple of times, matching my face to the photo. Stepping aside, he said, "This ward's closed."

"So I see. For how long?"

"Till they open it."

I walked past him and headed for the teak doors.

He said, "Looking for anything in particular?"

I stopped and faced him again. One hand rested on his holster; the other gripped his baton.

Resisting the urge to bark, "Draw, pardner," I said, "I came to see a *patient*. They used to treat them here."

I used a phone on the public ward to call Admissions and Discharge and confirmed that Cassie had been released an hour ago. I took the stairs down to the first floor and bought a watery cola from a vending machine. I was carrying it across the entrance lobby when I crossed paths with George Plumb and Charles Jones, Jr. They were laughing, keeping up a brisk pace that caused Jones's short bowlegs to pump. So much for concerned grandpa.

They got to the door just as I emerged. Jones saw me and his mouth stood still. A few seconds later his feet did the same. Plumb stopped, too, remaining just behind his boss. The pink in his complexion was more vivid than ever.

"Dr. Delaware," said Jones. His gravel voice made it sound like a warning growl.

"Mr. Jones."

"Do you have a moment, Doctor?"

Caught off guard, I said, "Sure."

Casting an eye at Plumb, he said, "I'll catch up with you later, George."

Plumb nodded and marched off, arms swinging.

When we were alone Jones said, "How's my granddaughter?"

"Last time I saw her she was looking better."

"Good, good. I'm on my way to see her."

"She's been discharged."

His grizzled eyebrows crinkled unevenly, each thatch of steely hair pointing randomly. Beneath the brows were lumps of scar tissue. His eyes got tiny. For the first time I noticed they were a watery brown.

"That so? When?"

"An hour ago."

"Damn." He squeezed his broken nose and jiggled the tip back and forth. "I came by expressly to see her because I didn't get a chance to see her yesterday—blasted meetings all day. She's my only grandchild, you know. Beautiful little thing, isn't she?"

"Yes, she is. Be nice if she were healthy."

He stared up at me. Put his hands in his pocket and tapped a wingtip on the marble floor. The lobby was nearly empty and the sound echoed. He repeated it. His posture had lost some of its stiffness, but he straightened quickly. The watery eyes sagged.

"Let's find a place to talk," he said, and barreled forward through the lobby, confident once more. A solid little fireplug of a man who carried himself as if self-doubt wasn't in his DNA. Jingling as he walked.

"I don't keep an office here," he said. "With all the money problems, the space shortage, last thing I want is to be seen as playing fast and loose."

As we passed the elevators one of them arrived. Tycoon's luck. He strode right in, as if he'd reserved the lift, and jabbed the basement button.

"How about the dining room?" he said as we rode down.

"It's closed."

"I know it is," he said. "I'm the one who curtailed the hours."

The door opened. He strode out and headed for the cafeteria's locked doors. Pulling a ring of keys out of his trouser pocket—the jingle—he thumbed and selected a key. "Early on we did a resource-utilization survey. It showed no one was using the room much during this time of day."

He unlocked the door and held it open.

"Executive privilege," he said. "Not too democratic, but democracy doesn't work in a place like this."

I stepped in. The room was pitch-dark. I groped the wall for a light switch but he walked right to it and flipped it. A section of fluorescent panels stuttered and brightened.

He pointed to a booth in the center of the room. I sat down and he went behind the counter, filled a cup with tap water, and dropped a lemon wedge in it. Then he got something from under the counter— a Danish—and put it on a plate. Moving briskly, familiarly, as if he were puttering in his own kitchen.

He came back, took a bite and a sip, and exhaled with satisfaction.

"She *should* be healthy, dammit," he said. "I really don't understand why the hell she isn't, and no one's been able to give me a straight story."

"Have you talked to Dr. Eves?"

"Eves, the others, all of them. No one seems to know a damn thing. You have anything to offer yet?"

"Afraid not."

He leaned forward. "What I don't understand is why they called you in. Nothing personal—I just don't see the point of a psychologist here."

"I really can't discuss that, Mr. Jones."

"Chuck. Mr. Jones is a song by that curly character, whatsisname—Bob Dylan?" Tiny smile. "Surprised I know that, right? Your era, not mine. But it's a family joke. From way back when. Chip's high school days. He used to ride me, fight everything. Everything was like this."

He made hooks of his hands, linked them, then strained to pull them apart, as if they'd become glued.

"Those were the days," he said, smiling suddenly. "He was my only one, but he was like half a dozen, in terms of rebellion. Anytime I'd try to get him to do something he didn't want to do, he'd rear up and buck, tell me I was acting just like the song by that Dylan Thomas character, that guy who doesn't know what's going on—Mr. Jones. He'd play it loud. I never actually listened to the lyrics, but I got the point. Nowadays he and I are best of friends. We laugh about those days."

Thinking of friendship cemented by real estate deals, I smiled.

"He's a solid boy," he said. "The earring and the hair are just part of the image—you know he's a college professor, don't you?"

I nodded.

"The kids he teaches *eat* that kind of thing up. He's a great teacher, won awards for it."

"That so?"

"Lots of them. You'll never hear him toot his own horn. He was always like that. Modest. I've got to do his bragging for him. He was winning them back when he was a student. Went to Yale. Always had a flair for it, teaching. Used to tutor the slow boys in his fraternity and get them up to grade. Tutored high school kids, too—got a commendation for it. It's a gift, like anything else."

His hands were still linked together, two stubby, fleshy grapples. He separated them, fanned them on the table. Closed the fingers. Scratched the Formica.

"Sounds like you're pretty proud of him," I said.

"I most certainly am. Cindy too. Lovely girl, no pretensions. They've created something solid—proof of the pudding is Cassie. I know I'm not objective but that little girl is adorable and beautiful and smart. Great disposition to boot."

"No mean feat," I said. "Considering."

His eyes wandered. Closed and opened.

"You know we lost one before her, don't you? Beautiful little boy—crib death. They still don't know why that happens, do they?"

I shook my head.

"That was *hell* on earth, Doctor. Clear out of the blue—one day he's here; the next . . . I just can't understand why no one can tell me what's wrong with this one."

"No one really knows, Chuck."

He waved that off. "I still don't understand why you're involved. Don't take that personally. I know you've heard all sorts of horror stories about why we abolished the Psychiatry division. But the truth is, that had nothing to do with approving or disapproving of mental health treatment. I certainly do approve—what's not to approve? Some people need help. But the fact is that the weak sisters running Psychiatry had no idea how to construct a budget and stick to it, let alone do their own jobs competently. The clear picture I got from the other doctors was that they were inept. Of course, to hear it now, they were all geniuses—we destroyed a center of psychiatric brilliance."

He rolled his eyes. "No matter. Hopefully, one day we'll be able to establish a good, solid department. Bring in some top people. You used to work here, didn't you?"

"Years ago."

"Would you ever consider returning?"

I shook my head.

"Why'd you leave?"

"Various reasons."

"The freedom of the private sector? Be your own boss?"

"That was part of it."

"So maybe if you step back you can be objective and understand what I mean. About the need for efficiency. Being realistic. In general, I'm finding doctors out in the private sector do understand. Because running a practice is running a business. It's only the ones who live off the— But no matter. Getting back to what I was saying, about your involvement with my granddaughter. No one's got the gall to say her problems are in her *head,* do they?"

"I really can't talk about details, Chuck."

"Why the hell not?"

"Confidentiality."

"Chip and Cindy don't keep secrets from me."

"I need to hear that from them. It's the law."

"You're a tough one, aren't you?"

"Not particularly." I smiled.

He smiled back. Linked his hands again. Drank hot water.

"All right. This is *your* business and you have to stick to your own rules. Guess I've got to get some kind of permission note from them."

"Guess so."

He smiled wide. His teeth were severely misaligned and brown.

"In the meantime," he said, "am *I* allowed to talk to *you?*"

"Sure."

He locked in on my face, studying it, with a mixture of interest and skepticism, as if it were a quarterly report. "I'll just assume no one seriously thinks Cassie's problems are mental, because that's just too ridiculous."

Pause. Assess. Hoping for a nonverbal clue?

I made sure not to move.

He said, "So, the only other thing I can come up with to explain your getting involved is that someone thinks something's wrong with Cindy or Chip. Which is ridiculous."

He sat back. Kept studying. A triumphant look came on his face. I was sure I hadn't even blinked. Wondered if he'd seen something or was just finessing.

I said, "Psychologists aren't called in only to analyze, Chuck. We also give support to people under stress."

"Being a hired friend, huh?" He jiggled his nose again, stood, smiled. "Well, then, be a *good* friend. They're good kids. All three of them."

I drove away trying to figure out what he'd been after and whether I'd given it to him.

Wanting me to see him as a concerned grandfather?

Chip and Cindy don't keep secrets from me.

Yet Chip and Cindy hadn't taken the trouble to inform him Cassie was being discharged. I realized that during all the contacts I'd had with both of them, his name hadn't come up once.

A tightly wound little man who was *all* business—even during our few minutes together, he'd mixed family matters with hospital affairs.

He hadn't wasted a moment on debate, had never tried to change my opinion.

Choosing, instead, to *shape* the conversation.

Even the choice of meeting place had been calculated. The dining room he closed and now treated as his personal galley. Getting refreshments for himself, but not me.

Brandishing a ring of keys to let me know he could open any

door in the hospital. Bragging about it, but letting me know he had too much integrity to grab office space.

Bringing my presumed hostility toward the despoiler of the Psychiatry department out in the open, then trying to neutralize me by appending a bribe just subtle enough to be taken as casual conversation:

Hopefully, one day we'll be able to establish a good, solid department. Bring in some top people . . . Would you ever consider returning?

When I'd demurred, he'd backed off immediately. Empathized with my good sense, then used it to support his point of view.

If he'd been a hog farmer, he'd have found a way to use the squeal.

So I had to believe that though ours had been a chance encounter, if we hadn't bumped into each other soon, he would have arranged a meeting.

I was too small a fry for him to care what I thought about him.

Except as it related to Cassie and Chip and Cindy.

Wanting to know what I'd learned about his family.

Meaning there was probably something to hide and he didn't know if I'd discovered it.

I thought of Cindy's worry: *People must think I'm crazy.*

Was there a breakdown in her past?

The entire family fearful of a psychological probe?

If so, what better place to avoid scrutiny than a hospital without a Psychiatry department?

Another reason not to transfer Cassie.

Then Stephanie had gone and ruined things by bringing in a free-lance.

I remembered Plumb's surprise when she told him what I was.

Now his boss had checked me out personally.

Shaping, molding. Painting a rosy picture of Chip and Cindy.

Mostly Chip—I realized he'd spent very little time on Cindy.

Paternal pride? Or directing me *away* from his daughter-in-law because the less said about her the better?

I stopped for a red light at Sunset and La Brea.

My hands were tight on the steering wheel. I'd cruised a couple of miles without knowing it.

When I got home I was in a bad mood and thankful that Robin wasn't there to share it.

The operator at my service said, "Nothing, Dr. Delaware. Isn't that nice?"

"You bet." We told each other to have a nice day.

Unable to get Ashmore and Dawn Herbert out of my head, I drove over to the university, hooking into the campus at the north end and continuing southward until I came to the Medical Center.

A new exhibit on the history of leeching lined the hallway leading to the Biomed library—medieval etchings and wax simulations of patients being feasted upon by rubbery parasites. The main reading room was open for another two hours. One librarian, a good-looking blond woman, sat at the reference desk.

I searched through a decade of the *Index Medicus* for articles by Ashmore and Herbert and came up with four by him, all published during the last ten years.

The earliest appeared in the World Health Organization's public-health bulletin—Ashmore's summary of his work on infectious diseases in the southern Sudan, emphasizing the difficulty of conducting research in a war-torn environment. His writing style was cool, but the anger leaked through.

The other three pieces had been published in biomathematics journals. The first, funded by a grant from the National Institutes of Health, was Ashmore's take on the Love Canal disaster. The second was a federally funded review of mathematical applications to the life sciences. Ashmore's final sentence: "There are lies, damn lies, and statistics."

The last report was the work Mrs. Ashmore had described: analyzing the relationship between soil-concentration of pesticides and rates of leukemia, brain tumors, and lymphatic and liver cancers in children. The results were less than dramatic—a small numerical link between chemicals and disease, but one that wasn't statistically significant. But Ashmore said if even one life was saved, the study had justified itself.

A little strident and self-serving for scientific writing. I checked the funding on the study: The Ferris Dixon Institute for Chemical Research, Norfolk, Virginia. Grant #37958.

It sounded like an industry front, though Ashmore's point of view wouldn't have made him a likely candidate for the chemical industry's largesse. I wondered if the absence of any more publications meant the institute had cut off his grant money.

If so, who paid his bills at Western Peds?

I went over to the librarian and asked her if there was a compilation of scientific grants issued by private agencies.

"Sure," she said. "Life science or physical?"

Not sure how Ashmore's work would be categorized, I said, "Both."

She got up and walked briskly back to the reference shelves. Heading straight for a case in the center of the section, she pulled down two thick soft-cover books.

"Here you go—these are the most recent. Anything prior to this year is bound, over there. If you want federally funded research, that's over there to the right."

I thanked her, took the books to a table, and read their covers. CATALOGUE OF PRIVATELY FUNDED RESEARCH: VOLUME I: THE BIOMEDICAL AND LIFE SCIENCES.

Ditto, VOLUME II: ENGINEERING, MATHEMATICS, AND THE PHYSICAL SCIENCES.

I opened the first one and turned to the "Grantee" section at the back. Laurence Ashmore's name popped out at me midway through the *A*s, cross-referenced to a page number in the "Grantor" section. I flipped to it:

THE FERRIS DIXON INSTITUTE FOR CHEMICAL RESEARCH
NORFOLK, VIRGINIA

The institute had funded only two projects for the current academic year:

#37959: Ashmore, Laurence Allan. Western Pediatric Medical Center, Los Angeles, CA. *Soil toxicity as a factor in the etiology of pediatric neoplasms: a follow-up study.* $973,652.75, three years.

#37960: Zimberg, Walter William. University of Maryland, Baltimore, MD. *Non-parametric statistics versus Pearson correlations in scientific prediction: the investigative, heuristic, and predictive value of* a priori *determination of sample distribution.* $124,731.00, three years.

The second study was quite a mouthful, but Ferris Dixon obviously wasn't paying by the word. Ashmore had received nearly 90 percent of its total funding.

Nearly a million dollars for three years.

Very big bucks for a one-man project that was basically a rehash. I was curious about what it took to impress the folks at Ferris Dixon. But it was Sunday and even those with deep pockets rested.

I returned home, changed into soft clothes, and puttered, pretending the fact that it was the weekend meant something to me. At six o'clock, no longer able to fake it, I called the Jones house. As the phone rang, the front door opened and Robin stepped in. She waved, stopped in the kitchen to kiss my cheek, then kept going toward the bedroom. Just as she disappeared from view Cindy's voice came on the line.

"Hello."

"Hi. It's Alex Delaware."

"Oh, hi. How are you, Dr. Delaware?"

"Fine. And you?"

"Oh . . . pretty good." She sounded edgy.

"Something the matter, Cindy?"

"No . . . Um, could you hold for just one second?"

She covered the receiver and the next time I heard her voice it was muffled and her words were unintelligible. But I made out another voice answering—from the low tones, Chip.

"Sorry," she said. "We're just getting settled. I thought I heard Cassie—she's taking a nap."

Definitely edgy.

"Tired from the ride?" I said.

"Um . . . that and just getting readjusted. She had a great big dinner, plus dessert, then just dropped off. I'm across the hall from her right now. Keeping my ears open . . . you know."

"Sure," I said.

"I keep her door open to our bathroom—it connects to our room—and a night light on inside. So I can look in on her regularly."

"How do you get any sleep that way?"

"Oh, I manage. If I'm tired, I nap when she does. Being together so much, we've kind of gotten on to the same schedule."

"Do you and Chip ever take shifts?"

"No, I couldn't do that—his course load's really heavy this semester. Are you coming out to visit us, soon?"

"How about tomorrow?"

"Tomorrow? Sure. Um . . . how about in the afternoon—around four?"

Thinking of the 101 freeway snarl, I said, "Would earlier be possible?"

"Um, okay—three-thirty?"

"I was thinking even earlier, Cindy, like two?"

"Oh, sure . . . I've got some things to do—would two-thirty be okay?"

"Fine."

"Great, Dr. Delaware. We're looking forward to seeing you."

I walked to the bedroom, thinking how much more nervous she sounded at home than in the hospital. Something about home setting her off—raising her anxiety and leading to Munchausen manipulation?

Though, even if she was virgin-innocent, I supposed it made sense for her house to spook her. For her, home was where the harm was.

Robin was slipping into a little black dress I'd never seen before. I zipped her up, pressed my cheek to the warmth between her shoulder blades, and finally managed to complete the process. We drove to the top of the Glen, to an Italian place in the shopping center just below Mulholland. No reservation, and we had to wait at a cold onyx bar. Frantic singles scene tonight, lots of tanned flesh and triple entendres. We enjoyed not being part of it, reveled in silence. I started to have real faith in our reunion—something pleasant to think about.

A half hour later we were seated at a corner table and ordering before the waiter could escape. We ate veal and drank wine for a peaceful hour, drove back home, got out of our clothes and straight into bed. Despite the wine, our union was quick, limber, almost jovial. Afterward, Robin ran a bath, got in, and called for me to join her. Just as I was about to, the phone rang.

"Dr. Delaware, this is Janie at your service. I've got a call from a Chip Jones."

"Thanks. Put him on, please."

"Dr. Delaware?"

"Hi, Chip, what's up?"

"Nothing—nothing medical, that is, thank God. I hope I'm not calling too late?"

"Not at all."

"Cindy just phoned me to say you're coming by, tomorrow afternoon. I'm checking to see if you need me to be there."

"Your input's always welcome, Chip."

"Hmm."

"Is there a problem?"

"I'm afraid there is. I've got an afternoon class at one-thirty, then a meeting with some of my students right afterward. Nothing earth-shattering—just routine office hours—but with finals approaching, the undergraduate panic level's been rising at a precipitous rate."

"No problem," I said, "I'll catch you the next time."

"Great—and if something comes up that you want to ask me about, just call. I gave you my number here, didn't I?"

"Yes, you did."

"Great. Then it's all set."

I hung up, bothered by his call but not sure why. Robin called from the bathroom and I went in. The light was dim and she was up to her neck in suds, head tilted back against the rim of the tub. A few clusters of bubbles dotted her pinned-up hair, shiny as gems. Her eyes were closed and she kept them that way as I got in.

Covering her breasts, she said, "Shudder, shudder—hope that's not Norman Bates."

"Norman preferred showers."

"Oh. Right. Norman's meditative brother, then."

"Norman's wet brother—Merman."

She laughed. I stretched out, closed my eyes too. She put her legs atop mine. I sank, feeling myself warm, massaging her toes, trying to loosen up. But I kept thinking of the conversation I'd just had with Chip and remained tight.

Cindy just phoned me to say you're coming by, tomorrow afternoon.

Meaning he hadn't been home when I'd called.

Hadn't been the man I'd heard Cindy speaking to.

The edginess . . .

Robin said, "What's the matter? Your shoulders are all bunched."

I told her.

"Maybe you're reading too much into it, Alex. It could have been a relative visiting—her father or her brother."

"She doesn't have either."

"So it was a cousin or an uncle. Or a service call—the plumber, the electrician, whatever."

"Try getting one of those guys on a Sunday evening," I said.

"They're rich. The rich get what they want when they want it."

"Yeah, maybe that's all it was. . . . Still, I thought she sounded nervous. As if I'd caught her off guard."

"Okay, let's say she's having a fling. You already suspect her of poisoning her kid. Adultery's a misdemeanor in comparison."

"Having a fling the first day back from the hospital?"

"Hubby didn't see anything wrong with flying off to his office the first day, did he? If that's his usual pattern, she's probably a lonely lady, Alex. He isn't giving her what she needs, so she's getting it elsewhere. Anyway, does adultery relate to this Munchausen business?"

"Anything that makes someone with those tendencies feel helpless could have an effect. But it's more than that, Robin. If Cindy's having an affair, that could provide a motive. Ditch hubby and kids, get free to be with her lover."

"There are easier ways to get free of your family."

"We're talking about someone sick."

"Really sick."

"I don't get paid to deal with healthy heads."

She leaned forward and touched my face. "This is really getting to you."

"Sure is. Cassie's so damned dependent and everyone's failing her."

"You're doing everything *you* can."

"I suppose."

We stayed in the water. I worked at relaxing again, settled finally for loose muscles and a tight mind. Soap-sud clouds gathered around Robin's shoulders like an ermine stole. She looked beautiful and I told her so.

She said, "What a flatterer, Mer." But her grin was deep and heartfelt. At least I'd made someone feel good.

We got back into bed and tackled the Sunday paper. I read carefully this time, searching for anything on Western Peds or Laurence Ashmore but finding nothing. The phone rang at ten forty-five. Robin answered. "Hi, Milo."

He said something that made her laugh. She said, "Absolutely," handed me the receiver, and returned to her crossword puzzle.

"Nice to hear her voice again," he said. "Finally, you show some good judgment." The connection was clear, but it sounded distant.

"Where are you?"

"Alley behind a leather-goods store, little pilfering surveillance, nothing so far. Am I interrupting something?"

"Domestic bliss," I said, stroking Robin's arm. She was concentrating hard on the puzzle, pencil in mouth, but her hand rose to meet mine and we laced fingers.

"Let's hear it for any kind of bliss," said Milo. "Got a couple of things for you. First, your Mr. Huenengarth has an interesting pattern. Valid driver's license and social security number, but the address on the license traces to a mail drop in Tarzana, and he's got no phone number, credit history, or IRS file. No county records either. No record of him in the military or on the voter roster. Similar pattern to a long-term con just out of the joint—someone who hasn't voted or paid taxes. Though he doesn't show up on NCIC or the parole rolls either, so maybe it's a computer glitch or I screwed up technically. I'll have Charlie try tomorrow."

"Phantom of the hospital," I said. "I feel so much better knowing he's head of Security."

Robin looked up briefly, then down again.

"Yeah," said Milo. "You'd be surprised how many strange types get into security—nutcases who try out for police departments, don't pass the psych evaluation. Meantime, keep your distance from him until I can find out more. Second thing is, I've been nosing around the Herbert file and plan to do a little late-night downtown prowl—talk to that bartender witness."

"Does he have something new to offer?"

"No, but Gomez and his partner didn't follow through enough for my taste. The guy has a serious dope record and they figured him for an unreliable witness. So they let him off easy, not enough questions. I got hold of his number, spoke to his girlfriend, and found out he got a job at another club nearby, over in Newton Division. Thought I'd go over and talk to him. Thought you might be interested in a tag-along. But you've obviously got better things to do."

Robin looked up. I realized my fingers had tightened around hers and eased my grip.

"When are you going?" I said.

"Hour or so. Figured I'd make it over there after midnight, when the scene just starts. I want to catch him in his element, but before it gets too intense. Anyway, enjoy your bliss."

"Wait. I've got a few things for *you*. Got time?"

"Sure. Nothing here in this alley but us cats. What's up?"

"I got buttonholed by Grandpa Chuck today, just as I left the hospital. He gave me a one-big-happy-family speech—defending the clan's honor, just like we discussed. Topped it off by offering me a job. The implication I got was I should behave myself, not dig too deeply."

"Not very subtle."

"Actually, he managed to do it quite subtly. Even if it had been taped, he could never have been pinned down. Not that the offer was worth much, because a job at Western Peds isn't likely to have much security."

I recounted Plumb's newspaper interview, and the financial-scheme hypotheses that had led me to look further into Laurence Ashmore's research. By the time I got to the Ferris Dixon Institute, Robin had put her puzzle down and was listening intently.

"Virginia," said Milo. "Been there a couple of times for fed training seminars. Pretty state, but anything down there always spells government to me."

"The institute's listed in a roster of private agencies. I figured it for some kind of corporate front."

"What kind of grant was it?"

"Pesticides in the soil, Ashmore analyzing his old data. Way too much money for that kind of thing, Milo. I thought I'd call the institute tomorrow morning, see what else I can learn. I'm also going to try to contact Mrs. Ashmore again. Find out if Huenengarth the Mystery Man's dropped by."

"Like I said, Alex, keep your distance."

"Don't worry, I won't get any closer than the phone. Afternoon I'll be doing what I went to school for over at Chip and Cindy's. Who may *not* be in a state of domestic bliss."

I reviewed my suspicions, including the caveats Robin had raised. "What do you think?"

"I think, who the hell knows? Maybe she did have a leaky faucet, or maybe she's the Hester Prynne of the San Fernando Valley. Tell you one thing, if she is stepping out on the Chipper, she's being pretty sloppy about it, wouldn't you say? Letting you hear Lover Boy's voice."

"Maybe she didn't mean to—I caught her off guard. She sounded antsy—covered the phone almost immediately. All I actually made out were a few low tones. And if she's a Munchausen type, flirting with another kind of danger would be right up her alley."

"Low tones, huh? Sure it wasn't the TV?"

"No, this was a real-life conversation. Cindy talked and the guy answered. I assumed it was Chip. If he hadn't called me later, I'd never have known it wasn't."

"Hmm," he said. "So what does it mean? In terms of Cassie?"

I repeated my motive theory.

He said, "Don't forget Chip's dough—that's one hell of an incentive."

"One hell of a family embarrassment, too, if it blows wide open and there's a nasty divorce. Maybe *that's* what Chuck's trying to keep me away from. He talked about Chip and Cindy creating something solid—called Cindy a lovely girl. Even though she doesn't seem like the girl a guy in his position would have wanted for his only daughter-in-law. On the other hand, from the look of his teeth, he came up the hard way himself. So maybe he's not a snob."

"His teeth?"

"They're crooked and discolored. No one ever shelled out on orthodontia on his account. Fact is, his entire manner's pretty rough."

"Self-made man," he said. "Maybe he respects Cindy for doing the same thing."

"Who knows? Anything on why she left the army?"

"Not yet. Gotta press Charlie on that . . . Okay, I'll check with you tomorrow."

"If you find out anything from the bartender, call me first thing."

There was a strain in my voice. My shoulders had bunched again.

Robin touched them and said, "What is it?"

I covered the phone and turned to her. "He's found a lead to something that may or may not be related to the case."

"And he called to invite you along."

"Yes, but—"

"And you want to go."

"No, I—"

"Is it anything dangerous?"

"No, just interviewing a witness."

She gave me a gentle shove. "Go."

"It's not necessary, Robin."

She laughed. "Go anyway."

"I don't need to. This is nice."

"Domestic bliss?"

"Mega-bliss." I put my arm around her.

She kissed it, then removed it.

"Go, Alex. I don't want to lie here listening to you toss."

"I won't."

"You know you will."

"Being alone is preferable?"

"I won't be. Not in my head. Not with what we've got going for us now."

I tucked her in bed and went out to the living room to wait. Milo knocked softly just before midnight. He was carrying a hard-shell case the size of an attaché and had on a polo shirt, twill pants, and windbreaker. All in black. Regular-guy parody of the L.A. hipster ensemble.

I said, "Trying to fade into the night, Zorro?"

"We're taking your car. I'm not bringing the Porsche down there."

I pulled out the Seville; he put the case in the trunk, got in the passenger seat. "Let's roll."

I followed his directions, taking Sunset west to the 405 south, merging with hurtling trucks and the red-eye crowd heading out to the airport. At the junction with the Santa Monica Freeway, I hooked over toward L.A. and traveled east in the fast lane. The highway was emptier than I'd ever seen it, softened to something impressionistic by a warm, moist haze.

Milo lowered the window, lit up a panatela, and blew smoke out at the city. He seemed tired, as if he'd talked himself out over the phone. I felt weary, too, and neither of us said a word. Near La Brea a loud, low sports car rode our tail, belched and flashed its brights before passing us at close to a hundred. Milo sat up suddenly—cop's reflex—and watched it disappear before settling back down and staring out the windshield.

I followed his gaze upward to an ivory moon, cloud-streaked and fat, though not quite full. It dangled before us like a giant yo-yo, ivory mottled with green-cheese verdigris.

"Three-quarter moon," I said.

"More like seven-eighths. That means *almost* all the nuts're out. Stay on the Ten past the interchange and get off at Santa Fe."

He kept grumbling directions in a low voice, taking us into a broad, silent district of storehouses, foundries, and wholesale jobbers. No streetlights, no movement; the only vehicles I spotted were penned behind prison-grade security fences. As we'd traveled away from the ocean, the haze had lifted and the downtown skyline had turned chiseled and crisp. But here I could barely make out the shapes, miragelike against the matte-black stasis of the city's outer limits. The silence seemed glum—a failure of spirit. As if L.A.'s geographical boundaries had exceeded its energy.

He directed me through a series of quick, sharp turns down asphalt strips that could have been streets or alleys—a maze that I'd never be able to reverse from memory. He'd allowed his cigar to go cold but the smell of tobacco stuck to the car. Though the breeze streaming in was warm and pleasant, he began raising the window. I realized why before he finished: A new smell overpowered the burnt-cloth stink of cheap leaf. Sweet and bitter at the same time, metallic, yet rotten. It leaked through the glass. So did noise—cold and resonant, like giant steel hands clapping—scraping the night-lull from somewhere far away.

"Packing houses," he said. "East L.A. all the way down to Vernon, but the sound carries. When I first came on the force I drove a cruiser down here, on the night watch. Sometimes they slaughtered the hogs at night. You could hear them howling, smashing into things, and rattling their chains. Nowadays I think they tranquilize them— Here, turn right, then immediately left. Go a block and park anywhere you can."

The maze ended on a skinny block-long straightaway bounded

on both sides by cyclone fencing. No sidewalks. Weeds erupted through the tar like hairs on a wen. Cars lined both sides of the street, pushed up close to the fence.

I pulled into the first space I saw, behind an old BMW with a K-ROQ window sticker and a rear deck piled high with trash. We got out of the Seville. The air had cooled but the slaughterhouse smell remained—dribs and drabs of stench, rather than a constant assault. Changing wind, probably, though I couldn't sense it. The machine scrape was gone, replaced by music—electric organ elf-squeaks and a murky bass, middle-range tones that might have come from guitars. If there was a beat, I couldn't sense that either.

"Party time," I said. "What's the dance of the week?"

"Felony lambada," said Milo. "Sidle up against your partner and rifle through his/her pockets." He shoved his hands in *his* pockets and slouched forward.

We began walking up the street. It dead-ended at a tall, windowless building. Pale-painted brick walls that a couple of red lights turned pink. Three stories—a trio of successively smaller cubes stacked atop one another. Flat roof, steel doors asymmetrically placed under a random assortment of shuttered windows. A tangle of fire-escape ladders hugged the facade like cast-iron ivy. As we got closer I saw huge, faded letters painted above the dock: BAKER FERTILIZER AND POTASH CO.

The music got louder. Heavy, slow, keyboard solo. Voices became audible in between notes. As we got closer, I saw a line of people S-curved in front of one of the doors—a fifty-foot ant-trail that dipped into the street and clogged it.

We began passing the line. Faces turned toward us sequentially, like animated dominoes. Black duds were the uniform, sullen pouts the mask. Boot chains, cigarettes—legal and otherwise—mumbles and shuffles and sneers, an amphetamine jerk here and there. Flashes of bare flesh, whiter than the moonlight. A rude comment harmonized with the organ and somebody laughed.

The age range was eighteen to twenty-five, skewed toward the lower end. I heard a cat snarl at my back, then more laughter. Prom from Hell.

The door that had drawn the crowd was a rust-colored sheet-metal rectangle blocked by a slide bolt. A big man wearing a sleeveless black turtleneck, green-flowered surfing shorts, and high-laced boots stood in front of it. He was in his early twenties, had clotted features, dreamy eyes, and skin that would have been florid even without the red bulb above his head. His black hair was trimmed to a buzz on top and engraved with lightning bolts of scalp on both sides. I noticed a couple of thin spots that hadn't been barbered—downy patches, as if he was recovering from chemo-therapy. But his body was huge and inflated. The hair at the back of his head was long and knotted in a tight, oiled queue that hung over one shoulder. The shoulder and its mate were graveled with acne. Steroid rash—that explained the hair loss.

The kids at the head of the line were talking to him. He wasn't answering, didn't notice our approach or chose to ignore it.

Milo walked up to him and said, "Evening, champ."

The bouncer kept looking the other way.

Milo repeated himself. The bouncer jerked his head around and growled. If not for his size, it would have been comical. The people at the head of the line were impressed.

Someone said, "Yo, kung-fu." The bouncer smiled, looked away again, cracked his knuckles and yawned.

Milo moved quickly, stepping up nose to nose with him while shoving his badge in the meaty face. I hadn't seen him remove it from his pocket.

The bouncer growled again but the rest of him was acquiescent. I looked over my shoulder. A girl with hair the color of deoxygenated blood stuck her tongue out at me and wiggled it. The boy fondling her chest spit and flipped me the bird.

Milo moved his badge back and forth in front of the bouncer's eyes. The bouncer followed it, as if hypnotized.

Milo held it still. The bouncer read laboriously.

Someone cursed. Someone else howled like a wolf. That caught on and soon the street sounded like something out of Jack London.

Milo said, "Open up, Spike, or we start checking IDs and health codes."

The lupine chorus grew louder, almost blotting out the music. The bouncer crunched his brows, digesting. It looked painful. Finally he laughed and reached behind himself.

Milo grabbed his wrist, big fingers barely making it around the joint. "Easy."

"Op'ning it, man," said the bouncer. "Key." His voice was unnaturally deep, like a tape played at slo-mo, but whiny nonetheless.

Milo backed away, gave him some space, and watched his hands. The bouncer pulled a key out of his surf-shorts, popped a lock on the bolt, and lifted the bar.

The door opened an inch. Heat and light and noise poured out through it. The wolf-pack charged.

The bouncer leaped forward, hands shaped into what he thought were karate blades, baring his teeth. The pack stopped, retreated, but a few protests sounded. The bouncer raised his hands high in the air and made pawing movements. The light from above turned his irises red. His armpits were shaven. Pimples there, too.

"The fuck back!" he bellowed.

The wolfies went still.

Milo said, "Impressive, Spike."

The bouncer kept his eyes fixed on the line. His mouth hung open. He was panting and sweating. Sound kept pouring out of the door crack.

Milo put his hand on the bolt. It creaked and stole the bouncer's attention. He faced Milo.

"Fuck him," said a voice from behind us.

"We're going in now, Spike," said Milo. "Keep those assholes calm."

The bouncer closed his mouth and breathed loudly through his nose. A bubble of snot filled one nostril.

"It's not Spike," he said. "It's James."

Milo smiled. "Okay. You do good work, James. Ever work at the Mayan Mortgage?"

The bouncer wiped his nose with his arm and said, "Huh?"

Working hard at processing.

"Forget it."

The bouncer looked injured. "Whaddya say, man? Seriously."

"I said you've got a bright future, James. This gig ever gets old, you can always run for Vice President."

*   *   *

The room was big, harshly lit in a few spots, but mostly dark. The floors were cement; the walls that I could see, painted brick. A network of conduits, wheels, gears, and pipes adhered to the ceiling, ragged in places, as if ripped apart in a frenzy.

Off to the left was the bar—wooden doors on sawhorses fronting a metal rack full of bottles. Next to the rack were half a dozen white bowls filled with ice.

Shiny porcelain bowls. Raised lids.

Toilets.

Two men worked nonstop to service a thirsty throng of minors, filling and squirting and scooping cubes from the commodes. No faucets; the soda and water came from bottles.

The rest of the space was a dance floor. No boundary separated the bar crowd from pressure-packed bodies writhing and jerking like beached grunion. Up close, the music was even more formless. But loud enough to keep the Richter scale over at Cal Tech busy.

The geniuses creating it stood at the back, on a makeshift stage. Five hollow-cheeked, leotarded things who could have been junkies had they been healthier-looking. Marshall Stacks big as vacation cabins formed a black felt wall behind them. The bass drum bore the legend OFFAL.

High on the wall behind the amps was another BAKER FERTILIZER sign, partially blocked by a hand-lettered banner tacked diagonally.

WELCOME TO THE SHIT HOUSE.

The accompanying artwork was even more charming.

"Creative," I said, loud enough to feel my palate vibrate, but inaudible.

Milo must have read my lips because he grinned and shook his head. Then he lowered it and charged through the dancers, toward the bar.

I dived in after him.

We arrived, battered but intact, at the front of the drinkers. Dishes of unshelled peanuts sat beside toilet paper squares improvising as napkins. The bartop needed wiping. The floor was carpeted with husks where it wasn't wet and slick.

Milo managed to bull his way behind the bar. Both of the barkeeps were thin, dark, and bearded, wearing sleeveless gray undershirts and baggy white pajama bottoms. The one closer to Milo was bald. The other was Rapunzel in drag.

Milo went over to Baldy. The bartender jabbed one hand defensively while pouring Jolt Cola into a glass quarter-filled with rum. Milo's hand fit all the way around this wrist. He gave it a short, sharp twist—not enough to cause injury, but the bartender's eyes and mouth opened and he put the cola can down and tried to jerk away.

Milo held fast, doing the badge thing again, but discreetly. Keeping the ID at an angle that hid it from the drinkers. A hand from the crowd reached out and snared the rum and cola. Several others began slapping the bartop. A few mouths opened in soundless shouts.

Baldy gave Milo a panicked look.

Milo talked in his ear.

Baldy said something back.

Milo kept talking.

Baldy pointed at the other mix-master. Milo released his grip. Baldy went over to Rapunzel and the two of them conferred. Rapunzel nodded and Baldy returned to Milo, looking resigned.

I followed the two of them on a sweaty, buffeted trek through and around the dance floor. Slow going—part ballet, part jungle clearance. Finally we ended up at the back of the room, behind the band's amps and a snarl of electric wires, and walked through a wooden door marked TOILETS.

On the other side was a long, cold, cement-floored hall littered with paper scraps and nasty-looking puddles. Several couples groped in the shadows. A few loners sat on the floor, heads lowered to laps. Marijuana and vomit fought for olfactory dominance. The sound level had sunk to jet-takeoff roar.

We passed doors stenciled STANDERS and SQUATTERS, stepped over legs, tried to skirt the garbage. Baldy was good at it, moving with a light, nimble gait, his pajama pants billowing. At the end of the hallway was yet another door, rusted metal, identical to the one the bouncer had guarded.

Baldy said, "Outside okay?" in a squeaky voice.

"What's out there, Robert?"

The bartender shrugged and scratched his chin. "The back." He was anywhere from thirty-five to forty-five. The beard was little more than fuzz and didn't conceal much of his face. It was a face worth concealing, skimpy and rattish and brooding and mean.

Milo pushed the door open, looked outside, and took hold of the bartender's arm.

The three of us went outside to a small fenced parking lot. A U-Haul two-ton truck was parked there, along with three cars. Lots more trash was spread across the ground in clumps, a foot high in places, fluttering in the breeze. Beyond the fence was the fat moon.

Milo led the bald man to a relatively clean spot near the center of the lot, away from the cars.

"This is Robert Gabray," he said to me. "Mixologist extraordinaire." To the bartender: "You've got fast hands, Robert."

The barkeep wiggled his fingers. "Gotta work."

"The old Protestant ethic?"

Blank look.

"You like working, Robert?"

"Gotta. They keep a record a everything."

"Who's they?"

"The owners."

"They in there watching you?"

"No. But they got eyes."

"Sounds like the CIA, Robert."

The bartender didn't answer.

"Who pays your salary, Robert?"

"Some guys."

"Which guys?"

"They own the building."

"What's the name on your payroll check?"

"Ain't no checks."

"Cash deal, Robert?"

Nod.

"You holding out on the Internal Revenue?"

Gabray crossed his arms and rubbed his shoulders. "C'mon, what'd I do?"

"You'd know that better than me, wouldn't you, Robert?"

"Bunch a A-rabs, the owners."

"Names."

"Fahrizad, Nahrizhad, Nahrishit, whatever."

"Sounds Iranian, not Arab."

"Whatever."

"How long you been working here?"

"Couple of months."

Milo shook his head. "No, I don't think so, Robert. Wanna give it another try?"

"What?" Gabray looked puzzled.

"Think back where you *really* were a couple of months ago, Robert."

Gabray rubbed his shoulders some more.

"Cold, Robert?"

"I'm okay . . . Okay, yeah, it's been a couple of *weeks*."

"Ah," said Milo, "that's better."

"Whatever."

"Weeks, months, it's all the same to you?"

Gabray didn't answer.

"It just *seemed* like months?"

"Whatever."

"Time goes quickly when you're having fun?"

"Whatever."

"Two weeks," said Milo. "That makes a lot more sense, Robert. Probably what you meant to say. You wouldn't think of giving me a hard time—you were just making an honest error, right?"

"Yeah."

"You forgot that two months ago you weren't working anywhere because you were at County lockup on a pissanty mary-joo-anna rap."

The bartender shrugged.

"Really bright, Robert, running those red lights with that brick in the trunk of your car."

"It wasn't my stuff."

"Ah."

"It's true, man."

"You took the heat for someone else?"

"Yeah."

"You're just a nice guy, huh? Real hero."

Shrug. Another rub of the shoulders. One of Gabray's arms rose higher and he scratched the bare skin atop his head.

"Got an itch, Robert?"

"I'm fine, man."

"Sure you're not dope-chilled?"

"I'm okay, man."

Milo looked at me. "Robert mixes powders as well as fluids. Quite an amateur chemist—isn't that right, Robert?"

Another shrug.

"Got a day job, Robert?"

Shake of the head.

"Your P.O. know you're working here?"

"Why shouldn't I?"

Milo leaned in closer and smiled patiently. "Because you, as a habitual although petty felon, are supposed to stay away from bad influences, and those folks in there don't look any too wholesome."

Gabray sucked his teeth and looked at the ground. "Who told you I was here?"

Milo said, "Spare me the questions, Robert."

"It was that bitch, wasn't it?"

"What bitch is that?"

"You know."

"Do I?"

"You musta—you knew I was here."

"Angry at her, Robert?"

"Nah."

"Not at all?"

"I don't get mad."

"What do you get?"

"Nothing."

"You get even?"

Gabray said, "Can I smoke?"

"She paid your bail, Robert. In my book that makes *her* the hero."

"I'll marry her. Can I smoke?"

"Sure, Robert, you're a free man. Least till your trial. 'Cause *the bitch* made your bail."

Gabray pulled a pack of Kools out of his p.j. pants. Milo was ready with a match.

"Let's talk about where you were *three* months ago, Robert."

Gabray smoked and gave another foggy look.

"A month before you got busted, Robert. March."

"What about it?"

"The Mayan Mortgage."

Gabray smoked and looked at the sky.

"Remember it, Robert?"

"What about it?"

"This."

Milo slid something out of his shirt pocket. Penlight and a color photo. He held the picture in front of Gabray's eyes and shined the light on it. I stepped behind Gabray and peered over his shoulder.

Same face as in the snapshot the Murtaughs had given me. Below the hairline. Above it, the skull was flattened to something that was incapable of holding a brain. What was left of the hair was a matted red-black cloud. Eggshell-colored skin. A black-red necklace encircled the throat. The eyes were two purple eggplants.

Gabray looked at it, smoked, said, "So?"

"Remember her, Robert?"

"Should I?"

"Her name's Dawn Herbert. She was offed near the Mayan and you told some detectives you saw her with some guy."

Gabray flicked ashes and smiled. "*That's* what this is about? Yeah, I told them. I guess."

"You guess?"

"It was a long time ago, man."

"Three months."

"That's a long time, man."

Milo moved closer to Gabray and stared down at the smaller man. "You gonna help me on this? Yes or no?" Waving the homicide photo.

"What happened to the other cops? One a them was a beaner, I think."

"They took early retirement."

Gabray laughed. "Where? In Tia Wanna?"

"Talk to me, Robert."

"I don't know nothing."

"You saw her with a guy."

Shrug.

"Did you lie to those poor hardworking detectives, Robert?"

"Me? Never." Smile. "Perish my thoughts."

"Tell me what you told them."

"Didn't they write it down?"

"Tell me anyway."

"It was a long time ago."

"Three months."

"That's long, man."

"Sure is, Robert. Ninety whole days, and think about this: Your record, even a little weed could put you away for two, three times that long. Think of three hundred cold days—that was a lot of grass in your trunk."

Gabray looked at the photo, turned his head, and smoked.

"It wasn't mine. The weed."

Milo's turn to laugh. "That gonna be your defense?"

Gabray frowned, pinched his cigarette, sucked smoke through it. "You're saying you can help me?"

"Depends on what you come up with."

"I seen her."

"With a guy?"

Nod.

"Tell me the whole thing, Robert."

"That's it."

"Tell it like a story. Once upon a time."

Gabray snickered. "Yeah, sure. Once upon a time . . . I seen her with a guy. The end."

"In the club?"

"Outside."

"Where outside?"

"Like . . . a block away."

"That the only time you saw her?"

Gabray contemplated. "Maybe I seen her another time, inside."

"Was she a regular?"

"Whatever."

Milo sighed and patted the barkeep's shoulder. "Robert, Robert, Robert."

Gabray flinched with each mention of his name. "What?"

"That's not much of a story."

Gabray ground out his cigarette and produced another. He waited for Milo to light it and when that didn't happen, pulled out a book of matches and did it himself.

"I seen her maybe one more time," he said. "That's it. I only worked there a couple of weeks."

"Trouble holding down a job, Robert?"

"I like to move around, man."

"A ramblin' guy."

"Whatever."

"Twice in a couple of weeks," said Milo. "Sounds like she enjoyed the place."

"Fuckheads," said Gabray with sudden passion. "All a them, rich dumb fucks, coming down to play street-life, then running back to Rodeo Drive."

"Dawn Herbert come across as a rich bitch?"

"They're all the same, man."

"Ever talk to her?"

Alarm in the barkeep's eyes. "Nah. Like I said, I only seen her once, maybe twice. That's it. I didn't know her from shit—I had nothing to do with her and nothing to do with *that*." Pointing at the photo.

"You're sure about that."

"Real sure. *Really* real sure, man. That is *not* my thing."

"Tell me about seeing her with this guy."

"Like I said, once upon a time I was working there and once upon a time I went to take a smoke and seen her. Only reason I remembered was 'cause a the guy. He wasn't one a them."

"One of who?"

"The fuckheads. *She* was, but not *him*. He, like, stood out."

"Stood out how?"

"Straight."

"Businessman?"

"Nah."

"What then?"

Gabray shrugged.

"Was he wearing a suit, Robert?"

Gabray smoked hard and thought. "Nah. Kinda like you—

Sears Roebuck, that kind of jacket." Drawing his hands across his
waist.

"A windbreaker?"

"Yeah."

"What color?"

"I dunno—dark. It was a long—"

"Time ago," said Milo. "What else was he wearing?"

"Pants, shoes, whatever. He looked like you." Smile. Smoke.

"In what way?"

"I dunno."

"Heavyset?"

"Yeah."

"My age?"

"Yeah."

"My height?"

"Yeah."

"Same hair as me?"

"Yeah."

"You have two dicks?"

"Ye— Huh?"

"Cut the crap, Robert. What was his hair like?"

"Short."

"Bald or a full head?"

Gabray frowned and touched his own bare dome. "He had hair,"
he said grudgingly.

"Beard or mustache?"

"I dunno. It was far."

"But you don't remember any facial hair?"

"No."

"How old was he?"

"I dunno—fifty, forty, whatever."

"You're twenty-nine and he was much older than you?"

"Eight. Next *month* I'm twenty-nine."

"Happy birthday. He was older than you?"

"A lot older."

"Old enough to be your father?"

"Maybe."

"Maybe?"

"Nah—not old enough. Forty, forty-five."

"Hair color?"

"I dunno—brown."

"Maybe or definitely?"

"Probably."

"Light or dark brown?"

"I dunno. It was nighttime."

"What color was *her* hair?"

"You got the picture there."

Milo shoved the photo in the barkeep's face. "Is this what she looked like when you saw her?"

Gabray pulled back and licked his lips. "Uh-uh—it was . . . her hair was different."

"Sure it was," said Milo. "It was sitting on an intact skull."

"Yeah—no—I mean the color. You know, yellow. Real yellow—like scrambled eggs. You could see it in the light."

"She was under a light?"

"I guess . . . yeah. The two a them were— a streetlight. Just for a sec, till they heard me and split."

"You didn't tell the other detectives about any light."

"They didn't ask."

Milo lowered the picture. Gabray smoked and looked away.

Milo said, "What were Ms. Herbert and this straight-looking guy doing under the light?"

"Talking."

"His hair wasn't blond?"

"I told you, *hers* was. You could *see* it, man—it was like a . . . banana." Gabray chuckled.

"And his was brown."

"Yeah. Hey, if this is so important, how come you're not writing it down?"

"What else do you remember about him, Robert?"

"That's it."

"Middle-aged, dark windbreaker, dark hair. That's not much to trade with, Robert."

"I'm telling you what I saw, man."

Milo turned his back on Gabray and looked at me. "Well, we tried to help him."

"You got someone, like tight?" said the bartender.

Milo kept his back turned. "What do you mean, Robert?"

"Tight *case,* man. I don't want to be telling you something and have some dude walk on some *Miranda* or something and come looking for me, you know?"

"You haven't told me much, Robert."

"You got someone tight?"

Milo pivoted slowly and faced him. "What I got is you, Robert, trying to jerk me around, withholding evidence on top of that brick in your trunk. I figure six months minimum—get the wrong judge, you might even be talking a year or so."

Gabray held out his hands. "Hey, I just don't want someone walking and coming after me. This guy was . . ."

"What?"

Gabray was silent.

"This guy was what, Robert?"

"A con—okay? He looked like serious business. A hard-case."

"You could tell that from far away?"

"Some things you can tell, okay? The way he stood, I dunno. He had these shoes—big and ugly, like you get in the joint."

"You could see his shoes?"

"Not up close—the light. But they were big—I seen shoes like that before. Whaddya want from me—I'm trying to help."

"Well, Robert, don't you worry. There's no one in custody."

"What *if?*" said Gabray.

"What if what?"

"I tell you and 'cause a that you *bust* him? How do I know he's not gonna get out and come looking for me?"

Milo held up the photo again. "Look what he did, Robert. What do you think? We're gonna let him walk?"

"That don't mean *nothing* to me, man. I don't have confidence in the system."

"That so?"

"Yeah. I see guys all the time, do bad stuff and walk on technos."

"Tsk, tsk," said Milo. "What's this world coming to? Listen, genius, we find him, he won't walk. And you tell me something that'll help me find him, you'll walk too. With brownie points. Hell,

Robert, all the points you'll have, you'll be able to screw up a couple *more* times and coast."

Gabray smoked and tapped his foot and frowned.

"What is it, Robert?"

"I'm *thinking*."

"Ah." To me: "Let's be real quiet."

"His face," said the bartender. "I seen it. But just for a second."

"That so? Was he angry or anything?"

"Nah, just talking to her."

"And what was she doing?"

"Listening. I thought when I saw it: this punk cunt's listening to Mr. Straight. Don't make sense."

"Mr. Con."

"Yeah. But he still didn't fit the scene—all you see down there at that hour is freaks and beaners and niggers. And cops—I thought first that he was a cop. Then I thought that he looked like a con. Same difference."

"What was he talking to her about?"

"I couldn't *hear* it, man! It was—"

"Was he holding anything?"

"Like what?"

"Like anything."

"You mean like to hurt her with? Nothing I saw. You really think he's the one did her?"

"What did his face look like?"

"Regular . . . uh, kinda . . . square." Gabray put the cigarette in his mouth and used his hands to frame a wobbly quadrangle. "A regular face."

"Complexion?"

"He was white."

"Pale, swarthy—on the dark side?"

"I dunno, just a white guy."

"Same color as her?"

"She had on makeup—that real white shit they like? He was darker than that. Regular white. Normal."

"Eye color?"

"I was too far away for that, man."

"How far?"

"I dunno, half a block."

"But you could see his shoes?"

"Maybe it was closer . . . I seen 'em. But I didn't see no eye color."

"How tall was he?"

"Taller than her."

"Taller than you?"

"Uh . . . maybe. Not much."

"What're you?"

"Five ten."

"So he was what, five eleven or six feet?"

"Guess so."

"Heavy build?"

"Yeah, but not fat, you know."

"If I knew I wouldn't be asking you."

"Heavy—big—you know—like from working out. On the yard."

"Muscular."

"Yeah."

"Would you remember this guy if you saw him again?"

"Why?" Another alarm flash. "You *do* got someone?"

"No. Would you remember him if you saw his picture?"

"Yeah, sure." Flippantly. "I got a good memory. Put him in a lineup and I'll give you a beaucoup ID, you treat me good."

"You trying to hustle me, Robert?"

Gabray smiled and shrugged. "Taking care of biz."

"Well," said Milo, "let's take care of some now."

We took Gabray across the rear lot, walked through a rubble-filled ditch on the east side of the building, and got back on the street. The line at the front door hadn't shrunk much. This time the bouncer noticed as we walked by.

Gabray said, "Yo, fuckin' King Kong," under his breath.

Milo said, "The guy with Ms. Herbert as big as James?"

Gabray laughed. "No—no way. That's not human. That they got outa the fuckin' zoo."

Milo pushed him forward, questioning him all the way to the car without extracting anything further.

"Nice wheels," said Gabray when we stopped at the Seville. "Get it from impound or something?"

"Hard work, Robert. That old Protestant ethic."

"I'm Catholic, man. Used to be, anyway. All of that religion shit's bullshit."

Milo said, "Shut up, Robert," and opened the trunk.

He removed the hard-shell case, put Gabray in the rear seat of the car, and got in next to him, leaving the door open for light. I stood outside and watched him open the case. Inside was a book that said IDENTIKIT. Milo showed Gabray transparencies with facial features drawn on them. Gabray selected some and put them together. When he was finished, a bland-looking Caucasian face gazed up. A face out of a *Dick and Jane* primer. Someone's dad.

Milo stared at it, fixed it in place, wrote something down; then he had Gabray designate spots on a street map with a yellow marker. After a few more questions, he got out of the car. Gabray followed. Despite the warm breeze, the barkeep's bare shoulders were fuzzed with goose bumps.

"Okay?" he said.

"For the time being, Robert. I'm sure I don't have to tell you this, but I'm gonna anyway: Don't change addresses. Stay where I can reach you."

"No prob." Gabray started to walk away.

Milo blocked him with a straight-arm. "Meanwhile, *I'm* gonna be writing letters. One to your P.O. saying you worked here without telling him, another to Mr. Fahrizad and his buddies informing them you finked on them and that's why the fire department's closing them down, and a third to the IRS telling them you've been taking cash for God knows how long and not declaring it."

Gabray bent at the waist as if seized by a cramp. "Oh, man—"

"Plus a report to the prosecutor on your weed thing, letting him know you were uncooperative and obstructive and a poor risk for plea bargain. I don't like writing letters, Robert. Writing letters makes me grumpy. If I have to waste my time looking for you, I'm gonna get even grumpier and all of those letters get hand-delivered. You behave yourself, I tear them up. *Comprende?*"

"Aw, man, that's *rude.* I been strai—"

"No problems if you behave yourself, Robert."

"Yeah, yeah, sure."

"Will you?"

"Yeah, yeah. Can I go now? I gotta work."

"Are you *hearing* me, Robert?"

"I'm hearing. Stay in one place, be a fucking boy scout. No jamming, no scamming. Okay? Can I go?"

"One more thing, Robert. Your lady."

"Yeah?" said Gabray, in a hard voice that turned him into something more than a sniveling loser. "What about her?"

"She's gone. Flew the coop. Don't even think about going after her. And *especially* don't think about hurting her for talking to me. Because I woulda found you anyway. You've got no gripe with her."

Gabray's eyes widened. "Gone? What the—whaddya mean?"

"Gone. She wanted out, Robert."

"Aw, shit—"

"She was packing her bags when I spoke to her. Pretty shaken up by your approach to domestic life."

Gabray said nothing.

Milo said, "She had enough of being pounded on, Robert."

Gabray dropped the cigarette and stomped it out hard.

"She *lies,*" he said. "Fucking *bitch.*"

"She made your bail."

"She *owed* me. She *still* owes me."

"Let it go, Robert. Think of those letters."

"Yeah," said Gabray, tapping his foot. "Whatever. I'm cool with it. I got a good attitude about life."

When we were out of the maze and back on San Pedro, Milo turned on his penlight and studied the Identikit face.

"Think he's reliable?" I said.

"Not very. But in the unlikely event a real suspect ever shows up, this might help."

I stopped for a red light and glanced at the composite. "Not very distinctive."

"Nope."

I leaned over and gave a closer look. "It could be Huenengarth, minus the mustache."

"That so?"

"Huenengarth's younger than the guy Gabray described—mid-thirties—and his face is a bit fuller. But he's thickly built and his hair's styled like that. His mustache could have been grown since March, and even if not, it's very faint—might have been hard to spot from a distance. And you said he might be an ex-con."

"Hmm."

The light turned green, and I headed back toward the freeway.

He chuckled.

"What?"

"Just thinking. If I ever actually make sense out of the Herbert thing, my troubles will just be beginning. Sneaking her file out. Moving in on Central's territory, offering Gabray protection I had no permission to authorize. Far as the department's concerned, I'm a goddam clerk."

"Solving a homicide wouldn't impress the department?"

"Not nearly as much as rank conformity—but hell, I suppose I can work something out if it comes to that. Give a gift to Gomez and Wicker—let them take the glory and hope for half a gold star. Gabray may get sold out in the process . . . Hell, he's no innocent—screw him. If his info turns out to be real, he'll do okay."

He closed the kit and placed it on the floor.

"Listen to me," he said, "talking like a goddam politician."

I drove up the ramp. All lanes were empty and the freeway looked like a giant drag strip.

He said, "Putting some bad guys out of commission should be enough satisfaction, right? What you guys call intrinsic motivation."

"Sure," I said. "Be good for goodness' sake and Santa will remember you."

We arrived back at my house just after three. He drove away in the Porsche and I slipped into bed, trying to be silent. Robin awoke anyway and reached for my hand. We locked fingers and fell asleep.

She was up and gone before my eyes cleared. A toasted English muffin and juice were at my place on the kitchen table. I finished them off while planning my day.

Afternoon at the Joneses'.

Morning on the phone.

But the phone rang before I could get to it.

"Alex," said Lou Cestare, "all those interesting questions. Branching out into investment banking?"

"Not yet. How was the hike?"

"Long. I kept thinking my little guy would tire but he wanted to play Edmund Hillary. Why do you want to know about Chuck Jones?"

"He's chairman of the board of the hospital where I used to work. He also manages the hospital's portfolio. I'm still on staff there, feel some affection for the place. Things aren't going well there financially, and there's been talk of Jones running the place down so he can dissolve it and sell the land."

"Doesn't sound like his style."

"You know him?"

"Met him a couple of times at parties. Quick hello-goodbye— he wouldn't remember. But I do know his style."

"Which is?"

"Building up, not tearing down. He's one of the best money managers around, Alex. Pays no attention to what other people are doing and goes after solid companies at cut-rate prices. True bargains—the stock-buys everyone dreams about. But *he* finds them better than anyone else."

"How?"

"He knows how to really figure out how a company's doing. Which means going way beyond quarterly reports. Once he ferrets out an undervalued stock about to pop, he buys in, waits, sells, repeats the process. His timing's impeccable."

"Does he ferret using inside information?"

Pause. "This hour of the morning and you're already talking dirty?"

"So he does."

"Alex, the whole inside trading thing has been blown way out of proportion. As far as I'm concerned, no one's even come up with a good definition."

"Come on, Lou."

"Do *you* have one?"

"Sure," I said. "Using data unavailable to the average person in order to make buy-and-sell decisions."

"Okay, then, what about an investor who wines and dines a key employee in order to find out if the company's doing its job properly? Someone who takes the time to really get into the nuts and bolts of company operations? Is that corrupt or just being thorough?"

"If bribery's involved, it's corrupt."

"What, the wining and dining? Why's that different from a reporter buttering up a source? Or a cop encouraging a witness with a doughnut and a cup of coffee? I don't know of any law that makes dinner between business people illegal. Theoretically, anyone could do it, if they were willing to put out the effort. *But no one ever bothers, Alex.* That's the thing. Even professional researchers usually rely on graphs and charts and the numbers the company gives them. Lots of them never even bother to visit the company they're analyzing."

"I guess it depends on what the investor learns from the wining and dining."

"Exactly. If the employee tells him someone's going to make a serious takeover bid on such and such a date, that's illegal. But if that same employee tells him the company's in a financial position that makes it ripe for takeover, that's valid data. It's a thin line—see what I mean? Chuck Jones does his homework, that's all. He's a bulldog."

"What's his background?"

"I don't think he even went to college. We're talking rags to riches. I think he shod horses or something when he was a kid. Doesn't that appeal to your sensibilities? The guy came out of Black Monday a hero because he dumped his stocks months before the crash and shifted to T-bills and metals. Even though his stocks were shooting *up*. If anyone had known, they would have thought he was going senile. But when the market crashed, he was able to bottom-fish, bought in again and made another fortune."

"Why didn't anyone know?"

"He's got a thing for privacy—his kind of strategy depends upon it. He buys and sells constantly, avoids big block trades, stays away from computerized trading. It wasn't until months later that I found out, myself."

"How'd you find out?"

"The scuttlebutt—twenty-twenty hindsight, while the rest of us licked our wounds."

"How was he able to predict the crash?"

"Prescience. The best players have it. It's a combination of a great data base and a kind of ESP you get from being in the game a long time. I used to think I had it, but I got chastened—no big deal. Life was getting boring, and rebuilding's more fun than just treading water. But Chuck Jones *does* have it. I'm not saying he never loses. Everyone does. But he wins a lot more than he loses."

"What's he into now?"

"I don't know—like I said, close-to-the-cuff's his style. Invests only for himself, so he's got no shareholders to deal with. I doubt, though, that he's high on real estate."

"Why's that?"

"Because real estate's a turkey. I don't mean for someone like you who bought in years ago and is just looking for some stable income. But for traders out for a quick profit, the party's over, at least for now. I divested myself a while ago, moved back into stocks. Jones is smarter than me, so odds to evens he got there before I did."

"His son owns a big block of land out in the Valley."

"Who said wisdom is genetic?"

"His son's a college professor. I don't think he was able to buy fifty parcels for himself."

"Probably his trust fund—I don't know. You'll still have to convince me Chuck's getting into r.e. in a big way. The land the hospital's on is Hollywood, right?"

"Several acres," I said. "Purchased a long time ago—the hospital's seventy years old—so it's probably all paid for. Even in a slump, a sale would be pure profit."

"Sure it would, Alex. But to the hospital itself. What's *Jones's* incentive?"

"Commission on the deal."

"How many acres are we talking about and where exactly are they?"

"Five or so." I told him Western Peds's address.

"Okay, so that's ten, fifteen million—let's even say twenty because of contiguous lots. Which is liberal, because that big of a chunk would be hard to unload, so you might have to subdivide into smaller parcels. That could take time—there'd be zoning hassles, hearings, permits, environmental shenanigans. The biggest cut Chuck could take for himself without attracting a commotion would be twenty-five percent—ten's more likely. Meaning two to five mil in his pocket . . . No, I can't see Chuck messing around for that kind of money."

"What if there's more to it?" I said. "What if he not only plans to close down one hospital but is also figuring to open up a new one on his son's land?"

"All of a sudden he's in the hospital business? I doubt it, Alex.

No offense, but health care's a turkey too. Hospitals have been going belly-up almost as fast as savings and loans."

"I know, but maybe Jones figures he can do a good job anyway, bucking the trend. You just said he doesn't pay attention to what everyone else is doing."

"Anything's possible, Alex, but once again you'd have to prove it to me. Where'd you come up with all this theorizing, anyway?"

I told him about Plumb's comments in the paper.

"Ah, the other name on your list. Him, I'd never heard of him, so I looked him up in every directory I've got. What emerges is your basic corporate drone: M.B.A., doctorate, a series of management jobs, climbing the ladder. His first job was at a national accounting firm named Smothers and Crimp. Then he moved into the head office at another place."

"Where?"

"Hold on—I wrote it down somewhere . . . Here we go. Plumb, George Haversford. Born, '34; married Mary Ann Champlin, '58; two kids, blah blah blah . . . out of grad school in '60 with a D.B.A.; Smothers and Crimp, 1960 through '63, left as a partner. Controller, Hardfast Steel in Pittsburgh, '63 till '65; Controller and chief operating officer, Readilite Manufacturing, Reading, Pennsylvania, '65 through '68; a step up to CEO at an outfit called Baxter Consulting, stayed there till '71; '71 through '74 at Advent Management Specialists; went out on his own with the Plumb Group, '74 till '77; then back into the corporate world in '78 at a place called Vantage Health Planning, CEO till '81—"

"The guy hops around a lot."

"Not really, Alex. Moving around every couple of years in order to up your ante is your basic corporate drone pattern. It's one of the main reasons I dropped out of it early. Hell on the family—lots of booze-hound wives who smile a lot and kids who turn delinquency into an art form. . . . Where was I? Vantage Health till '81; then it looks as if he began specializing in medical stuff. Arthur-McClennan Diagnostics for three years, NeoDyne Biologicals for another three, then MGS Healthcare Consultants—the Pittsburgh place you asked me to look up."

"What'd you find out about it?"

"Small-to-medium hospital outfit specializing in acute-care facilities in small-to-medium cities in the northern states. Established in '82 by a group of doctors, went public in '85, OTC issue, poor stock performance, got reprivatized the next year—bought out by a syndicate and shut down."

"Why would a syndicate buy it, then shut it down?"

"Could be any number of reasons. Maybe they discovered buying it was a mistake and tried to cut their losses fast. Or they wanted the company's resources, rather than the company itself."

"What kinds of resources?"

"Hardware, investments, the pension fund. The other group you asked about—BIO-DAT—was originally a subsidiary of MGS. The data analysis arm. Before the buy-out it got sold to another concern—Northern Holdings, in Missoula, Montana—and was maintained."

"Is it a public company?"

"Private."

"What about the other companies Plumb worked for? Are you familiar with any of them?"

"Not a one."

"Are any of *them* public?"

"One second and I'll tell you. . . . Got the old PC cooking. Let me make a scan list. You want to go all the way back to the accountants—Smothers and whatever?"

"If you've got the time."

"Got more time than I'm used to. Hold on just one second."

I waited, listening to keyboard clicks.

"All right," he said, "now let's scroll up the exchanges and run a search . . . here we go."

Beep. "Nothing on the New York."

Beep. "No Amex listings on any of them, either. Let's see about the Nasdaq . . ."

Beep. Beep. Beep. Beep.

"No listings, Alex. Let me check the list of private holdings."

Beep.

"Doesn't look like it, Alex." A slight edge in his voice.

"Meaning none of them are in business?"

"Looks like it."

"Do you find that unusual?"

"Well," he said, "businesses do fail or close down at a pretty high rate, but this Plumb guy does seem to be the kiss of death."

"Chuck Jones hired him to run the hospital, Lou. Care to revise your thinking about his intentions?"

"Think he's a spoiler, huh?"

"What happened to the other companies Plumb was associated with?"

"That would be hard to find out—they were all small, and if they were privately held, there'd be no stock ramifications, little or no coverage in the business press."

"What about the local press?"

"If it was a company town with lots of people being thrown out of work, maybe. But good luck tracking that down."

"Okay, thanks."

"Is this really important, Alex?"

"I don't know."

"It would be a hell of a lot easier for *me* to track," he said, "knowing the ropes. Let me play Tarzan and climb a few."

After he hung up, I called Virginia Information and got the number of the Ferris Dixon Institute for Chemical Research. A pleasant female voice answered, "Ferris Dixon, good afternoon, how may I help you?"

"This is Dr. Schweitzer from Western Pediatric Medical Center in Los Angeles. I'm an associate of Dr. Laurence Ashmore."

"Just one second, please."

Long pause. Music. The Hollywood Strings doing The Police's *Every Breath You Take.*

The voice returned: "Yes, Dr. Schweitzer, how may I help you?"

"Your institute funds Dr. Ashmore's research."

"Yes?"

"I was just wondering if you knew he was deceased."

"Oh, how horrible," she said, but she didn't sound surprised. "But I'm afraid the person who can help you with that isn't in."

I hadn't asked for help, but I let that pass. "Who might that be?"

"I'm not exactly sure, Doctor. I'd have to check that."

"Could you, please?"

"Certainly, but it may take a while, Doctor. Why don't you give me your number and I'll get back to you."

"I'll be moving around. How about if I get back to you?"

"Certainly, Doctor. Have a nice—"

"Excuse me," I said. "As long as we're talking, could you give me some information on the institute? For purposes of my own research?"

"What would you like to know, Dr. Schweitzer?"

"What kinds of projects do you prefer to fund?"

"That would be a technical question, sir," she said. "I'm afraid I can't help you with that, either."

"Is there some kind of brochure you could send me? A list of previous studies you've funded?"

"I'm afraid not—we're a fairly young agency."

"Really? How young?"

"One moment, please."

Another long break. More Muzak, then she was back.

"Sorry for taking so long, Doctor, and I'm afraid I can't stay with you—I've got several other incoming calls. Why don't you get back to us with *all* your questions. I'm sure the right person will be able to help you."

"The right person," I said.

"Exactly," she said with sudden cheer. "Have a nice day, Doctor."

Click.

I called back. The line was busy. I asked the operator to put through an emergency interruption, and waited until she came back on the line.

"I'm sorry, sir, that number's out of order."

I sat there, still hearing the pleasant voice.

Smooth . . . well rehearsed.

One word she'd used jumped out at me.

"We're a fairly young *agency.*"

Odd way to describe a private foundation.

Virginia . . . anything down there always spells government to me.

I tried the number again. Still off the hook. Checked my notes for the other study the institute had funded.

Zimberg, Walter William. University of Maryland, Baltimore. Something to do with statistics in scientific research.

The med school? Mathematics? Public health?

I got the university's number and called it. No Zimbergs on the medical school faculty. Same at the math department.

At Public Health a male voice answered.

"Professor Zimberg, please."

"Zimberg? No such person here."

"Sorry," I said. "I must have gotten the wrong information. Do you have a faculty roster handy?"

"One moment . . . I've got a Professor *Walter* Zimberg but he's in the Department of Economics."

"Could you please connect me to his office?"

Click. Female voice: "Economics."

"Professor Zimberg, please."

"Hold, please."

Click. Another female voice: "Professor Zimberg's office."

"Professor Zimberg, please."

"I'm afraid he's out of town, sir."

I threw out a guess: "Is he over in Washington?"

"Um . . . Who is this, please?"

"Professor Schweitzer, an old colleague. Is Wal—Professor Zimberg at the convention?"

"What convention is that, sir?"

"National Association of Biostatisticians—over at the Capital Hilton? I heard he was going to present some new data on nonparametrics. The study the Ferris Dixon Institute's funding."

"I'm— The professor should be calling in soon, sir. Why don't you give me your number and I'll have him get back to you."

"Appreciate the offer," I said, "but I'm about to hop on a plane myself. That's why I didn't make the convention. Did the professor write up an abstract on his paper before he left? Something I could read when I get back?"

"You'd have to talk to the professor about that."

"When do you expect him back?"

"Actually," she said, "the professor's on sabbatical."

"No kidding? I didn't hear that. . . . Well, he's due, isn't he? Where's he off to?"

"Various places, Professor . . ."

"Schweitzer."

"Various places, Professor Schweitzer. However, as I said, he does call in frequently. Why don't you give me your number and I'll have him get back to you."

Repeating, almost word for word, what she'd just said a minute ago.

Word for word what another friendly female voice had said, *five* minutes ago, speaking from the hallowed offices of the Ferris Dixon Institute for Chemical Research.

25

To hell with Alexander Graham Bell.

I drove back to some hallowed halls I could see and touch.

There was one parking meter free near the university administration building. I went to the registrar's office and asked an Indian clerk in a peach-colored sari to look up Dawn Kent Herbert.

"Sorry, sir, we don't give out personal information."

I flashed my clinical faculty card from the med school across town. "I don't want anything personal—just need to know in which department she's enrolled. It has to do with a job. Verification of education."

The clerk read the card, had me repeat Herbert's name, and walked away.

A moment later she returned. "I show her as a graduate student in the School of Public Health, sir. But her enrollment's been terminated."

I knew Public Health was in the Health Sciences building, but I'd never actually been there. Shoving more money in the meter, I headed toward south campus, passing the Psych building, where I'd learned to train rats and listen with the third ear, crossing the Science quad, and entering the Center at the west end, near the Dental School.

The long hall that led to Public Health was a quick jog from the library, where I'd just studied Ashmore's academic history. Walls on both sides were lined with group photos of every class the medical school had graduated. Brand-new doctors looking like kids. The white-coats milling in the halls seemed just as young. By the time I reached the School of Public Health, the corridor had quieted. A woman was leaving the main office. I caught the door for her and stepped in.

Another counter, another clerk working in cramped space. This one was very young, black, with straightened hennaed hair and a smile that seemed real. She wore a fuzzy lime-green sweater with a yellow-and-pink parrot embroidered on it. The bird was smiling too.

"I'm Dr. Delaware from Western Pediatric Hospital. One of your graduate students worked at our hospital and I'd like to know who her faculty adviser is."

"Oh, sure. Her name, please."

"Dawn Herbert."

No reaction. "What department is she in?"

"Public Health."

The smile broadened. "This is the *School* of Public Health, Doctor. We have several departments, each with its own faculty." She lifted a brochure from a stack near my elbow, opened it and pointed to the table of contents.

DEPARTMENTS OF THE SCHOOL

BIOSTATISTICS

COMMUNITY HEALTH SCIENCES

ENVIRONMENTAL HEALTH SCIENCES

ENVIRONMENTAL SCIENCE AND ENGINEERING

EPIDEMIOLOGY

HEALTH SERVICES

Thinking of the kind of work Ashmore had done, I said, "Either Biostatistics or Epidemiology."

She went to the files and pulled down a blue fabric loose-leaf folder. The spine was lettered BIOSTAT.

"Yes, here we go. She's in the Ph.D. program in Biostat and her adviser's Dr. Yanosh."

"Where can I find Dr. Yanosh?"

"One floor down—office B-three-forty-five. Would you like me to call and see if she's in?"

"Please."

She picked up a phone and punched an extension. "Dr. Yanosh? Hi. Merilee here. There's a doctor from some hospital wanting to talk to you about one of your students . . . Dawn Herbert . . . Oh . . . Sure." Frowning. "What was your name again, sir?"

"Delaware. From Western Pediatric Medical Center."

She repeated that into the receiver. "Yes, of course, Dr. Yanosh . . . Could I see some identification, please, Dr. Delaware?"

Out came the faculty card again.

"Yes, he does, Dr. Yanosh." Spelling my name. "Okay, Doctor, I'll tell him."

Hanging up, she said, "She doesn't have much time but she can see you right now." Sounding angry.

As I opened the door, she said, "She was *murdered*?"

"I'm afraid so."

"That's really *ugly*."

There was an elevator just past the office, next to a darkened lecture hall. I rode it down one flight. B-345 was a few doors to the left.

Closed and locked. A slide-in sign said ALICE JANOS, M.P.H., PH.D.

I knocked. Between the first and second raps a voice said, "One minute."

Heel-clicks. The door opened. A woman in her fifties said, "Dr. Delaware."

I held out my hand. She took it, gave an abrupt shake, and let go. She was short, plump, blond, bubble-coiffed, and expertly made up and wore a red-and-white dress that had been tailored for her. Red shoes, matching nails, gold jewelry. Her face was small and attractive in a chipmunkish way; when she was young she'd probably been the cutest girl in school.

"Come in, please." European accent. The intellectual Gabor sister.

I stepped into the office. She left the door open and came in after me. The room was pin-neat, minimally furnished, scented with perfume, and hung with art posters in chromium frames. Miró and Albers and Stella and one that commemorated a Gwathmey-Siegel exhibit at the Boston Museum.

An open box of chocolate truffles sat on a round glass table. Next to it was a sprig of mint. On a stand perpendicular to the desk were a computer and a printer, each sheathed with a zippered cover. Atop the printer was a red leather designer purse. The desk was university-issue metal, prettified with a diagonally set lace coverlet, a floral-patterned Limoges blotter, and family photos. Big family. Albert Einstein look-alike husband and five good-looking, college-age kids.

She sat close to the chocolate and crossed her legs at the ankles. I faced her. Her calves were ballet-thick.

"You are a physician?"

"Psychologist."

"And what connection do you have to Ms. Herbert?"

"I'm consulting on a case at the hospital. Dawn obtained a medical chart belonging to the patient's sibling and never returned it. I thought she might have left it here."

"This patient's name?"

When I hesitated, she said, "I can't very well answer your question without knowing what I'm looking for."

"Jones."

"Charles Lyman Jones the Fourth?"

Surprised, I said, "You have it?"

"No. But you are the second person who's come asking for it. Is there a genetic issue at stake that makes this so urgent? Sibling tissue typing or something like that?"

"It's a complex case," I said.

She recrossed her legs. "The first person didn't give me an adequate explanation either."

"Who was that?"

She gave me an analytic look and sat back in her chair. "Forgive me, Doctor, but I'd appreciate seeing the identification you just showed Merilee upstairs."

For the third time in half an hour I presented my faculty card, augmenting it with my brand-new full-color hospital badge.

Putting on gold-framed half-glasses, she examined both, taking her time. The hospital ID held her interest longer.

"The other man had one of these too," she said, holding it up. "He said he was in charge of hospital security."

"A man named Huenengarth?"

She nodded. "The two of you seem to be duplicating each other's efforts."

"When was he here?"

"Last Thursday. Does Western Pediatrics generally give this type of personal service to all its patients?"

"As I said, it's a complex case."

She smiled. "Medically or socio-culturally?"

"I'm sorry," I said. "I can't get into details."

"Psychotherapeutic confidentiality?"

I nodded.

"Well, I certainly respect that, Dr. Delaware. Mr. Huenengarth used another phrase to protect *his* secrecy. 'Privileged information.' I thought that sounded rather cloak-and-dagger and told him so. He wasn't amused. A rather grim fellow, actually."

"Did you give him the chart?"

"No, because I don't *have* it, Doctor. Dawn left no medical charts of any kind behind. Sorry to have misled you, but all the attention she's generated lately has led me to be cautious. That and her murder, of course. When the police came by to ask questions, I cleaned out her graduate locker personally. All that I found were some textbooks and the computer disks from her dissertation research."

"Have you booted up the disks?"

"Is that question related to your complex case?"

"Possibly."

"Possibly," she said. "Well, at least you're not getting pushy the way Mr. Huenengarth did. Trying to pressure me to turn them over."

Removing her glasses, she got up, returned my ID, closed the door. Back in her chair, she said, "Was Dawn involved in something unsavory?"

"She may have been."

"Mr. Huenengarth was a bit more forthcoming than you, Doctor. He came right out and said Dawn had *stolen* the chart. Informed me it was my *duty* to see that it was returned—quite imperious. I had to ask him to leave."

"He's not Mr. Charm."

"An understatement—his approach is pure KGB. More like a policeman than the real policemen who investigated Dawn's murder, as far as I'm concerned. *They* weren't pushy *enough*. A few cursory questions and goodbye—I grade them C-minus. Weeks later I called to see what kind of progress was being made, and no one would take my call. I left messages and none were returned."

"What kind of questions did they ask about her?"

"Who her friends were, had she ever associated with criminal types, did she use drugs. Unfortunately, I wasn't able to answer any of them. Even after having her as my student for four years, I knew virtually nothing about her. Have you served on any doctoral committees?"

"A few."

"Then you know. Some students one really gets close to; others pass through without making a mark. I'm afraid Dawn was one of the latter. Not because she wasn't bright. She was *extremely* sharp, mathematically. It's why I accepted her in the first place, even though I had reservations about her motivation. I'm always looking for women who aren't intimidated by numbers and she had a true gift for math. But we never . . . jelled."

"What was the matter with her motivation?"

"She didn't *have* any. I always got the feeling she'd drifted into grad school because it was the path of least resistance. She'd applied to medical school and gotten rejected. Kept applying even after she enrolled here—a lost cause, really, because her non-math grades weren't very good and her M-CAT scores were significantly below average. Her math scores were so high I decided to accept her, though. I went so far as to get her funding—a Graduate Advanced Placement fellowship. This past fall, I had to cut that off. That's when she found the job at your hospital."

"Poor performance?"

"Poor progress on her dissertation. She finished her course work with adequate grades, submitted a research proposal that looked promising, dropped it, submitted another, dropped that, et cetera. Finally she came up with one that she seemed to like. Then she just froze. Went absolutely nowhere with it. You know how it is— students either zip through or languish for years. I've been able to help plenty of the languishers and I tried to help Dawn. But she rejected counseling. Didn't show up for appointments, made excuses, kept saying she could handle it, just needed more time. I never felt I was getting through to her. I was at the point of considering dropping her from the program. Then she was . . ."

She rubbed a fingertip over one blood-colored nail. "I suppose none of that seems very important now. Would you like a chocolate?"

"No, thanks."

She looked down at the truffles. Closed the box.

"Consider that little speech," she said, "as an elongated answer to your question about her disks. But yes, I did boot them up, and there was nothing meaningful on them. She'd accomplished *nothing* on the dissertation. As a matter of fact, I hadn't even bothered to look at them when your Mr. Huenengarth showed up—had put them away and forgotten about them, I was so upset by her death. Going through that locker felt ghoulish enough. But *he* made such a point of trying to get them that I booted them up the moment he was gone. It was worse than I'd imagined. All she'd produced, after all my encouragement, were statements and restatements of her hypotheses and a random numbers table."

"A random numbers table?"

"For random sampling. You know how it's done, I'm sure."

I nodded. "Generate a collection of random numbers with a computer or some other technique, then use it to select subjects from a general pool. If the table says five, twenty-three, seven, choose the fifth, twenty-third, and seventh people on the list."

"Exactly. Dawn's table was huge—thousands of numbers. Pages and pages generated on the department's mainframe. What a foolish waste of computer time. She was nowhere near ready to select her sample. Hadn't even gotten her basic methodology straight."

"What was her research topic?"

"Predicting cancer incidence by geographical location. That's as specific as she'd gotten. It was really pathetic, reading those disks. Even the little bit she had written was totally unacceptable. Disorganized, out of sequence. I had to wonder if indeed she *had* been using drugs."

"Did she show any other signs of that?"

"I suppose the unreliability could be considered a symptom. And sometimes she did seem agitated—almost manic. Trying to convince me—or herself—that she was making progress. But I know she wasn't taking amphetamines. She gained lots of weight over the last four years—at least forty pounds. She was actually quite pretty when she enrolled."

"Could be cocaine," I said.

"Yes, I suppose so, but I've seen the same things happen to students who *weren't* on drugs. The stress of grad school can drive anyone temporarily mad."

"How true," I said.

She rubbed her nails, glanced over at the photos of her family. "When I found out she'd been murdered, it changed my perception of her. Up till then I'd been absolutely *furious* with her. But hearing about her death—the way she'd been found . . . well, I just felt sorry for her. The police told me she was dressed like some kind of punk-rocker. It made me realize she'd had an outside life she'd kept hidden from me. She was simply one of those people to whom the world of ideas would never be important."

"Could her lack of motivation have been due to an independent income?"

"Oh, no," she said. "She was poor. When I accepted her she begged me to get her funding, told me she couldn't enroll without it."

I thought of the carefree attitude about money she'd shown the Murtaughs. The brand-new car she'd died in.

"What about her family?" I said.

"I seem to remember there was a mother—an alcoholic. But the policemen said they hadn't been able to locate anyone to claim the body. We actually took up a collection here at the school in order to bury her."

"Sad."

"Extremely."

"What part of the country was she from?" I said.

"Somewhere back east. No, she wasn't a rich girl, Dr. Delaware. Her lack of drive was due to something else."

"How did she react to losing her fellowship?"

"She didn't react at *all*. I'd expected some anger, tears, anything—hoped it would help clear the air and we'd reach an understanding. But she never even tried to contact me. Finally, I called *her* in, asked her how she was planning to support herself. She told me about the job at your hospital. Made it sound like something prestigious—was quite snotty, actually. Though your Mr. Huenengarth said she'd been little more than a bottle washer."

No bottles in Ashmore's lab. I was silent.

She looked at her watch, then over at her purse. For a moment I thought she was going to get up. But instead, she moved her chair closer and stared at me. Her eyes were hazel, hot, unmoving. An inquisitive heat. Chipmunk searching for the acorn hoard.

"Why all the questions, Doctor? What are you really after?"

"I really can't give any details because of the confidentiality issue," I said. "I know it doesn't seem fair."

She said nothing for a moment. Then: "She *was* a thief. Those textbooks in her locker had been stolen from another student. I found other things too. Another student's sweater. A gold pen that had belonged to me. So I won't be surprised if she *was* involved in something unsavory."

"She may have been."

"Something that led to her being murdered?"

"It's possible."

"And what's *your* involvement with all of this, Doctor?"

"My patient's welfare may be at stake."

"Charles Jones's sister?"

I nodded, surprised that Huenengarth had revealed that much.

"Is some type of child abuse suspected?" she said. "Something Dawn found out about and tried to profit from?"

Swallowing my amazement, I managed to shrug and run a finger across my lips.

She smiled. "I'm no Sherlock Holmes, Dr. Delaware. But Mr.

Huenengarth's visit made me very curious—all that pressure. I've studied health-care systems too long to believe anyone would go to that kind of effort for an average patient. So I asked my husband to make inquiries about the Jones boy. He's a vascular surgeon, has privileges at Western Peds, though he hasn't operated there in years. So I know who the Joneses are and the role the grandfather's playing in the turmoil the hospital's going through. I also know that the boy died of SIDS and another child keeps getting sick. Rumors are floating. Put that together with the fact that Dawn stole the first child's chart and went from abject student poverty to being quite cavalier about money, add two separate visits from professionals personally looking for that chart, and one doesn't need to be a detective."

"I'm still impressed."

"Are you and Mr. Huenengarth working at cross-purposes?"

"We're not working together."

"Whose side are you on?"

"The little girl's."

"Who's paying your fee?"

"Officially, the parents."

"Don't you consider that a conflict of interest?"

"If it turns out to be, I won't submit a bill."

She studied me for several moments. "I do believe you might mean that. Now tell me this: Does possession of the disks put *me* in any danger?"

"I doubt it, but it can't be ruled out."

"Not a very comforting answer."

"I don't want to mislead you."

"I appreciate that. I survived the Russian tanks in Budapest in '56, and my survival instincts have been well developed ever since. What do you suspect might be the importance of the disks?"

"They may contain some kind of coded data," I said, "imbedded in the random number table."

"I must say I thought of the same thing—there really was no logical reason for her to have generated that table at such an early stage of her research. So I scanned it, ran a few basic programs, and no obvious algorithms jumped out. Do you have any cryptographic skills?"

"None whatsoever."

"Neither do I, though good decoding programs do exist, so one no longer needs to be an expert. However, why don't we take a look right now, and see if our combined wisdom produces anything. After that, I'll hand the disks over to you and be rid of them. I'll also be sending a letter to Huenengarth and the police, carbon-copied to my dean, stating that I passed the disks along to you and have no interest in them."

"How about just to the police? I can give you a detective's name."

"No." She walked back to the desk, picked up the designer purse and unclasped it. Removing a small key, she fit it into the lock of the top desk drawer.

"I usually don't lock up like this," she said. "That man made me feel as if I were back in Hungary."

Sliding open a left-hand file drawer, she looked down into it. Frowned. Stuck her arm in, moved it around, pulled it out empty.

"Gone," she said, looking up. "How interesting."

The two of us went up to the department office and Janos asked
Merilee to get Dawn Herbert's student file. Five-by-eight index card.

"This is all of it?" she said, frowning.

"We recycle all the old paper now, Dr. Janos, remember?"

"Ah, yes. How politically correct . . ." Janos and I read the card:
DE-ENROLLED stamped at the top in red. Four typed lines under that:

> Herbert, D.K. Prog: Ph.D., Bio-St.
> D.O.B.: 12/13/63
> POB: Poughkeepsie, N.Y.
> A.B., Math, Poughkeepsie Coll.

"Not much," I said.

Janos gave a cold smile and handed the card back to Merilee.
"I've got a seminar, Dr. Delaware, if you'll please excuse me."

She left the office.

Merilee stood there holding the card, looking as if she'd been an
unwilling witness to a marital spat.

"Have a nice day," she said, then turned her back on me.

*   *   *

I sat in the car and tried to untangle the knots the Jones family had
tied in my head.

Grandpa Chuck, doing something to the hospital.

Chip and/or Cindy doing something to their kids.

Ashmore and/or Herbert learning about some or all of it. Ash-
more's data confiscated by Huenengarth. Herbert's data stolen by
Huenengarth. Herbert probably murdered by a man who looked like
Huenengarth.

The blackmail scenario obvious even to a casual observer like
Janos.

But if Ashmore and Herbert had both been up to something,
why had she been the first to die?

And why had Huenengarth waited so long after her death to
search for her disks, when he'd moved in on Ashmore's computers the
day after the toxicologist's murder?

Unless he'd only *learned* about Herbert's data after reading
Ashmore's files.

I stayed with that for a while and came up with a possible
chronology:

Herbert the first to suspect a tie-in between Chad Jones's death
and Cassie's illnesses—student leading the teacher, because the
teacher couldn't care less about patients.

She pulled Chad's chart, confirmed her suspicions, recorded her
findings—encoded as random numbers—on the university computer, printed out a floppy disk, stashed it in her graduate locker, and
put the squeeze on the Jones family.

But not before making a duplicate record and filing it in one of
Ashmore's computers, *without* Ashmore's knowledge.

Two months after her murder, Ashmore found the file and tried
to use it too.

Greedy, despite his million-dollar grant.

I thought of the Ferris Dixon money. Way too much for what
Ashmore claimed to be doing with it. Why had the largesse of a
chemical foundation extended to a man who criticized chemical
companies? A foundation no one seemed to know much about,

supposedly dedicated to life-science research, but its only other grantee was an *economist*.

The elusive Professor Zimberg . . . the sound-alike secretaries at his office and Ferris Dixon.

Some kind of game . . .

The waltz.

Maybe Ashmore and Herbert had worked *different* angles.

He, leaning on Chuck Jones because he'd latched on to a financial scam. She, trying to milk Chip and Cindy on the child-abuse secret.

Two blackmailers operating out of one lab?

I worked with it a while longer.

Money and death, dollars and science.

I couldn't get it to mesh.

The parking meter's red VIOLATION flag popped up like toast. I looked at my watch. Just after noon. Over two hours until my appointment with Cassie and mommy.

In the meantime, why not a visit with daddy?

I used a pay phone in the administration building to call West Valley Community College and get directions.

Forty-five-minute drive, if traffic was thin. Leaving the campus and heading north, I turned west on Sunset and got onto the 405. At the interchange I transferred to the Ventura Freeway, drove toward the western end of the Valley, and got off at Topanga Canyon Boulevard.

The northward cruise took me through a commercial cross-section: upscale shopping plazas still pretending trickle-down economics was working, shabby storefront businesses that had never believed it in the first place, insta-bilt strip malls without any ideological underpinnings.

Up above Nordhoff, the street turned residential and I was treated to a lean stretch of budget-box apartments and motor courts, condo complexes plastered with happy-talk banners. A few citrus groves and U-pick farms had resisted progress. Essences of manure, petroleum, and lemon leaves mingled, not quite masking the burnt-supper smell of simmering dust.

I drove to the Santa Susanna Pass, but the road was closed for no apparent reason and blockaded by CalTrans barriers. I kept going to the end of Topanga, where a jumble of freeway overpasses butted up against the mountains. Off to the right a group of sleek women cantered on beautiful horses. Some of the riders wore fox-hunting garb; all looked content.

I found the 118 on-ramp within the concrete pretzel, traveled west for a few miles, and got off on a brand-new exit marked COLLEGE ROAD. West Valley C.C. was a half-mile up—the only thing in sight.

Nothing at all like the campus I'd just left. This one was announced by a huge, near-empty parking lot. Beyond that, a series of one-story prefab bungalows and trailers were distributed gracelessly over a ten-acre patchwork of concrete and dirt. The landscaping was tentative, unsuccessful in places. A sprinkling of students walked on plain-wrap concrete pathways.

I got out and made my way to the nearest trailer. The midday sun cast a tinfoil glare over the Valley and I had to squint. Most of the students were walking alone. Very little conversation filtered through the heat.

After a series of false starts, I managed to locate someone who could tell me where Sociology was. Bungalows 3A through 3F.

The departmental office was in 3A. The departmental secretary was blond and thin and looked just out of high school. She seemed put-upon when I asked her where Professor Jones's office was, but said, "Two buildings up, in Three-C."

Dirt separated the bungalows, cracked and trenched. So hard and dry that not a single footprint showed. A far cry from the Ivy League. Chip Jones's office was one of six in the small pink stucco building. His door was locked and the card listing his office hours was marked:

ALWAYS

FIRST COME, FIRST SERVED.

All the other offices were locked too. I went back to the secretary and asked her if Professor Jones was on campus. She consulted a schedule and said, "Oh, yeah. He's teaching Soc One-oh-two over in Five-J."

"When's the class over?"

"In an hour—it's a two-hour seminar, twelve to two."

"Do they take a break in the middle?"

"I don't know."

She turned her back on me. I said, "Excuse me," managed to get her to tell me where 5J was, and walked there.

The building was a trailer, one of three on the western edge of the campus, overlooking a shallow ravine.

Despite the heat, Chip Jones was conducting class outside, sitting on one of the few patches of grass in sight, in the partial shade of a young oak, facing ten or so students, all but two of them women. The men sat at the back; the women circled close to his knees.

I stopped a hundred feet away.

His face was half-turned away from me and his arms were moving. He had on a white polo shirt and jeans. Despite his position, he was able to inject a lot of body English into his delivery. As he moved from side to side the students' heads followed and a lot of long female hair swayed.

I realized I had nothing to say to him—had no reason to be there—and turned to leave.

Then I heard a shout, looked over my shoulder and saw him waving.

He said something to the class, sprang to his feet, and loped toward me. I waited for him and when he got to me, he looked scared.

"I thought it was you. Is everything okay?"

"Everything's fine," I said. "Didn't want to alarm you. Just thought I'd drop by before heading over to your house."

"Oh—sure." He blew out breath. "Well, that's a relief. I just wish you'd told me you were coming, so I could've scheduled some time for us to talk. As it stands, I've got a two-hour seminar until two—you're welcome to sit in, but I don't imagine you want to hear about the structure of organizations. And after that there's a faculty meeting till three and another class."

"Sounds like a busy day."

He smiled. "My kind of day." The smile vanished. "Actually, Cindy's the one with the tough job. *I* can escape."

He smoothed his beard. Today's earring was a tiny sapphire, inflamed by the sun. His bare arms were tan and hairless and sinewy.

"Is there anything specific you wanted to talk to me about?" he said. "I can have them break for a few minutes."

"No, not really." I looked around at all the empty space.

"Not exactly Yale," he said, as if reading me. "I keep telling them a few trees would help. But I like being on the cutting edge— building something from scratch. This whole area's *the* high-growth region of the L.A. basin. Come back in a few years and it'll be teeming."

"Despite the slump?"

He frowned, tugged on his beard, and said, "Yes, I think so. The population can only go one way." Smile. "Or at least that's what my demographer friends tell me."

He turned toward the students, who were staring at us, and held up a hand. "Do you know how to get to the house from here?"

"Approximately."

"Let me tell you exactly. Just get back on the freeway—on the One-eighteen—and get off at the seventh exit. After that you can't miss it."

"Great. I won't keep you," I said.

He looked at me but seemed to be somewhere else.

"Thanks," he said. Another backward glance. "This is what keeps me sane—gives me the illusion of freedom. I'm sure you know what I mean."

"Absolutely."

"Well," he said, "I'd better be getting back. Love to my ladies."

The ride to the house wouldn't take more than fifteen minutes, leaving forty-five to go before my two-thirty with Cassie.

Remembering Cindy's odd resistance to my coming out any earlier, I decided to head over there right now. Do things on my terms, for a change.

Each exit on the 118 took me farther into the isolation of brown mountains, deforested by five years of drought. The seventh was marked Westview, and it deposited me on a gently curving road of red clay darkened by the mountain's hulk. A few minutes later the clay turned to twin lanes of new asphalt, and red pennants on high metal poles began appearing at fifty-foot intervals. A yellow backhoe was parked on a turnoff. No other vehicles were in sight. Baked hillside and blue sky filled my eyes. The pennant poles flashed by like jail bars.

The asphalt tabled at a hundred square feet of brick, shaded by olive trees. High metal gates were rolled wide open. A big wooden sign to the left of the aperture read WESTVIEW ESTATES in red block letters. Below the legend was an artist's rendition of a spreading pastel-hued housing development set into too-green alps.

I rolled close enough to the sign to read it. A timetable beneath the painting listed six construction phases, each with "twenty to a hundred custom estate homesites, 1/2 to 5 acres." According to the dates, three phases should have been completed. When I looked through the gates I saw a sprinkle of rooftops, lots of brown. Chip's comments about population growth, a few minutes ago, seemed a bit of wishful thinking.

I drove past an untended guardhouse whose windows still bore masking-tape Xs, into a completely empty parking lot fringed with yellow gazania. The exit from the lot fed to a wide, empty street named Sequoia Lane. The sidewalks were so new they looked white-washed.

The left side of the street was an ivy-covered embankment. A half-block in, to the right, sat the first houses, a quartet of big, bright, creatively windowed structures, but unmistakably a tract.

Mock Tudor, mock hacienda, mock Regency, mock Ponderosa Ranch, all fronted by sod lawns crosscut with beds of succulents and more gazania. Tennis court tarp backed the Tudor house; peacock-blue pool water glimmered behind the open lots of the others. Signs on the doors of all four read MODEL. Business hours were posted on a small billboard on the lawn of the Regency, along with the phone number of a real estate company in Agoura. More red pennants. All four doors were closed and the windows were dark.

I kept going, looking for Dunbar Court. The side streets were all "Courts"—wide, squat strips ending in cul-de-sacs, and ribbing east-ward from Sequoia. Very few cars were parked along curbs and in driveways. I saw a bicycle on its side in the center of a half-dead lawn, a garden hose that lay unfurled like a somnolent snake—but no people. A momentary breeze produced sound but no relief from the heat.

Dunbar was the sixth Court. The Jones house was at the mouth of the dead end, a wide, one-story ranch, white stucco trimmed with used-brick. In the center of the front yard a wagon wheel leaned against a young birch tree too thin to support it. Flower beds edged the facade. The windows sparkled. The loom of mountains behind the house made it look like something constructed from a child's kit. The air smelled of grass pollen.

A gray-blue Plymouth Voyager van was parked in the driveway. A brown pickup truck with a bed full of hoses, nets, and plastic bottles was idling in the driveway of the house next door. The sign on the door said VALLEYBRITE POOL SERVICE. Just as I pulled up to the curb the truck shot out. The driver saw me and stopped short. I waved him on. A young, shirtless, ponytailed man stuck his head out and stared. Then he grinned suddenly and gave me the thumb-up, instant buddy sign. Dropping a bronze arm over the driver's door, he finished backing up and was off.

I walked to the front door. Cindy opened it before I had a chance to knock, brushing hair out of her face and glancing at her Swatch.

"Hi," she said. Her voice sounded choked, as if she'd just caught her breath.

"Hi." I smiled. "Traffic was better than I thought."

"Oh . . . sure. C'mon in." The hair was unbraided but still waved by constriction. She wore a black T-shirt and very short white shorts. Her legs were smooth and pale, a little skinny but well-shaped above narrow bare feet. The sleeves of the T-shirt were cut high and on the bias, revealing lots of slender arm and a bit of shoulder. The bottom hem of her shirt barely reached her waist. As she held the door open she hugged herself and looked uncomfortable. Showing more skin than she'd intended for me, I supposed.

I walked in and she closed the door after me, taking care not to slam it. A modest entry hall ended at ten feet of wall papered in a teal-blue miniprint and hung with at least a dozen framed photographs. Cindy and Chip and Cassie, posed and candid, and a couple of a pretty, dark-haired baby in blue.

Smiling baby boy. I looked away from him and let my eyes settle on an enlarged snapshot of Cindy and an older woman. Cindy appeared around eighteen. She wore a white bare-midriff blouse and tight jeans tucked into white boots, and her hair was a wide, windblown fan. The older woman was leathery-looking, thin but wide-hipped, and had on a red-and-white striped sleeveless knit top over white stretch pants and white shoes. Her hair was dark-gray and cut very short, her lips so skinny they were nearly invisible. Both she and Cindy wore sunglasses; both were smiling. The older woman's smile said No Nonsense. Boat masts and gray-green water backgrounded the shot.

"That's my Aunt Harriet," said Cindy.

Remembering she'd grown up in Ventura, I said, "Where is this, Oxnard Harbor?"

"Uh-huh. Channel Islands. We used to go there for lunch, on her days off. . . ." Another look at her watch. "Cassie's still sleeping. She takes her nap around now."

"Back to routine pretty quickly." I smiled. "That's good."

"She's a good girl. . . . I guess she'll be up soon."

She sounded edgy again.

"Can I get you something to drink?" she said, moving away from the picture wall. "There's iced tea in the fridge."

"Sure, thanks."

I followed her through a generously dimensioned living room lined on three sides with floor-to-ceiling mahogany bookshelves and furnished with oxblood leather couches and club chairs that looked new. The shelves were full of hardcovers. A brown afghan was draped over one of the chairs. The fourth wall had two curtained windows and was papered in a black-and-green plaid that darkened the room further and gave it a clubby look, unmistakably masculine.

Chip's dominance? Or indifference to interior decorating on her part? I trailed slightly behind her, watching her bare feet sink into brown plush carpet. A grass stain spotted one buttock of her shorts. She had a stiff stride and held her arms pressed to her sides.

A dining room papered in a brown mini-print led to a white-tile and oak kitchen large enough to accommodate a distressed pine table and four chairs. The appliances were chrome-fronted and spotless. Glassed cabinets revealed neatly stacked crockery and size-ordered glassware. The dish drainer was empty; the counters, bare.

The window above the sink was a greenhouse affair filled with painted clay pots stuffed with summer flowers and herbs. A larger window to the left afforded a view of the backyard. Flagstone patio, rectangular pool covered with blue plastic and fenced with wrought iron. Then a long, perfect strip of grass, interrupted only by a wooden play-set, that ended at a hedge of orange trees espaliered against a six-foot cinder-block wall. Beyond the wall the ubiquitous mountains hung like drapery. Maybe miles away, maybe yards. I tried to get some perspective, couldn't. The grass began looking like a runway to eternity.

She said, "Please, have a seat."

Setting a place mat before me, she put a tall glass of iced tea upon it. "Just a mix—hope that's all right." Before I could answer, she returned to the refrigerator and touched the door.

I drank and said, "It's fine."

She picked up a washcloth and ran it over clean counter tiles, avoiding my eyes.

I sipped a bit, waited till we finally made contact, and tried another smile.

Her return smile was quick and tight and I thought I saw some color in her cheeks. She tugged her shirt down, kept her legs pressed together as she wiped the counter some more, washed the cloth, rung it out, folded it. Held it in both hands as if unsure what to do with it.

"So," she said.

I looked out at the mountains. "Beautiful day."

She nodded, snapped her face to the side, cast a downward glance, and placed the washcloth over the faucet spout. She ripped a square of paper towel from a wooden roller and began wiping the spigot. Her hands were wet. A Lady Macbeth thing or just her way of dealing with the tension?

I watched her clean some more. Then she gave another downward look and I followed it. To her chest. Nipples poking sharply through the thin black cotton of her shirt, small but erect.

When she looked up, my eyes were elsewhere.

"She should be up soon," she said. "She usually sleeps from about one to two."

"Sorry for coming so early."

"Oh, no, that's okay. I wasn't doing anything anyway."

She dried the spigot and stowed the paper towel in a wastebasket beneath the sink.

"While we wait," I said, "do you have any questions about Cassie's development? Or anything else?"

"Um . . . not really." She bit her lip, polished the faucet. "I just wish I . . . someone could tell me what's going on—not that I expect you to."

I gave a nod, but she was looking out the greenhouse window and didn't notice it.

Suddenly she leaned over the sink on tiptoe and adjusted one of the potted plants. Her back was to me and I saw her shirt ride up, revealing a couple of inches of tight waist and spine-knob. As she puttered, her long hair swayed like a horsetail. The stretch made her calves ride up and her thighs tighten. She straightened the pot, then another, stretched farther, and fumbled. One of the planters fell, hitting the rim of the sink, shattering, and showering planter's mix onto the floor.

She was down on all fours in an instant, scooping and collecting. Dirt crusted her hands and streaked her shorts. I got up but before I could help her, she bounded to her feet, hurried to a utility closet and retrieved a broom. Her sweeping was hard and angry. I tore a paper square off the roller and handed it to her after she put the broom away.

She was flushed now, and her eyes were wet. She took the towel without looking at me. Wiping her hands, she said, "I'm sorry—I have to go change."

She left the kitchen through a side door. I used the time to walk around the room, opening drawers and doors and feeling like an imbecile. Nothing more ominous in the cupboards than housekeeping aids and convenience foods. I looked out the door through which she'd left, found a small bathroom and service porch, and checked them out too. Washer and dryer, cabinets choked with detergents and cleansers, softeners and brighteners—a treasury of things promising to make life shiny and sweet-smelling. Most of them toxic, but what did that prove?

I heard footsteps and hurried back to the table. She came in wearing a loose yellow blouse, baggy jeans, sandals—her hospital uniform. Her hair was loosely braided and her face looked scrubbed.

"Sorry. What a klutz," she said.

She walked to the refrigerator. No independent movement from her chest region, no nipples.

"More iced tea?"

"No, thanks."

She took a can of Pepsi, popped it open, and sat down facing me.

"Did you have a nice ride over?"

"Very nice."

"It's good when there's no traffic."

"Yes, it is."

"I forgot to tell you, they closed off the pass to widen the road. . . ."

She continued to talk. About the weather and gardening, creasing her forehead.

Working hard at being casual.

But she seemed a stranger in her home. Talking stiffly, as if she'd rehearsed her lines but had no confidence in her memory.

Out the big window, the view was static as death.

Why were they living here? Why would Chuck Jones's only son choose exurban quarantine in his own faltering housing development when he could have afforded to live anywhere?

Proximity to the junior college didn't explain it. Gorgeous ranchland and plenty of country-club communities dotted the west end of the Valley. And funk-chic was still alive in Topanga Canyon.

Some kind of rebellion? A bit of ideology on Chip's part— wanting to be part of the community he planned to build? Just the kind of thing a rebel might use to dampen any guilt over making big profits. Though, from the looks of it, profits were a long way off.

Another scenario fit, too: abusive parents often secreted their families from the prying eyes of potential rescuers.

I became aware of Cindy's voice. Talking about her dishwasher, letting out words in a nervous stream. Saying she rarely used it, preferred gloving up and using steaming water so that the dishes dried almost instantly. Getting animated, as if she hadn't talked to anyone in a long time.

She probably hadn't. I couldn't imagine Chip sitting around for chitchat about housework.

I wondered how many of the books in the living room were hers. Wondered what the two of them had in common.

When she paused for breath, I said, "It really is a nice house."

Out of context, but it perked her up.

She gave a big smile, sloe-eyed, lips moist. I realized how good-looking she could be when she was happy.

"Would you like to see the rest of it?" she said.

"Sure."

We retraced our steps to the dining room and she pulled pieces of wedding silver out of a hutch and showed them to me, one by one. Next came the book-lined living room, where she talked about how hard it had been to find skilled carpenters to build solid shelving, no plywood. "Plywood gasses out—we want the house to be as clean as possible."

I pretended to listen while inspecting the books' spines.

Academic texts: sociology, psychology, political science. A bit of fiction, but none of it dated after Hemingway.

Interspersed among the volumes were certificates and trophies. The brass plate on one was inscribed: SINCERE THANKS TO MR. C. L. JONES III, FROM LOURDES HIGH SCHOOL ADVANCED PLACEMENT CLUB. YOU SHOWED US THAT TEACHING AND LEARNING WERE JUST PART OF FRIENDSHIP. Dated ten years ago.

Right below it was a scroll presented by the Yale Tutorial Project to CHARLES "CHIP" JONES FOR DEDICATED SERVICES TO THE CHILDREN OF THE NEW HAVEN FREE CLINIC.

On a higher shelf was yet another tutoring award, issued by a fraternity at Yale. Two more plasticized plaques, granted by the College of Arts and Sciences at the University of Connecticut at Storrs, attested to Chip's excellence in graduate teaching. Papa Chuck hadn't lied.

Several more recent testimonials from West Valley Junior College: the Department of Sociology's Undergraduate Teaching Citation, a gavel on a plaque from the WVJC Student Council thanking PROF. C. L. JONES FOR SERVING AS FACULTY ADVISOR, a group photo of Chip and fifty or so smiling, shiny-cheeked sorority girls on an athletic field, both he and the girls in red T-shirts emblazoned with Greek letters. The picture was autographed: "Best, Wendy." "Thanks, Prof. Jones—Debra." "Love, Kristie." Chip was squatting on a baseline, arms around two of the girls, beaming, looking like a team mascot.

Cindy's got the tough job. I can escape.

I wondered what Cindy did for attention, realized she'd stopped talking, and turned to see her looking at me.

"He's a great teacher," she said. "Would you like to see the den?"

More soft furniture, crammed shelves, Chip's triumphs preserved in brass and wood and plastic, plus a wide-screen TV, stereo components, an alphabetized rack of classical and jazz compact discs.

That same clubby feel. The sole strip of wall not covered with shelves was papered in another plaid—blue and red—and hung with

Chip's two diplomas. Below the foolscaps, placed so low I had to kneel to get a good look, were a couple of watercolors.

Snow and bare trees and rough-wood barns. The frame of the first was labeled NEW ENGLAND WINTER. The one just above the floor molding was SYRUP TAPPING TIME. No signature. Tourist-trap quality, done by someone who admired the Wyeth family but lacked the talent.

Cindy said, "Mrs. Jones—Chip's mom—painted those."

"Did she live back east?"

She nodded. "Years ago, back when he was a boy. Uh-oh, I think I hear Cassie."

She held up an index finger, as if testing the wind.

A whimper, distant and mechanical, came from one of the bookcases. I turned toward it, located the sound at a small brown box resting on a high shelf. Portable intercom.

"I put it on when she sleeps," she said.

The box cried again.

We left the room and walked down a blue-carpeted hall, passing a front bedroom that had been converted into an office for Chip. The door was open. A wooden sign nailed to it said SKOLLAR AT WIRK. Yet another book-filled leathery space.

Next came a deep-blue master bedroom and a closed door that I assumed led to the connecting bathroom Cindy had told me about. Cassie's room was at the end of the hall, a generous corner space done up in rainbow paper and white cotton curtains with pink trim. Cassie was sitting up in a canopied crib, wearing a pink nightshirt, hands fisted, crying halfheartedly. The room smelled baby-sweet.

Cindy picked her up and held her close. Cassie's head was propped on her shoulder. Cassie looked at me, closed her eyes, flopped her face down.

Cindy cooed something. Cassie's face relaxed and her mouth opened. Her breathing became rhythmic. Cindy rocked her.

I looked around the room. Two doors on the southern wall. Two windows. Bunny and duck decals appliquéd to furniture. A wicker-back rocker next to the crib. Boxed games, toys, and enough books for a year's worth of bedtime reading.

In the center three tiny chairs surrounded a circular play table. On the table were a stack of paper, a new box of crayons, three sharpened pencils, a gum eraser, and a piece of shirt cardboard hand-lettered WELCOME DR. DELAWARE. LuvBunnies—more than a dozen of them—sat on the floor, propped against the wall, spaced as precisely as cadets at inspection.

Cindy settled in the rocker with Cassie in her arms. Cassie molded to her like butter on bread. Not a trace of tension in the little body.

Cindy closed her eyes and rocked, stroking Cassie's back, smoothing sleep-moistened strands of hair. Cassie took a deep breath, let it out, nestled her head under Cindy's chin, and made high-pitched contented sounds.

I lowered myself to the floor and sat cross-legged—shrink's analytical lotus—watching, thinking, suspecting, imagining worst-cases and beyond.

After a few minutes my joints began to ache and I got up and stretched. Cindy's eyes followed me. We traded smiles. She pressed her cheek to Cassie's head and shrugged.

I whispered, "Take your time," and began walking around the room. Running my hands along the dustless surfaces of furniture, inspecting the contents of the toy case while trying not to look too inquisitive.

Good stuff. The right stuff. Each game and plaything safe, and age-appropriate, and educational.

Something white caught the corner of my eye. The buckteeth of one of the LuvBunnies. In the dim light of the nursery the critter's grin and those of its mates seemed malevolent—mocking.

I remembered those grins from Cassie's hospital room and a crazy thought hit me.

Toxic toys. *Accidental* poisoning.

I'd read about a case in a child health journal—stuffed animals from Korea that turned out to be filled with waste fibers from a chemical plant.

Delaware solves the mystery and everyone goes home happy.

Picking up the nearest bunny—a yellow one—I squeezed its belly, felt the give-and-rebound of firm foam. Raising the toy to my nose, I smelled nothing. The label said MADE IN TAIWAN OF LUV-PURE AND FIREPROOF MATERIALS. Below that was an approval seal from one of the family magazines.

Something along the seam—two snaps. A trapdoor flap that could be undone. I pulled it open. The sound made Cindy turn. Her eyebrows were up.

I poked around, found nothing, fastened the snap, and put the toy back.

"Allergies, right?" she said, talking just above a whisper. "To the stuffing—I thought of that too. But Dr. Eves had her tested and she's not allergic to anything. For a while, though, I washed the bunnies every day. Washed all her cloth toys and her bedding with Ivory Liquid. It's the gentlest."

I nodded.

"We pulled up the carpeting, too, to see if there was mold in the padding or something in the glue. Chip had heard of people getting sick in office buildings—'sick buildings,' they call them. We had a company come out and clean the air-conditioning ducts, and Chip had the paint checked, to see if there was lead or chemicals."

Her voice had risen and taken on an edge again. Cassie squirmed. Cindy rocked her quiet.

"I'm always looking," she whispered. "All the time—ever since . . . the beginning."

She covered her mouth with her hand. Removed the hand and slapped it down to her knee, pinkening the white skin.

Cassie's eyes shot open.

Cindy rocked harder, faster. Fighting for composure.

"First one, now the other," she whispered—loud, almost hissing. "Maybe I'm just not supposed to be a mother!"

I went over and placed my hand on her shoulder. She slid out from under it, shot up out of the rocker, and thrust Cassie at me. Tears streamed from her eyes, and her hands shook.

"Here! Here! I don't know what I'm doing. I'm not meant to be a mother!"

Cassie began whimpering, then gulping air.

Cindy thrust her at me again and, when I took her, ran across the room. My hands were around Cassie's waist. She was arching her back. Wailing, fighting me.

I tried to comfort her. She wouldn't let me.

Cindy threw open a door, exposing blue tile. Running into the bathroom, she slammed the door. I heard the sound of retching, followed by a toilet flush.

Cassie squirmed and kicked and screamed louder. I got a firm grasp around her middle and patted her back. "It's okay, honey. Mommy's coming right back. It's okay."

She coiled more violently, punching at my face, continuing to caterwaul. I tried to contain her while providing comfort. She jerked and turned scarlet, threw her little head back and howled, nearly slipping out of my grasp.

"Mommy's coming right back, Cass—"

The bathroom door opened and Cindy rushed out, wiping her eyes. I expected her to grab Cassie away but she just held out her hands and said, "Please," mouthing the word over Cassie's shrieks and looking as if she expected me to withhold her child.

I handed Cassie back to her.

She hugged the little girl and started to circle the room very fast. Taking large, hard steps that made her thin thighs quiver, and muttering things to Cassie that I couldn't hear.

Two dozen circuits and Cassie's cries got softer. Another dozen and she was quiet.

Cindy kept moving, but as she passed me she said, "I'm sorry—I really am. I'm sorry."

Her eyes and cheeks were wet. I told her it was okay. The sound of my voice made Cassie crank up again.

Cindy began walking faster, saying, "Baby, baby, baby."

I went over to the play table and sat as best I could on one of the tiny chairs. The welcome cardboard stared up at me like some kind of sick joke.

A few moments later, gasps and sucking sobs took the place of Cassie's cries. Then she silenced and I saw that her eyes were closed.

Cindy returned to the rocking chair and began to whisper harshly: "I'm really, really, really sorry. I'm so— That was— God, I'm a *horrible* mother!"

Barely audible, but the anguish in her voice opened Cassie's eyes. The little girl stared up at her mother and mewled.

"No, no, baby, it's okay. I'm sorry—it's okay."

Mouthing to me: "I'm horrible."

Cassie started to cry again.

"No, no, it's okay, honey. I'm good. If you want me to be good, I'm good. I'm a *good* mommy, yes, I am, yes—yes, honey, everything's okay. Okay?"

Forcing herself to smile down at Cassie. Cassie reached up and touched one of Cindy's cheeks.

"Oh, you are *so* good, little girl," said Cindy, in a crumbling voice. "You are *so* good to your mommy. You are *so, so good!*"

"Ma ma."

"Mama *loves* you."

"Ma ma."

"You're so good to your mama. Cassie Brooks Jones is the best girl, the sweetest girl."

"Ma ma. Mamama."

"Mama loves you *so* much. Mama loves you *so* much." Cindy looked at me. Looked at the play table.

"Mama loves you," she said into Cassie's ear. "And Dr. Delaware's a very good friend, honey. Here, see?"

She turned Cassie's head toward me. I tried another smile, hoping it looked better than it felt.

Cassie shook her head violently and said, "Nuh!"

"Remember, he's our friend, honey? All those pretty drawings he did for you at the hospita—"

"Nuh!"

"The animals—"

"Nuh *nuh!*"

"C'mon, honey, there's nothing to be scared of—"

"*Nuuuh!*"

"Okay, okay. It's okay, Cass."

I got up.

"Are you going?" said Cindy. Alarm in her voice.

I pointed to the bathroom. "May I?"

"Oh. Sure. There's one just off the entry hall too."

"This is fine."

"Sure . . . Meantime, I'll try to calm her down. . . . I'm really, really sorry."

*   *   *

I locked the door and the one leading to the master bedroom, flushed the toilet, and let out my breath. The water was as blue as the tiles. I found myself staring down at a tiny azure whirlpool. Turning on the water, I washed my face and dried it, catching a glimpse of myself in the mirror.

Dire and old with suspicion. I tried on a few smiles, finally settled on one that didn't approximate the leer of a used-car salesman. The mirror was the face of a medicine cabinet.

Child-proof latch. I undid it.

Four shelves. I turned the water up full blast, rifled quickly, starting at the top and working down.

Aspirin, Tylenol, razor blades, shaving cream. Men's cologne, deodorant, an emery board, a bottle of liquid antacid. A small yellow box of spermicidal jelly capsules. Hydrogen peroxide, a tube of earwax-dissolving ointment, suntan lotion . . .

I closed the cabinet. When I turned off the water I heard Cindy's voice through the door, saying something comforting and maternal.

Until she'd thrust Cassie at me, the little girl had accepted me.

Maybe I'm not supposed to be a mother. . . . I'm a horrible mother.

Stretched past the breaking point? Or trying to sabotage my visit?

I rubbed my eyes. Another cabinet beneath the sink. Another child-proof latch. Such careful parents, pulling up the carpets, washing the toys . . .

Cindy was cooing to Cassie.

Silently, I got down on my knees, freed the latch, and opened the door.

Beneath the snake of the drainpipe were boxes of tissues and rolls of plastic-wrapped toilet paper. Behind those sat two bottles of green mint mouthwash and an aerosol can. I examined the can. Pine-scented disinfectant. As I replaced it, it fell and my arm shot forward to catch it and mask the noise. I succeeded but the back of my hand knocked against something, off to the right, with sharp corners.

I pushed the paper goods aside and drew it out.

White cardboard box, about five inches square, imprinted on top with a red-arrow logo above stylized red script that read HOLLO-WAY MEDICAL CORP. Above that was an arrow-shaped gold foil sticker: SAMPLE, PRESENTED TO: *Ralph Benedict, M.D.*

A string-and-disc tie held the box shut. I unwound it, pushed back the flaps, and exposed a sheet of corrugated brown paper. Under that was a row of white plastic cylinders the size of ballpoint pens, nestled in a bed of Styrofoam peanuts. A folded slip of printed paper was rubber-banded to each one.

I fished out a cylinder. Feather-light, almost flimsy. A numbered ring girdled the bottom of the shaft. At the tip was a hole surrounded by screw thread; on the other end, a cap that twisted but didn't come off.

Black letters on the barrel said INSUJECT. I removed the printed paper. Manufacturer's brochure, copyrighted five years ago. Holloway Medical's home office was in San Francisco.

The first paragraph read:

INSUJECT (TM) is a dose-adjustable ultra-lightweight delivery system for the subcutaneous administration of human or purified pork insulin in 1 to 3 unit doses. INSUJECT should be used in conjunction with other components of the Holloway INSU-EASE (TM) system, namely, INSUJECT disposable needles and INSUFILL (TM) cartridges.

The second paragraph highlighted the selling points of the system: portability, an ultra-thin needle that reduced pain and the risk of subdermal abscesses, increased "ease of administration and precise calibration of dosage." A series of boxed line drawings illustrated needle attachment, loading of the cartridge into the cylinder, and the proper way to inject insulin beneath the skin.

Ease of administration.

An ultra-thin needle would leave a minuscule puncture wound, just as Al Macauley had described. If the injection site was concealed, the mark just might escape detection.

I groped around inside the box, looking for needles.

None, just the cylinders. Shoving my hands into the recesses of the cabinet yielded nothing more.

Probably cool enough to store insulin, but maybe someone was picky. Could Insufill cartridges be sitting on one of the shelves of the chrome-faced refrigerator in the kitchen?

Standing, I placed the box on the counter and the brochure in my pocket. The water in the toilet bowl had just stopped spinning. I cleared my throat, coughed, flushed again, looking around the room for another hiding place.

The only possibility I could see was the toilet tank. I lifted the cap and peered in. Just plumbing and the gizmo that dyed the water.

Ultra-thin needle . . . The bathroom was an ideal hiding place—perfect conduit from the master suite to the nursery.

Perfect for fixing up a middle-of-the-night injection:

Lock the door to the master suite, fetch the gear from beneath the sink, assemble it, and tiptoe into Cassie's room.

The bite of the needle would startle the little girl awake, probably make her cry, but she wouldn't know what had happened.

Neither would anyone else. Waking up in tears was normal for a child her age. Especially one who'd been sick so often.

Would darkness conceal the needle-wielder's face?

On the other side of the nursery door Cindy was talking, sounding sweet.

Then again, maybe there was an alternative explanation. The cylinders were meant for her. Or Chip.

No—Stephanie had said she'd tested both of them for metabolic disease and found them healthy.

I looked at the door to the master bedroom, then down at my watch. I'd spent three minutes in this blue-tile dungeon, but it felt like a weekend. Unlocking the door, I padded across the threshold into the bedroom, grateful for thick, tight-weave carpeting that swallowed my footsteps.

The room was darkened by drawn shutters and furnished with a king-size bed and clumsy Victorian furniture. Books were stacked high on one of the nightstands. A phone sat atop the stack. Next to the table was a brass-and-wood valet over which hung a pair of jeans. The other stand bore a Tiffany revival lamp and a coffee mug. The bedcovers were turned down but folded neatly. The room smelled of the pine disinfectant I'd found in the bathroom.

Lots of disinfectant. Why?

A double chest ran along the wall facing the bed. I opened a top drawer. Bras and panties and hose and floral sachet in a packet. I felt around, closed the drawer, got to work on the one below, wondering what thrill Dawn Herbert had gotten from petty theft.

Nine drawers. Clothing, a couple of cameras, canisters of film, and a pair of binoculars. Across the room was a closet. More clothes, tennis rackets and canisters of balls, a fold-up rowing machine, garment bags and suitcases, more books—all on sociology. A telephone directory, light bulbs, travel maps, a knee brace. Another box of contraceptive jelly. Empty.

I searched garment pockets, found nothing but lint. Maybe the dark corners of the closet concealed something but I'd been there too long. Shutting the closet door, I snuck back to the bathroom. The toilet had stopped gurgling and Cindy was no longer talking.

Had she grown suspicious about my prolonged absence? I cleared my throat again, turned on the water, heard Cassie's voice—some kind of protest—then the resumption of mommy-talk.

Detaching the toilet paper holder, I slid off the old roll and tossed it into the cabinet. Unwrapping a refill, I slipped it onto the dispenser. The ad copy on the wrapper promised to be gentle.

Picking up the white box, I pushed open the door to Cassie's room, wearing a smile that hurt my teeth.

They were at the play table, holding crayons. Some of the papers were covered with colored scrawl.

When Cassie saw me she gripped her mother's arm and began whining.

"It's okay, hon. Dr. Delaware's our friend." Cindy noticed the box in my hands and squinted.

I came closer and showed it to her. She stared at it, then up at me. I stared back, searching for any sign of self-indictment.

Just confusion.

"I was looking for toilet paper," I said, "and came across this."

She leaned forward and read the gold sticker.

Cassie watched her, then picked up a crayon and threw it. When that didn't capture her mother's attention, she whined some more.

"Shh, baby." Cindy's squint tightened. She continued to look baffled. "How strange."

Cassie threw her arms up and said, "Uh uh uh!"

Cindy pulled her closer and said, "Haven't seen those in a long time."

"Didn't mean to snoop," I said, "but I knew Holloway made equipment for diabetics and when I saw the label I got curious—thinking about Cassie's blood sugar. Are you or Chip diabetic?"

"Oh, no," she said. "Those were Aunt Harriet's. *Where* did you find them?"

"Beneath the sink."

"How odd. No, Cass, these are for drawing, not throwing." She picked up a red crayon and drew a jagged line.

Cassie followed the movement, then buried her head in Cindy's blouse.

"Boy, I haven't seen those in a really long time. I cleaned out her house, but I thought I threw all her medicines out."

"Was Dr. Benedict her doctor?"

"And her boss."

She bounced Cassie gently. Cassie peeked out from under her arm, then began poking her under the chin.

Cindy laughed and said, "You're tickling me. . . . Isn't that odd, under the sink all this time?" She gave an uneasy smile. "Guess that doesn't make me much of a housekeeper. Sorry you had to go looking for paper—I usually notice when the roller's low."

"No problem," I said, realizing there'd been no dust on the box.

Pulling out a cylinder, I rolled it between my fingers.

Cassie said, "Peh-il."

"No, it's not a pencil, honey." No anxiety. "It's just a . . . thing."

Cassie reached for it. I gave it to her and Cindy's eyes got wide. Cassie put it to her mouth, grimaced, lowered it to the paper and tried to draw.

"See, I told you, Cass. Here, if you want to draw, use this."

Cassie ignored the proffered crayon and kept looking at the cylinder. Finally she threw it down on the table and began to fuss.

"C'mon, sweetie, let's draw with Dr. Delaware."

My name evoked a whimper.

"Cassie *Brooks*, Dr. Delaware came all the way to play with you, to draw animals—hippos, kangaroos. Remember the kangaroos?"

Cassie whimpered louder.

"Hush, honey," said Cindy, but without conviction. "No, don't break your crayons, honey. You can't— C'mon, Cass."

"Uh uh uh." Cassie tried to get off Cindy's lap.

Cindy looked at me.

I offered no advice.

"Should I let her?"

"Sure," I said. "I don't want to be associated with confining her."

Cindy released her and Cassie made her way to the floor and crawled under the table.

"We did a little drawing while we were waiting for you," said Cindy. "I guess she's had enough."

She bent and looked under the table. "Are you tired of drawing, Cass? Do you want to do something else?"

Cassie ignored her and picked at the carpet fibers.

Cindy sighed. "I'm really sorry—for before. I . . . it just . . . I really blew it, didn't I? I really, really screwed things up—don't know what came over me."

"Sometimes things just pile up," I said, shifting the Insuject box from one hand to another. Keeping it in her view, looking for any sign of nervousness.

"Yes, but I still blew it for you and Cassie."

"Maybe it's more important for you and me to talk, anyway."

"Sure," she said, touching her braid and casting a glance under the table. "I could sure use some help, couldn't I? How about coming out now, Miss Cassie?"

No answer.

"Could I trouble you for another iced tea?" I said.

"Oh, sure, no trouble at all. Cass, Dr. Delaware and I are going into the kitchen."

Cindy and I walked to the door of the nursery. Just as we reached the threshold, Cassie crawled out, tottered upright, and came running toward Cindy, arms outstretched. Cindy picked her up and carried her on one hip. I followed, carrying the white box.

In the kitchen Cindy opened the refrigerator door with one hand and reached in for the pitcher. But before she could pull it out, Cassie slipped lower and Cindy needed both hands to hold her.

"Why don't you concentrate on her," I said, placing the box on the kitchen table and taking hold of the pitcher.

"Let me at least get you a glass." She went to the open cupboards across the room.

The moment her back was turned, I conducted a manic visual scan of the fridge. The most medicinal thing on the shelves was a tub of no-cholesterol margarine. Butter was in the butter compartment, the one marked CHEESE held a packet of sliced American.

Taking hold of the pitcher, I closed the door. Cindy was setting a glass on a place mat. I poured it half-full and drank. My throat felt raw. The tea tasted sweeter than before—almost sickly. Or maybe it was just my mind, lingering on thoughts of sugar.

Cassie watched me with a child's piercing suspicion. My smile caused her to frown. Wondering if trust could ever be regained, I put the glass down.

"Can I get you something else?" said Cindy.

"No, thanks. Better be going. Here." Offering her the box.

"Oh, I don't need it," she said. "Maybe someone at the hospital can use it. They're very expensive—that's why Dr. Ralph used to give us samples."

Us.

"That's very nice of you." I picked up the box.

"Well," she said, "we sure can't use them." She shook her head. "How strange, your finding them—kind of brings back memories."

Her mouth turned down. Cassie saw it, said, "Uh," and squirmed.

Cindy replaced the pout with a wide, abrupt smile. "Hello, sweetie."

Cassie poked at her mouth. Cindy kissed her fingers. "Yes, Mama loves you. Now let's walk Dr. Delaware bye-bye."

When we got to the entrance I stopped to look at the photos, realizing there were none of Chip's parents. My eyes settled back on the shot of Cindy and her aunt.

"We were walking that day," she said softly. "Along the dock. She used to take lots of walks. Long ones, for her diabetes—the exercise helped her control it."

"Did she have it pretty much under control?"

"Oh, yes—that wasn't what . . . what took her. That was an S-T-R-O-K-E. She had really great control—careful about everything that went into her mouth. When I lived with her, I wasn't allowed any sweets or junk. So I never developed a taste for it, and we don't keep much around the house."

She kissed Cassie's cheek. "I figure if she doesn't get a taste of it now, maybe she won't want it later."

I turned away from the photo.

"We do everything," she said, "to keep her healthy. Without health, there's . . . nothing. Right? That's the kind of thing you hear when you're young but it's only later that you start to believe it."

Anguish filled her eyes.

Cassie wiggled and made wordless sounds.

"True," I said. "How about you and me getting together tomorrow, right here."

"Sure."

"When would be a good time?"

"With or without . . . H-E-R?"

"Without, if possible."

"Then it would have to be when she's asleep. She generally naps from one to two or two-thirty, then goes down for the night at seven or eight. How about eight, in order to play it safe? If that's not too late for you."

"Eight's fine."

"Chip will probably be able to be here, too—that should be good, don't you think?"

"Absolutely," I said. "See you then."

She touched my arm. "Thanks for everything, and I'm really sorry. I know you'll help us get through this."

Back on Topanga, I pulled into the first gas station I saw and used the pay phone to call Milo at work.

"Perfect timing," he said. "Just got off the phone with Fort Jackson. Seems little Cindy was sick all right. *And* back in '83. But not pneumonia or meningitis. *Gonorrhea*. They drummed her out because of it, on an ELS—entry-level status. That means she served less than a hundred and eighty days and they wanted to get rid of her before they had to pay benefits."

"Just because of a dose?"

"A dose plus what led up to it. Seems during the four months she was there, she set some kind of record for sexual promiscuity. So if she's fooling around on hubby, that just means she's being consistent."

"Promiscuity," I said. "I just finished my home visit and this was the first time I got a sense of her sexuality. I arrived early, on purpose—curious about why she didn't want me out there until two-thirty. She'd let her hair down. Literally. Was wearing short shorts and a T-shirt with no bra."

"Coming on to you?"

"No. In fact she seemed really uncomfortable. A few minutes later she spilled some dirt on her clothes, hurried off to change and came back dowdied up."

"Maybe you just missed her boyfriend."

"Could be. She told me one-to-two was Cassie's nap time and Chip teaches a class that day from twelve to two, so what better time for an affair? And the bedroom smelled of disinfectant."

"Masking the smell of love," he said. "You didn't see anyone? Pass any cars speeding away?"

"Just the pool man pulling out of the driveway next door— Oh, shit, you don't think?"

"Sure I do." He laughed. "I see the worst in everyone." More laughter. "The pool man. Now there's your basic SoCal *thang*."

"He was next door, not at her house."

"So what? It's not unusual for those guys to service several pools on one block—that far out of town, he might do the whole damned neighborhood. More ways than one. Do the Joneses have a pool?"

"Yes, but it was covered."

"Get a look at Mr. Chlorine?"

"Young, tan, ponytail. The sign on his truck said ValleyBrite Pool Service, with an I-T-E."

"He see you pull up?"

"Yup. He stopped short, stuck his head out the window and stared, then gave this big grin with the thumb-up sign."

"Friendly, huh? Even if he'd just screwed her, he may not be the only one. Back in the army she was no nun."

"How'd you find out about it?"

"Wasn't easy. The army buries stuff just on principle. Charlie spent a lot of time trying to get into her file and couldn't. Finally, I swallowed my pride and called the colonel—only for you, bucko."

"Much appreciated."

"Yeah . . . To his credit, the asshole didn't gloat. Hooked me right up with an unlisted military number in D.C. Some kind of archive. They had no details—just name, rank, serial number, and her ELS designation, but I was lucky to get a records officer who'd done rice-paddy duty same time as me, and I convinced him to call South Carolina and find me someone to talk to. He came up with a female captain who'd been a corporal back when Cindy was a grunt. She remembered Cindy very well. Seems our gal was the talk of the barracks."

"It's an all-female base," I said. "Are we talking lesbian promiscuity?"

"Nope. She messed around in town—used to go on leave and party in the local bars. It ended, according to this captain, when Cindy hooked up with a bunch of teenagers and one of them happened to be the son of a local big shot. She gave him the clap. Mayor paid a visit to the base commander, and bye-bye. Sordid little tale, huh? Any relevance to the Munchausen thing?"

"Promiscuity's not part of the profile, but if you consider it another form of attention seeking, I guess it would be consistent. Also, Munchausens often report incest in childhood, and promiscuity could be another reaction to that. What *definitely* fits the profile is early experience with serious illness, and V.D. wasn't *her* first. The aunt who raised her was diabetic."

"Sugar screw-up. Interesting."

"Wait, there's more." I told him about finding the Insujects and showing them to Cindy.

"I thought it might be the confrontation we've been waiting for. But she didn't show any guilt or anxiety. Just puzzlement about what they were doing beneath the sink. She said they were leftovers from the aunt—something she thought she'd gotten rid of when she cleaned out the aunt's house after she died. But there was no dust on the box, so that's probably another lie."

"How long ago did the aunt die?"

"Four years. The doctor the samples were sent to was the aunt's physician and boss."

"Name?"

"Ralph Benedict. Hell, for all I know, *he's* the mystery lover.

Who'd be better at faking illnesses than a doctor? And we know she goes for older men—she married one."

"Younger ones too."

"Yeah. But it makes sense, doesn't it—a doctor boyfriend? Benedict could be supplying her with drugs and apparatus. Coaching her in faking illness."

"What's his motive?"

"True love. He sees the kids as encumbrances, wants to get rid of them and have Cindy all to himself. Maybe with some of Chip's money thrown in. As an M.D., he'd know how to set it up. Know how to be careful. Because two kids from one family dying, one right after another, is suspicious, but if the deaths were different and each looked medically valid, it could be pulled off."

"Ralph Benedict," he said. "I'll check with the medical board."

"Cindy grew up in Ventura. He might still be there."

"What's the name of the company who shipped him these cylinders?"

"Holloway Medical. San Francisco."

"Let's see what else they sent him and when. Cylinders—like empty tubes?"

"They're part of a kit." I described the Insuject system.

"No needles or drugs under the sink?"

"Nope, the needles and the insulin spansules come separately." I recounted my search of the bedroom and the refrigerator. "But they could be anywhere in that house. Any possibility of getting a search warrant now?"

"Just on the basis of tubes? Doubtful. With needles attached and the insulin all loaded up, maybe. That would be evidence of premeditation, though she could still claim the stuff was left over from the aunt."

"Not if the insulin was still fresh. I'm not sure of insulin's exact shelf life, but it's not four years."

"Yeah. So find me some fresh insulin and I'll visit a judge. Right now, there's no evidentiary chain."

"Even with Cassie's low sugar?"

"Even with. Sorry. Wonder why she left it under the sink like that."

"She probably never imagined anyone would look there. It was stuck in a corner—you'd have to be groping around to find it."

"And she wasn't pissed at all that you were snooping in her john?"

"If she was, she didn't show it. I made up a story about running out of toilet paper and going under the sink for a fresh roll. She apologized for not being a better housekeeper."

"Eager to please, huh? The boys back in South Carolina sure took advantage of it."

"Or she gets people to do what she wants by playing dumb and passive. I didn't walk out of that house feeling in control."

"Ye olde bathroom detective. Sounds like you're ready for the Vice Squad."

"I'll pass. The whole thing was surreal. Not that I was doing much good as a therapist."

I told him how Cindy had thrust Cassie at me, and Cassie's subsequent panic.

"Up till then my rapport with Cassie had been progressing pretty well. Now, it's shot to hell, Milo. So I have to wonder if Cindy was deliberately trying to sabotage me."

"Waltzing and leading, huh?"

"Something she told me suggests that control is a big issue for her. When she was a kid, the aunt wouldn't let her eat any sweets at all, even though there was nothing wrong with *her* pancreas. That's a far cry from Munchausen, but there is a hint of pathology there—not allowing a healthy child to have an occasional ice cream."

"Aunt projecting the diabetes onto her?"

"Exactly. And who knows if there were other aspects of the disease the aunt projected—like injections. Not insulin, but maybe some kind of vitamin shots. I'm just guessing. Cindy also told me that she restricts Cassie's sweets. At face value, that sounds like good mothering. Reasonable health-consciousness from someone who's already lost one child. But maybe there's a whole weird thing going on with regard to sugar."

"Sins of the mothers," he said.

"The aunt was *Cindy's* functional mother. And look at the role model she provided: a health professional who had a chronic disease and *controlled* it—Cindy spoke of that with pride. She may have grown up associating being female—being *maternal*—with being sick and emotionally rigid: controlled and control*ling*. It's no surprise she chose the military right after high school—from one structured environment to another. When that didn't work out, her next step was respiratory tech school. Because Aunt Harriet told her it was a good profession. Control and illness—it keeps repeating itself."

"She ever mention why she didn't finish respiratory tech school?"

"No. What are you thinking—more promiscuity?"

"I'm a big believer in patterns. What'd she do after that?"

"Junior college. Where she met Chip. She dropped out, got married. Got pregnant right away—more big changes that might have made her feel out of control. The marriage was a step up for her socially, but she ended up living in a very lonely place."

I described Dunbar Court and the surrounding tract.

"Slow death for someone who craves attention, Milo. And when Chip gets home, I'll bet the situation doesn't change much. He's really into the academic life—big fish in a small pond. I dropped by the J.C. before I went to the house and caught a glimpse of him teaching. Guru on the grass, disciples at his feet. A whole world she's not part of. The house reflects it—room after room of *his* books, *his* trophies, masculine furniture. Even in her own home she hasn't made an imprint."

"So she makes an imprint on the kid."

"Using familiar tools, things she remembers from her childhood. Insulin, needles. Other poisons—manipulating what goes into Cassie's mouth the same way her aunt controlled her."

"What about Chad?"

"Maybe he actually did die of SIDS—yet another traumatic illness in Cindy's life—and *that* was the stress that drove her over the edge. Or maybe she smothered him."

"You think your finding the cylinders will scare her off?"

"That would be logical, but with Munchausen, the whole power game, I suppose it could do just the opposite—raise the ante, challenge her to get the better of me. So maybe I just made things more dangerous for Cassie—hell if I know."

"Don't flog yourself. Where are the cylinders now?"

"Right here. In the car. Can you have them dusted for prints?"

"Sure, but Cindy's or Chip's prints on it wouldn't mean much— one of them stashed it years ago and forgot about it."

"What about the lack of dust?"

"It's a clean cabinet. Or you knocked off whatever dust was on it when you took it out. I'm talking like a defense attorney now, though we're not even close to making anyone need one. And if this Benedict guy touched it, that's cool too. They were sent to him in the first place."

"With the aunt dead, there'd be no reason for him to give them to Cindy."

"True. If we can pin down this shipment to him *after* the aunt died, that would be great. Any serial numbers on the things? Or an invoice?"

"Let me check . . . no invoice. But there are serial numbers. And the copyright on the manufacturer's brochure is five years old."

"Good. Give me those numbers and I'll get on it. In the meantime, I still think your best bet is to continue playing with Cindy's head. Give her a taste of her own medicine."

"How?"

"Pull her in for a meeting, without the kid—"

"That's already set up for tomorrow evening. Chip'll be there too."

"Even better. Confront her, straight on. Tell her you think someone is making Cassie sick and you know *how*. Hold up a cylinder and say you're not buying any of this leftover crap. You want to take chances, go for a big bluff: say you've talked to the D.A. and he's ready to file charges for attempted murder. Then pray she cracks."

"And if she doesn't?"

"You get thrown off the case, but at least she'll know someone's wise to her. I don't see what you can gain by waiting any longer, Alex."

"What about Stephanie? Do I clue her in? Are we eliminating her as a suspect?"

"Like we said before, she could be Cindy's secret lover, but there's no sign of that. And if she *was* involved, why would Cindy mess with Benedict? Stephanie's a doctor—she could get the same stuff he could. Anything's possible, but far as I can tell, the mom started out looking good and she keeps getting better."

"If Stephanie's off the hook," I said, "I should let her in on it—she's the primary doc. Pulling something this strong without her knowledge is probably unethical."

"Why don't you just sound her out and see how she reacts? Tell her about the cylinders and see where she goes with it. If you're satisfied she's clean, take her along with you when you play with Cindy's head. Strength in numbers."

"Play with her head? Sounds fun."

"It rarely is," he said. "If I could do it for you, I would."

"Thanks. For everything."

"Anything else?"

Finding the Insujects had pushed the visit to Dr. Janos's office out of my head.

"Plenty," I said, and told him how Huenengarth had beat me to Dawn Herbert's computer disks. Then I threw in my calls to Ferris Dixon and Professor W. W. Zimberg's office, and my updated blackmail theories on Herbert and Ashmore.

"High intrigue, Alex—maybe some of it's even true. But don't let yourself get distracted from Cassie. I'm still checking on Huenengarth. Nothing yet, but I'll stay on it. Where will you be in case something does come up?"

"I'll call Stephanie soon as we hang up. If she's in her office I'll run over to the hospital. If not, I'll be home."

"All right. How about we get together later tonight, trade miseries. Eight okay?"

"Eight's fine. Thanks again."

"Don't thank me. We're a long way from feeling good about this one."

The General Peds receptionist said, "Dr. Eves stepped out. Let me page her."

I waited, looking out through the clouded walls of the phone booth at traffic and dust. The equestrians came into view again, cantering up a side street, heading back from what must have been a circuit. Slim jodhpured legs clamped around glistening torsos. Lots of smiles.

Probably heading back to the club for cold drinks and conversation. I thought of all the ways Cindy Jones could have chosen to fill her time.

Just as the horses vanished, the receptionist came back on the line. "She's not answering, Doctor. Would you like to leave a message?"

"Any idea when she'll be back?"

"I know she's coming back for a five o'clock meeting—you might try her just before then."

Five P.M. was almost two hours away. I drove down Topanga

thinking of all the damage that could be done to a child in that time. Kept heading south to the on-ramp.

Traffic was backed up to the street. I nosed into the snail-trail and oozed eastward. Nasty drive to Hollywood. At night, though, the ambulance would fairly zip.

I pulled into the doctors' lot just before four, clipped my badge to my lapel, and walked to the lobby, where I paged Stephanie. The anxiety that had hit me only a week ago was gone. In its place, a driving sense of anger.

What a difference seven days make . . .

No answer. I phoned her office again, got the same receptionist, the same answer, delivered in a slightly annoyed tone.

I went up to the General Peds clinic and walked into the examination suite, passing patients, nurses, and doctors without notice.

Stephanie's door was closed. I wrote a note for her to call me and was bending to slip it under the door when a husky female voice said, "Can I help you?"

I straightened. A woman in her late sixties was looking at me. She had on the whitest white coat I'd ever seen, worn buttoned over a black dress. Her face was deeply tanned, wrinkled, and pinch-featured under a helmet of straight white hair. Her posture would have made a marine correct his own.

She saw my badge and said, "Oh, excuse me, Doctor." Her accent was Marlene Dietrich infused with London. Her eyes were small, green-blue, electrically alert. A gold pen was clipped to her breast pocket. She wore a thin gold chain from which a single pearl dangled, set in a golden nest like a nacreous egg.

"Dr. Kohler," I said. "Alex Delaware."

We shook hands and she read my badge. Confusion didn't suit her.

"I used to be on the staff," I said. "We worked together on some cases. Crohn's disease. Adaptation to the ostomy?"

"Ah, of course." Her smile was warm and it made the lie inoffensive. She'd always had that smile, wore it even while cutting down a resident's faulty diagnosis. Charm planted by an upper-class Prague childhood cut short by Hitler, then fertilized by marriage to The Famous Conductor. I remembered how she'd offered to use her connections to bring funds to the hospital. How the board had turned her down, calling that kind of fund-raising "crass."

"Looking for Stephanie?" she said.

"I need to talk to her about a patient."

The smile hung there but her eyes iced over. "I happen to be looking for her myself. She's scheduled to be here. But I suppose our future division head must be busy."

I feigned surprise.

"Oh, yes," she said. "Those in the know say her promotion is imminent."

The smile got wider and took on a hungry cast. "Well, all the best to her . . . though I hope she learns to anticipate events a bit better. One of her teenage patients just showed up without an appointment and is creating a scene out in the waiting room. And Stephanie left without checking out."

"Doesn't sound like her," I said.

"Really? Lately, it's *become* like her. Perhaps she sees herself as having already ascended."

A nurse passed by. Kohler said, "Juanita?"

"Yes, Dr. Kohler?"

"Have you seen Stephanie?"

"I think she went out."

"Out of the hospital?"

"I think so, Doctor. She had her purse."

"Thank you, Juanita."

When the nurse had gone, Kohler pulled a set of keys out of a pocket.

"Here," she said, jamming one of the keys into Stephanie's lock and turning. Just as I caught the door, she yanked the key out sharply and walked away.

The espresso machine was off but a half-full demitasse sat on the desk, next to Stephanie's stethoscope. The smell of fresh roast overpowered the alcohol bite seeping in from the examining rooms. Also on the desk were a pile of charts and a memo pad stuffed with drug company stationery. As I slipped my note under it I noticed writing on the top sheet.

Dosages, journal references, hospital extensions. Below that, a solitary notation, scrawled hastily, barely legible.

> B, Brwsrs, 4

Browsers—the place where she'd gotten the leather-bound Byron. I saw the book, up in the shelf.

B for Byron? Getting another one?

Or meeting someone at the bookstore? If it meant today, she was there now.

It seemed an odd assignation in the middle of a hectic afternoon. Not like her.

Until recently, if Kohler was to be believed.

Something romantic that she wanted segregated from the hospital rumor mill? Or just seeking out some privacy—a quiet moment among the mildew and the verse.

Lord knew she was entitled to her privacy.

Too bad I was going to violate it.

Only a half-mile from the hospital to Los Feliz and Hollywood, but traffic was lobotomized and it took ten minutes to get there.

The bookstore was on the west side of the street, its facade the same as it had been a decade ago: cream-colored sign with black gothic letters spelling out ANTIQUARIAN BOOK MERCHANT above dusty windows. I cruised past, looking for a parking space. On my second go-round I spotted an old Pontiac with its back-up lights on, and waited as a very small, very old woman eased away from the curb. Just as I finished pulling in, someone came out of the bookstore.

Presley Huenengarth.

Even at this distance his mustache was nearly invisible.

I slumped low in the car. He fiddled with his tie, took a pair of sunglasses out, slipped them on, and shot quick looks up and down the street. I ducked lower, pretty sure he hadn't seen me. He touched his tie again, then began walking south until he came to the corner. Turning right, he was gone.

I sat up.

Coincidence? There'd been no book in his hand.

But it was hard to believe he was the one Stephanie was meeting. Why would she call him "B"?

She didn't like him, had called him spooky.

Gotten *me* thinking of him as spooky.

Yet *his* bosses were promoting her.

Had she been talking the rebel line while fraternizing with the enemy?

All for the sake of career advancement?

Do you see me as a division head, Alex?

Every other doctor I'd spoken to was talking about leaving, but *her* eye was on a promotion.

Rita Kohler's hostility implied it wouldn't be a bloodless transition. Was Stephanie being rewarded for good behavior—treating the chairman's grandchild without making waves?

I remembered her absence at the Ashmore memorial. Her showing up late, claiming she'd been tied up.

Maybe true, but in the old days she'd have found a way to be there. Would have been up on the dais.

I kept thinking about it as I sat there, wanting to see it another way. Then Stephanie came out of the store and I knew I couldn't.

Satisfied smile on her face.

No books in her hand either.

She looked up and down the block the same way he had.

Big plans for Dr. Eves.

Rat jumping *onto* a sinking ship?

I'd driven over intending to show her the Insuject cartridges. Ready to study her reaction, declare her innocent and make her a part of tomorrow night's confrontation of Cindy Jones.

Now, I didn't know where she stood. Milo's first suspicions of her began to solidify.

Something wrong—something off.

I lowered my head again.

She began walking. In the same direction *he* had.

Came to the corner, looked to the right. Where *he'd* gone.

She lingered there for a while. Still smiling. Finally crossed the street and kept going.

I waited until she was out of sight, then drove away. The moment I cleared the space, someone zipped in.

First time all day I'd felt useful.

When I got home, just before five, I found a note from Robin saying she'd be working late unless I had something else on my mind. I had plenty, but none of it included fun. I called her, got a machine and told her I loved her and that I'd be working too. Though as I said it, I realized I didn't know at what.

I phoned Parker Center. A nasal, high-pitched male voice answered.

"Records."

"Detective Sturgis, please."

"He's not *he-ere*."

"When will he be back?"

"Who is this?"

"Alex Delaware. A friend."

He pronounced my name as if it were a disease, then said, "I have absolutely no *ide-a*, Mr. Delaware."

"Do you know if he's gone for the day?"

"I wouldn't know that *either*."

"Is this Charlie?"

Pause. Throat clear. "This is *Charles* Flannery. Do I *know* you?"

"No, but Milo's talked about how much you've taught him."

Longer pause, more throat clears. "How *grand* of him. If you're interested in your *friend's* schedule, I suggest you call the deputy chief's office."

"Why would they know?"

"Because he's *there*, Mr. Delaware. As of half an hour ago. And please don't ask me why, because I don't *kno-ow*. No one tells me *anything*."

*   *   *

The deputy chief's. Milo in trouble again. I hoped it wasn't because of something he'd done for me. As I thought about it, Robin called back.

"Hi, how's the little girl?"

"I may have pinned down what's happening to her, but I'm worried it may have made things worse for her."

"How could that be?"

I told her.

She said, "Have you told Milo yet?"

"I just tried to reach him and he's been called into the deputy chief's office. He's been free-lancing for me on the department computer. I hope it didn't mess him up."

"Oh," she said. "Well, he can handle himself—he's shown that."

"What a mess," I said. "This case is bringing back too many memories, Robin. All those years at the hospital—eighty-hour weeks and all the suffering you can eat. So much garbage I couldn't do anything *about*. The doctors weren't always effective either, but at least they had their pills and their scalpels. All I had were words and nods and meaningful pauses and some fancy behavioral technology that I rarely got a chance to use. Half the time I walked around the wards feeling like a carpenter with bad tools."

She said nothing.

"Yeah, I know," I said. "Self-pity's a bore."

"You can't suckle the world, Alex."

"Now there's an image for you."

"I mean it. You're as masculine as they come but sometimes I think you're a frustrated mother—wanting to *feed* everyone. Take *care* of everything. That can be good—look at all the people you've helped. *Including* Milo, but—"

"Milo?"

"Sure. Look at what he's got to deal with. A gay *cop* in a department that denies there's any such thing. Officially, he doesn't exist. Think of the alienation, day in and day out. Sure he's got Rick, but that's his other world. Your friendship's a connection for him—an extension to the rest of the world."

"I'm not his friend out of charity, Robin. It's no big political thing. I just like him as a human being."

"Exactly. He knows the kind of friend you are—he once told me it took him six months to get used to having a straight friend. Someone who would just take him at face value. Told me he hadn't had a friend like that since junior high. He also appreciates the fact that you don't play therapist with him. That's why he extends himself for you. And if he's gotten in trouble because of it, he can deal with it. Lord knows he's dealt with worse— Oops, gotta turn off the saw. That's all the profundity you get out of me today."

"When did you get so wise?"

"It's always been there, Curly. You just have to have your eyes open."

Alone again, I felt like jumping out of my skin. I called my service. Four messages: a lawyer asking me to consult on a child custody case, someone with an M.B.A. promising to help me build my practice, the county psychological association wanting to know if I was going to attend the next monthly meeting and, if so, did I want chicken or fish. The last, from Lou Cestare, letting me know he'd found nothing new on George Plumb's former employers but would keep trying.

I tried Milo again, on the off chance he'd returned from the deputy chief's office. Charles Flannery's voice came on and I hung up.

What *was* Stephanie up to, meeting with Huenengarth?

Just malignant careerism or had someone leaned on her, too— the old drunk-driving arrest.

Or maybe her drinking wasn't ancient history. What if the drinking was still out of control and they were exploiting *that*?

Exploiting while grooming her for division head?

It didn't make sense—but maybe it did.

If I was right about Chuck Jones wanting to dissolve the hospital, hiring an impaired division head would fit beautifully.

Rat climbing aboard a sinking ship . . .

I thought of someone who'd jumped off.

What *had* made Melendez-Lynch finally leave?

I didn't know if he'd talk to me. Our last contact, years ago, had been tainted by his humiliation—a case gone very bad, a lapse of ethics on his part that I'd learned about without wanting to.

But what was there to lose?

Miami Information had one listing for him. Our Lady of Mercy Hospital. It was eight-thirty in Florida. His secretary would be gone, but unless Raoul had undergone a personality transplant, he'd still be working.

I dialed. A recorded voice, female and cultured, informed me I'd reached the chief physician's office, which was now closed, and enunciated a series of touch-tone codes for reaching Dr. Melendez-Lynch's voice mail.

I pressed the Instant Page code and waited for a callback, wondering when machines were going to start calling one another and eliminating the messiness of the human factor.

A still-familiar voice said, "Dr. Melendez-Lynch."

"Raoul? It's Alex Delaware."

"*Ahleex?* No keeding. How *are* you?"

"Fine, Raoul. And you?"

"Much too fat and much too busy, but otherwise superb . . . What a surprise. Are you here in Miami?"

"No, still in L.A."

"Ahh . . . So tell me, how have you been spending the last few years?"

"Same as before."

"Back in practice?"

"Short-term consults."

"Short term . . . still retired, eh?"

"Not exactly. How about you?"

"Also more of the same, Alex. We are doing some very exciting things—advanced cell-wall permeability studies in the carcinogenesis lab, several pilot grants on experimental drugs. So tell me, to what do I owe the honor of this call?"

"I've got a question for you," I said, "but it's personal, not professional, so if you don't want to answer it, just say so."

"Personal?"

"About your leaving."

"What do you want to know about it?"

"Why you did it."

"And why, may I ask, are you suddenly so curious about my motivation?"

"Because I'm back at Western Peds, consulting on a case. And

the place looks really *sad*, Raoul. Low morale, people quitting—
people I never thought would leave. You're the one I know best, so
I'm calling you."

"Yes, that is personal," he said. "But I don't mind answering."
He laughed. "The answer is very simple, Alex. I left because I was
unwanted."

"By the new administration?"

"Yes. The Visigoths. The choice they gave me was simple.
Leave, or die professionally. It was a matter of survival. Despite what
anyone will tell you, money had nothing to do with it. No one ever
worked at Western Peds for the money—you know that. Though the
money got worse, too, when the Visigoths took control. Wage
freezes, hiring freezes, eating away at our secretarial staff, a totally
arrogant attitude toward the physicians—as if we were their servants.
They even stuck us out on the street in trailers. Like derelicts. I could
tolerate all of that because of the *work*. The research. But when that
ended, there was simply no reason to stay on."

"They cut off your research?"

"Not explicitly. However, at the beginning of the last academic
year the board announced a new policy: Because of financial difficulties, the hospital would no longer chip in for overhead on research
grants. You know how the government works—on so many grants,
any money they give you depends upon the host institution contrib-
uting expenses. Some of the private foundations are also insisting
upon it now. All of my funding came from NCI. A no-overhead rule
essentially *nullified* all of my projects. I tried to argue, yelled,
screamed, showed them figures and facts—what we were trying to *do*
with our research; this was pediatric *cancer,* for God's sake. No use. So
I flew to Washington and talked with *government* Visigoths, trying to
get them to suspend the rules. That, too, was futile. Our kinder and
gentler bunch, eh? None of them functions at a human level. So what
were my options, Alex? Stay on as an overeducated technician and
give up fifteen years of work?"

"Fifteen years," I said. "Must have been hard."

"It wasn't easy, but it turned out to be a *fantastic* decision. Here,
at Mercy, I sit on the board as a voting member. There are plenty of
idiots here, too, but I can ignore them. As a bonus, my second
child—Amelia—is enrolled at the medical school in Miami and lives

with me. My condominium overlooks the ocean and on the rare occasion I visit Little Havana, it makes me feel like a little boy. It was like surgery, Alex. The process was painful but the results were worth it."

"They were stupid to lose you."

"Of course they were. Fifteen years and not even a gold watch." He laughed. "These are not people who hold physicians in awe. All that matters to them is money."

"Jones and Plumb?"

"And that pair of dogs trailing after them—Novak and whatever. They may be accountants but they remind me of Fidel's thugs. Take my advice, Alex: Don't get too involved there. Why don't you come out to Miami and put your skills to use where they'll be appreciated? We'll write a grant together. The AIDS thing is paramount now—so much sadness. Two thirds of our hemophiliacs have received infected blood. You could be useful here, Alex."

"Thanks for the invitation, Raoul."

"It's a sincere one. I remember the good we did together."

"So do I."

"Think about it, Alex."

"Okay."

"But of course you won't."

Both of us laughed.

I said, "Could I ask you one more thing?"

"Also personal?"

"No. What do you know about the Ferris Dixon Institute for Chemical Research?"

"Never heard of it. Why?"

"It funded a doctor at Western Peds. *With* overhead."

"Really. And which guy is this?"

"A toxicologist named Laurence Ashmore. He's done some epidemiologic work on childhood cancer."

"Ashmore . . . never heard of him either. What kind of epidemiology does he do?"

"Pesticides and malignancy rates. Mostly theoretical stuff, playing with numbers."

He snorted. "How much did this institute give him?"

"Nearly a million dollars."

Silence.

"What?"

"It's true," I said.

"With *overhead*?"

"High, huh?"

"Absurd. What's the name of this institute?"

"Ferris Dixon. They only funded one other study, much smaller. An economist named Zimberg."

"With overhead . . . Hmm, I'll have to check into that. Thank you for the tip, Alex. And think about my offer. The sun shines here too."

I didn't hear from Milo and had doubts if he'd make our eight o'clock meeting. When he hadn't shown up by twenty after, I figured whatever had held him up at Parker Center had gotten in the way. But at 8:37 the bell rang, and when I opened the door it was him. Someone was standing behind him.

Presley Huenengarth. His face floated over Milo's shoulder like a malignant moon. His mouth was as small as a baby's.

Milo saw the look in my eyes, gave an it's-okay wink, put his hand on my shoulder, and walked in. Huenengarth hesitated for a moment before following. His hands were at his sides. No gun. No bulge in his jacket; no sign of coercion.

The two of them could have been a cop team.

Milo said, "Be right with you," and went into the kitchen.

Huenengarth stood there. His hands were thick and mottled and his eyes were everywhere. The door was still open. When I closed it, he didn't move.

I walked into the living room. Though I couldn't hear him, I knew he was following me.

He waited for me to sit on the leather sofa, unbuttoned his jacket, then sank into an armchair. His belly bulged over his belt, straining the white broadcloth of his button-down shirt. The rest of him was broad and hard. His neck flesh was cherry-blossom pink and swelled over his collar. A carotid pulse plinked through, steady and rapid.

I heard Milo messing in the kitchen.

Huenengarth said, "Nice place. Any view?"

It was the first time I'd heard his voice. Midwest inflections, medium-pitched, on the reedy side. On the phone it would conjure a much smaller man.

I didn't answer.

He put a hand on each knee and looked around the room some more.

More kitchen noise.

He turned toward it and said, "Far as I'm concerned, people's personal lives are their own business. As long as what he is doesn't get in the way of the job, I could care less. Matter of fact, I can help him."

"Great. You want to tell me who you are?"

"Sturgis claims you know how to keep a secret. Few people do."

"Especially in Washington?"

Blank stare.

"Or is it Norfolk, Virginia?"

He pursed his lips and turned his mouth into a peeved little blossom. The mustache above it was little more than a mouse-colored stain. His ears were close-set, lobeless, and pulled down into his bull neck. Despite the season, the gray suit was a heavy worsted. Cuffed pants, black oxfords that had been resoled, blue pen in his breast pocket. He was sweating just below the hairline.

"You've been trying to follow me," he said. "But you really have no idea what's going on."

"Funny, I felt followed."

He shook his head. Gave a stern look. As if he were the teacher and I'd guessed wrong.

"So educate me," I said.

"I need a pledge of total discretion."

"About what?"

"Anything I tell you."

"That's pretty broad."

"That's what I need."

"Does it have to do with Cassie Jones?"

The fingers on his knees began drumming. "Not directly."

"But indirectly."

He didn't answer.

I said, "You want a pledge from me, but you won't give an inch. You've *got* to work for the government."

Silence. He examined the pattern of my Persian rug.

"If it compromises Cassie," I said, "I can't pledge anything."

"You're wrong," he said, and gave another headshake. "If you really cared about her, you wouldn't obstruct me."

"Why's that?"

"I can help her too."

"You're a pretty helpful guy, aren't you?"

He shrugged.

"If you're able to stop the abuse, why haven't you?"

He ceased drumming and touched one index finger to the other. "I didn't say I was *omniscient*. But I can be useful. *You* haven't made much progress so far, have you?"

Before I could answer, he was up and headed for the kitchen. He returned with Milo, who was carrying three cups of coffee.

Taking one for himself, Milo put the remaining two on the coffee table and settled on the other end of the sofa. Our eyes met. He gave a small nod. Trace of apology.

Huenengarth sat back down, in a different chair from the one he'd just gotten out of. Neither he nor I touched our coffee.

Milo said, "Skoal," and drank.

"Now what?" I said.

"Yeah," said Milo. "He's low on charm, but maybe he can do what he says he can."

Huenengarth turned toward him and glared.

Milo sipped, crossed his legs.

I said, "You're here of your own free will, huh?"

Milo said, "Well, everything's relative." To Huenengarth: "Stop playing Junior G-man and give the man some data."

Huenengarth glared some more. Turned to me. Looked at his coffee cup. Touched his mustache.

"This theory you have," he told me, "about Charles Jones and George Plumb destroying the hospital—who've you discussed it with so far?"

"It's not *my* theory. The entire staff thinks the administration's screwing the place over."

"The entire staff hasn't taken it as far as you have. Who've you talked to besides Louis B. Cestare?"

I hid my surprise and my fear. "Lou's not involved in this."

Huenengarth half-smiled. "Unfortunately, he is, Doctor. A man in his position, all those links to the financial world—he could have turned out to be a knotty problem for me. Fortunately, he's being cooperative. At this very moment. Conferring with one of my colleagues up in Oregon. My colleague says Mr. Cestare's estate is quite lovely."

Full smile. "Don't worry, Doctor, we only bring out the thumb-screws as a last resort."

Milo put down his coffee. "Why don't you just cut to the chase, bucko?"

Huenengarth's smile vanished. He sat up straighter and looked at Milo.

Silent stare.

Milo gave a disgusted look and drank coffee.

Huenengarth waited a while before turning back to me. "Is there anyone else you've spoken to in addition to Mr. Cestare? Not counting your girlfriend, Ms.—uh—Castagna. Don't worry, Doctor. From what I know about her, she isn't likely to leak a story to *The Wall Street Journal*."

"What the hell do you want?" I said.

"The names of anyone you've included in your fantasy. Specifically, people with business connections or a reason to harbor a grudge against Jones or Plumb."

I glanced at Milo. He nodded, though he didn't look happy.

"Just one other person," I said. "A doctor who used to work at Western Peds. Now he lives in Florida. But I didn't tell him anything he didn't already know and we didn't go into any details—"

"Dr. Lynch," said Huenengarth.

I swore. "What'd you do, tap my phone?"

"No, that wasn't necessary. Dr. Lynch and I talk once in a while. Have been talking for a while."

"*He* tipped you off?"

"Let's not get sidetracked, Dr. Delaware. The main thing is *you* told me about speaking to *him*. That's good. Admirably frank. I also like the way you wrestled with it. Moral dilemmas mean something to you—I don't get to see that too often. So now I trust you more than when I walked into this room, and that's good for both of us."

"Gee, I'm touched," I said. "What's my reward? Learning your real name?"

"Cooperation. Maybe we can be mutually helpful. To Cassie Jones."

"How can you help her?"

He folded his arms across his barrel chest. "Your theory—the *entire staff's* theory—is appealing. For a one-hour TV episode. Greedy capitalists sucking the lifeblood out of a beloved institution; the good guys come in and clean it up; cut to commercial."

"Who're the good guys here?"

He put a hand to his chest. "I'm hurt, Doctor."

"What are you, FBI?"

"A different collection of letters—it wouldn't mean anything to you. Let's get back to your theory: appealing, but wrong. Do you remember Cestare's first reaction when you floated it by him?"

"He said it was unlikely."

"Why?"

"Because Chuck Jones was a builder, not a destroyer."

"Ah."

"But then he looked up *Plumb's* job history and found out companies *he's* been associated with tend not to live long. So maybe Jones has changed his style and is going for slash and burn."

"Plumb *is* a slash-and-burn man," he said. "Got a long history of setting up companies for raiders, then taking fat commissions on the buy-out. But those were companies backed up by *assets* that made them worth plundering. Where's the incentive to destroy a nonprofit money-loser like Western Pediatrics? Where are the *assets*, Doctor?"

"The real estate the hospital sits on, for a start."

"The real estate." Another headshake, accompanied by a finger wag. The guy had a definite tutorial bent. "As a matter of fact, the land is owned by the city and leased to the hospital under a ninety-nine-year contract, the contract's renewable for another ninety-nine at the hospital's request, and the rent's a dollar a year. Public record—look it up at the assessor's office, just as I did."

"You're not here because Jones and his gang are innocents," I said. "What are they after?"

He moved forward on his chair. "Think *convertible* assets, Doctor. A massive supply of high-quality stocks and bonds at Chuck Jones's disposal."

"The hospital's investment portfolio—Jones manages it. What's he doing, skimming?"

Yet another headshake. "Proximate but no panatela, Doctor. Though that's also a reasonable assumption. As it turns out, the hospital's portfolio is a joke. Thirty years of dipping into it to balance the operating budget has stripped it down to bare bones. In fact, Chuck Jones has built it up some—he's a very savvy investor. But rising costs keep eating away at it. There'll never be enough in there to make it worth fooling with—not at Jones's level."

"What's his level?"

"Eight figures. Major-league financial manipulation. Fisk and Gould would have counted their fingers after shaking hands with Chuck Jones. His public image is that of a financial wizard and he's even saved a few companies along the way. But it's his *plundering* that fuels it all. The man's destroyed more businesses than the Bolsheviks."

"So he's a slash-and-burn man, too, as long as the price is high enough."

Huenengarth looked up at the ceiling.

"Why doesn't anyone know about it?" I said.

He scooted forward a bit more. Very little of him was touching the chair.

"They will soon," he said quietly. "I've been on his trail for four and a half years and the end's finally in sight. No one's going to fuck it up—that's why I need total discretion. I *won't* get derailed. Understand?"

The pink of his neck had deepened to tomato-aspic. He fingered his collar, loosened his tie and opened it.

"*He's* discreet," he said. "Covers himself beautifully. But I'm going to beat him at his own game."

"Covers himself how?"

"Layers of shadow corporations and holding companies, phony syndicates, foreign bank accounts. Literally *hundreds* of trading accounts, operating simultaneously. Plus battalions of lackeys like Plumb and Roberts and Novak, most of whom only know a small part of each picture. It's a screen so effective that even people like Mr. Cestare don't see through it. But when he falls, he's going to fall hard, Doctor, I promise you. He's made mistakes and I've got him in my sights."

"So what's he plundering at Western Peds?"

"You really don't need to know the details."

He picked up his coffee cup and drank.

I thought back to my conversation with Lou.

Why would a syndicate buy it, then shut it down?

Could be any number of reasons . . . They wanted the company's resources, rather than the company itself.

What kinds of resources?

Hardware, investments, the pension fund . . .

"The doctors' pension fund," I said. "Jones manages that, too, doesn't he?"

He put down the cup. "The hospital charter says it's his responsibility."

"What's he done with it? Turned it into his personal cashbox?"

He said nothing.

Milo said, "Shit."

"Something like that," said Huenengarth, frowning.

"The pension fund is eight figures?" I said.

"A healthy eight."

"Come on, how's that possible?"

"Some luck, some skill, but mostly just the passage of time, Doctor. Ever calculate what a thousand dollars left in a five percent savings account for seventy years would be worth? Try it some time. The doctors' pension fund is seventy years' worth of blue chip stocks and corporate bonds that have increased ten, twenty, fifty, hundreds of times over, split and resplit dozens of times, and paid out dividends that are reinvested in the fund. Since World War Two the stock market's been on a steady upward swing. The fund's full of gems like IBM purchased at two dollars a share, Xerox at one. And, unlike a commercial investment fund, almost nothing goes out. The rules of the fund say it can't be used for hospital expenses, so the only outflow is payments to doctors who retire. And that's only a trickle, because the rules also minimize payments to anyone who leaves before twenty-five years."

"The actuarial structure," I said, remembering what Al Macauley had said about not collecting any pension. "Anyone who leaves before a certain period gets paid nothing."

He gave an enthusiastic nod. The student was finally getting things right.

"It's called the fractional rule, Doctor. Most pension funds are set up that way—supposedly to reward loyalty. When the medical school agreed to contribute to the fund seventy years ago, it stipulated that a doctor who left before five years wouldn't get a penny. Same goes for one who leaves after *any* time period and continues to work as a physician at a comparable salary. Doctors are very employable, so those two groups account for over eighty-nine percent of cases. Of the remaining eleven percent, very few doctors serve out the full twenty-five and qualify for full pension. But the money paid into the fund for every doctor who's ever worked at the hospital stays right there, earning interest."

"Who contributes besides the med school?"

"You were on staff there. Didn't you read your benefits package?"

"Psychologists weren't included in the fund."

"Yes, you're right. It does stipulate M.D. . . . Well, count yourself lucky to be a Ph.D."

"Who contributes?" I repeated.

"The hospital kicks in the rest."

"The doctors don't pay anything?"

"Not a penny. That's why they accepted such strict regulations. But it was very shortsighted. For most of them, the pension's worthless."

"Stacked deck," I said. "Giving Jones an eight-figure cashbox— that's why he's making the staff's lives miserable. He doesn't want to destroy the hospital—he wants to keep it limping along with no doctor staying very long. Keep turnover high—staff leaving before five years or when they're young enough to get comparable jobs. The pension keeps accruing dividends, he doesn't have to pay out, and he's able to rape the surplus."

He nodded with passion. "Gang rape, Doctor. It's happening all over the country. There are over nine hundred thousand corporate pension funds in the U.S. Two *trillion* dollars held in trust for eighty million workers. When this last bull market created billions of dollars of surplus, corporations got Congress to ease up on how surpluses can be used. The money's now considered a *company* asset, rather than the property of the workers. Last year alone, the sixty largest corporations in the U.S. had sixty billion dollars to play around with. Some companies have started buying insurance policies so they can use the *principal*. It's part of what fueled the whole takeover mania—pension status is one of the first things raiders look at when they choose their targets. They dissolve the company, use the surplus to buy the next company, and dissolve *it*. And so on and so on. People get thrown out of jobs—too bad."

"Getting rich with other people's money."

"Without having to create any goods or services. Plus, once you start thinking you own something, it gets easier to bend the rules. Illegal pension manipulations have skyrocketed—embezzlement, taking personal loans out of the fund, awarding management contracts to cronies and taking kickbacks while the cronies charge outrageous management fees—that's organized crime's contribution. Up in Alaska we had a situation where the mob cleaned out a union fund and workers lost every cent. Companies have also changed the rules in the middle of the game by switching over to defined-contribution plans. Instead of monthly payments the retiree gets one lump sum based on his life expectancy, and the company buys itself predictability. It's legal, for the time being, but it defeats the whole purpose of pensions—old-age security for working people. Your average blue-collar guy doesn't have any idea how to invest. Only five percent ever do. Most defined-benefit payouts get frittered away on miscellaneous expenses, and the worker's left high and dry."

"Surpluses," I said. "Bull markets. What happens when the economy slows, like right now?"

"If the company goes belly-up and the plan's been looted, the workers have to collect from any private insurance companies that hold paper. There's also a federal fund—PBGC. Pension Benefits Guarantee Corporation. But just like FDIC and FSLIC, it's grossly underfunded. If enough companies with looted plans start folding, you'll have a crisis that'll make the S and L thing look like a picnic. But even with PBGC functioning, it can take years for a worker to collect on a claim. The employees with the most to lose are the oldest and sickest—the loyal ones who gave their lives to the company. People go on welfare, waiting. Die."

His whole face had gone red and his hands were big mottled fists.

"Is the doctors' fund in jeopardy?" I said.

"Not yet. As Mr. Cestare told you, Jones saw Black Monday coming and turned mega-profits. The hospital board of directors loves him."

"Building up his cashbox, for future plundering?"

"No, he's plundering right now. As he's putting dollars in, he's slipping them out."

"How can he get away with it?"

"He's the only one who's got a handle on each and every transaction—the total picture. He's also using the fund as leverage for personal purchases. Parking stock in it, merging fund accounts with his own—moving money around hourly. *Playing* with it. He buys and sells under scores of aliases that change daily. *Hundreds* of transactions daily."

"Lots of commission for him?"

"Lots. Plus, it makes it incredibly difficult to keep track of him."

"But you have."

He nodded, still flushed—the hunter's glow. "It's taken me four and a half years but I've finally gained access to his data banks, and so far, he doesn't know it. There's no reason for him to suspect he's being watched, because normally the government doesn't pay any attention to nonprofit pension funds. If he hadn't made some mistakes with some of the corporations he killed, he'd be home free, in fiduciary heaven."

"What kinds of mistakes?"

"Not important," Huenengarth barked.

I stared at him.

He forced himself to smile and held out one hand. "The point is, his shell's finally cracked and I'm prying it open—getting *exquisitely* close to shattering it. It's a crucial moment, Doctor. That's why I get cranky when people start following me. Understand? Now, are you satisfied?"

"Not really."

He stiffened. "What's your problem?"

"A couple of murders, for starts. Why did Laurence Ashmore and Dawn Herbert die?"

"Ashmore," he said, shaking his head. "Ashmore was a weird bird. A doctor who actually understood economics and had the technical skills to put his knowledge to use. He got rich, and like most rich people he started to believe he was smarter than anyone else. So smart he didn't have to pay his share of taxes. He got away with it for a while, but the IRS finally caught on. He could've gone to jail for a long time. So I helped him."

"Go west, young swindler," I said. "He was your hacker into Jones's data, wasn't he? The perfect wedge—an M.D. who doesn't see patients. Was his degree real?"

"Hundred percent."

"You bought him a job with a million-dollar grant, plus overhead. Basically, the hospital got *paid* to hire him."

He gave a satisfied smile. "Greed. Works every time."

"You're IRS?" I said.

Still smiling, he shook his head. "Very occasionally, one tentacle strokes the other."

"What'd you do? Just put your order in to the IRS? Give me a physician in tax trouble who also has computer skills—and they filled it?"

"It wasn't that simple. Finding someone like Ashmore took a long time. And finding him was one of the factors that helped convince . . . my superiors to fund my project."

"Your superiors," I said. "The Ferris Dixon Institute for Chemical Research—FDIC. What does the R stand for?"

"Rip-off. It was Ashmore's idea of a joke—everything was a game with him. What he really wanted was something that conformed to PBGC—the Paul Bowles Garden Club was his favorite. He prided himself on being literary. But I convinced him to be subtle."

"Who's Professor Walter William Zimberg? Your boss? Another hacker?"

"No one," he said. "Literally."

"He doesn't exist?"

"Not in any real sense."

"Munchausen man," Milo muttered.

Huenengarth shot him a sharp look.

I said, "He's got an office at the University of Maryland. I spoke to his secretary."

He lifted his cup, took a long time drinking.

I said, "Why was it so important for Ashmore to work out of the hospital?"

"Because that's where Jones's main terminal is. I wanted him to have direct access to Jones's hardware and software."

"Jones is using the hospital as a business center? He told me he doesn't have an office there."

"Technically that's true. You won't see his name on any door. But his apparatus is buried within some of the space he's taken away from the doctors."

"Down in the sub-basement?"

"Let's just say buried deeply. Somewhere hard to find. As head of Security, I made sure of that."

"Getting *yourself* in must have been quite a challenge."

No answer.

"You still haven't answered me," I said. "Why'd Ashmore die?"

"I don't know. Yet."

"What'd he do?" I said. "Make an end-run around you? Use what he'd learned working for you to extort money from Chuck Jones?"

He licked his lips. "It's possible. The data he collected are still being analyzed."

"By whom?"

"People."

"What about Dawn Herbert? Was she in on it?"

"I don't know what her game was," he said. "Don't know if she had one."

His frustration seemed real.

I said, "Then why'd you chase down her computer disks?"

"Because *Ashmore* was interested in them. After we started to decode *his* files, her name came up."

"In what context?"

"He'd made a coded notation to take her seriously. Called her a 'negative integer'—his term for someone suspicious. But she was already dead."

"What else did he say about her?"

"That's all we've gotten so far. He put everything in code—complex codes. It's taking time to unravel them."

"He was your boy," I said. "Didn't he leave you the keys?"

"Only some of them." Anger narrowed the round eyes.

"So you stole her disks."

"Not stole, appropriated. They were mine. She compiled them while working for Ashmore, and Ashmore worked for me, so legally they're my property."

He blurted the last two words. The possessiveness of a kid with a new toy.

I said, "This isn't just a job with you, is it?"

His gaze flicked across the room and back to me. "That's exactly what it is. I just happen to love my work."

"So you have no idea why Herbert was murdered."

He shrugged. "The police say it was a sex killing."

"Do *you* think it was?"

"I'm not a policeman."

"No?" I said, and the look in his eyes made me go on. "I'll bet you were some kind of cop before you went back to school. Before you learned to talk like a business school professor."

He gave another eye-flick, quick and sharp as a switchblade. "What's this, free psychoanalysis?"

"Business administration," I said. "Or maybe economics."

"I'm a humble civil servant, Doctor. Your taxes pay my salary."

"Humble civil servant with a false identity and over a million dollars of phony grant money," I said. "You're Zimberg, aren't you? But that's probably not your real name, either. What does the 'B' on Stephanie's note pad stand for?"

He stared at me, stood, walked around the room. Touched a picture frame. The hair on his crown was thinning.

"Four and a half years," I said. "You've given up a lot to catch him."

He didn't answer but his neck tightened.

"What's Stephanie's involvement in all this?" I said. "Besides true love."

He turned and faced me, flushed again. Not anger this time— embarrassment. A teenager caught necking.

"Why don't you ask her?" he said softly.

She was in a car parked at the mouth of my driveway, dark Buick Regal, just behind the hedges, out of sight from the terrace. A dot of light darted around the interior like a trapped firefly.

Penlight. Stephanie sat in the front passenger seat, using it to read. Her window was open. She wore a gold choker that caught starlight, and had put on perfume.

"Evening," I said.

She looked up, closed the book, and pushed the door open. As the penlight clicked off, the dome-light switched on, highlighting her as if she were a soloist onstage. Her dress was shorter than usual. I thought: heavy date. Her beeper sat on the dashboard.

She scooted over into the driver's seat. I sat where she'd just been. The vinyl was warm.

When the car was dark again, she said, "Sorry for not telling you, but he needs secrecy."

"What do you call him, Pres or Wally?"

She bit her lip. "Bill."

"As in Walter William."

She frowned. "It's his nickname—his friends call him that."

"He didn't tell *me*. Guess I'm not his friend."

She looked out the windshield and took hold of the wheel. "Look, I know I misled you a bit, but it's personal. What I do with my private life is really none of your concern, okay?"

"Misled me a bit? Mr. Spooky's your main squeeze. What else haven't you told me about?"

"Nothing—nothing to do with the case."

"That so? He says he can help Cassie. So why didn't you get him to pitch in sooner?"

She put her hands on the steering wheel. "Shit."

A moment later: "It's complicated."

"I'll bet it is."

"Look," she said, nearly shouting, "I told you he was spooky because that's the image he wants to project, okay? It's important that he be seen as a bad guy to get the job done. What he's doing is *important*, Alex. As important as medicine. He's been working on it for a long time."

"Four and a half years," I said. "I've heard all about the noble quest. Is getting you in as division head part of the master plan?"

She turned and faced me. "I don't have to answer that. I *deserve* that promotion. Rita's a dinosaur, for God's sake. She's been coasting on her reputation for years. Let me tell you a story: A couple of months ago we were doing rounds up on Five East. Someone had eaten a McDonald's hamburger at the nursing station and left the box up on the counter—one of those Styrofoam boxes for takeout? With the arches embossed right on it? Rita picks it up and asks what it is. Everyone thought she was kidding. Then we realized she wasn't. *McDonald's,* Alex. That's how out of touch she is. How can she relate to our patient mix?"

"What does that have to do with Cassie?"

Stephanie held her book next to her, like body armor. My night-accustomed eyes made out the title. *Pediatric Emergencies.*

"Light reading?" I said. "Or career advancement?"

"Damn you!" She grabbed the door handle. Let go. Sank back. "Sure it'd be good for him if I was head—the more friends he can get close to *them,* the better chance he has of picking up more information to nail them with. So what's wrong with that? If he doesn't get them, there'll be no hospital at all, soon."

"Friends?" I said. "You sure he knows what that means? Laurence Ashmore worked for him, too, and he doesn't speak very fondly of him."

"Ashmore was a jerk—an obnoxious little schmuck."

"Thought you didn't know him very well."

"I didn't—didn't have to. I told you how he treated me—how blasé he was when I needed help."

"Whose idea was it to have him review Chad's chart in the first place? Yours? Or *Bill's*? Trying to dish up some additional dirt on the Joneses?"

"What's the difference?"

"Be nice to know if we're doing medicine or politics here."

"What's the difference, Alex? What's the damned *difference*! The important thing is results. Yes, he's my friend. Yes, he's helped me a lot, so if I want to help him back, that's okay! What's *wrong* with that! Our goals are *consistent*!"

"Then why not help *Cassie*?" Shouting myself. "I'm sure the two of you have discussed her! Why put her through one more second of misery if Mr. *Helpful* can put an end to it?"

She cowered. Her back was up against the driver's door. "What the hell do you *want* from me? Perfection? Well, sorry, I can't fill that bill. I tried that—it's a short road to misery. So just lay off, okay? *Okay?*"

She began to cry.

I said, "Forget it. Let's just concentrate on Cassie."

"I *am*," she said in a small voice. "Believe me, Alex, I *am* concentrating on her—always have been. We couldn't do anything, because we didn't *know*—had to be sure. That's why I called you in. Bill didn't want me to, but I insisted on that. I put my foot down—I really did."

I kept silent.

"I needed your help to find out," she said. "To know for sure that Cindy was really doing it to her. *Then* Bill could help. At that point, we could confront them."

"*Then?*" I said. "Or were you just waiting until Bill gave the signal? Until his plan was in place and he was ready to take down the whole family?"

"No! He . . . We just wanted to do it in a way that would . . . be effective. Just jumping in and accusing them wouldn't be . . ."

"Strategic?"

"*Effective!* Or ethical—it wouldn't be the right thing. What if she wasn't guilty?"

"Something organic? Something metabolic?"

"Why not! I'm a doctor, dammit, not God. How the hell could I know? Just because Chuck's a piece of slime didn't mean Cindy was! I wasn't *sure,* dammit! Getting to the bottom of it is *your* job—that's why I called you in."

"Thanks for the referral."

"Alex," she said plaintively, "why are you making this so *painful* for me? You know the kind of doctor I am."

She sniffed and rubbed her eyes.

I said, "Since you called me in, I feel I've been running a maze."

"Me too. You think it's easy having meetings with those sleaze-balls and pretending to be their little stooge? Plumb thinks his hand was created in order to rest on my knee."

She grimaced and pulled her dress lower. "You think it's easy being with a bunch of docs, passing Bill in the hall and hearing what they say about him? Look, I know he's not your idea of a nice guy, but you don't really know him. He's *good.* He *helped* me."

She looked out the driver's window. "I had a problem. . . . You don't need to know the details. Oh, hell, why not? I had a *drinking* problem, okay?"

"Okay."

She turned around quickly. "You're not surprised? Did I show it—did I act pathologic?"

"No, but it happens to nice people too."

"I never showed it at all?"

"You're not exactly a drooling drunk."

"No." She laughed. "More like a *comatose* drunk, just like my mom—good old genetics."

She laughed again. Squeezed the steering wheel.

"Now my dad," she said, "there was your *angry* drunk. And my brother, Tom, he was a *genteel* drunk. Witty, charming—very Noel Cowardish. Everyone loved it when *he'd* had a few too many. He was an industrial designer, much smarter than me. Artistic, creative. He died two years ago of cirrhosis. He was thirty-eight."

She shrugged. "I postponed becoming an alcoholic for a while—always the contrary kid. Then, during my internship, I finally decided to join the family tradition. Binges on the day off. I was really good at it, Alex. I knew how to clean up just in time to look clever-and-together on rounds. But then I started to slip. Got my timing mixed up. Timing's always a tricky thing when you're a closet lush. . . . A few years ago I got busted for drunk driving. Caused an accident. Isn't that a pretty picture? Imagine if I'd killed someone, Alex. Killed a kid. Pediatrician turns toddler into road pizza—what a headline."

She cried again. Dried her eyes so hard it looked as if she were hitting herself.

"Shit, enough with the self-pity—my AA buddies always used to get on me for that. I did AA for a year. Then I broke away from it—no spare time and I was doing fine, right? Then last year, with all the stress—some personal things that didn't work out—I started again. Those teeny little bottles you get on airplanes? I picked some up on a flight, coming home from an AMA convention. Just a nip before bed. Then a few more . . . then I started taking the little buggers to the office. For that *mellow* moment at the end of the day. But I was cool, always careful to put the empties back in my purse, leave no evidence. See, I'm good at subterfuge. You didn't know that about me till now, did you? But I got you, too, didn't I? Oh, shit!"

She hit the wheel, then rested her head on it.

"It's okay," I said. "Forget it."

"Sure, it is. It's okay, it's great, it's terrific, it's wonderful. . . . One night—a really shitty one, sick kids up the wazoo—I polished off a *bunch* of little bottles and passed out at my desk. Bill was making a security check and found me at three in the morning. I'd vomited all over my charts. When I saw him standing over me I thought I was going to die. But he held me and cleaned me up and took me home— took *care* of me, Alex. *No* one ever did that for me. I was always taking care of my mother because she was always . . ."

She rolled her brow on the steering wheel.

"It's because of him that I'm pulling it together. Did you notice all the weight I've lost? My hair?"

"You look great."

"I learned how to dress, Alex. Because it finally mattered. Bill bought me my coffee machine. He *understood,* because *his* family was also . . . His dad was a *real* nasty drunk. Weekend lush, but he held down a job in the same factory for twenty-five years. Then the company got taken over and dissolved, and his dad lost his job, and they found out the pension fund had been looted. Completely stripped. His dad couldn't find another job and drank himself to death. Bled out, right in his bed. Bill was in high school. He came home from football practice and found him. Do you see why he understands? Why he needs to do what he's doing?"

"Sure," I said, wondering how much of the story was true. Thinking of the Identikit face of the man seen walking into the darkness with Dawn Herbert.

"He raised *his* mom, too," she said. "He's a natural problem solver. That's why he became a cop, why he took the time to go back to school and learn about finance. He has a Ph.D., Alex. It took him ten years because he was working." She lifted her head and her profile was transformed by a smile. "But don't try calling him Doctor."

"Who's Presley Huenengarth?"

She hesitated.

"Another state secret?" I said.

"It . . . Okay, I'll tell you because I want you to trust me. And it's no big deal. Presley was a friend of his when he was a kid. A little boy who died of a brain tumor when he was eight years old. Bill used his identity because it was safe—there was nothing on file but a birth certificate, and the two of them were the same age, so it was perfect."

She sounded breathless—excited—and I knew "Bill" and his world had offered her more than just succor.

"Please, Alex," she said, "can we just forget all this and work together? I know about the insulin injectors—your friend told Bill. You see, *he* trusts him. Let's put our heads together and get her. Bill will help us."

"How?"

"I don't know, but he will. You'll see."

She hooked her beeper over her belt and the two of us went back up to the house. Milo was still on the couch. Huenengarth/Zimberg/Bill was standing across the room, in a corner, leafing through a magazine.

Stephanie said, "Hi, guys," in a too-chirpy voice.

Huenengarth closed the magazine, took her by the elbow, and seated her in a chair. Pulling another one close to her, he sat down.

She didn't take her eyes off him. He moved his arm as if to touch her, but unbuttoned his jacket instead.

"Where are Dawn Herbert's disks?" I said. "And don't tell me it's not relevant, because I'll bet you it is. Herbert may or may not have latched on to what Ashmore was doing for you, but I'm pretty sure she had suspicions about the Jones kids. Speaking of which, have you found Chad's chart?"

"Not yet."

"What about the disks?"

"I just sent them over to be analyzed."

"Do the people analyzing even know what they're looking at? The random number table?"

He nodded. "It's probably a substitution code—shouldn't be too much of a problem."

"You haven't unscrambled all of Ashmore's numbers yet. What makes you think you'll do better with Herbert's?"

He looked at Stephanie and gave another half-smile. "I like this guy."

Her return smile was nervous.

"Man raises a good point," said Milo.

"Ashmore was a special case," said Huenengarth. "Real puzzle-freak, high IQ."

"Herbert wasn't?"

"Not from what I've learned about her."

"Which is?"

"Just what you know," he said. "Some smarts in math, but basically she was a klepto and a lowlife—doper and a loser."

As he spat out each noun, Stephanie flinched. He noticed it, turned and touched her hand briefly, let go.

"If something comes up on the disk that concerns you," he said, "rest assured I'll let you know."

"We need to know now. Herbert's information could give us some direction." I turned to Milo. "Did you tell him about our friend the bartender?"

Milo nodded.

"Everything?"

"Don't bother being subtle," said Huenengarth. "I saw the

masterpiece your junkie bartender produced and no, it's not me. I don't hack up women."

"What are you talking about?" said Stephanie.

"Stupidity," he told her. "They've got a description of a murder suspect—someone who may or may not have murdered this Herbert character—and they thought it bore a resemblance to yours truly."

She put her hand to her mouth.

He laughed. "Not even close, Steph. Last time I was that thin was back in high school." To me: "Can we get to work now?"

"I've never stopped," I said. "Do you have any information on Vicki Bottomley?"

Huenengarth waved a hand at Milo. "Tell him."

"We've done phone traces from her home to the Jones house and Chip's office."

"We?" said Huenengarth.

"Him," said Milo. "Federal warrant. Next week he sprouts a fucking pair of wings."

"Find anything?" I said.

Milo shook his head. "No calls. And none of Bottomley's neighbors have seen Cindy or Chip around, so if there is a link, it's pretty damn hidden. My intuition is she's got nothing to do with it. She's certainly not the main poisoner. Once the chips fall, we'll see if she fits in, anywhere."

"So where do we go now?"

Milo looked at Huenengarth. Huenengarth looked at me and held his hand out toward the couch.

"Been sitting all day," I said.

He frowned and touched his tie. Stared at everyone else.

Milo said, "Any more federal doublespeak and I'm outa here."

"All right," said Huenengarth. "First, I want to reiterate my demand of total discretion—total cooperation from both of you. *No* improvisation. I mean it."

"In return for what?" I said.

"Probably enough technical support to bust Cindy. Because I've got federal warrants on Chuck Jones, and with a two-minute phone call I can include Junior and everything *he* owns in the deal. We're talking audio, video, home, place of business—they go bowling, I can have someone peeking from behind the pins. Give me two hours alone in their house and I can rig it with peep-toys you wouldn't believe. Got a camera that goes right in their TV so when they're watching it, it's watching them. I can toss the house for insulin or whatever crap you're looking for and they'll never know it. All you have to do is keep your mouths shut."

"Cassie's room is the one that needs to be rigged," I said. "And the bathroom connecting it to the master bedroom."

"Tile walls in the bathroom?"

"Tile walls and one window."

"No problem—whatever toys I don't have at hand, I can have delivered in twenty-four hours."

Milo said, "Your tax dollars busy at work."

Huenengarth frowned. "Sometimes they are."

I wondered if he knew what a joke was. Stephanie didn't care if he did; her expression said he danced on water.

"I've got a meeting scheduled at the house tomorrow night," I said. "I'll try to change it to the hospital. Can you have your equipment ready by then?"

"Probably. If not, it will be soon after—day or two. But can you assure me the house will be totally empty? I'm ready to pounce on Daddy, I can't afford *any* screwups."

I said to Stephanie, "Why don't you call Chip and Cindy in for a meeting? Tell them something came up on the lab tests, you need to examine Cassie and then speak with them. Once they get there, make sure they stay for a long time."

"Fine," she said. "I'll keep them waiting, tell them the labs got lost or something."

"Action, camera," said Huenengarth.

"How come you can get Chip included in the warrant?" I asked him. "Is he involved in his father's financial dealings?"

No answer.

I said, "I thought we were being frank."

"He's a sleaze, too," Huenengarth said, irritated.

"The fifty parcels he owns? Is that really one of Chuck's deals?"

He shook his head. "The land deal's for shit—Chuck's too smart for that. Junior's a loser, can't hold on to a dollar. Gone through plenty of Daddy's already."

"What's he spending it on besides land?" I said. "His life-style's pretty ordinary."

"Sure, on the surface it is. But that's just part of the image: Mr. Self-made. It's a crock. That dinky junior college he teaches at pays him twenty-four thousand a year—think you can buy a house in *Watts* on that, let alone that entire tract? Not that he owns it, anymore."

"Who does?"

"The bank that financed the deal."

"Foreclosure?"

"Any minute." Big smile. "Daddy bought the land at a bargain price, years ago. Gave it to Junior, the idea being that Junior would sell at the right time and get rich on his own. He even told Junior when the right time was, but Junior didn't listen."

The smile became a lottery-winner's grin. "Not the first time, either. Back when Junior was at Yale, he started his own business: competition with Cliff Notes because he could do it better. Daddy bankrolled him, hundred thousand or so. Down the drain, because apart from its being a harebrained scheme, Junior lost interest. That's his pattern. He has a problem with finishing things. A few years later, when he was in graduate school, he decided he was going to be a publisher—start a sociology magazine for the lay public. Another quarter of a million of Daddy's dough. There've been others, all along the same lines. By my calculation, around a million or so urinated away, not including the land. Not much by Daddy's standards, but you'd figure someone with half a brain could do something constructive with that kind of grubstake, right? Not Junior. He's too *creative*."

"What went wrong with the land?" I said.

"Nothing, but we're in a recession and property values dropped. Instead of cashing in and cutting his losses, Junior decided to go into the construction business. Daddy knew it was stupid and refused to bankroll it, so Junior went out and got a loan from a bank using Daddy's name as collateral. Junior lost interest as usual, the sub-contractors saw they had a real chicken on their hands and started plucking. Those houses are built like garbage."

"Six phases," I said, remembering the architectural rendering. "Not much completed."

"Maybe half of one phase. The plan was for an entire city. Junior's own personal Levittown." He laughed. "You should see the

proposal he wrote up when he sent it to Daddy. Like a term paper—
delusions of grandeur. No doubt the bank'll go to Daddy first, before
taking over the deed. And Daddy may just divvy up. Because he *loves*
Junior, tells everyone who'll listen what a scholar his baby boy is—
another joke. Junior changed his major a bunch of times in college.
Didn't finish his Ph.D.—the old boredom thing."

"One thing he has stuck with is teaching," I said. "And he seems
to be good at it—he's won awards."

Huenengarth let his tongue protrude through his small lips as
he shook his head. "Yeah. Formal Organizations, New Age Management Techniques. We're talking Marxist theory and rock 'n' roll. He's
an *entertainer.* I've got tapes of his lectures, and basically what he does
is pander to the students. Lots of anti-capitalist rhetoric, the evils of
corporate corruption. You don't have to be Freud to figure *that* one
out, right? He likes rubbing the old man's face in it—even the wife's
part of that program, wouldn't you say?"

"In what way?"

"C'mon, Doctor. Milo, here, told me you found out about her
military *career.* The woman's a *slut.* A lowlife *loser.* On *top* of what she's
doing to the kid. Can't exactly be what the old man had in mind for
Junior."

He grinned. Scarlet again, and sweating heavily. Nearly levitat-
ing off his chair in rage and delight. His hatred was tangible,
poisonous. Stephanie felt it; her eyes were thrilled.

"What about Chip's mother?" I said. "How did she die?"

He shrugged. "Suicide. Sleeping pills. Entire family's fucked
up. Though I can't say I blame her. Don't imagine living with Chuck
was any barrel of primates. He's been known to play around—likes
'em in groups of three or four, young, chesty, blond, borderline
intelligence."

I said, "You'd like to get all of them, wouldn't you?"

"I've got no use for them," he said quickly. Then he got up, took
a few steps, turned his back on us, and stretched.

"So," he said. "Let's aim for tomorrow. You get 'em out, we
move in and play Captain Video."

"Great, Bill," said Stephanie. Her beeper went off. She removed
it from her belt and examined the digital readout. "Where's your
phone, Alex?"

I walked her into the kitchen and hung around as she punched numbers.

"This is Dr. Eves. I just got . . . What? . . . When? . . . All right, give me the resident on call. . . . Jim? This is Stephanie. What's up? . . . Yes, yes, there's a history of that. It's all in the chart. . . . Absolutely, keep that drip going. Sounds like you're doing everything right, but get me a full tox panel, stat. Make sure to check for hypoglycemic metabolites. Check all over for puncture wounds, too, but don't let on, okay? It's important, Jim. Please. . . . Thanks. And keep her totally isolated. *No* one goes in. . . . Especially not them . . . What? . . . Out in the hall. Leave the drapes open so they can see her, but *no one goes inside.* . . . I don't care. . . . I know. Let it be on my head, Jim. . . . What? . . . *No.* Keep her in ICU. Even *if* things lighten up . . . I don't *care,* Jim. Find a bed somewhere. This one's crucial. . . . What? . . . Soon. Soon as I can— maybe an hour. Just— What? . . . Yes, I will. . . . Okay. Thanks. I owe you."

She hung up. Her face was white and her chest heaved.

"Again," I said.

She looked past me. Held her head.

"Again," she said. "This time she's unconscious."

31

Quiet night on Chappy Ward. No shortage of empty rooms.

This one was two doors down from 505W. Cassie's room.

That cold, clean hospital smell.

The images on the TV I was watching were black-and-white and fuzzy and small, a miniaturized, capsulated reality.

Cold and clean and a medicinal staleness—though no one had been in this room for a long time.

I'd been in it most of the day and all of the evening.

Into the night . . .

The door was bolted shut. The room was dark, except for a focused yellow parabola from a corner floor lamp. Double drapes blotted out Hollywood. I sat on an orange chair, as confined as a patient. The piped music barely leaked through from the hallway.

The man who called himself Huenengarth sat across the room, near the lamp, cradled by a chair identical to mine that he'd pushed up to the empty bed. A small black hand radio rested in his lap.

The bed was stripped down to the mattress. Resting on the ticking was a sloping paper ramp. Government documents.

The one he was reading had kept his interest for more than an hour. Down at the bottom was a line of numbers and asterisks and a word that I thought was UPDATE. But I couldn't be sure because I was too far away and neither of us wanted to change that.

I had things to read, too: the latest lab reports on Cassie and a brand-new article Huenengarth had shoved at me. Five typed pages on the subject of pension fraud by Professor W. W. Zimberg, written in starchy legalese with lots of words blacked out by a broad-tipped marker.

My eyes went back to the TV. No movement on the screen other than the slow drip of sugar-water through plastic tubing. I inspected the small, colorless world from edge to edge. For the thousandth time . . .

Bedclothes and railings, a blur of dark hair and puffy cheek. The I.V. gauge, with its inlets and outlets and locks . . .

I sensed movement across the room without seeing it. Huenengarth took out a pen and crossed something out.

According to documents he showed Milo in the deputy chief's office, he'd been in Washington, D.C., the night Dawn Herbert was butchered in her little car. Milo told me he'd corroborated it, as the two of us drove to the hospital just before sunrise.

"Who exactly is he working for?" I said.

"Don't know the details but it's some sort of covert task force, probably in cahoots with the Treasury Department."

"Secret agent man? Think he knows our friend the colonel?"

"Wondered about that myself. He found out pretty damn fast that I was playing computer games. After we got out of the D.C.'s office, I shot the colonel's name at him and got a blank stare, but it wouldn't surprise me if the two of them attended some of the same parties. Tell you one thing, Alex—asshole's more than just a field agent, got some real juice behind him."

"Juice and motivation," I said. *"Four and a half years to avenge his father. How do you think he managed the million-dollar budget?"*

"Who knows? Probably kissed the right ass, stabbed the right back. Or maybe it was just a matter of the right person's ox getting gored. Whatever, he's a smart cookie."

"Good actor, too—getting that close to Jones and Plumb."

"So one day he'll run for President. Did you know you were going twenty over the limit?"

"*If I get a ticket, you can fix it for me, right? Now that you're a real policeman again.*"

"*Yeah.*"

"*How'd you pull it off?*"

"*I didn't pull off anything. When I got to the D.C.'s, Huenengarth was already there. He gets right in my face, demands to know why I've been tracing him. I think about it and tell him the truth, because what's my choice? Play hard to get and have the department cite me for improper use of departmental time and facilities? He then proceeds to ask me lots of questions about the Jones family. All this time, the D.C. is just sitting behind his desk, hasn't said a word, and I figure this is it, start thinking private enterprise. But soon as I finish, Huenengarth thanks me for my cooperation, says it's a shame, the crime rate being what it is, that a guy with my experience is sitting in front of a screen instead of working cases. The D.C. looks as if he just sucked pigshit through a straw, but he keeps quiet. Huenengarth asks if I can be assigned to his investigation—LAPD liaison to the Feds. D.C. squirms and says sure, getting me back on active duty was the department's plan all along. Huenengarth and I leave the office together and the minute we're alone he tells me he doesn't give a fuck about me personally, but his case on Jones is just about to break and I'd better not get in his way while he moves in with the killing thrust.*"

"*Killing thrust, huh?*"

"*Gentle soul, probably doesn't wear fur . . . Then he said, 'Maybe we can cut a deal. Don't fuck me up and I'll help you.' Then he told me how he knew about Cassie from Stephanie, but hadn't done anything because there wasn't enough evidence, but maybe now there was.*"

"*Why all of a sudden?*"

"*Probably because he's close enough to getting Grandpa and wouldn't mind doing a total destruct on the family. I also wouldn't be surprised if on some level he enjoys seeing Cassie suffer—the curse of the Jones family. He really hates them, Alex. . . . On the other hand, where would we be without him? So let's use the hell out of him, see what happens. How does this look on me?*"

"*High fashion, Ben Casey.*"

"*Yeah. Take a picture. When it's over.*"

Movement on the screen.

Then nothing.

My neck was stiff. I shifted position while keeping my eyes on the TV.

Huenengarth continued to do his homework. It had been hours since anything I did caught his attention.

Time passed, slothfully cruel.

More movement.

Shadowing one corner. Upper right-hand.

Then nothing, for a long time.

Then . . .

"Hey!" I said.

Huenengarth peered over his pamphlet. Bored.

The shadow grew. Lightened.

Took shape. White and fuzzy.

Starfish . . . human hand.

Something grasped between thumb and forefinger.

Huenengarth sat up.

"Go!" I said. "This is it!"

He smiled.

The hand on the screen advanced. Grew larger. Big, white . . .

"C'mon!" I said.

Huenengarth put down his article.

The hand jabbed . . . poking at something.

Huenengarth seemed to be savoring the picture.

He looked at me as if I'd interrupted a terrific dream.

The thing between the fingers probed.

Huenengarth's smile stretched under his little mustache.

"Damn you," I said.

He picked up the little black radio and held it to his mouth. "On your mark," he said.

The hand was at the I.V. gauge now, using the thing between its fingers to nuzzle a rubber-tipped inlet.

Sharp-tipped thing.

White cylinder, much like a pen. Ultra-thin needle.

It darted, a bird pecking a wormhole.

Plunged.

Huenengarth said, "Go," to the radio.

It was only later that I realized he'd skipped "Get set."

He moved toward the door, but I threw the bolt and was out first. All those years of jogging and treadmilling finally paid off.

The door to 505 W was already wide open.

Cassie was on her back in the bed, breathing through her mouth.

Post-seizure slumber.

She was covered to the neck. I.V. tubing curled from under the blankets.

Cindy was sleeping, too, flat on her stomach, one arm dangling.

Milo stood next to the I.V. pole, baggy in green surgical scrubs. A hospital ID badge was pinned to his shirt. M. B. STURGIS, M.D., his photographed face cross and bearish.

The real face was policeman-stoic. One of his big hands was clamped over Chip Jones's wrist. The other bent Chip's arm behind his back. Chip cried out in pain.

Milo ignored him and told him his rights.

Chip had on a camel-colored jogging suit and brown suede running shoes with diagonal leather stripes. His back was arched in Milo's grip and his eyes were splayed and bright, sick with terror.

It was his fear that made me want to kill him.

I ran to the bed and checked the I.V. gauge. Locked—sealed with Krazy Glue. Stephanie's idea. None of what was in the cylinder was entering Cassie's bloodstream. Creative, but a risk: seconds later, Chip would have felt the pressure build behind the needle. And known.

Milo had him cuffed now. Chip started crying, then stopped.

Huenengarth licked his lips and said, "You're fucked, Junior." I hadn't seen him come in.

Chip stared at him. His mouth was still open. His beard trembled. He dropped something on the floor. White cylinder with a tiny, sharp tip. It rolled on the carpet before coming to a stop. Chip raised a foot and tried to step on it.

Milo yanked him away. Huenengarth put on a surgical glove and picked up the cylinder.

He waved it in front of Chip's face.

Chip made a whimpering noise and Huenengarth responded with a masturbatory movement of one arm.

I went over to Cindy and nudged her. She rolled and didn't waken. A shake of her shoulders failed to rouse her. I shook harder, said her name. Nothing.

A cup was on the floor, near her dangling hand. Half-filled with coffee.

"What did you drug her with?" I asked Chip.

He didn't answer. I repeated the question and he looked at the floor. His earring tonight was an emerald.

"What'd you give her?" I said, dialing the phone.

He pouted.

The page operator came on and I called for an emergency resuscitation.

Chip watched, wide-eyed.

Huenengarth advanced toward him again. Milo stilled him with a look and said, "If she's in danger and you don't tell us, you're only making matters worse for yourself."

Chip cleared his throat, as if preparing for an important announcement. But he said nothing.

I went to Cassie's bed.

"Okay," said Milo, "let's go to jail." He pushed Chip forward. "We'll let the lab figure it out."

Chip said, "Probably diazepam—Valium. But I didn't give it to her."

"How much?" I said.

"Forty milligrams is what she usually takes."

Milo looked at me.

"Probably not lethal," I said. "But it's a heavy dose for someone her size."

"Not really," said Chip. "She's habituated."

"Bet she is," I said, lacing my fingers to keep my hands still.

"Don't be stupid," said Chip. "Search me—see if you find drugs of any kind."

"You're not holding because you gave it all to her," said Huenengarth.

Chip managed to laugh, though his eyes were frightened. "Go ahead, search."

Huenengarth patted him down, turned his pockets inside out, and found only a wallet and keys.

Chip looked at him, shook hair out of eyes, and smiled.

"Something funny, Junior?"

"You are making a big mistake," said Chip. "If I wasn't the victim, I'd really feel sorry for you."

Huenengarth smiled. "That so?"

"Very much so."

"Junior, here, thinks this is funny, gents." He wheeled on Chip: "What the fuck do you think is going on here? You think one of Daddy's *attorneys* is going to get you out of this? We've got you on videotape trying to kill your kid—everything from loading the needle to sticking it in. Want to guess where the camera is?"

Chip kept smiling but panic fueled his eyes. They blinked, popped, raced around the room. Suddenly he shut them and dropped his head to his chest, muttering.

"What's that?" said Huenengarth. "What'd you say?"

"Discussion closed."

Huenengarth came closer. "Atttempted murder's not some dinky-shit Chapter Eleven. What kind of scum would do this to his own flesh and blood?"

Chip kept his head down.

"Well," said Huenengarth, "you can always start a new project—Cliff Notes for jailhouse lawyers. Those big bucks in maximum lockup are gonna love your educated anus."

Chip didn't move. His body had gone loose—meditative—and Milo had to work at holding him upright.

A sound came from the bed. Cassie shifting position. Chip looked at her.

She moved again, but remained asleep.

A terrible look came onto his face—disappointment at an unfinished job.

Enough hatred to fuel a war.

All three of us saw it. The room got very small.

Huenengarth reddened and puffed like a bullfrog.

"Happy rest of your life, fuckhead," he whispered. Then he stomped out.

When the door closed, Chip snickered, but it sounded forced.

Milo pushed him toward the door. They got out just before Stephanie arrived with the emergency team.

I watched Cassie sleep. Stephanie left with the team, but came back about a half hour later.

"How's Cindy doing?" I said.

"She'll probably have a monster headache but she'll survive."

"She may need to be detoxed," I said, lowering my voice to a whisper. "He said she was habituated, though he denied dosing her—made a real big point of saying he didn't have any drugs on him. But I'm sure he slipped it in her coffee, did it plenty of times before tonight. Every time I saw him here, he had a cup with him."

She shook her head, sat on the bed, and pulled her stethoscope from around her neck. Warming the disk with her breath, she placed it on Cassie's chest and listened.

When she was through, I said, "Any dope in Cassie's system?"

"No, just low sugar." Her whisper was weak. She lifted Cassie's free arm and took a pulse. "Nice and regular." She put the arm down.

She sat there for a moment, then tucked the covers up around Cassie's neck and touched a soft cheek. The drapes were open. I saw her look out at the night with tired eyes.

"It makes no sense," she said. "Why did he use insulin, right after you found the injectors? Unless Cindy didn't tell him you found them. Was their communication that bad?"

"I'm sure she did tell him, and that's *exactly* why he used them. He planted them there for me to find. Made a special call to verify that I was coming out and making sure he wouldn't be there. Playing concerned daddy, but he was really pinpointing the time. Because he knew we had to suspect Munchausen by now, and he was hoping I'd snoop, discover the cylinders, and suspect Cindy, just as I did. What could be more logical: They were *her* aunt's samples. *She* was in charge of the house, so she'd be the most likely one to hide them there. And she was the *mother*—that stacked the deck against her from the beginning. The first time I met him he made a point of telling me they had a traditional marriage—child rearing was her bailiwick."

"Pointing a finger at her right from the beginning." She shook her head in disbelief. "So . . . orchestrated."

"Meticulously. And if I hadn't found the cylinders during yesterday's visit, there would have been plenty of other opportunities for him to set her up."

"What a monster," she said.

"The devil wears jogging clothes."

She hugged herself.

I said, "How big of a dosage was loaded into the Insuject?"

She looked at Cassie and lowered her voice to a whisper. "More than enough."

"So tonight was to be the final chapter," I said. "Cassie seizing fatally, Cindy right there snoozing, with all of us suspecting her. If we hadn't caught him he probably would have stashed the needle in her purse or somewhere else incriminating. And the Valium in her system would have added to the picture of guilt: suicide attempt. Remorse for killing her baby, or just an unbalanced mind."

Stephanie rubbed her eyes. Rested her head on one hand. "What an incredible prick . . . How'd he get in without going through Security?"

"Your friend Bill said he didn't enter the hospital through the front door, so he probably used one of his father's keys and came in through the back. Maybe one of the loading docks. At this hour there'd be no one there. We know from the hallway camera that he took the stairs up and waited until the Five East nurse went into the back room before entering Chappy. Probably did the same thing when Cassie had that first seizure here in the hospital. Dress rehearsal. Sneaking up in the wee hours, injecting her with just enough insulin to provide a delayed reaction, then driving home to the Valley and waiting for Cindy's call before coming back to comfort her in the E.R. The fact that Chappy's nearly always empty made it easier for him to come and go unnoticed."

"And all this time I was obsessing on Cindy. Brilliant, Eves."

"I zeroed in on her too. We all did. She was a perfect Munchausen suspect. Low self-esteem, easygoing manner, early experiences with serious illness, health-care training. He probably came across the syndrome in his readings, saw the fit, and realized he had an opportunity to get her. *That's* why he didn't have Cassie transferred to another hospital. He wanted to give us time to develop our suspicions. Worked us like an audience—the way he works his students. *He's* the exhibitionist, Steph. But we never saw it because the books say it's always a woman."

Silence.

"He killed Chad, didn't he?" she said.

"It's a strong possibility."

"Why, Alex? Why use his own kids to get at Cindy?"

"I don't know, but I'll tell you one thing. He hates Cassie. Before they took him away he gave her a look that was really disturbing. Pure contempt. If the tape caught it and it's ruled admissible in court, it's all the prosecutor will need."

Shaking her head, she returned to the bed and stroked Cassie's hair.

"Poor little baby. Poor little innocent baby."

I sat there, not wanting to think or do or talk or feel.

A trio of LuvBunnies sat on the floor near my feet.

I picked one up. Passed it from hand to hand. Something hard in the belly.

Undoing the flap, I poked around the foam stuffing, just as I had in Cassie's bedroom. This time, I found something tucked into a fold near the groin.

I drew it out. A packet. About an inch in diameter. Tissue paper fastened with cellophane tape.

I unwrapped it. Four pills. Pale-blue, each with a heart-shaped cutout.

Stephanie said, "Valium."

"Here's our secret stash." I rewrapped the packet and set it aside for Milo. "He made such a big deal about not having any dope with him. Everything's a game with him."

"Vicki bought those bunnies," Stephanie said. "Vicki's the one who got Cassie started on them."

"Vicki will be talked to after this," I said.

"Too weird," she said. "The stuff they don't teach you in sch—"

A squeak came from the bed. Cassie's eyes blinked spasmodically, then opened. Her little mouth turned down. She blinked some more.

"It's okay, baby," said Stephanie.

Cassie's mouth worked, finally producing a sound:

"Eh eh eh."

"It's okay, honey. Everything's gonna be fine. You're gonna be fine now."

"Eh eh eh eh."

More blinks. A shudder. Cassie tried to move, failed, cried out in frustration. Scrunched her eyes. Crinkled her chin.

Stephanie held her and rocked her. Cassie tried to twist away from Stephanie's caress.

I remembered the way she'd fought me in her bedroom.

Reacting to her mother's anxiety? Or memories of another man who came in the night, shrouded by darkness, and hurt her?

But then, why hadn't she panicked whenever she saw Chip? Why had she jumped up into his arms, so willingly, the first time I'd seen them together?

"Eh eh eh . . ."

"Shh, baby."

"Eh . . . eh eh . . . eh."

"Go back to sleep, honey. Go back to sleep."

Very faintly: "Eh . . ."

"Shh."

"Eh . . ."

Closed eyes.

Soft snores.

Stephanie held her for several moments, then slipped her hands free.

"Must be the magic touch," she said sadly. Looping her stethoscope over her neck, she walked out of the room.

34

A nurse and a policewoman arrived soon after.

I gave the cop the packet of pills and sleepwalked my way to the teak doors.

Out in Five East, people were moving and talking, but I didn't focus on them. I rode the elevator down to the basement. The cafeteria was closed. Wondering if Chip had a key to that, too, I bought coffee from a machine, found a pay phone, and sipped as I asked information for a number on a Jennifer Leavitt. Nothing.

Before the operator could break the connection, I had him check for any Leavitts in the Fairfax district. Two. One of them matched my vague memory of Jennifer's parents' home number.

My watch said 9:30. I knew Mr. Leavitt went to sleep early in order to make it to the bakery by 5:00 A.M. Hoping it wasn't too late, I punched numbers.

"Hello."

"Mrs. Leavitt? It's Dr. Delaware."

"Doctor. How *are* you?"

"Fine, and you?"

"Very good."

"Am I calling too late?"

"Oh, no. We're just watching television. But Jenny's not here. She has her own apartment now—my daughter the doctor, very independent."

"You must be proud of her."

"What's not to be proud of? She's always made me proud. Do you want her new number?"

"Please."

"Hold on . . . She's in Westwood Village, right near the U. With another girl, a nice girl . . . Here it is. If she's not there, she's probably in her office—she's got an office, too." Chuckle.

"That's great." I copied down the numbers.

"An office," she said. "You know, raising a child like that, it's a privilege. . . . I miss her. For my taste, the house is too quiet."

"I'll bet."

"You were very helpful to her, Dr. Delaware. College at her age wasn't so easy—you should be proud of *yourself*."

No one answered at Jennifer's apartment. But she picked up her office phone after one ring: "Leavitt."

"Jennifer, it's Alex Delaware."

"Hi, Alex. Did you solve your Munchausen by proxy?"

"The *who*dunit," I said. "But the whydunit's not clear yet. It turned out to be the father."

"Well, *that's* a twist," she said. "So it isn't *always* the mother."

"He was counting on our assuming it was. He set her up."

"How Machiavellian."

"He fancies himself an intellectual. He's a professor."

"Here?"

"No, at a junior college. But he does his serious research at the U, which is why I'm calling you. My bet is he read up exhaustively on the syndrome in order to create a textbook case. His first child died of SIDS. Another textbook case, so I'm wondering if he set that up too."

"Oh, no—this sounds *grotesque*."

"I was thinking about the SAP system," I said. "If he's got a faculty account, would there be some way to find out?"

"The library keeps a record of all users, for billing."

"Do the bills list which articles were pulled?"

"Absolutely. What time is it? Nine forty-seven. The library's open till ten. I could call down there and see if anyone I know is working. Give me the bastard's name."

"Jones, Charles L. Sociology, West Valley Community College."

"Got it. I'm going to put you on hold and call them on the other line. Just in case we get cut off, give me your number."

Five minutes later she clicked in.

"*Voilà,* Alex. The idiot left a beautiful paper trail. Pulled everything the system's got on three topics—Munchausen, sudden infant death, and the sociological structure of hospitals. Plus a few isolated articles on two other topics: diazepam toxicity and—are you ready for this?—women's fantasies about penis size. It's all there: names, dates, exact hour. I'll get a printout for you tomorrow."

"Fantastic. I really appreciate it, Jennifer."

"One more thing," she said. "He's not the only one who used the account. There's another signature on some of the searches—a Kristie Kirkash. Know anyone by that name?"

"No," I said, "but I wouldn't be surprised if she's young, cute, and one of his students. Maybe even plays sorority softball."

"Sleazy affair for the prof? How do you figure?"

"He's a creature of habit."

Hot morning and the Valley was frying. A big rig had overturned on the freeway, showering all lanes with eggs. Even the shoulder was blocked and Milo cursed until the highway patrolman waved us through.

We arrived at the junior college ten minutes behind schedule. Made it to class just as the last students were entering.

"Damn," said Milo. "Improv time." We climbed the stairs to the trailer. I remained in the doorway and he went up to the black-board.

It was a small room—half the trailer, partitioned by an accordion wall and set up with a conference table and a dozen folding chairs.

Ten of the chairs were occupied. Eight women, two men. One of the women was in her sixties; the rest were girls. Both men were fortyish. One was white, with a full head of light-brown hair; the other, Hispanic and bearded. The white man looked up briefly, then buried himself in a book.

Milo picked up a pointer and tapped the board. "Mr. Jones won't be making it today. I'm Mr. Sturgis, your substitute."

All eyes on him, except those of the reader.

One of the girls said, "Is he okay?" in a strained voice. She had very long, dark, frizzy hair, a thin, pretty face, and wore dangling earrings constructed of lavender-and-white plastic balls on nylon fishing line. Her black tube top showed off a big chest and smooth, tan shoulders. Too-blue eye shadow, too-pale lipstick, too much of both.

Despite that, better-looking than the photo in her student file. Milo said, "Not really, Kristie."

She opened her mouth. The other students looked at her.

She said, "Hey, what's going on?" and grabbed her purse.

Milo reached into his pocket and pulled out his police badge. "You tell me, Kristie."

She froze. The other students gawked. The reader's eyes floated above the pages of his book. Moving slowly.

I saw Milo look at him. Look down at the floor.

Shoes.

Clunky black oxfords with bubble toes. They didn't go with his silk shirt and his designer jeans.

Milo's eyes narrowed. The reader's fixed on mine, then sank out of view as he raised the book higher.

Theories of Organizations.

Kristie started to cry.

The other students were statues.

Milo said, "Yo Joe! Cavity check!"

The reader looked up reflexively. Just for a second, but it was enough.

Bland face. Dick and Jane's dad from a half-block distance. Up close, details destroyed the paternal image: five o'clock shadow, pockmarks on the cheeks, a scar across the forehead. Tattoo on one hand.

And the sweat—a coat of it, shiny as fresh lacquer.

He stood up. His eyes were hard and narrow; his hands huge, the forearms thick. More tattoos, blue-green, crude. Reptilian.

He picked up his books and stepped away from the table while keeping his head down.

Milo said, "Hey, c'mon, stay. I'm an easy grader."

The man stopped, began to lower himself, then he threw the books at Milo and made a rush for the door.

I stepped in front of him, locking my hands in a double-arm block.

He shouldered me full-force. The impact slammed me against the door and pushed it open.

I fell backward onto the cement, landing hard and feeling my tailbone hum. Reaching out, I grabbed two handfuls of silk. He was on top of me, clawing and punching and spraying sweat.

Milo pulled him off, hit him very fast in the face and the belly and shoved him hard against the bungalow. The man struggled. Milo kidney-punched him, hard, and cuffed him as he sank, groaning.

Milo forced him down on the ground and put one foot on the small of his back.

A pat-down produced a wad of cash, a flick-knife with a black handle, a vial of pills, and a cheap plastic billfold stamped RENO: NEVADA'S PLAYGROUND. Milo pulled three different driver's licenses out of the fold.

"Well, well, well, what have we here? Sobran comma Karl with a K, Sebring comma Carl with a C, and . . . Ramsey comma Clark Edward. Which one's real, turkey, or are you suffering from multiple personality syndrome?"

The man said nothing.

Milo nudged one of the black shoes with a toe.

"Good old prison clumpers. County or state?"

No answer.

"You need new heels, genius."

The man's back muscles moved under his shirt.

Milo turned to me. "Find a phone and call the Devonshire substation. Tell them we've got a suspect on a Central Division homicide and give them Dawn Herbert's full name."

The man on the ground said, "Bullshit." His voice was deep and muddy.

One of the young students came out onto the stairs. Twenty or twenty-one, short blond pageboy, sleeveless white dress, Mary Pickford face.

She said, "Kristie's pretty upset," in a very timid voice.

"Tell her I'll be with her in a minute," said Milo.

"Um . . . sure. What did Karl do?"

"Sloppy homework," said Milo.

The man on the ground growled and the girl looked startled.

Milo kept his knee on the man's back and said, "Shut up."

The blond girl gripped the doorjamb.

Softening his voice, Milo said, "It's okay—nothing to worry about. Just go inside and wait."

"This isn't some kind of experiment or anything, is it?"

"Experiment?"

"A role-play. You know? Professor Jones likes to use them to raise our awareness."

"Bet he does. No, miss, this is real. Sociology in action. Take a good look—it'll be on the final."

The envelope arrived by messenger at 7:00 P.M., just before Robin got home. I put it aside and tried to have a normal evening with her. After she went to sleep, I took it to the library. Turned on all the lights and read.

TRANSCRIPT OF INTERROGATION

DR# 102—789 793
DR# 64—458 990
DR# 135—935 827

PLACE: L.A.C. JAIL, BLOCK: HIGH-POWER
T/DATE: 6/1/89, 7:30 P.M.

SUSPECT: JONES, CHARLES LYMAN III, MW, 6'3",
BRO, BLU
AGE: 38

DEF ATTORNEY: TOKARIK, ANTHONY M., ESQ.

LAPD: MILO B. STURGIS #15994, WLA
(SPEC. ASSIGNMENT)
STEPHEN MARTINEZ, #26782, DEVSHR.

DET. STURGIS: This is video-audiotape session number two with Suspect Charles Lyman Jones the Third. Suspect was informed of his rights at the time of arrest for attempted murder. Miranda warning was repeated and taped at a previous session, eleven A.M. June 1, 1989, and transcribed on that day at two P.M. Said session was terminated on advice of suspect's counsel, Mr. Anthony Tokarik, Esquire. This session represents resumption of interview at request of Mr. Tokarik. Do I need to re-Mirandize him, Counselor, or does that second warning hold for this session?

MR. TOKARIK: It will hold, unless Professor Jones requests re-Mirandization. Do you want to be warned again, Chip?

MR. JONES: No. Let's get on with this.

MR. TOKARIK: Go ahead.

DET. STURGIS: Evening, Chip.

MR. TOKARIK: I'd prefer that you address my client respectfully, Detective.

DET. STURGIS: Professor be okay?

MR. TOKARIK: Yes. However, if that's too difficult for you, "Mr. Jones" would suffice.

DET. STURGIS: You just called him Chip.

MR. TOKARIK: I'm his lawyer.

DET. STURGIS: Uh-huh . . . okay . . . sure. Hey, I'd even call him "Doctor," but he never finished his Ph.D., did you, Chip—Mr. Jones? What's that? Can't hear you.

MR. JONES: (unintelligible)

DET. STURGIS: Got to speak up, Mr. Jones. Grunts don't make it.

MR. TOKARIK: Hold on, Detective. Unless the tone of this interview changes, I'm going to call a halt to it immediately.

DET. STURGIS: Suit yourself—your loss. I just thought you guys might want to hear some of the evidence we've compiled against old Chip, here. 'Scuse me—Mister Jones.

MR. TOKARIK: I can get anything you have from the district attorney under the rules of recovery, Detective.

DET. STURGIS: Fine. Then wait till the trial. Let's go, Steve.

DET. MARTINEZ: Sure.

MR. JONES: Hold on. (unintelligible)

MR. TOKARIK: Wait, Chip. (unintelligible) I'd like to confer with my client privately, if you don't mind.

DET. STURGIS: If it doesn't take too long.

Tape off: 7:39 P.M.
Tape on: 7:51 P.M.

MR. TOKARIK: Go ahead, show us what you've got.

DET. STURGIS: Yeah, sure, but is Mr. Jones going to be answering questions or is it gonna be a one-way show-and-tell?

MR. TOKARIK: I reserve my client's right to refuse to answer any questions. Proceed if you wish, Detective.

DET. STURGIS: What do you think, Steve?

DET. MARTINEZ: I don't know.

MR. TOKARIK: Decision, gentlemen?

DET. STURGIS: Yeah, okay . . . Well, Chip—Mr. Jones—I'm glad you've got yourself a high-priced lawyer like Mr. Tokarik here, 'cause you're sure gonna—

MR. TOKARIK: This is definitely getting off on the wrong foot. My fees have nothing to—

DET. STURGIS: What are we doing here, Counselor, interrogating a suspect or critiquing my style?

MR. TOKARIK: I strenuously object to your—

DET. STURGIS: Object all you want. This isn't court.

MR. TOKARIK: I request another conference with my client.

DET. STURGIS: No way. Let's split, Steve.

DET. MARTINEZ: You bet.

MR. JONES: Hold on. Sit down.

DET. STURGIS: You ordering me around, Junior?

MR. TOKARIK: I object to—

DET. STURGIS: Come on, Steve, we're outa here.

MR. JONES: Hold on!

MR. TOKARIK: Chip, it's—

MR. JONES: Shut up!

MR. TOKARIK: Chip—

MR. JONES: Shut up!

DET. STURGIS: Uh-uh, no way do I proceed with this kind of friction going on between the two of you. Then he complains he wasn't represented by counsel of choice? No way.

MR. TOKARIK: Don't play lawyer with me, Detective.

MR. JONES: Just shut the hell up, Tony! This whole thing is preposterous!

DET. STURGIS: What is, Professor Jones?

MR. JONES: Your supposed case.

DET. STURGIS: You didn't attempt to inject your daughter, Cassandra Brooks, with insulin?

MR. JONES: Of course not. I found the needle in Cindy's purse, got upset because it confirmed my suspicions about her, and was trying to see if she'd already—

MR. TOKARIK: Chip—

MR. JONES: . . . jected it into Cassie's I.V. Stop giving me looks, Tony—it's my future at stake here. I want to hear what kind of folderol they think they've got, so I can clear it up once and for all.

DET. STURGIS: Folderol?

MR. TOKARIK: Chip—

DET. STURGIS: I don't want to continue if—

MR. JONES: He's my attorney of choice, okay? Go on.

DET. STURGIS: You're sure?

MR. JONES: (unintelligible)

DET. STURGIS: Speak right into that mike over there.

MR. JONES: Get on with it. I want out of here, posthaste.

DET. STURGIS: Yes, sir, massah sir.

MR. TOKARIK: Detecti—

MR. JONES: Shut up, Tony.

DET. STURGIS: Everyone ready? Okay. First of all, we've got you on videotape, trying to shoot insulin into—

MR. JONES: Wrong. I told you what that was about. I was just trying to see what Cindy was up to.

DET. STURGIS: Like I said, we've got you on videotape, trying to shoot insulin into your daughter's intravenous line. Plus video logs of the cameras at the entrance to Western Pediatric Medical Center confirming that you didn't enter the hospital through the front door. One of the keys on your ring has been identified as a hospital master. You probably used it to sneak in through the—

MR. TOKARIK: I obj—

MR. JONES: Tony.

MR. TOKARIK: I request a brief conference with my—

MR. JONES: Cut it out, Tony. I'm not one of your idiot sociopaths. Go on with your fairy tale, Detective. And you're right, I did use one of Dad's keys. So what? Whenever I go to that place I avoid the front door. I try to be inconspicuous. Is discretion an egregious felony?

DET. STURGIS: Let's go on. You bought two cups of coffee from a hospital machine, then took the stairs up to the fifth floor. We've got you on video up there too. Out in the hall where Five East meets Chappell Ward, carrying the coffee and looking through a crack in the door. What it looks like to me is you're waiting until the nurse on duty goes into a back room. Then you go into room 505 West where you stay for fifty-five minutes until I come in and find you jabbing that needle into your daughter's I.V. line. We're going to show you all those videotapes now, okay?

MR. JONES: Seems eminently superfluous, but suit yourself.

DET. STURGIS: Action, camera.

Tape off: 8:22 P.M.

Tape on: 9:10 P.M.

DET. STURGIS: Okay. Any comments?

MR. JONES: Godard it's not.

DET. STURGIS: No? I thought it had a lot of *vérité.*

MR. JONES: Are you a fan of *cinéma vérité,* Detective?

DET. STURGIS: Not really, Mr. Jones. Too much like work.

MR. JONES: Hah, I like that.

MR. TOKARIK: Is that it? That's your evidence, in toto?

DET. STURGIS: In toto? Hardly. Okay, so now we've got you jabbing that needle—

MR. JONES: I told you what that was about—I was testing it. Checking the I.V. inlet to see if Cindy'd already injected Cassie.

DET. STURGIS: Why?

MR. JONES: Why? To protect my child!

DET. STURGIS: Why did you suspect your wife of harming Cassie?

MR. JONES: Circumstances. The data at hand.

DET. STURGIS: The data.

MR. JONES: Exactly.

DET. STURGIS: Want to tell me more about the data?

MR. JONES: Her personality—things I noticed. She'd been acting strange—elusive. And Cassie always seemed to fall ill after she'd spent time with her mother.

DET. STURGIS: Okay . . . We've also got a puncture wound in the fleshy part of Cassie's armpit.

MR. JONES: No doubt you do, but I didn't put it there.

DET. STURGIS: Aha . . . what about the Valium you put in your wife's coffee?

MR. JONES: I explained it in the room, Detective. I didn't

give it to her. It was for her nerves, remember. She's been really on edge—been taking it for a while. If she denies that, she's lying.

DET. STURGIS: She does indeed deny it. She says she was never aware you were dosing her up.

MR. JONES: She lies habitually—that's the point. Accusing me based purely on what she says is like constructing a syllogism based on totally false premises. Do you understand what I mean by that?

DET. STURGIS: Sure, Prof. Valium tablets were found in one of Cassie's toys—a stuffed bunny.

MR. JONES: There you go. How would I know anything about that?

DET. STURGIS: Your wife says you bought several of them for Cassie.

MR. JONES: I bought Cassie all sorts of toys. Other people bought LuvBunnies too. A nurse named Bottomley—very iffy personality. Why don't you check her out, see if she's involved.

DET. STURGIS: Why should she be?

MR. JONES: She and Cindy seem awfully close—too close, I always thought. I wanted her transferred off the case, but Cindy refused. Check her out—she's strange, believe me.

DET. STURGIS: We did. She's passed a polygraph and every other test we threw at her.

MR. JONES: Polygraphs are inadmissible in court.

DET. STURGIS: Would you take one?

MR. TOKARIK: Chip, don't—

MR. JONES: I don't see any reason to. This whole thing is preposterous.

DET. STURGIS: Onward. Did you have a prescription for the Valium we found at your campus office?

MR. JONES: (laughs) No. Is that a crime?

DET. STURGIS: As a matter of fact, it is. Where'd you get it?

MR. JONES: Somewhere—I don't remember.

DET. STURGIS: One of your students?

MR. JONES: Of course not.

DET. STURGIS: A student named Kristie Marie Kirkash?

MR. JONES: Uh—absolutely not. I may have had it around from before.

DET. STURGIS: For yourself?

MR. JONES: Sure. From years ago—I was under some stress.

Now that I think about it, I'm sure that's what it was. Someone lent it to me—a faculty colleague.

DET. STURGIS: What's this colleague's name?

MR. JONES: I don't remember. It wasn't that significant. Valium's like candy nowadays. I plead guilty to having it without a prescription, okay?

DET. STURGIS: Okay.

MR. TOKARIK: What did you just take out of your briefcase, Detective?

DET. STURGIS: Something for the record. I'm going to read it out loud—

MR. TOKARIK: I want a copy first. Two copies—for myself and for Professor Jones.

DET. STURGIS: Duly noted. We'll get the Xerox going soon as we're finished here.

MR. TOKARIK: No, I want it simultaneous with your—

MR. JONES: Stop obstructing, Tony. Let him read whatever it is. I want out of here today.

MR. TOKARIK: Chip, nothing's of greater importance to me than your imminent release, but I—

MR. JONES: Quiet, Tony. Read, Detective.

MR. TOKARIK: Not at all. I'm unhappy with thi—

MR. JONES: Fine. Read, Detective.

DET. STURGIS: That settled? Sure? Okay. This is a transcript of an encoded computer floppy disk, 3M Brand, DS, DD, RH, double-sided, double-density, Q Mark. Further designated with Federal Bureau of Investigation Evidence Tag Number 133355678345 dash 452948. The disk was decoded by the cryptography division of the FBI National Crime Laboratory in Washington, D.C., and was received at Los Angeles Police Department Headquarters, this morning, 6:45 A.M., via government pouch. Once I start, I'm going to read it in its entirety, even if you choose to leave the room with your client, Counselor. In order to make it clear that this evidence was offered to you and you declined to hear it. Understood?

MR. TOKARIK: We exercise all of our rights without prejudice.

MR. JONES: Read on, Detective. I'm intrigued.

DET. STURGIS: Here goes:

> I'm putting this in code to protect myself, but it's not a
> complicated code, just a basic substitution—numbers for

letters with a couple of reversals, so you should be able to handle that, Ashmore. And if something's happened to me, have fun with it.

Charles Lyman Jones the Third, known as Chip, is a monster.

He came to my high school as a volunteer tutor and seduced me sexually and emotionally. This was ten years ago. I was seventeen and a senior and in the honors program in math, but I needed help with English and Social Sciences because I found it boring. He was twenty-eight and a graduate student. He seduced me and we had sex repeatedly over a six-month period at his apartment and at the school, including activities that I found personally repulsive. He was frequently impotent and did sick things to me in order to arouse himself. Eventually, I got pregnant and he said he'd marry me. We never got married, just lived together in a dive near the University of Connecticut, at Storrs. Then it got worse.

1. He didn't tell his family about me. He kept another apartment in town and went there whenever his father came to visit.

2. He started to act really crazy. Doing things to my body—putting drugs in my drinks and sticking me with needles when I was sleeping. At first I wasn't sure what was happening, used to wake up with marks all over, feeling sore. He said I was anemic and it was petechiae—broken capillaries due to pregnancy. Since he told me he'd been pre-med at Yale, I believed him. Then one time I woke up and caught him trying to inject me with something brown and disgusting-looking—I'm sure now it was feces. Apparently he hadn't given me enough dope to put me out, or maybe I'd become hooked and needed more to pass out. He explained the needle by saying it was all for my good—some kind of organic vitamin tonic.

I was young and I believed all his lies. Then it got too weird and I left and tried to live with my mother but she was drunk all the time and wouldn't take me in. Also, I think he paid her off, because right around then she got lots of new clothes. So I went back to him and the more pregnant I got, the meaner and more vicious he got. One time he pulled a really hysterical fit and told me the baby would ruin everything between us and that it had to go. Then he claimed it wasn't even his, which was ridiculous because I was a virgin when I met him and never fooled around with anyone else. Eventually, the stress he put me through made me miscarry. But that didn't make him

happy either, and he kept sneaking up on me when I was
sleeping, shouting in my ear and sometimes sticking me.
I was getting fevers and bad headaches and hearing voices
and becoming dizzy. For a while I thought I was going
crazy.

I finally left Storrs and went back to Poughkeepsie.
He followed me and we had a real screaming fit in Victor
Waryas Park. Then he gave me a check for ten thousand
dollars and told me to get out of his life and stay there.
That was a lot of money to me at the time and I agreed. I
was feeling too down and screwed up to work, so I got out
on the street and got ripped off and ended up marrying
Willie Kent, a black guy who pimped once in a while.
That lasted about six months. Then I got into detox and
got my equivalency and got into college.

I majored in math and computer science and did
really well and then I got seduced by another teacher
named Ross M. Herbert and was married to him for two
years. He wasn't a monster like Chip Jones but he was
boring and unhygienic and I divorced him and left college
after three years.

I got a job in computers but that was pretty noncrea-
tive so I decided to be a doctor and went back to school to
study pre-med. I had to work nights and squeeze in my
studying. That's why my grades and my M-CAT scores
weren't as high as they should have been, but I did get
straight As in math.

I finally finished and applied to a bunch of medical
schools but didn't get in. I worked as a lab assistant for a
year and took the M-CATs again and did better. So I
applied again and made some waiting lists. I also applied
to some Public Health programs in order to get a related
degree, and the best one that accepted me was in Los
Angeles, so I came out here.

I scraped by for four years, kept applying to med
school. Then I was reading the paper and saw an article on
Charles Lyman Jones, Jr., and realized it was his father.
That's when I realized how rich they were and how I'd
been ripped off. So I decided to get some of what was
coming to me. I tried to call his father but couldn't get
through to him, even wrote letters he never answered. So I
looked up Chip in city records and found he was living out
in the Valley and went out to see what his house looked
like. I did it at night, so no one could see me. I did it a
bunch of times and got a look at his wife. What freaked
me out was how much like me she looked, before I gained

weight. His little daughter was real cute, and boy, did I feel sorry for the two of them.

I really didn't want to hurt them—the wife and the little girl—but I also felt I should warn them what they were up against. And he owed me.

I went back there several times, thinking about what to do, and then one night I saw an ambulance pull up in front of the house. He came out right afterward, in his Volvo, and I followed him at a distance, to Western Pediatric Medical Center. I stayed behind him all the way to the Emergency Room and heard him ask about his daughter, Cassie.

The next morning I went back, to Medical Records, wearing my white lab coat and saying I was Dr. Herbert. It was really easy, no security. Later, they beefed things up. Anyway, the daughter: her chart was gone but a card was there listing all these other admissions for her, so I knew he was up to his tricks. The poor little thing.

That's what really got me going—it wasn't just the money. Believe it or don't, Ashmore, but it's the truth. When I saw that card on the little girl, I knew I had to get him. So I went to Personnel and applied for a job. Three weeks later they called and offered me a half-time. With you, Ashmore. Shitty job, but I could watch Chip without him knowing. I finally got hold of Cassie's chart and found out everything he was doing to her. I also read in there that they'd had a boy who died. So I looked up his chart and found out he'd had crib death. So Chip had finally murdered someone. Next time I saw Cassie's name on the A and D sheets, I watched for him and finally saw him and followed him out to the parking lot and said, "Surprise."

He was really freaked out, tried to pretend he didn't know me. Then he tried to put me on the defensive by saying how much weight I'd gained. I just told him I knew what he was up to and that he'd better stop. Also, if he didn't give me a million dollars, I'd go to the police. He actually started crying, said he never meant to hurt anyone—just like he used to do when we were together. But this time it didn't work. I said no dice.

Then he said he'd give me a good-will payment of ten thousand dollars and try to come up with some more, but I had to give him time and it wouldn't be anything near a million—he didn't have that kind of money. I said fifty up front and we finally agreed on twenty-seven five. The next day he met me up at Barnsdale Park in Hollywood and gave me the money in cash. I told him he'd better come up with at least two hundred thousand more by the end of the month. He started crying again and said he'd do his best. Then he asked me to forgive him. I left and used the money to buy a new car because my old one was broken down, and in L.A. you're nothing without a good car. I put Chad Jones's chart in a locker at the airport—LAX, United Airlines, Number 5632—and the next day I quit the hospital.

So now I'm waiting till the end of the month and writing this down as collateral. I want to be rich and I want to be a doctor. I deserve all that. But just in case he tries to renege, I'm leaving this floppy in a locked drawer each night, then collecting it in the morning. There's also a copy in my locker at school. If you're reading it, I'm probably in Dutch, but so what. I've got no other alternatives.

March 7, 1989
Dawn Rose Rockwell Kent Herbert

DET. STURGIS: That's it.

MR. TOKARIK: Are we supposed to be impressed? Decoded hocus-pocus? You know this is totally inadmissible.

DET. STURGIS: If you say so.

MR. TOKARIK: Come on, Chip, let's get out of here—Chip?

MR. JONES: Uh-huh.

DET. STURGIS: Sure you wanna go? There's more.

MR. TOKARIK: We've heard quite enough.

DET. STURGIS: Suit yourself, Counselor. But don't waste your time asking for bail. D.A.'s filing Murder One as we speak.

MR. TOKARIK: Murder One! That's outrageous. Who's the victim?

DET. STURGIS: Dawn Herbert.

MR. TOKARIK: Murder One? On the basis of that fantasy?

DET. STURGIS: On the basis of eyewitness testimony, Counselor. Collaborator testimony. Upstanding citizen named Karl Sobran. You do have a thing for your students, don't you, Prof.

MR. TOKARIK: Who?

DET. STURGIS: Ask the prof.

MR. TOKARIK: I'm asking you, Detective.

DET. STURGIS: Karl Edward Sobran. We've got a windbreaker with blood on it and a confession implicating your client. And Sobran's credentials are impeccable. Bachelor's degree in interpersonal violence from Soledad, postgraduate training from numerous other institutions. Your client hired him to kill Ms. Herbert and make it look like a sex thing. Not much of a challenge, because Sobran likes to get violent with women—did time for rape and assault. His last paid vacation was for larceny and he spent it up in the Ventura County Jail. That's where old Professor Chip, here, met him. Volunteer tutoring—a class project his sociology students were doing. Sobran got an A. Old Chip sent a letter recommending parole, calling Sobran graduate-school material and promising to keep him under his wing. Sobran got out and enrolled at West Valley Community College as a sociology major. What he did to Dawn— What was that, Prof? Fieldwork?

MR. TOKARIK: This is the most ridiculous thing I've ever heard of.

DET. STURGIS: D.A. doesn't think so.

MR. TOKARIK: The D.A. is totally politically motivated. If my client was any other Jones, we wouldn't even be sitting here.

DET. STURGIS: Okay . . . have a nice day. Steve?

DET. MARTINEZ: See y'all.

MR. TOKARIK: Coded disks, the alleged testimony of a convicted felon—absurd.

DET. STURGIS: Ask your client if it's absurd.

MR. TOKARIK: I'll do no such thing. Let's go, Chip. Come on.

MR. JONES: Can you get me bail, Tony?

MR. TOKARIK: This isn't the place to—

MR. JONES: I want out of this place, Tony. Things are piling up. I've got papers to grade.

MR. TOKARIK: Of course, Chip. But it may take—

DET. STURGIS: He's not going anywhere and you know it, Counselor. Level with him.

MR. JONES: I want out. This place is depressing. I can't concentrate.

MR. TOKARIK: I understand, Chip, but—

MR. JONES: No buts, Tony. I want out. *A l'extérieur.* O.U.T.

MR. TOKARIK: Of course, Chip. You know I'll do everything I—

MR. JONES: I want out, Tony. I'm a good person. This is totally Kafkaesque.

DET. STURGIS: Good person, huh? Liar, torturer, murderer . . . Yeah, I guess if you don't count those minor technicalities, you're up for sainthood, Junior.

MR. JONES: I am a good person.

DET. STURGIS: Tell that to your daughter.

MR. JONES: She's not my daughter.

MR. TOKARIK: Chip—

DET. STURGIS: Cassie's not your daughter?

MR. JONES: Not strictly speaking, Detective. Not that it's relevant—I wouldn't hurt anyone's child.

DET. STURGIS: She's not yours?

MR. JONES: No. Even though I've raised her as if she were. All the responsibility but none of the ownership.

DET. MARTINEZ: Whose is she, then?

MR. JONES: Who knows? Her mother's such a compulsive roundheels, jumps anything with a— In pants. God only knows who the father is. I sure don't.

DET. STURGIS: By "her mother" you're referring to your wife? Cindy Brooks Jones.

MR. JONES: Wife in name only.

MR. TOKARIK: Chip—

MR. JONES: She's a barracuda, Detective. Don't believe that innocent exterior. Pure predator. Once she snagged me, she reverted to type.

DET. STURGIS: What type is that?

MR. TOKARIK: I'm calling this session to a halt right now. Any further questions are at your legal risk, Detective.

DET. STURGIS: Sorry, Chip. Your legal beagle, here, says zip the lip.

MR. JONES: I'll talk to whom I want, when I want, Tony.

MR. TOKARIK: For God's sake, Chip—

MR. JONES: Shut up, Tony. You're growing tedious.

DET. STURGIS: Better listen to him, Prof. He's the expert.

MR. TOKARIK: Exactly. Session ended.

DET. STURGIS: Whatever you say.

MR. JONES: Stop infantilizing me—all of you. I'm the one stuck in this hellhole. My rights are the ones being abridged. What do I have to do to get out of here, Detective?

MR. TOKARIK: Chip, at this point there's nothing you can do—

MR. JONES: Then what do I need you for? You're fired.

MR. TOKARIK: Chip—

MR. JONES: Just shut up and let me get a thought out, okay?

MR. TOKARIK: Chip, I can't in good conscience—

MR. JONES: You don't have a conscience, Tony. You're a lawyer. Quoth the Bard: "Let's kill all the lawyers." Okay? So just hold on . . . okay . . . Listen, you guys are cops—you understand street people, how they lie. That's the way Cindy is. She lies atavistically—it's an ingrained habit. She fooled me for a long time because I loved her—"When my love swears that she is made of truth, I do believe her, though I know she lies." Shakespeare—everything's in Shakespeare. Where was I . . . ?

MR. TOKARIK: Chip, for your own sake—

MR. JONES: She's amazing, Detective. Could charm the bark off a tree. Serve me dinner and smile and ask me how my day had been—and an hour before, she was in our marital bed, screwing the pool man. The pool man, for God's sake. We're talking urban legend here. But she lived it.

DET. STURGIS: By "the pool man" you're referring to Greg Worley of ValleyBrite Pool Service?

MR. JONES: Him, others—what's the difference? Carpenters, plumbers, anything in jeans and a tool belt. No trouble getting tradesmen out to our place—oh, no. Our place was Disneyland for every blue-collar cocksman in town. It's a disease, Detective. She can't help herself. Okay, rationally, I can understand that. Ungovernable impulses. But she destroyed me in the process. I was the victim.

MR. TOKARIK: (unintelligible)

DET. STURGIS: What's that, Counselor?

MR. TOKARIK: I register my objection to this entire session.

MR. JONES: Suppress your ego, Tony. I'm the victim—don't exploit me for your ego. That's my problem in general— people tend to take advantage of me because they know I'm fairly naïve.

DET. STURGIS: Dawn Herbert do that?

MR. JONES: Absolutely. That folderol you read was absolute fantasy. She was a dope addict when I found her. I tried to help her and she paid me back with paranoia.

DET. STURGIS: What about Kristie Kirkash?

MR. JONES: (unintelligible)

DET. STURGIS: What's that, Prof?

MR. JONES: Kristie's my student. Why? Does she say it's more than that?

DET. STURGIS: Actually she does.

MR. JONES: Then she's lying—another one.

DET. STURGIS: Another what?

MR. JONES: Predator. Believe me, she's old beyond her years. I must attract them. What happened with Kristie is that I caught her cheating on a test and was working with her on her ethics. Take my advice and don't accept anything she says at face value.

DET. STURGIS: She says she rented a post office box for you out in Agoura Hills. You have the number handy, Steve?

DET. MARTINEZ: Mailboxes Plus, Agoura, box number 1498.

MR. JONES: That was for research.

DET. STURGIS: What kind of research?

MR. JONES: I've been thinking of a possible project: pornography research—recurrent images in an overly organized society—as a form of ritual. Obviously, I didn't want material sent to my home or my campus office—you get on pervert lists, and I didn't want a flood of garbage coming in. So Kristie rented the POB for me.

DET. STURGIS: Any reason you didn't rent it yourself?

MR. JONES: I was busy, Kristie lived out there, and it just seemed convenient.

DET. STURGIS: Any reason you rented it under the name of Ralph Benedict, M.D.? A physician who's been dead for two and a half years and just happened to have treated your wife's aunt for diabetes?

MR. TOKARIK: Don't answer that.

DET. STURGIS: Any reason you had medical apparatus shipped out to that post office box using Ralph Benedict, M.D.'s name and medical license number?

MR. TOKARIK: Don't answer that.

DET. STURGIS: Any reason you had insulin and Insuject insulin-delivery systems, such as the one we found in your hand in your daughter's hospital room, shipped to that post office box in Ralph Benedict, M.D.'s name?

MR. TOKARIK: Don't answer that.

MR. JONES: Ridiculous. Cindy knew about the POB, too. I gave her my spare key. She must have used it for that.

DET. STURGIS: She says she didn't.

MR. JONES: She's lying.

DET. STURGIS: Okay, but even so, why'd *you* use Benedict's name to *get* the box? It's your name on the application form.

MR. TOKARIK: Don't answer that.

MR. JONES: I want to—I want to clear my name, Tony. In all honesty, Detective, I can't really answer that one. It must have been subconscious. Cindy must have mentioned Benedict's name—yes, I'm sure she did. As you said, he was her aunt's doctor, she talked about him a lot, and it stuck in my mind—so when I needed a name for the box, it just popped into my head.

DET. STURGIS: Why'd you need an alias in the first place?

MR. JONES: I already explained that. For the pornography—some of the stuff I received was really disgusting.

DET. STURGIS: Your wife says she knew nothing about the box.

MR. JONES: Of course she does. She's lying. Really, Detective, it's all a matter of context—seeing things in a different light, using a new lens.

DET. STURGIS: Uh-huh.

MR. TOKARIK: Now what are you pulling out?

DET. STURGIS: I think it's obvious. This is a mask.

MR. TOKARIK: I fail to see—

MR. JONES: No big deal. It's from the carnival—Delta Psi's carnival. They dressed me up as a witch. I kept the mask for a souvenir.

DET. STURGIS: Kristie Kirkash kept it. You gave it to her last week and told her to keep it.

MR. JONES: So?

DET. STURGIS: So I think you put this on when you injected Cassie. So you'd look like a woman—the wicked witch.

MR. TOKARIK: Ridiculous.

MR. JONES: I agree with you there, Tony.

DET. STURGIS: A souvenir, huh? Why'd you give it to Kristie?

MR. JONES: She's a Delta Psi. I thought the sorority would like to have it.

DET. STURGIS: Considerate.

MR. JONES: I'm their faculty adviser. What's the big—

DET. STURGIS: You have a thing for your students, don't you? That's how you met your wife, isn't it? She was your student.

MR. JONES: It's not unusual—the teacher-student relationship . . .

DET. STURGIS: What about it?

MR. JONES: Often . . . sometimes it leads to intimacy.

DET. STURGIS: You tutor her, too? Your wife?

MR. JONES: As a matter of fact, I did. But she was hopeless—not very bright at all.

DET. STURGIS: But you married her anyway. How come? A smart guy like you.

MR. JONES: I was smitten—"this spring of love."

DET. STURGIS: You met in the spring?

MR. JONES: It's a quotation—

DET. STURGIS: Shakespeare?

MR. JONES: As a matter of fact, yes. I fell deeply in love and was taken advantage of. A romantic nature. My bête noire.

DET. STURGIS: What about Karl Sobran? He take advantage of you too?

MR. JONES: With Karl it was different—with him, ironically, I wasn't naïve. I knew what he was, right away, but I felt I could help him channel his impulses.

DET. STURGIS: What did you know he was?

MR. JONES: Classic antisocial sociopath. But contrary to popular belief, those types don't lack consciences. They merely suspend them at their convenience—read Samenow. As a police officer, you really should. Where was I? Karl. Karl is very bright. I was hoping to direct his intelligence in a constructive manner.

DET. STURGIS: Like murder for hire?

MR. TOKARIK: Don't answer that.

MR. JONES: Stop sighing, Tony. That's ridiculous. Of course not. Did Karl actually say that?

DET. STURGIS: How else would I know about him, Prof?

MR. JONES: Ludicrous. But he is a sociopath—don't forget that. Genetic liar. At worst I'm guilty of underestimating him—not realizing how truly dangerous he was. As much as I didn't respect Dawn as a human being, I was horrified to find out she was murdered. If I'd known, I'd never have written that letter to Karl's parole board. Never have . . . Oh, my God.

DET. STURGIS: Never have what?

MR. JONES: Talked idly to Karl.

DET. STURGIS: About Dawn?

MR. TOKARIK: Don't answer that.

MR. JONES: You're sighing again—it's very wearisome, Tony. Yes, about her, as well as other things. I'm afraid I must have thrown out idle comments about Dawn that Karl must have misinterpreted horribly.

DET. STURGIS: What kinds of comments?

MR. JONES: Oh, no, I can't believe he actually— How she was harassing me. He misunderstood. God, what a horrible misunderstanding!

DET. STURGIS: You're saying he misunderstood your comments and killed her on his own?

MR. JONES: Believe me, Detective, the thought makes me sick. But it's an inescapable conclusion.

DET. STURGIS: What exactly did you tell Sobran about Dawn?

MR. JONES: That she was someone from my past who was bothering me.

DET. STURGIS: That's it?

MR. JONES: That's it.

DET. STURGIS: There was no solicitation? To kill or hurt her?

MR. JONES: Absolutely not.

DET. STURGIS: But there was payment, Prof. Two thousand dollars that Sobran deposited in his account the day after her murder. He had some of it in his pocket when I arrested him. He says he got it from you.

MR. JONES: No problem. I've been helping Karl for a long time—so he could get on his feet, wouldn't have to revert.

DET. STURGIS: Two thousand dollars?

MR. JONES: Sometimes I get a little loose with the purse strings. It's an occupational hazard.

DET. STURGIS: Of being a sociology professor?

MR. JONES: Of growing up wealthy—it can be a real curse, you know. That's why I always tried to live my life as if the money didn't exist. Keeping my life-style unpretentious— keeping away from all the things that have the potential to corrupt.

DET. STURGIS: Like real estate deals?

MR. JONES: My investments were for them—Cindy and the kids. I wanted them to have some kind of financial stability, because teaching school sure won't give you that. That was before I realized what she was doing.

DET. STURGIS: By "doing," you mean sexual behavior?

MR. JONES: Exactly. With everything that walked in through the door. The children weren't even mine, but I took care of them anyway. I'm a soft touch—it's something I need to work on.

DET. STURGIS: Uh-huh . . . Was Chad yours?

MR. JONES: Not a chance.

DET. STURGIS: How do you know?

MR. JONES: One look at him. He was the spitting image of a roofer we had working out on the tract. Spitting image—total clone.

DET. STURGIS: Is that why you killed him?

MR. JONES: Don't be tedious, Detective. Chad died of sudden infant death syndrome.

DET. STURGIS: How can you be sure?

MR. JONES: Textbook case. I read up on it—SIDS—after the little guy died. Trying to understand—to work it through. It was a horrible time for me. He wasn't my flesh and blood, but I still loved him.

DET. STURGIS: Okay, let's move on. Your mother. Why'd you kill her?

MR. TOKARIK: I object!

MR. JONES: You fuck—

DET. STURGIS: See, I did some studying, too—

MR. JONES: You fat fu—

MR. TOKARIK: I object! I most strenuously object to thi—

DET. STURGIS: —trying to understand you, Prof. Talked to people all about your mom. You'd be amazed at how willing people are to talk once someone's down—

MR. JONES: You are stupid. You are psychotic and . . . and . . . egregiously stupid and ignorant. I should have known better than to bare my soul to someone like—

MR. TOKARIK: Chip—

DET. STURGIS: One thing they all agree on was that old Mom was a hypochondriac. Healthy as a horse but convinced she was terminally ill. One person I spoke to said her bedroom was like a hospital room—that she actually had a hospital bed. With the little table? All these pills and syrups lying around. Needles too. Lots of needles. She stick herself, or get you to do it?

MR. JONES: Oh, God . . .

MR. TOKARIK: Take my handkerchief, Chip. Detective, I demand that you cease this line of questioning.

DET. STURGIS: Sure. Bye.

MR. JONES: She was the one who did the sticking! Herself and me—she hurt me! Vitamin B-12 shots twice a day. Protein shots. Antihistamine shots, even though I wasn't allergic to anything! My bottom was her fucking pincushion! Antibiotics the minute I coughed. Tetanus shots if I got a scrape. I was the Azazel goat—cod liver oil and castor oil, and if I threw it up, I had to clean it up and to take a double dosage. She could always get hold of medicine because she used to be a nurse—that's how she met him. Army hospital, he was wounded at Anzio—big hero. She took care of him, but to me she was a sadistic maniac—you have no idea what it was like!

DET. STURGIS: Sounds like no one protected you.

MR. JONES: No one! It was a living hell. Every day brought a new surprise. That's why I hate surprises. Hate them. Detest them.

DET. STURGIS: You prefer everything planned out, huh?

MR. JONES: Organization. I like organization.

DET. STURGIS: Sounds like your dad let you down.

MR. JONES: (laughs) That's his hobby.

DET. STURGIS: So you go your own way.

MR. JONES: Mother's the— Necessity's the mother of invention. (laughs) Thank you, Herr Freud.

DET. STURGIS: Getting back to mom for a minute—

MR. JONES: Let's not.

DET. STURGIS: The way she died—Valium O.D., plastic bag over the head—guess we'll never prove it wasn't suicide.

MR. JONES: That's because it was. And that's all I have to say about that.

DET. STURGIS: Want to say anything about why you hung two pictures she painted in your house but really low to the ground? What was that, a symbolic demeaning or something?

MR. JONES: I have nothing to say about that.

DET. STURGIS: Uh-huh . . . yeah . . . So what you're trying to tell me is, you're the victim and this is all a big misunderstanding.

MR. JONES: (unintelligible)

DET. STURGIS: What?

MR. JONES: Context, Detective. Context.

DET. STURGIS: New lens.

MR. JONES: Exactly.

DET. STURGIS: Your reading up on sudden infant death·was because you were trying to understand your . . . Chad's death?

MR. JONES: Exactly.

DET. STURGIS: Did you read up on Munchausen syndrome by proxy because you were trying to understand Cassie's illnesses?

MR. JONES: As a matter of fact, I did. Research is what I'm trained to do, Detective. All the experts seemed to be baffled by Cassie's symptoms. I figured I'd learn what I could.

DET. STURGIS: Dawn Herbert said you were once pre-med.

MR. JONES: Very briefly. I lost interest.

DET. STURGIS: Why?

MR. JONES: Too concrete, no imagination involved. Doctors are really nothing more than glorified plumbers.

DET. STURGIS: So . . . you read up on Munchausen syndrome—doing the old professor thing.

MR. JONES: (laughs) What can I tell you? In the end we all revert. . . . It was a revelation, believe me. Learning about the syndrome. Not that I ever imagined, in the beginning, that Cindy might be doing something to her— Perhaps I was too slow to suspect, but my own childhood . . . too painful. I suppose I repressed. But then . . . when I read . . .

DET. STURGIS: What? Why are you shaking your head?

MR. JONES: It's hard to talk about . . . so cruel . . . You think you know someone and then . . . But the fit—everything started to fit. Cindy's history. Her obsession with health. The techniques she must have used . . . disgusting.

DET. STURGIS: Such as?

MR. JONES: Smothering to simulate asphyxia. Cindy was always the one who got up when Cassie cried—she only called me when things got bad. Then those terrible GI—gastrointestinal—problems and fevers. Once I saw something brown in Cassie's baby bottle. Cindy said it was organic apple juice and I believed her. Now I realize it must have been some sort of fecal matter. Poisoning Cassie with her own filth so that she'd get an infection but it would be an autologous one—self-infection, so that no foreign organism would show up on the blood tests. Disgusting, isn't it?

DET. STURGIS: That it is, Prof. What's your theory on the seizures?

MR. JONES: Low blood sugar, obviously. Overdose of insulin. Cindy knew all about insulin, because of her aunt. I guess I should have figured it out—she talked about her aunt's diabetes all the time, wouldn't let Cassie have any junk food—but it really didn't sink in. I guess I really didn't want to believe it, but . . . the evidence. I mean, at some point one simply has to stop denying, doesn't one? But still . . . Cindy had—*has*—her frailties, and sure, I was furious with her for her sexual acting-out. But her own child . . .

DET. STURGIS: Hers, only.

MR. JONES: Yes, but that's beside the point. Who wants to see any child suffer?

DET. STURGIS: So you went over to the university and pulled medical articles out of the SAP data bank.

MR. JONES: (unintelligible)

DET. STURGIS: What's that?

MR. JONES: No more questions, okay? I'm getting a little tired.

DET. STURGIS: Did I say something that offended you?

MR. JONES: Tony, make him stop.

MR. TOKARIK: Session ended.

DET. STURGIS: Sure. Absolutely. But I just don't get it. We're having a good talk, all convivial, and then all of a sudden I say something about the SAP data bank—that great computerized system they've got, where you can pull articles right off the computer and Xerox them? Something just click about that, Professor? Like the fact that professors can open an account and get an itemized monthly bill?

MR. TOKARIK: My client and I have no idea what you're talking abou—

DET. STURGIS: Steve?

DET. MARTINEZ: Here you go.

MR. TOKARIK: Ah, more tricks from the police bag.

DET. STURGIS: Here. You look at it, Counselor. The articles with the red stars are on sudden infant death. Check the dates your client and Ms. Kirkash pulled 'em out of the computer. Six months before Chad died. The blue ones are on

Munchausen syndrome. Check those dates and you'll see he pulled those two months after Cassie was born—long before her symptoms started. To me that spells premeditation, don't you think, Counselor? Though I have enjoyed the little comedy routine he's just done for us—maybe the fellas on cell block will enjoy it, too. Hell, maybe you can get him off High-Power and into the main population, Counselor. So he can teach those sociopaths some sociology—what do you say? What's that?

MR. JONES: (unintelligible)

MR. TOKARIK: Chip—

DET. STURGIS: Are those tears I see, Chipper? Poor baby. Speak up—I can't hear you.

MR. JONES: Let's deal.

DET. STURGIS: Deal? For what?

MR. JONES: Reduced charges: assault—assault with a deadly weapon. That's all you've got evidence of, anyway.

DET. STURGIS: Your client wants to negotiate, Counselor. I suggest you advise him.

MR. TOKARIK: Don't say anything, Chip. Let me handle this.

MR. JONES: I want to deal, goddamit! I want out!

DET. STURGIS: What do you have to deal with, Chipper?

MR. JONES: Information—hard facts. Things my dad's been doing. Real murder. There was a doctor at the hospital named Ashmore—he must have been bothering my dad about something. Because I overheard my dad and one of his lackeys—a worm named Novak—I heard them talking about it when I went to visit my dad at his house. They were in the library and didn't know I was standing right outside the door—they never paid much attention to me. They were saying this guy, this doctor, would have to be handled. That with all the security problems at the hospital it shouldn't be a problem. I didn't really think much of it, but then a month later, Ashmore was murdered in the hospital parking lot. So there had to be a connection, right? I'm sure my dad had him killed. Take a close look at it—believe me, it'll make all this nonsense look trivial.

DET. STURGIS: All this folderol, huh?

MR. JONES: Believe me, just investigate.

DET. STURGIS: Selling the old man down the river, huh?

MR. JONES: He never did a thing for me. Never protected me—not once, not a single time!

DET. STURGIS: Hear that, Counselor? There's your defense: a bad childhood. Bye, Chip. C'mon, Steve.
DET. MARTINEZ: See y'all in court.
MR. JONES: Wait—
MR. TOKARIK: Chip, there's no nee—

END OF TAPE

The indictment made the third page of a news-thin Saturday paper. The headline was PROFESSOR CHARGED WITH MURDER AND CHILD ABUSE, and an old college photo of Chip was included. In it, he looked like a happy hippie; the article described him as a "sociological researcher and recipient of several teaching awards." The mandatory sample of disbelieving colleagues was quoted.

Next week's story swallowed that one up: Chuck Jones and George Plumb's arrests for conspiracy to commit the murder of Laurence Ashmore.

A co-conspirator named Warren Novak—one of the gray accountants—had cut a deal and was telling all, including the fact that Plumb had instructed him to draw cash out of a hospital account to pay a hired killer. The man who'd actually cracked Ashmore's skull was described as a former bodyguard for Charles Jones named Henry Lee Kudey. A photo showed him being escorted to jail by an unnamed federal agent. Kudey was big and heavy and sloppy-looking and appeared to have just woken up. The marshal was blond and wore black-framed spectacles. His face was a nearly equilateral triangle. As a Western Peds Security guard he'd called himself A. D. Sylvester.

I wondered why a government agent would be doing the arresting on a homicide until I came to the final paragraph: Federal charges against Chuck Jones and his gang for "alleged financial wrongdoings based upon a lengthy government probe" were imminent. Anonymous "federal officials" were quoted. The names Huenengarth and Zimberg never appeared.

At four o'clock on a Tuesday, I made my fourth attempt to reach Anna Ashmore. The first three times, no one had answered at the house on Whittier Drive. This time, a man did.

"Who's calling?" he said.

"Alex Delaware. I'm on the staff at Western Pediatric Hospital. Paid a condolence call last week and just wanted to see how she's doing."

"Oh. Well, this is her attorney, Nathan Best. She's doing as well as can be expected. Left for New York last night to visit with some old friends."

"Any idea when she'll be back?"

"I'm not sure she will."

"Okay," I said. "If you speak to her, give her my best."

"All right. What did you say your name was?"

"Delaware."

"Are you a doctor?"

"Psychologist."

"You wouldn't be in the market for some bargain real estate, would you, Doctor? The estate will be divesting itself of several properties."

"No, thanks."

"Well, if you know someone who is, tell them. Bye."

At five o'clock, I stuck to a recently acquired routine and drove to a small white house on a shady dead-end street in West L.A., just east of Santa Monica.

This time Robin came along with me. I parked and got out. "Shouldn't be long."

"Take your time." She pushed the seat back, put her feet up on the dash, and began sketching pearl-inlay designs on a piece of Bristol board.

As usual, the house was curtained. I walked up the path of railroad ties that split the lawn. Vermilion-and-white petunias struggled in the borders. A Plymouth Voyager van was parked in the driveway. Behind it was a dented copper-colored Honda. The heat was really settling in and the air felt thick and greasy. I couldn't detect any breeze. But something was causing the bamboo chimes over the doorway to clank.

I knocked. The peephole slid open and a pretty blue eye filled it. The door swung back and Vicki Bottomley stood aside and let me pass. She wore a lime-green nurse's smock over white stretch pants. Her hair was sprayed tight. A pumpkin-colored mug was in her hand.

"Coffee?" she said. "There's a little left."

"No, thanks. How's it going today?"

"Seems to be better, actually."

"Both of them?"

"Mostly the little one—she's really come out of her shell. Running around like a real little bandit."

"Good."

"Talking to herself, too—is that okay?"

"I'm sure it is."

"Yeah. That's what I thought."

"What's she talking about, Vicki?"

"Can't make it out—mostly babbling. She looks happy enough, though."

"Tough little kid," I said, walking in.

"Most kids are. . . . She's looking forward to seeing you."

"That so?"

"Yup. I mentioned your name and she smiled. 'Bout time, huh?"

"Sure is. Must have earned my stripes."

"Got to, with the little ones."

"How's she sleeping?"

"Good. Cindy's not sleeping so good, though. I keep hearing her get up and turn on the TV a bunch of times every night. Maybe the Valium withdrawal, huh? Though I don't notice any other symptoms."

"Maybe that, or just plain anxiety."

"Yeah. Last night she fell asleep in front of the TV, and I woke her and sent her back to her room. But she'll be okay. Doesn't have much choice, does she?"

"Why's that?"

"Being a mother."

The two of us began walking through the living room. White walls, beige carpet, brand-new furniture barely out of the rental warehouse. The kitchen was to the left. Straight ahead were sliding glass doors that had been left wide open. The backyard was a strip of Astroturfed patio followed by real grass, pale in comparison. An orange tree heavy with ripening fruit served as a centerpiece. At the rear was a scallop-topped redwood fence backed by phone wires and the roofline of the neighboring garage.

Cassie sat on the grass, sucking her fingers while inspecting a pink plastic doll. Doll clothes were strewn on the grass. Cindy sat nearby, cross-legged.

Vicki said, "Guess so."

"What's that?"

"Guess you've earned your stripes."

"Guess we both have."

"Yeah . . . You know I wasn't too happy having to take that lie detector."

"I can imagine."

"Answering all those questions—being *thought* of like that." She shook her head. "That was really hurtful."

"The whole thing was hurtful," I said. "He set it up that way."

"Yeah . . . I guess he knocked us all around—using my bunnies. They should have capital punishment for people like that. I'm gonna *enjoy* getting up on the stand and telling the world about *him*. When do you think that'll happen—the trial?"

"Probably within a few months."

"Probably . . . Okay, have fun. Talk to you later."

"Any time, Vicki."

"Any time what?"

"Any time you want to talk."

"I'll bet." She grinned. "I'll just bet. You and me talky-talking—wouldn't that be a hoot?"

She slapped me lightly on the back and turned around. I stepped out onto the patio.

Cassie looked at me, then returned to the naked doll. She was barefoot and had on red shorts and a pink T-shirt patterned with silver hearts. Her hair was topknotted and her face was grimy. She appeared to have gained a little weight.

Cindy uncrossed her legs and stood without effort. She wore shorts, too. The skimpy white ones I'd seen at her house, below a white T-shirt. Her hair was loose and brushed straight back from her forehead. She'd broken out a bit on her cheeks and chin, and tried to patch it with makeup.

"Hi," she said.

"Hi." I smiled and got down on the ground with Cassie. Cindy stood there for a moment, then walked into the house. Cassie turned to watch her, lifted her chin and opened her mouth.

"Mommy'll be right back," I said, and lifted her onto my lap.

She resisted for a moment. I let go. When she made no attempt to get off, I put one hand around her soft little waist and held her. She didn't move for a while; then she said, "Ho-ee."

"Horsey ride?"

"Ho-ee."

"Big horsey or little horsey?"

"Ho-ee."

"Okay, here we go, little horsey." I bounced her gently. "Gid-dyap."

"Gi-ap."

She bounced harder and I moved my knee a little faster. She giggled and threw her arms up into the air. Her topknot tickled my nose on each assent.

"Giii-ahp! Giii-*ahhp*!"

When we stopped, she laughed, scrambled off my lap, and toddled toward the house. I followed her into the kitchen. The room was half the size of the one on Dunbar Drive and furnished with tired-looking appliances. Vicki stood by the sink, one arm elbow-deep in a chromium coffeepot.

She said, "Well, look what the wind blew in." The arm in the pot kept rotating.

Cassie ran to the refrigerator and tried to pull it open. She wasn't successful and began to fuss.

Vicki put the pot down, along with a piece of scouring cloth, and placed her hands on her hips. "And what do *you* want, young lady?"

Cassie looked up at her and pointed to the fridge.

"We have to *talk* to get things around here, Miss Jonesy."

Cassie pointed again.

"Sorry, I don't understand pointy-language."

"Eh!"

"What kind of *eh*? Potato or tomato?"

Cassie shook her head.

"Lamb or jam?" said Vicki. "Toast or roast, juice or moose?"

Giggle.

"Well, what is it? An ice cream or a sunbeam?"

"Eye-ee."

"What's that? Speak up."

"Eye-ee!"

"I *thought* so."

Vicki opened the freezer compartment and took out a quart container.

"Mint chip," she said to me, frowning. "Frozen toothpaste, if you ask me, but she loves it—all the kids do. You want some?"

"No, thanks."

Cassie danced a quick little two-step of anticipation.

"Let's sit down at the table, young lady, and eat like a human being."

Cassie toddled to the table. Vicki put her on a chair, then pulled a tablespoon out of a drawer and began to scoop ice cream.

"Sure you don't want some?" she asked me.

"I'm sure, thanks."

Cindy came in, drying her hands on a paper towel.

"Snack time, Mom," said Vicki. "Probably ruin her dinner, but she did pretty good on lunch. Okay with you?"

"Sure," said Cindy. She smiled at Cassie, kissed the top of her head.

"I cleaned out the coffeepot," said Vicki. "Down to the dregs. Want some more?"

"No, I'm fine."

"Probably go out later to Von's. Need anything?"

"No, I'm fine, Vicki. Thanks."

Vicki set a bowl of ice cream in front of Cassie and pressed the round part of the spoon into the green, speckled mass.

"Let me soften this up—then you can go at it."

Cassie licked her lips again and bounced in her chair. "Eye-ee!"

Cindy said, "Enjoy, sweetie-pie. I'll be outside if you need me."

Cassie waved bye-bye and turned to Vicki.

Vicki said, "Eat up. Enjoy yourself."

I went back outside. Cindy was standing against the fence. Dirt was clumped up around the redwood slats and she imbedded her toes in it.

"God, it's hot," she said, brushing hair out of her eyes.

"Sure is. Any questions today?"

"No . . . not really. She seems to be fine. . . . I guess it'll be . . . I guess when he's on trial is when it's going to be hard, right? All the attention."

"Harder for you than her," I said. "We'll be able to keep her out of the limelight."

"Yeah . . . I guess so."

"Not that the press won't try to get pictures of both of you. It may mean moving around a bit—more rented houses—but she can be shielded."

"That's okay—that's all I care about. How's Dr. Eves?"

"I spoke to her last night. She said she'd be coming by this evening."

"When's she leaving for Washington?"

"Couple of weeks."

"Was moving something she planned or just . . ."

"You'd have to ask her that," I said. "But I know it didn't have anything directly to do with you."

"Directly," she said. "What does that mean?"

"Her moving was personal, Cindy. Nothing to do with you or Cassie."

"She's a nice lady—kind of . . . intense. But I liked her. I guess she'll be coming back for the trial."

"Yes, she will."

A citrus smell drifted over from the orange tree. White blossoms dusted the grass at the tree's base, fruit that would never be. She opened her mouth to speak, but shielded her lips with her hand instead.

I said, "You suspected him, didn't you?"

"Me? I— Why do you say that?"

"The last couple of times we talked, before the arrest, I felt you wanted to tell me something but were holding back. You just had that same look now."

"I— It really wasn't *suspicion*. You just wonder—I started to wonder, that's all."

She stared at the dirt. Kicked it again.

"When did you start wondering?" I said.

"I don't know—it's hard to remember. You think you know someone and then things happen. . . . I don't know."

"You're going to have to talk about all of it, eventually," I said. "For lawyers and policemen."

"I know, I know, and it scares me, believe me."

I patted her shoulder. She moved away and hit the fence with her back. The boards vibrated.

"I'm sorry," she said. "I just don't want to think about that now. It's just too . . ."

She looked down at the dirt again. It wasn't until I saw the tears drip from her face and dot the soil that I realized she was crying.

I reached out and held her. She resisted, then relented, leaning her full weight against me.

"You think you know someone," she said, between sobs. "You think you— You think someone loves you and they're . . . and then . . . your whole world falls apart. Everything you thought was real is just . . . *fake*. Nothing— Everything's wiped out. I . . . I . . ."

I could feel her shaking.

Pausing for breath, she said "I" again.

"What is it, Cindy?"

"I— It's . . ." Shaking her head. Her hair brushing against my face.

"It's okay, Cindy. Tell me."

"I should have— It didn't make sense!"

"What didn't?"

"The time— He was . . . *he* was the one who found Chad. *I* was always the one who got up when Chad cried or was sick. *I* was the mother—that was *my* job. He *never* got up. But that night he *did*. I didn't hear a thing. I couldn't *understand* that. Why didn't I hear a *thing*? *Why?* I *always* heard when my babies cried. I was always getting up all the *time* and letting him *sleep*, but this time I *didn't*. I should have *known*!"

She punched my chest, growled, rubbed her head against my shirt as if trying to grind her pain away.

"I should've known it was wrong when he came to get me and told me Chad didn't look good. Didn't *look* good! He was *blue*! He was . . . I went in and found him *lying* there—just lying there, not moving. His color . . . it was . . . all . . . It was wrong! He *never* was the one to get up when they cried! It was *wrong*. It was *wrong*— I should have . . . I should have known from the beginning! I could have . . . I . . ."

"You couldn't have," I said. "No one could have known."

"I'm the *mother*! I *should* have!"

Tearing away from me, she kicked the fence, hard.

Kicked it again, even harder. Began slapping the boards with the flats of her hands.

She said, "Ohhh! Oh, God, oh!" and kept striking out.

Redwood dust rained down on her.

She gave out a wail that pierced the heat. Pushed herself up against the fence, as if trying to force herself through it.

I stood there, smelling oranges. Planning my words and my pauses and my silences.

When I got back to the car, Robin had filled the board with designs and was studying them. I got behind the wheel and she put them back in her folio.

"You're *drenched,*" she said, wiping sweat from my face. "Are you okay?"

"Hanging in. The heat." I started the car.

"No progress?"

"Some. It's going to be a marathon."

"You'll make it to the finish."

"Thanks," I said. Hanging a three-point turn, I drove away.

Halfway down the block I pulled over to the curb, jammed the transmission into PARK, leaned across the seat, and kissed her hard. She flung both arms around me and we held each other for a long time.

A loud "ahem" broke us apart.

We looked up and saw an old man watering his lawn with a dribbling hose. Watering and scowling and mumbling. He wore a wide-brimmed straw hat with a ragged crown, shorts, rubber sandals. Bare-chested—his teats sagged like those of a woman wasted by famine. His upper arms were stringy and sunburnt. The hat shadowed a pouchy, sour face but couldn't conceal his disgust.

Robin smiled at him.

He shook his head and the water from his hose arced and sprayed the sidewalk.

One of his hands gave a dismissive wave.

Robin stuck her head out the window and said, "Whatsamatter, don't you approve of true love?"

"Goddam *kids,*" he said, turning his back on us.

We drove away without thanking him.